I0735195

Paul D. Escudero

MAN OF BIRDS
TRAVELING TO THE STARS

WORKBOOK PRESS LLC
187 E Warm Springs Rd,
Suite B285, Las Vegas, NV 89119, USA

Website: https://workbookpress.com/
Hotline: 1-888-818-4856
Email: admin@workbookpress.com

Ordering Information:
Quantity sales. Special discounts are available on quantity purchases by corporations, associations, and others.
For details, contact the publisher at the address above.

Library of Congress Control Number:

ISBN-13:   000-0-000000-00-0 (Paperback Version)
                000-0-000000-00-0 (Digital Version)

REV. DATE: 22/07/2022

Man of Birds
Traveling to the Stars

By

Paul D. Escudero

保罗·道格拉斯·埃斯库德罗

Bǎoluó·Dàogélāsī·Āisīkùdéluó

Copyright June 27, 2022

PREFACE

My day starts out taking long walks every morning at Ski Beach, part of Mission Bay Park in San Diego. I've done these walks for many years and in the past when I pushed myself, I usually walked ten miles every day. In recent years as I started publishing quite a few books and needed the brain power to get through all that, I cut the miles back to six or seven. A writer who sits all day long working, definitely, needs to exercise to keep up their physical well being as it plays into stamina and creativity.

Why would a writer need stamina? Before we submit a Novel manuscript most likely we have read and edited that book possibly a dozen times. Then the publisher gets the manuscript, and their editors work on it and send you back the edited manuscript for review. You may not agree to all the changes and there is a possibility they missed something that you also missed previously. You get another shot now to make further corrections, so this review is quite important. Based on my experiences, the editors usually did a decent job and a lot of the issues they missed are things I created.

After you approve all the changes in the edited manuscript that word file (usually in word) goes to a book builder who transfers the word file to publishing software the printing press can understand and also to fulfill the requirements of eBooks, since most paperbacks and hard bound books also sell as eBooks. That process does not always work well.

In a lot of my books, I use Chinese or Japanese names, words, and phrases, mainly to spice up the book. Chinese PINYIN is the alphabetical spelling of the Chinese Characters. Japanese has something similar called Romaji that does the same thing.

There are 35 finals (vowels) in Mandarin: 6 simple vowels, 13 compound vowels and 16 nasal vowels. Each vowel in Chinese Pinyin has one of four possible tonal markers above it as well as the neutral tone that has no marker. Vowels with tonal markers above them are simply called first tone through fourth tone. Thus, Chinese vowels have 5 possible tones as it's a tonal language.

In one of my Novels, none of the vowels with tonal markers above them got transferred but instead a space was inserted. So, you see an author must review the "page proofs." If the publisher does corrections, you must review it again to make sure something in the document didn't get damaged in the process.

So, by now you are starting to see the point I'm going to make. By the time you are finishing reviewing the page proofs, you have read that Novel about a dozen or more times and it takes a lot of stamina to read it again in a very careful manner and be fully coherent during that review process. If I did not do all the walking at SKI BEACH, I'm not sure I would have the stamina to get the job done. Every time every day I walk, I say to myself, "How bad do you want it?" Today as I completed ten miles, I asked myself that question.

As I'm walking around Ski Beach, I'm observing the many birds that are there. I've known some of these birds that have markings on them I can recognize for ten years. The blackbirds have adopted me and follow me around the park. I can't confirm nor deny I ever gave them treats.

Those many years of walking around the beach day dreaming created some of the books or parts of the books I've published. One day recently I daydreamed a scenario where a guy like me is walking around the beach and interacting with the birds. And if you ever go with me, you will discover those birds have emotions. I wanted to write a fiction based on those walks and that resulted in this book.

This Novel is about aliens observing a man walking around Ski Beach interacting with the birds who develops an emotional bond to them. The aliens that are visiting planet earth spot this man interacting with the birds. These Aliens have advanced telepathic abilities and can sense what the birds are thinking as well as the man. The alien princess who is part of this expedition had never experienced interactions between birds and humans like this before and decides she wants to have a conversation with that Earth person. In the proximity of the human the alien utilizes telepathic abilities to discover what the man is thinking and what is in his heart and why he has his love for the birds.

That encounter resulted in the Earth Person offered the opportunity to travel with the Aliens back to their home planet and experience life in advanced culture in one of the most powerful empires in the galaxy. The story then unfolds, and the *man of birds'* experiences galactic scale scenarios and a transcendence into relationship with birds, espionage, and galactic strife that only a fiction like this could suggest.

Would you accept a similar offer? *To Travel to the Stars…..*

About the Author: Paul D. Escudero lives in San Diego close to SKI BEACH and after a career in electronics and aerospace, spends his time enjoying the beach and observing all the new discoveries mankind is making especially with the Hubbell and Webb Telescopes. He spends a lot of time enjoying classical music and remains interested in trains.

In almost all my Novels I sneak in a train scene. This book is no exception. However, the train action is not robust like some of my other novels such as Pluto II Voyage to the Edge of the Universe.

TABLE OF CONTENTS

Chapter One

Man of Birds and Earth

The Lìsztbrùnést Royal Space Yacht started its slowdown when the Navigation Coefficients determined the distance was 100 Astronomical Units from planet Earth. This would create uncomfortable time for Princess Lì Alìgrāwná. But she understood it was part of the requirement of long-distance space travel. Without the unpleasant periods of acceleration and deacceleration, it would not be possible to travel long distances in the galaxy without transiting far faster than light speed. Another positive attribute of arriving above light speed and slowing down in this manner is it prevented possible enemies from setting up an ambush since they didn't know you were coming.

The crew all now latched in their deaccelerate chairs that had security netting holding their bodies in place in the event the ship tumbled during slowdown which could occur if a propulsion anomaly unexpectedly caused the Lìsztbrùnést Royal Space Yacht to tumble. With the security web and seat and chest restraints in place, interlocks closed allowing propulsion controls to commence breaking.

As the Lìsztbrùnést Royal Space Yacht slowed while it dropped below the speed of light while passing the first gas giant Saturn. The spacecraft continued breaking passing by the second gas giant Jupiter just above half the speed of light heading directly towards Earth, the only planet with lit up sections of the dark side of the planet. Hence Earth was assumed to be the only inhabited planet in the solar system.

Princess Lì Alìgrāwná visited Earth ten years before and found it rather boring but was curious if there had been much change in that period. During that visit the Lìsztbrùnést recorded substantial Earth communications and subsequently Princess Lì Alìgrāwná became emersed in several Earth languages and could effectively communicate in English should should there be an opportunity to explore the civilization and converse with a living human.

Mars was quite a distance away and offset from the track of the Lìsztbrùnést Royal Space Yacht, but with the space telescope they could observe it with great clarity as they passed the closest point of approach. The image of Mars was inspiring, but it simply appeared to be a dead planet with no vegetation or reason to visit.

"Dead and desolate planet Mars has nothing special to offer," Princess Lì Alìgrāwná stated observing the holograph of the planet.

The Lìsztbrùnést Royal Space Yacht's captain stated, "Photonics does show spot some exploratory activity on the planet that appear extremely small in scale."

Perhaps when we leave, we might take a closer look, Princess Lì Alìgrāwná thought.

Slowdown and Earth observations continued with great concentration. It seemed just a short while when they reached 50,000 miles per hour at the Closest Point of Approach to Earth and began the wide orbit burning off speed in preparation to penetrate the ionosphere on the dark side of the planet fully cloaked. Earth Forces would not detect their arrival.

Meanwhile as they orbited and slowly moved the orbit closer to the planet, the vast sensor array mapped all military threats on the planet including radars, observatories, and space tracking stations.

Finally, the moment Princess Lì Alìgrāwná was looking forward too, they slowed to twenty thousand miles per hour and approached the dark side of the planet, then maneuvered straight down towards the Pacific Ocean halfway between the West Coast and Hawaii. At 100,000 feet the Lìsztbrùnést Royal Space Yacht leveled off and went on a heading of 064 degrees pointing at the City of San Diego.

At fifty miles from the coast the Royal Space Yacht slipped below radar and continued to slow burning off speed. After a random selection, they slowly eased down in the middle of Ski Beach fully cloaked on the deserted sprawling luscious green park several hours before sunrise, fully cloaked. Nobody knew they were arriving in the manner they came thanks to the sophisticated cloaking device now employed.

The crew could get comfortable for a while as Artificial Intelligence kept the watch for them in case there were intruders coming after them.

Princess Lì Alìgrāwná went to her sleeping chamber where she quickly fell into a nap that would rejuvenate her so that she would feel more energetic during the festivities later in the day after sunrise.

There was no specific reason to pick this spot. It was randomly selected. They had never been here before and had no reason to be at this location other than it was simply an arbitrary selection based on the area topology.

<p align="center">~~~~~~</p>

Several hours passed and finally a beautiful sunrise came. About a half hour after sunrise an automobile pulled up into the parking lot near a couple trees. Pigeons slowly started to appear. Many of them were walking around the parking lot pavement and as soon as that car parked and a man and a woman got out of the automobile, the pigeons seemed to approach the two humans in large numbers. Artificial Intelligence observed and recorded the event for Princess Lì Alìgrãwná to observe after she returned to the control room.

Artificial Intelligence of the spacecraft analyzing the humans and bird interactions noted an extraordinary interaction between the birds and the two humans that seemed to be giving the birds something to eat. The pigeons acted very excited and came right up to the two humans and exhibited no fear.

Artificial Intelligence recorded and analyzed this extraordinary event. Eventually the humans deposited all the food and apparently packed some additional food to carry as they walked around the park.

Black Birds suddenly showed up calling out to the two humans who responded by placing food in trees the blackbirds immediately sought.

Princess Lì Alìgrãwná having strange sensations could not sleep and left her sleeping chamber and went to the spacecraft control room where Artificial Intelligence started briefing her and showing her video of the birds' interactions with the humans. She saw the interaction with black birds and observed them following the two humans giving them snacks along the way. *Perhaps this is what was giving me the strange sensation?* Princess Lì Alìgrãwná thought as she received many birds' mental telepathy.

Princess Lì Alìgrãwná now felt the strangest sensation via her mental telepathy ever encountered in her entire life. The black birds loved that human!

The blackbirds didn't seem to be much in thought about the female but there was a very strong emotional spike with the birds towards the man. It was more than just the food he was giving them. The emotional bond was incredibly strong. It almost seemed almost supernatural to Princess Lì Alìgrãwná.

The two Earth people walked down the road giving the blackbirds the treats as they continued their walk. Princess Lì Alìgrāwná grew more astonished as this all unfolded. Her mental telepathy was almost on overload, the birds were transmitting their emotions like nothing she ever experienced before. Princess Lì Alìgrāwná was emotionally struck observing all this. The crew members who could sense Princess Lì Alìgrāwná could not help but feel similar emotions. They all were empaths to some extent and dedicated their lives to the Princess. When she was emotional it affected them greatly. This was one of the most extraordinary events in all their lives.

As the two Earth people were walking a distance away, Princess Lì Alìgrāwná directed the Royal Space Yacht captain, "Go airborne and follow the couple so I can watch them."

"Your Highness, as you wish."

After doing all the proper controls and engaging the silent propulsion system, the ship's captain said, "I'm going airborne now and will follow the couple so you can observe."

The couple crisscrossed the park and walked near the waterline at the beach park where a flock of black colored birds with red eyes were floating along and as soon as they spotted the two Earth people they suddenly got animated and flew and ran towards the humans.

"Look at the feet of those birds. They look like reptiles," Princess Lì Alìgrāwná said with a curious look on her face.

Then it hit her hard. Getting fifty emotional spikes from those strange birds in parallel almost overloaded her thoughts and she had to tune them down. These strange birds approached the man who gave them items out of his coat pocket. Some of the birds were pecking at his pantleg as a form of communication demanding food and attention.

"These birds love that human. This is quite extraordinary," Princess Lì Alìgrāwná said growing more fascinated by the moment.

Princess Lì Alìgrāwná felt the love the man had for these birds. Their affection towards him felt extraordinary. Their birds' emotional spikes seemed unbelievable!

The two humans then walked on with other birds now coming into the picture. Small seagulls with beautiful colors were soon vectoring in on the humans and were repeating what happened before. In virtually moments the princess realized several hundred birds loved this human. And she could partially read the human's mind she felt he had great affection for the birds. It was a form of love that was quite extraordinary and unlike anything she experienced in her lifetime.

Never before had Princess Lì Alìgrāwná experienced rarefied human and bird penetrating interactions. It felt spiritual. Her emotions gripped her and in utter astonishment to the crew she started crying. The tears were coming down. It was an emotional transcendence like none of them ever expected to experience in their lifetimes.

The cloaked ship followed the couple around the park observing them interacting with the birds. It quickly became obvious there was one particular male blackbird that stayed close to the couple. There was a compelling attraction as the blackbird felt a sense of family being close to these two humans.

After about two miles the couple returned to their car, gave some crackers to a few pigeons that were super animated again. The entire flock had an emotional attraction to the two humans.

Soon the humans got into their car and drove off, ostensibly returning to their home.

Princess Lì Alìgrāwná now sensed the entire flock of pigeons felt sadness as the two humans left in their automobile. A combination of bewilderment and sadness permeated the pigeons. It was now crystal clear to Princess Lì Alìgrāwná the pigeons desired the humans to come back to them. It was an amazing revelation to her. What was more amazing was their thoughts lingered. It was as if the birds all had feelings towards these humans imbedded in their hearts. For such small creatures with small brains, it astonished Princess Lì Alìgrāwná these birds could retain those thoughts as long as they did.

The Captain and the Princess' governess Drákōlìné knew it would be best if they left the area to give Princess Lì Alìgrāwná some distance to escape the thoughts of all the birds in the park as they had really unnerved the princess earlier.

"Your Highness, we have a lot of places to go and see. I recommend we leave now and start exploring all those locations we planned," Drákōlìné suggested.

"Alright, us continue on the planned route," Princess Lì Alìgrāwná stated feeling slightly paralyzed. Then she surprised everyone and said, "Lock in these coordinates, I want to come back here in the morning."

The Royal Space Yacht Captain responded, "Coordinates are recorded, and we can come back whenever you desire."

"Thank you."

The Lìsztbrùnést Royal Space Yacht started climbing in altitude and even though it was cloaked based on experience if it were possible to fly in the proximity of another spacecraft or passenger jet, they could avoid radar until they got up in altitude. Knowing the airliners flying nearby leaving Lindberg Field would be cruising up to 30,000 feet, it would simplify their hidden posture flying under the airline a few feet.

Planes were flying by every few minutes and soon the pilot guided the Lìsztbrùnést Royal Space Yacht under an American

Airlines passenger jet and to his surprise it went out over the Pacific Ocean and banked into a course reversal. This airliner was heading to the East Coast on a course of zero eight zero and continued to climb. By the time it passed over into Arizona, the American Airlines jet was already flying at 25,000 feet. It wasn't long afterwards, the captain changed course and the Lìsztbrùnést Royal Space Yacht flew North following the General direction of the Colorado river. Their destination would be in the Grand Canyon. It would not take them long.

Looking out to the west the Salton Sea was easily recognized. This man-made sea created by a manmade disaster around 1906 slowly passed to the rear and the rough landscape lay ahead. Soon they were pointed downwards as the captain planned on getting down around one thousand feet above the ground to dump all their wastewater over the desert area and soon while hovering over the water at the Hoover Dam, take on a load of fresh water their reverse osmosis equipment would clean up very efficiently.

A short while later, a Navajo tribe member sitting up on the rocks overlooking the dam area and smoking his pipe loaded with peyote, saw strange shimmering and exposing what appeared to be an outline of a spacecraft. *Was he having a trip from those mushrooms and the pipe contents or was this vision real?*

The Lìsztbrùnést Royal Space Yacht water recyclers and reverse osmosis equipment was flushed with the fresh water from the lake. They now had sufficient water to travel home to Empire planets without the need to stop over anywhere.

The day continued as they flew up the Colorado River and looked at the impressive imagery and with superior photonics all the wildlife around the rim of the Grand Canyon. After traveling up the Colorado River beyond the canyon, they veered off and flew up into Utah in the Zion area. The landscape and natures tapestry engulfed their sentiments. But one thing was perfect clear to the princess:

Not a single animal had emotions directed at any humans like they experienced this morning. Princess Lì Alìgrāwná now knew she wanted to meet the man. She would observe him a few more days and determine how to do it without frightening him.

Princess Lì Alìgrāwná had traveled to many worlds and seen many incredible things, but none of them struck her with the emotions like she felt this morning.

The Lìsztbrùnést traveled great distances showing the princess many more sights and soon sunset occurred signaling the end of the day.

"Should we find a remote area and park the Royal Space Yacht for the night?" Drákōlìné asked.

"I would like to travel back to where we were this morning and observe the bird man in the morning," Princess Lì Alìgrāwná responded.

Drákōlìné nodded at the ship's captain, and he understood vividly that was the new operational plan because the princess could be very stubborn at times, and they all learned a long time ago its better to make her happy than to suffer her might over the next few days.

The spacecraft flew out over the Pacific Ocean where the captain detected an airliner flying south ostensibly to Los Angeles or San Diego.

A lot of Airliners had reported a lot of turbulence all the way along the coast and the Alaskan Airlines jet had experienced a lot of turbulence but suddenly it stopped. It was eerily smooth. Another strange thing happened. The auto throttles cut back. They were flying virtually on idle!

The Alaskan Airline Jet knew nobody on the ground would believe them, but when they showed up with a lot of extra fuel, they might realize something spectacular happened. But what was it?

The Lìsztbrùnést Royal Space Yacht had the Airliner in an invisible tractor beam to prevent collision while using it to help obscure their presence from radar. When the Airliner landed in San Diego, it only used 1500 gallons of fuel flying to San Diego when they normally burn 3,600 gallons per hour. This became one of the biggest mysteries in Airline history.

When the Lìsztbrùnésts arrived at Ski Beach there were a couple campfires at the North end of the park far away from where the Lìsztbrùnést Royal Space Yacht would sit down with their cloaking device on and the Artificial Intelligence fully vigilant to the surroundings. The parking lot area adjacent to the Lìsztbrùnést Royal Space Yacht parking area not far from the bridge at the South end of the park was now mostly empty. A few homeless people were camping out under the bridge getting high for the night coping with their miserable lives.

"Your highness, sunrise is not for another five hours. I recommend you get some rest," Drákōlìné stated.

"Alright, get me up at sunrise, I don't want to miss the Earth person with the birds."

"Understand your highness, I will make sure you are awake and have something to eat and drink before the Earth person shows up."

Soon the princess was in her sleeping chamber resting peacefully happy to experience what she felt when they first arrived.

The princess could not help but have vivid dreams as the multitudes of birds had saturated her thoughts with quite an extensive emotional outpour. Normally birds are not like that. Their thoughts are casual and barely intermittent almost as if its a second thought, except for those who are attempting breeding. But even then, its more animalistic in nature and not emotional like experienced with the Earth person.

The emotions detected the previous day from the Coots felt

rather incredible. The Coots had completely befriended this human. There were no other emotions towards any other human. This was a singularity. The affection the human felt for the birds exhibited unquestioningly strong affection especially when they got near him.

Princess Lì Alìgrāwná planned on eventually meeting this earth person. *I wonder how he will feel about me when he discovers I have wings?*

The man's image was indelibly etched in her mind. He had more impact on her psyche than any other man for her entire life, including somewhat her own father. She almost felt like crying again as her memories of the episode the previous morning now flooded her dreams.

Somehow the princess was able to ease off into a nice dream world where she met the man. Since she already read his mind, she knew a lot about him. He gave her great satisfaction in her dreams.

She was just about to cross over into a romantic interlude with the human when Drákōlìné was gently awakening the princess as to not startle and get her poised for her morning activity.

After her morning activities that included nutrition and drinks, the Princess changed into her Royal Garments and proceeded to the control room where the captain was present, and all the appropriate sensors were ready to observe the Earth person when he drove his car to his typical parking spot next to approximately forty pigeons now waiting and uncharacteristically walking around the pavement of the parkinglot.

As expected, when the two Earth people showed up and parked their automobile in the same spot as the previous day, the pigeons became energetic and flooded Princess Lì Alìgrāwná's thoughts with extraordinary levels of telepathic activity.

Many pigeons had been walking around the parking lot which

seemed rather odd. Pigeons usually fly everywhere but here, and they simply didn't spend a lot of time walking around on asphalt covered roads. Soon as the couple got out of the automobile those pigeons and more on the light poles were swooping down in a raucous outpour showing expectation and emotional spikes. It was almost deafening to Princess Lì Alìgrāwná as the birds' thoughts were profound. Their affection towards this earth person was unquestioningly strong.

In the previous day, Princess Lì Alìgrāwná was tuned in to the birds and missed a lot of the man's thoughts. Today she ignored the noise and focused on the human and felt his compassion for the birds. The human's love for the birds was real and genuine. It was clear to Princess Lì Alìgrāwná this man probably arrived here every single day. This was his passion in life.

Just like the previous day, the blackbirds started showing up. They stood their distance almost in a very reserved polite manner. They had such warm feelings for this human. It was astonishing for Princess Lì Alìgrāwná.

After the couple took care of the pigeons, they took off walking around the park just like the previous day. The blackbirds flew into the trees in exact spots they knew he would approach and leave behind treats for them. Some of the blackbirds were crying out to the human. They were communicating in the most effective manner they could.

In several trees, they received plenty of treats and the couple walked on as the man gave out more treats systematically to the fifteen or more blackbirds following. As he approached the middle of the park and made the predictable turn, the spacecraft was airborne and cloaked and following him. It was a repeat of the previous day with all the birds having huge emotions for the human.

The man whistled in a peculiar manner to the birds, and they reacted in a positive manner. As he approached the North end of the beach park, the Coots were in the water and as soon as he did his strange whistle they came running and ascended upon him very abruptly in combination of walking and running. There was nobody else around and the birds were exploding in emotion which was quite unusual for these very calm and quiet birds. Just like the previous day some of them were pecking at his pantlegs to signal to him they wanted his attention.

Again, the princess was overwhelmed. The love between the birds and the human was unquestionably strong.

Drákōlìné closely observing Princess Lì Alìgrāwná saw the tears appear again. This was truly remarkable. Everyone thought Princess Lì Alìgrāwná had a hard heart. It would not be unusual for Princess Lì Alìgrāwná to raise entire enemy villages, killing everyone there in some of their past wars. To see this incredible change in Princess Lì Alìgrāwná utterly stunned Drákōlìné.

They followed the couple back to their automobile and detected the disappointment in the birds when the couple left.

"Follow them to their home. I want to see where they live in case, I decide I want to visit."

That comment really shook up Drákōlìné as she thought it would be reckless for Princess Lì Alìgrāwná to put herself at risk by doing such a foolish activity.

But the Captain and Drákōlìné knew better than to argue with Princess Lì Alìgrāwná who had a ruthless reputation and had a strong will as much or more than her father who everyone greatly feared.

They followed the Earth person's automobile going back to their residence. Instead of parking and getting out, the car stopped in the street in front of the home and the female got out and went to the residence. The man then made a U-turn at the end of the street and drove back to the park. It was evident the female only walked approximately two miles, and the male came back for more walking.

The birds were excited to see the man again. It was clear the birds had quite an emotional bond to this human. They were definitely emotionally bonded to the human. With the female gone all the telepathic transcendence was far clearer as it now all unfolded. Every single bird loved this man, and *the affection was bidirectional and strong.*

Now it all unfolded, the man walked many miles and after each lap loaded up more treats again and the birds knew what to expect. Today the man walked ten miles, but at the eight-mile mark over at Paradise Cove on the other side of the city street with the Lìsztbrùnést Royal Space Yacht following overhead fully cloaked, Princess Lì Alìgrāwná sensed the human was feeling quite physically fatigued.

Princess Lì Alìgrāwná could more easily telepathically enter the man's mind as there were only a handful of birds on this adjacent park, accessible by going under the bridges at each end of the park.

The human was struggling, and Princess Lì Alìgrāwná wondered if he was going to give up his walk and leave the park.

Out of nowhere came several Mallard Ducks that approached the man. The Mallard Ducks also emanated telepathically profound love for the human. The man stopped and gave them treats and gave them a couple soft whistles as it seemed it was his way to communicate to them.

The next major revelation in this event now surprised Princess Lì Alìgrāwná. There was some type of metaphysical response in the human as if the ducks were giving him energy. It was unmistakable, his entire physiology was changing. It was as if these ducks healed him and gave him a second wind. He then continued walking appearing fully refreshed!

Drákōlìné and the captain observing this human now picking up the pace knew something extraordinary happened. They also could not miss the betrayal of Princess Lì Alìgrāwná's emotions as she was in a vulnerable state not guarding her thoughts as well as she should have from others prying. They knew the obvious, she was captivated by this human like they have never seen before. If Princess Lì Alìgrāwná wasn't careful she could transition to ovulation and suddenly be like a woman in heat wanting a man and no doubt it would be this Earth person she would go after with the vigor of the will of an emperor in conquest.

The man finished walking ten miles, went to his car. By now the pigeons had mostly dispersed. This was probably typical as the pigeons now went about their business fully satisfied with the man and feeling whole.

Again, the Lìsztbrùnést Royal Space Yacht followed the man home, but he stopped at a shopping mall and went inside a store. They were curious as to what he was doing and waited. In a brief period, he went back to his automobile with a shopping care with a couple bags of articles.

Princess Lì Alìgrāwná sensed his thoughts to determine what items now existed in the two bags of articles in his automobile. Some of it was snacks for the birds for the next day. Other items he and his spouse would consume.

The Earth person then drove home and took the two bags inside his home and was now going to commence work on his writing. This added a fresh new curiosity to Princess Lì Alìgrāwná.

Princess Lì Alìgrāwná knew the human was finished going outside for the day, so she said, "lets continue with our journey. We were due to travel to Asia today, let's go."

It was a relief to the Captain and Drákōlìné that Princess Lì Alìgrāwná abruptly shifted out of that mental condition that seemed fixated on the *man of birds*. Soon they were speeding up leaving the atmosphere gliding above the ionosphere on their way to their destination in central China. They did not transition to high-speed transit until outside the atmosphere as to not leave behind any wakes that would enable Earth forces to observe a phenomenon and track them.

Even though it seemed rather innocuous, a KH-14 satellite did get a sniff of the alien spacecraft. This super-secret satellite put up specifically to search for aliens and bandwidths beyond processing abilities of most countries. The main reason for this satellite was the United States Space Force observed Aliens transitioning in and out of a cloaked profile. Thanks to the successful recovery of aliens and wrecked spacecraft there was a degree of knowledge in how to penetrate a cloaked field if the precise wavelengths were utilized, previously out of the range of human processing.

The American Space Force controllers in Cheyenne Mountain had no idea where the alien ship headed as it sped away so abruptly, they lost track via the KH-14 and as soon as they rotated the satellite's imaging system it was too late, the aliens were gone with no idea where the alien ship went.

~~~~~~
~~~~~~

CHAPTER TWO

HEARTBREAKING DEPARTURE

Stanley arrived home just soon enough to see his wife Ami before she departed to work at the company she owned. She was a one-woman band doing her thing enjoying being the big wheel slowly growing in stature and fame.

Up until a year prior Ami did not go on walks with Stanley in the morning, but after he informed Ami, she was starting to develop a dragon ass, she took it to heart and decided she needed to get some exercises. She also thought this would be an excellent time to verify there wasn't some bikini clad women down at Ski Beach where Stanley might be involved in some nefarious activity.

Stanley had discussed the birds often with Ami who just could not accept the fact this man who seduced her and later impregnated her wouldn't lay his charm on the number of beautiful women that showed up at the beach in the summer.

Then to discover his passion was the birds really surprised her. Every morning except when she got super busy, Ami was down at the beach with Stanley taking it all in. It surprised Ami how the Mallard ducks would sometimes fly right up to Stanley and start their quacking.

During certain parts of the year, as Geese were migrating North, Ski Beach was one of their stopovers to rest for a few days.

And as Stanley explained to Ami those birds had facial recognition and great memories and would walk right up to Stanley knowing he had treats for them.

Often Stanley fed the Geese out of his hands otherwise the nasty seagulls would swoop in and attempt to get the treats.

Stanley was gentle to all the birds and some of the eager seagulls would be down at his feet eating the food slated for the Coots and small migratory seagulls. In doing so it made it easy for Stanley to bend over and grab the sea gulls then lift them up in the air and stair in their faces. The Seagulls were dumbfounded they were caught!

The seagulls get highly emotional and demand their fair share, but because of the brutal treatment they do to the black birds and the small migratory seagulls, Stanley rarely fed them. There was no hope for them. They simply had bad manors and would never change.

The blackbirds on the otherhand were very patient and respectful with one exception. One of the blackbirds that Stanley named Rascal often interacted awfully bad with the Mallard Ducks who got close to Stanley. But handling Rascal was easy. Throw him his favorite snack (hot dog pieces) and Rascal would fly to an area that usually had standing water in the curb, wash the hot dogs or crackers than eat it. It was rather clever the blackbirds would soften up the crackers in the standing water and eat them.

Ami always hugged Stanley before bed or when she went to work. Their long-lasting love was unquestionably strong and permanent. This special feeling of love is an emotion Princess Lì Alìgrāwná discovered in Stanley that drew her even closer. But she also knew another deep dark secret. Ami didn't love Stanley nearly as strong as he loved Ami.

There was the initial romance after Stanley and Ami met and after becoming partners, something happened. That spark quickly went out and for many years it was just existence on the part of Ami. But after twenty years observing her friends married to undesirable men who did not make their wives feel worthy, she slowly realized how her friends' lives were truly miserable and none of them had a mate that was nearly as compassionate and caring. She slowly evolved as reality and old age set in. But as time passed it wasn't really love as it seemed status and security as Ami dreaded getting older and vulnerable. Ami feared how her life would be disrupted without Stanley's financial support. Princess Lì Alìgrāwná had a growing knowledge of Ami and the composite psychological condition of a one-sided love and emotions would later affect the outcome of circumstances to come.

Stanley had a day job but eventually retired after an impressive career and became a novelist publishing books very quickly and soon, he had quite a few of them selling. Ami slowly realized he was someone special and the uniqueness struck her.

When Ami started observing all the gold diggers going after Stanley on Facebook, she started worrying that some day Stanley might dump her for a thirty-year-old. She regretted being a bitch for so many years. Ami had no idea previously what she could lose and now that fear grew as Stanley's long list of Facebook female friends grew with nice breasts, pretty faces, and rear ends that would entice most mere mortals.

The situation was now evolving for Stanley as his wife slowly realized how much was now at stake after Stanley's twenty third Novel started selling. But as Princess Lì Alìgrāwná analyzed Ami, she understood Ami's bond to Stanley was about everything except passionate love. Princess Lì Alìgrāwná really felt sorry for Stanley who had no way of knowing Ami's real motives.

That night Ami approached Stanley as she was getting ready to go to bed and said, "I can walk with you in the morning." Hence another typical day.

One thing Stanley felt was this past day had some unusual

feelings. He couldn't quite figure out what it was, but he felt weird, and it was as if somehow sadness was pumped into his mind for a few minutes. Then today, he felt the extra gusto as he fed the Mallard Ducks. But he already knew they had some magical powers over him and seemed to refresh him allowing him to finish his ten miles.

In the morning the two copied their normal activity. All the birds were as they expected and very friendly. Stanley could not but help but think the pigeons were close to him, emotionally by the way they carried on. The squirrels often joined in. The squirrels and pigeons did not fear each other and seemed to get along just fine. Occasionally, Stanley would feed a squirrel out of his hand. They had no fear of Stanley and had positive feelings for him.

In due time the Blackbirds were happy again getting their snacks. As expected on the North leg of the walk, Rascal was there as always at a spot the two always met. During multiple laps, Rascal always appeared and had some easily identifiable markings. These blackbirds knew Stanley quite well and had no fear of him, some coming within a few feet quite often. They had bonded and the facial recognition was quite advanced. These birds never approached other humans.

Just like any other day, Stanley took Ami home and came back for more and because of pressing issues with a publisher did only six miles and went home.

The next day Ami had clients coming in early and could not walk in the morning. Stanley went by himself.

~~~~~~

In due time, Princess Lì Alìgrāwná observed enough of Asia and was more than ready to go back to Ski Beach to check up on her new fascination. At her request they lifted off and went into space and came down vertically over Ski Beach and parked in the empty park by the parking lot as they had before.
~~~~~~

Drákōlìné decided to let Princess Lì Alìgrāwná sleep until the Earth person showed up. This morning it was slightly unusual as he arrived by himself and fed the pigeons land started walking with the blackbirds.

As before they followed Stanley all the way to the North End of Ski Beach. This time the control room was in for a huge shock. Princess Lì Alìgrāwná said, "I want someone to go down and invite him up in the ship. I wish to talk with him."

"You can't be serious?" Drákōlìné responded.

"This person has affected me like no other. I've played diplomat for lesser men in the past. This is all for me this time. I want to talk with him."

The captain knew how difficult life would get if they didn't fulfill Princess Lì Alìgrāwná's wishes interjected, "I'm willing to send down my top interpreter to invite him aboard the ship."

"Do it." Princess Lì Alìgrāwná quickly responded.

Just as Stanley was rounding the area by the Gazebo on the Northeast corner of Ski Beach, the Lìsztbrùnést Royal Space Yacht uncloaked directly ahead of Stanley.

The ship hanging over the bay was quite large and soon a type of ramp came down and a humanoid looking entity seemed to glide down this ramp and approached Stanley directly.

"Excuse me sir, but Princess Lì Alìgrāwná of the Lìsztbrùnést Empire would like you to come with me to the ship as she has some questions for you concerning all your bird friends."

Stanley realizing this was quite an extraordinary event, decided to risk fate and go with the man back in the ship hoping he would not be abducted.

"Sure, I'll go with you, but I hope you plan on returning me here after the discussions?"

"Certainly, your safety is also our concern."

"Alright let's go."

The interpreter led Stanley into the alien ship that quickly recloaked and left the area realizing others on the ground might have seen it and made reports.

The translator led Stanley into Princess Lì Alìgrāwná's private suite where she was eagerly awaiting.

Stanley had a sense of decorum and gave a long slow bow towards Princess Lì Alìgrāwná who sat in her space throne where she could order the destruction of empires if she wanted. A chair had been placed directly in front of Princess Lì Alìgrāwná so she could talk privately with a man that now gripped her heart.

"Please be seated."

"Thank you."

Princess Lì Alìgrāwná telepathically directed all the bodyguards and other individuals to leave her suite. Soon the two were alone.

"Thank you for visiting me."

"My pleasure."

"May I ask you what your name is?" Princess Lì Alìgrāwná already knew the answer but asked to create the essence of dignified discovery, she had to ask it anyway.

"My name is Stanley."

Stanley remembering what the Alien who invited him said was the princess's name, so he said, "Princess Lì Alìgrāwná, I've never met an Alien before or a Princess. Please forgive me, but what is the name you wish me to address you with?"

"Stanley, when I'm alone with you it's our private affair that nobody else is entitled to know about. I want to be comfortable with you, so please just refer to me as Lì."

"Alright Lì. That makes it quite simple and nice for me."

Princess Lì Alìgrāwná now probed deeper into Stanley's mind including capturing all his carnal knowledge. It wasn't wise for her to do such deep penetration because she was suddenly feeling her body respond to an ovulation peak. She now was terribly vulnerable and would not be able to resist Stanley if he even slightly suggested copulation of any sort. As best as she maintained her dignity, the fact was internally she was now melting and knew in her heart it would only be a matter of time before she succumbed to her growing desires for this Earth man who made her cry several times in the past few days. She however calmed herself as she wanted to discuss this rather bizarre situation with Stanley and the birds.

After reaching a calm interlude, and regaining her self-control, Princess Lì Alìgrāwná asked, "Stanley, why do all the birds love you?"

"Lì, I sense there is some type of bond between us. I'm not sure. Perhaps they can feel what is inside my heart."

"They can."

"How can you tell."

Lì felt her ovulation spiking again and her desires now climbing that majestic plateau of transcendental evoculations and decided now she would expose the essence of who she was. She was willing to take the risk of rejection to quantify and expose her desires for Stanley that was now reaching a critical point. She now stood tall and dropped her robe that exposed her nude body and her wings that she now spread out for Stanley. Other than the wings, Princess Lì Alìgrāwná was as beautiful and sexy as any movie star with perfect geometries on her breasts, hips, and beautiful legs with normal feet instead of claws.

Stanley took it all in with a sense of adventure and intrigue.

"Stanley, I can read your mind and your heart. I know what you are thinking now. Your lust and desires are real and if you want me, come to me now and I will give you a different experience in love."

Lì knew that Stanley would not be able to navigate the journey to the quintessential immersion into love making with one of the most powerful women in the galaxy. He was of a primative mind, so he needed help to cross the void. Lì knew she was violating her own moral and ethical philosophy, but the vast emotional attraction created out of this freak of nature drove her to do what she normally would detest others doing as she took control of Stanley's mind and helped him disrobe and accompany her to her sleeping chamber where she positioned him for the best coitus possible. Stanley was feeling a rarefied transcendence into a psychophysical response he never felt before in his life.

From the time Stanley's manhood entered Lì up until he fully expired, the feeling was total gratification that never ended. Lì wrapped her wings around Stanley who was now a mere cocoon fully unfurling his manliness into Lì as his mind was ensonified with harmony and emotional oscillations.

Until this moment, Lì was a virgin. She had never copulated before and had the strange experience not unfolded the way it did, there is a good probability she might have gone another three hundred years before finding a mate, and that would not be unusual for a Royal.

Eventually the couple extended their gratification to a slowly descending climax that reached the fulfillment and satisfaction that made this a milestone in the Royal Court's legacy.

The two were now psychologically hitched and Lì cried a little as she felt the love, she knew was real because Stanley could not hide his thoughts from her probing. Stanley was floating in love and compassion and feeling rather unusual, unlike never in his life.

Lì wanted to do something special for Stanley and knew soon they would part company, perhaps forever, but before that separation happened, she would give him a special gift he could enjoy for a while. His own set of wings.

Stanley slowly put his clothes back on wondering what just happened. It seemed so surreal to him having sex with an Alien Princess with wings.

One day he would have to confess to his wife, but Ami would laugh at him think his story was totally ridiculous.

Then came the set of wings.

"Stanley, if you want, I can arrange for you to have a pair of wings and the ability to fly. If in the future you no longer want to keep the wings, all you must do is think you want them removed and after a few days they will simply fall off and your body would revert to normal without any scars."

"I wouldn't mind having the ability to chase a few hawks away from my pigeons at Ski Beach."

"I'll call in Drákōlìné and ask her to make the arrangements."

"How long will this take?"

"A couple hours."

"Alright."

In a short while Stanley was in for the biggest change in his life. He needed the wings added and wired up to his brain that also needed flight controls added to his neurological functions. He was in a deep sleep when all this activity went on feeling extremely refreshed when he woke up from the procedure.

Princess Lì Alìgrāwná was there when he was awakened, and the Lìsztbrùnést Royal Space Yacht was landing in an Amazon rain forest area that had been cleared by gold miners and abandoned.

The purpose of landing here was to allow Stanley to test his new ability to fly.

The two medical and transform specialists had cloned Princess Lì Alìgrāwná's wings at her request to fit them on Stanley. The advanced alien three-dimensional biological printing created the set of wings in virtually fifteen minutes. The surgery to add them to Stanley's body only required thirty minutes but the reprogramming of his brain for flight ability took up the remainder of the time.

The two specialists helped Stanley to his feet and one of them said, "We are going to walk with you off the Royal Space Yacht to make sure you feel stable, then we want you to test your wings."

Stanley knew in his mind he felt his wings. He also had his arms and hands to independently work as before.

A few feet away from the Royal Space Yacht, Stanley spread his wings. Stanley felt as if he always had the wings. The wings seemed quite large. Stanley mentally knew how to control the wings and began flapping and took to flight. Princess Lì Alìgrāwná then flapped her wings and took to air with Stanley and the two flew like a couple birds that were mates for life.

This was an incredible thrill for Stanley. He felt exhilaration like never before in his lifetime. But he also knew he probably crossed the threshold of another reality. Back home he had Ami. This would be a tumultuous period in his life. He didn't quite know how he was going to deal with Ami. He didn't know how he let all this unwind into a transcendence into the most bizarre experience in his life. Was his life's timeline irrevocably changed forever?

Soon Stanley's future life started to unfold in front of him. The most powerful female in the galaxy, Princess Lì Alìgrāwná was now recharting his future and her massive manipulation in his thoughts were slowly changing everything.

Princess Lì Alìgrāwná decided while flying with Stanley he would be her mate forever and take him with her on his life journey to the stars. Princess Lì Alìgrāwná would at least allow Stanley a few precious moments with Ami before she whisked him away to the vast Lìsztbrùnést Empire near the center of the Milky Way Galaxy. Stanley would be with her when her child was born as she knew that due to her ovulation and love making with Stanley had most likely conceived the heir to the throne.

Drákōlìné and the Lìsztbrùnést Royal Space Yacht Captain were utterly stunned of how this all transpired. This event was impossible to predict, and the repercussions would be enormous when they returned to Empire Worlds.

After flying around for a while, the two decided they had enough of that activity and Princess Lì Alìgrāwná it was now time for another big event in Stanley's life. He needed to visit Ami and explain he would be departing this world to go explore the Universe. Would she understand and forgive him?

Everyone boarded the Lìsztbrùnést Royal Space Yacht, and they were soon on their way back to Ski Beach in San Diego. Had Stanley not had the extensive mental modifications, none of the activities that soon transpired would have occurred.

"Go home and visit Ami, then come back here and we will leave for the Empire Worlds where your presence is essential."

"What if I chose not to go?" Stanley asked.

"You no longer have that option. The minute you made love to me and agreed to get the wings, your timeline was irrevocably altered. You now have responsibility to the Empire as you have created the inheritor to the Empire, and you must present yourself to the Lìsztbrùnést Emperor Cornelius."

"What if one day I want to come back to Earth?"

"When our child has reached the age of plausible governorship, then you will be permitted to come back if that's what you desire."

"I kind of want to grow old and die here."

"Because of what we did to your body, you will not be growing old very quickly now. You will outlive every human on planet Earth."

Stanley didn't quite understand why he wasn't feeling remorse about Ami. He had no idea the level of mental intrusions Princess Lì Alìgrāwná now performed. She had completely emotionally bonded with Stanley and now she would take him away from this world and show him the universe in ways he could never expect.

Stanley drove his car home. He was under great observation by the Lìsztbrùnést. They left nothing to chance. He parked his car in front of his home and walked indoors. It was already evening, and Ami had wondered where he went for so long a period.

When Stanley entered the home, he looked completely different. He had a sheen to him that Ami had never observed before. And he had on some strange type of cloak.

Ami had not fully appreciated Stanley over the years. She took him for granted and never conveyed love to him. It was always Stanley exhibiting and transmitting the signals of love. *Was she just role playing?*

Princess Lì Alìgrāwná tuned into Ami's mind and discovered the gaping hole in the emotional bonding Ami had for Stanley. It wasn't love it was simply polite coexistence all these years. The only love in the family was Stanley's radiance of it. Princess Lì Alìgrāwná was quite surprised in the revelation. But it also helped her not feel guilt over taking the man out of Ami's life, since the level of appreciation and reciprocal emotions were slim to none.

They had a long talk and Ami asked Stanley, "Why do you have on the costume?"

"This is not a costume. I now have wings."

"Don't be ridiculous."

Stanley then stood and unfurled his wings and spread them which took up an impressive amount of room.

"I can fly now."

Ami didn't know what to think. *Is this some type of joke?*

Stanley then said the heart-breaking message: "When I leave in a few minutes. You can watch me fly away. I'm not sure when I'm coming back. It may be forever. If you open my laptop after I'm gone, the password is this. Stanley grabbed a notepad off his desk and wrote down the sequence of numbers. You will find a file called Stanley's Essential Information. It has my passwords for everything so you will have access to all my bank accounts and be able to transfer any money you need or sell stocks to survive. You will discover I planned well. You will be financially alright."

"Is this for real Stanley?" Ami asked as her eyes were watering up.

Stanley was starting to feel the heart break, but Princess Lì Alìgrāwná was nearby manipulating him, so he didn't break down and cancel all her efforts in a brisk explosion of emotions.

Stanley approached Ami and put his arms around her as her emotional dam broke and the flood gate of tears began.

"Goodbye Ami."

Stanley released Ami then walked out the front door out to the sidewalk next to the street, spread his wings and took to the air. Ami saw it all, so did a couple neighbors who were dumbfounded.

~~~~~~
~~~~~~

CHAPTER THREE

TRAVELING TO THE STARS

Stanley flew to ski beach and landed in the grass near where he often met the pigeons and blackbirds. There were as many as 30 people in the area observed Stanley come down. A few of the observers knew Stanley as the *man of birds* in Pacific Beach who interacted with the birds in strange mannerisms.

The individuals observing Stanley were super animated in what they saw. Then to add to their amazement, the Lìsztbrùnést Royal Space Yacht uncloaked, and a ramp came down which Stanley walked up meeting Princess Lì Alìgrāwná holding her hands out to Stanley.

Stanley and Princess Lì Alìgrāwná went inside the space craft. The ramp receded and the spacecraft entrance shut and sealed, and it went airborne and headed straight up into the air causing nearby Lindberg Field air traffic controllers some consternation.

F18 Super Hornets taking off from Miramar Marine Corp Air Base saw the UFO ascend then quickly gather speed as it quickly left them behind heading out to space and on its way to travel to the Lìsztbrùnést Empire home worlds.

Stanley and Princess Lì Alìgrāwná entered and remained in the control room with the Captain and Drákōlìné where they were observed with great interest. This was an extraordinary moment in

Lìsztbrùnést History where the future direction of the Empire was seeded by a man simply feeding birds at Ski Beach.

When the last glimpse of planet Earth was fading from the ships sensors, Princess Lì Alìgrāwná knew it was time to take Stanley to their private royal quarters and begin the indoctrination he needed as well as telepathic training so that Stanley would be able to function in the Empire and be prepared for the inevitable of the Royal Court, including meeting the most powerful man in the Galaxy, Princess Lì Alìgrāwná's father Emperor Cornelius who would find this extraordinary development quite a surprise.

Emperor Cornelius was starting to get impatient about his daughter Princess Lì Alìgrāwná delivering him an heir to the throne. Emperor Cornelius would of course be quite intrigued in how Princess Lì Alìgrāwná out of the blue manifested this relationship with an off-worlder after many years of disappointment. Should Princess Lì Alìgrāwná deliver Emperor Cornelius a healthy grandson, her father would be eternally grateful as the boy would soon start extensive indoctrination in the processes of how to oversee a vast Empire that was constantly dealing with issues that were quite compelling as well complex. It would take most of the emperor's life left to complete this task.

The journey from Earth's solar system to a solar system 2000 light years away from the Black Hole in the center of the Galaxy was intentionally done at slow speed taking three weeks. During this time Stanley received tremendous indoctrination from Princess Lì Alìgrāwná.

Stanley was a freak of nature. Perhaps this is what led to his strong bonding with the birds at Ski Beach. In the center of all human brains is photo receptors, exactly like in our eyes. There were several theories as to why these photo receptor cells existed in the center of the brain which Earth Scientists could never comprehend, but the study was intense. The Lìsztbrùnést knew the purpose of those photo receptors.

Primarily the photo receptors located directly in the center of the brain enabled humans to receive telepathic communications. But there were also other functions. Some scientists believed those photo receptors were the main conduit between the hemispheres of the brain. Yet another group spawned out of the Monroe Institute who developed Hemi-Sync wherewithal, determined it was the pathway to the universe allowing our minds to time travel and experience the Gateway Experience. A few theologians with vast scientific training, determined that's how God interacted with people.

In the case of Stanley, his photoreceptor network in the middle of his brain was almost twice as large as the normal person. How Stanley's photoreceptors grew to such dimensions, seemed a huge mystery to Princess Lì Alìgrāwná. But she realized one plausible consequence of this freak of nature, Stanley, and the vast number of birds at Ski Beach telepathically connected without knowing it. Stanley was communicating his love to the birds, and they responded. The feedback was spontaneous and wholesome.

It did not escape Princess Lì Alìgrāwná that her actions created two tragedies. First of course was the destruction of Ami's world, which she felt some remorse, but the second was she knew it would be rough on the birds for a while because someone they loved as precious to them as anyone else was suddenly gone and they would never experience Stanley again for the rest their lives.

The indoctrination and telepathic training tested Stanley's stamina to the extreme. At one point Princess Lì Alìgrāwná triggered a Gateway Experience in Stanley. His mind went to the universe, and he did not come back for several hours. During this time Princess Lì Alìgrāwná was terribly frightened as she feared he might never come back. She had no idea what was happening as Stanley sat there oblivious to the outside world.

But Stanley did come back after living five hundred years in another dimension and another time. Stanley's holographic reality returned with a much greater and expansive awareness of the

Universe. He clearly wasn't the same person that departed when he returned. His mind was far more advanced and sophisticated than Princess Lì Alìgrāwná would ever imagine. The change was rather incredible. Stanley was now a renaissance man with a metaphysical awareness that encapsulated transcenditional fabric of life woven with the tapestry of his mind that mere mortals would never understand.

The most remarkable result of Stanley's venture into the holographic journey to the universe is he returned fully telepathic. Princess Lì Alìgrāwná had achieved a miracle when she met the father of the future Emperor, put wings on him and developed his telepathic abilities. Stanley would now have the opportunity to flourish in the Lìsztbrùnést Empire where he would slowly watch his creation become the most powerful man in the galaxy.

The Hemi-Sync experience created a very humble man. His only ambition in life now centered around the celebration of the majestic nature of life and the spiritual awareness of the creator that may have touched his soul in his travels to the Universe. During that journey he visited Ami and healed her heart. She now understood his journey in life now evolved in ways humans would never understand.

Ami continued going to Ski Beach Park every day. The birds were just as heart broken as she was. They adopted her and gave her their love and care and concern because they knew part of her life was stripped from her heart. Her wings were broken, and her heart was shattered, and they did their upmost to repair her. She felt invigorated as she left the park each day. The birds saved her.

As the Lìsztbrùnést Royal Space Yacht came near planet Neflatraceous, the capital of the Lìsztbrùnést Empire, escorts were there to take them to the Capitol.

Word had spread, Princess Lì Alìgrāwná brought with her the future emperor's father. It was a festive environment with few knowing what to expect.

Stanley's venture into Hemi-Sync converted him to a surreal manifestation of a cross between a sage and an alchemist. Stanley's wisdom and temperament evolved quite extraordinary, and his persona bolstered traveling through the universe five hundred years.

Emperor Cornelius had great analytical power to size up individuals very quickly. Stanley would be the biggest challenge of his life. The enigma had no easy soft points to penetrate.

Thanks to Princess Lì Alìgrāwná's indoctrination and psyche manipulations, Stanley was slowly mentally shielded preventing others from mental telepathic trespassing of his thoughts. This new posture not only protected Stanley, but it also added a measure of security for Princess Lì Alìgrāwná.

Emperor Cornelius would quickly discover Stanly had no points of vulnerability. He was genuine, real, and a great mystery in now he arrived fully indoctrinated and primed for the Royal Court.

Very few space craft or air transports were allowed any where near the Royal Palace. The Lìsztbrùnést Royal Space Yacht was one of the few. Long before the Royal Space Yacht entered the planetary atmosphere, communications were sent to Emperor Cornelius that his daughter, Princess Lì Alìgrāwná was arriving with a special person in her life. This caught Emperor Cornelius completely by surprise as up until now Princess Lì Alìgrāwná had not shown any interest in males and stubbornly rejected every Knight or Prince Emperor Cornelius presented to her for a possible arranged unification.

Drákōlìné knew better than to allow Emperor Cornelius to be blind sighted on events and the fact that Princess Lì Alìgrāwná was bringing ostensibly her significant other required some substantial notifications. In the most private communications to Emperor Cornelius, Drákōlìné reported Princess Lì Alìgrāwná had consummated her love with Stanley and was most likely pregnant!

At first Emperor Cornelius was almost in a fit of rage and would have had Stanley executed with a laser rifle squad had Drákōlìné not sent secretly recorded video and sound showing the emotional outpour of Princess Lì Alìgrāwná and the interactions between Stanley and the multitudes of birds. Then the biggest shock of all to Emperor Cornelius was observing the transformation of Stanley in just a few weeks from a noble savage on a primative world to a *man of birds* with wings and a disposition that enraptured Princess Lì Alìgrāwná into a cosmic transcendence of ethereal plateaus and significant emotional bonding.

It was now crystal clear to Emperor Cornelius that Princess Lì Alìgrawná would likely have irreparable emotional destruction if something happened to her prince, Stanley. Thus, Emperor Cornelius was forced to modify his stance and let time figure things out for him until he discovered more about Stanley.

Thanks to Princess Lì Alìgrāwná's grooming of Stanley, his IQ raised over 1000 points. But even more so, Stanley's new profound ability of mental telepathy thanks to his exceptionally large number of photo receptors in the center of his brain, that only a freak of nature would have, facilitated powerful telepathic abilities to the point in due time Stanley could penetrate Princess Lì Alìgrāwná's thoughts as easily as she could his. She soon had no secrets she could keep from Stanley. Hence Stanley became adaptive as time went by. He would learn his place in the Royal Court very abruptly and be almost a fixture that most took for granted.

Some of the consequences of Stanley's evolution reversed his age considerably. By all appearances he looked twenty-five years younger when they reached Neflatraceous, the capital of the Lìsztbrùnést Empire. The masses of Lìsztbrùnésts would consider the couple ideal based on looks. In reality, Princess Lì Alìgrāwná was much older than Stanley. She simply aged much slower. Even though she had a youthful appearance, Princess Lì Alìgrāwná had experienced life and travels to many worlds and locations learning much about the galaxy.

Emperor Cornelius only had one issue with Princess Lì Alìgrāwná, which now seemed to be resolved by Stanley's arrival: her negligence in providing a successor to the throne. Drákōlìné made report that portrayed an accurate picture of what transpired on this journey to planet Earth, considered a cosmic Zoo.

All future emperors were raised and indoctrinated by significant members of the Royal Court. They left nothing to chance. But soon there would be a new paradigm as Stanley was different and would insist on influencing and nurturing the child. Never in a long history had a young emperor received direct love and compassion from parents. Their lives were all synthetic to create the development deemed necessary to maintain the empire.

Stanley had an infusion of multiple societies. His evolution appearing quite remarkable also gave him great insights that Lìsztbrùnést had never experienced. Even though he wasn't as old as Princess Lì Alìgrāwná who was at least one hundred years older, he had unique experiences that sculptured his forbearing and rational thinking.

Now it was all unfolding as the Lìsztbrùnést Royal Space Yacht slowly settled down in the private landing zone in front of the entrance to the Emperor Cornelius Palace. The color guard and Royal Court members invited for this auspicious event were lined up in perfect choreography. No less than two hundred Lìsztbrùnésts were present and lined up in the most impressive formation.

Just like a dress rehearsal, a moment after the Lìsztbrùnést Royal Space Yacht fully settled down onto the royal landing pad, the front door to the Mansion opened and Emperor Cornelius stepped forward with his two most trusted Valets Octavrator and Lucas on each side and walked down that open stretch directly towards the Royal Space Yacht that deployed its ramp and opened the doorway.

Princess Lì Alìgrāwná was dressed in immaculate Royal Clothing nobody else in the empire would ever be allowed to wear.

Beside her stood Stanley now given the title of *Duke Ravik* in honor of his great achievement towards the birds' transcendence in their hearts, minds, and souls.

Emperor Cornelius was somewhat mystified in the relationship of Duke Ravik (aka Stanley), in how that relationship spawned and evolved. Duke Ravik left behind many broken hearts, not just Ami. Despite what many might not understand, just like Ami, those birds would never forget Stanley. He left a gaping hole in all their hearts. They couldn't reason why they just accepted he was gone. Some of those birds knew Stanley for over ten years. They would not soon forget him.

Princess Lì Alìgrāwná was forever grateful she could telepathically instruct Duke Ravik in all his actions approaching the emperor. Their tightly coupled telepathic intercourse could not be heard by others. They had complete privacy in what they transmitted to each other's thoughts.

As such, Emperor Cornelius could tell the future father of an Emperor was highly polished. He was subtle and he was decisive. He was clearly not a coward, nor was he arrogant. His reserved quality bestowed on others a sense of rarified charm. The fact his daughter picked this man clearly demonstrated he was worthy. The INTEL provided by Drákōlìné was an extraordinary report by ever measure. Emperor Cornelius was curious as to how Duke Ravik would inter-relate to birds on this planet which didn't seem to have much affection for Lìsztbrùnésts.

The couple stopped a few feet in front of Emperor Cornelius who had on his poker face. He would not divulge his findings or his decisions to anyone but his two valets. If he decided, within hours Stanley would be led off to some discrete location and placed before a laser firing squad to remove him from the scene. That decision was deferred until further inquiry was accomplished. There was no reason to be hasty until he saw firsthand how far the relationship between Duke Ravik and Princess Lì Alìgrāwná had developed.

The couple did a long deep bow out of respect and in the most precise Lìsztbrùnést language Princess Lì Alìgrāwná as she was straightening up from her bow in perfect precision with Stanley stated, "My Dear Father, I wish to introduce to you my most significant other, Stanley, who I've given the Title Duke Ravik. I've chosen him to be my mate for the rest of our lives. He is a kind and gentle soul whom I love and adore."

By the words of Princess Lì Alìgrāwná, the emperor knew this was his final chance to end it or allow it to simply move forward and thus laid out his cards in front of God and everyone.

"Duke Ravik, as my daughter has named you, do you wish to remain with her the rest of your life."

"Your highness, I've given my heart and my life to Princess Lì Alìgrāwná. I now live for her sake and her happiness."

Time seemed to stand still while Emperor Cornelius thought about Stanley's (aka Duke Ravik) comments. He knew Stanley's complete history thanks to his very capable spy Drákōlìné who divulged to him everything. He looked at Stanley in a full gaze, fully evaluating the circumstances that Princess Lì Alìgrāwná arrived. She invited Stanley; it wasn't the other way. The fact Princess Lì Alìgrāwná picked Stanley was a huge mystery.

As such it was time to invite his daughter and significant other into the mansion where they would slowly come to terms with the new revelations as to how expectations of the Lìsztbrùnést Royal Court would manifest and complete the determinations and estimations as to how to proceed from here.

"Will Duke Ravik and my lovely daughter Lì please follow me into the Emperor's Mansion where we can relax and have some discussions."

The couple bowed and as the emperor turned towards the palace, they dutifully followed along not knowing what bestowed upon them.

In a respectful distance behind the couple, Drákōlìné followed as her role would not be terminated any time soon. She would be with the Princess for the rest of her life or until the Princess departed life for some unexpected reason.

Drákōlìné knew better than to interfere with Princess Lì Alìgrāwná's dreams because the consequence could be fatal. Princess Lì Alìgrāwná had made her critical life decision. The manner she picked her mate was rather extraordinary. It also demonstrated the level of ambition and decisive actions she could make. Only one other person in the entire galaxy had more power than the Princess, her father, Emperor Cornelius.

Princess Lì Alìgrāwná could wield considerable power and Drákōlìné knew she would order the execution of anyone that crossed her. In fact, Princess Lì Alìgrāwná witnessed some executions her father ordered for some of his enemies, and she stood there observing with no remorse whatsoever.

The fact Princess Lì Alìgrāwná picked Stanley (Duke Ravik) was obviously quite bizarre to Drákōlìné, but she knew the psychological intrigue that evolved in front of her eyes when a clairvoyant and sensitive telepath like Princess Lì Alìgrāwná could read the birds minds and discover that mystery of life extremely rare if not impossible. Drákōlìné knew beyond the shadow of a doubt that Stanley owned Princess Lì Alìgrāwná's heart. She loved Stanley dearly and in every passing day that love grew as Drákōlìné monitoring the situation measured and quantified the extent that seemed rather remarkable.

Drákōlìné was in a key position to observe Princess Lì Alìgrāwná's telepathic influences on Stanley and started molding him. Stanley was slowly becoming that Macro with the tapestry Princess Lì Alìgrāwná wanted. The stakes were extremely high. Princess Lì Alìgrāwná left nothing to chance. She more than paved the way for Stanley to evolve into a sustainable and firmly evolved asset in her life. Stanley was now the source of her full attention until the young future emperor was born. Then she would evolve to help develop the next emperor her son, so the Lìsztbrùnést would retain their influence in the galaxy leaving no real challenges to their supremacy and easy access to the hegemony it derived.

Emperor Cornelius fully equipped with his own telepathy had never experienced Princess Lì Alìgrāwná in such a state of mind. In some ways it was frightening, but in other ways it provided solace in that it conveyed to him she was quite serious in extending the longevity of the monarchy. Emperor Cornelius had his doubts about Princess Lì Alìgrāwná until she arrived with her significant other, Duke Ravik. Now he knew she really was all business and took her responsibility quite seriously. For that he would be eternally grateful to Stanley who manifested all this.

Emperor Cornelius felt quite surprised how polished Stanley (aka Duke Ravik) appeared as they strolled through the emperor's palace. Nevertheless, some of the secret files Drákōlìné sent the emperor, showed the amount of change Princess Lì Alìgrāwná facilitated as she was determined to make Stanley her lifetime companion and exhibit the qualities the Royal Court would appreciate. Princess Lì Alìgrāwná's success in indoctrinating and developing Stanley was nothing short of astonishing if one observed the secret files Drákōlìné shared with the emperor. The emperor would never underestimate his daughter ever again.

Princess Lì Alìgrāwná's love for her father was profound. Emperor Cornelius gave much of himself to Princess Lì Alìgrāwná especially after the tragedy of her mother whose life was abruptly taken in a coup, where her final act was to save the life of the emperor and her child. The emperor hence knew the meaning of true love and devotion his wife displayed at that critical moment in time. His daughter of course was devastated, and he had to deal with her for many years to help her psychologically heal from that tragedy.

It was quite apparent to the emperor that observing the two,

Stanley filled a huge void his daughter carried with her during most of her life. And finally in the blossom of her life, the special glow radiated the boundless happiness manifested from a quirk of nature that brought two into a covalence nobody would ever predict possible.

Even though the two and consummated the relationship in a permanent relationship neither would ever want to break, there was a political reason to put on a public display and show the Princess and her significant other in a moment of pomp and circumstance to make it fully final and codified in Royal Court proceedings. The two Valets would soon be preparing for that event soon to be on the horizon. But for this moment, it would simply be the family quietly rejoicing the changes of Princess Lì Alìgrāwná with the future spectacle of a child. Would there be a second or third? How far would this go?

A significant burden was now lifted off the emperor's shoulders as he could now slowly develop a successor plan. There would be a generational jump in that Princess Lì Alìgrāwná would never sit on the throne reserved for her child. The emperor hoped he would see the young man sitting on the throne with wisdom and effectiveness before he passed.

The reception with a couple dozen members of the Royal Court gave a feel of acceptance and accommodation. None of the court members knew much about Princess Lì Alìgrāwná's significant other. Duke Ravik was no doubt an enigma and Princess Lì Alìgrāwná's closeness to him conveyed a moderate spectacle to behold their vast inquisitiveness.

A line was formed, and Princess Lì Alìgrāwná took Duke Ravik down the line introducing him to each of the few assembled Royal Court members. Duke Ravik was dressed and made up in the most spectacular fashion including the sheen to his skin that left an impressive impression on those gathered. With his cape they were unaware Duke Ravik had wings. That was the next big surprise. After completing the pass through the court members,

Princess Lì Alìgrāwná took Stanley to a short platform where they could face the crowd and leave an everlasting image along with the appropriate number of holographic recordings to be used in the future.

Drákōlìné knew what was in store and accompanied the couple to the platform to assist. She first took of the princes" cape. Then Drákōlìné walked over to Stanley and undid his cape then stood back. The couple were approximately four feet apart from each other and they unfurled their wings, which reached out eight feet from one end to the other. The silver white wings glistened in the lighting. The crowd was speechless, including the emperor. This was one of the greatest revelations in Empire history. Princess Lì Alìgrāwná's most important person in her life was a *birdman with wings*. And Duke Ravik as the name he was given, had those silver white shiny wings that by themselves looked mystical.

When Emperor Cornelius later observed Duke Ravik flying, he would then know the extraordinary aspect of Princess Lì Alìgrāwná's true love.

Then came the next big surprise as Princess Lì Alìgrāwná asked her precious Duke Ravik to tell the group a little about his life journey and what his favorite pastime was.

To the utter amazement of the crowd, Duke Ravik had been fully programmed in the Lìsztbrùnést language with the most perfect Neflatraceous dialect. To a lot of Lìsztbrùnést people with the Neflatraceous dialect were considered snobs as the upper crust of society spoke in that dialect.

"Ladies and Gentlemen of the Royal Court, I come from the far away distant solar system where the planet Earth exists."

Stanley looked at all the Royal Court members and was making eye contact with them directly as he spoke.

"My focus and spare time centered around the study and

development of friendships with numerous bird species."

Princess Lì Alìgrāwná nodded at Drákōlìné who then directed the holographic technicians to begin showing a short program of approximately fifteen minutes.

The court members now see the strange planet Earth with many of its majestic buildings and landscape. They then saw the birds interacting with Duke Ravik and appeared mesmerized.

Looking at the couple now had a greater measure of why they were a couple. The man from Earth was handsome and majestic and it was clear he had a significant influence over wild animals like they would never believe had the video not showed the essence of his being.

Soon the video completed, and the Valet Octavrator nodded at the emperor who then stated, "Members of the Royal Court and my dear friends, please join me with my family for a nice feast to celebrate Princess Lì Alìgrāwná's return and to welcome Duke Ravik."

Drákōlìné helped the Duke and Princess cover their majestic wings with their royal capes and escorted them to their position next to the emperor sitting next to each other.

While Stanley traveled on the Lìsztbrùnést Royal Space Yacht, he had some samplings of the exquisite tasting food the staff prepared out of frozen foods. He knew they were exceptional chefs, and this meal would be no exception. The elixirs provided were quite appealing which supplanted fine wines and sparkling drinks also available. The twenty-four-course meal was substantial and impressive.

Stanley knew his role was not to consume and bask in the pleasures of the court. Princess Lì Alìgrāwná left nothing to chance as she continuously giving him telepathic instructions. She was the grand puppet master and knew how best for Stanley to interact with the Royal Court, engaging them in conversation and respond in a mannerism that would make court members appreciate his demeaner.

Emperor Cornelius thought Duke Ravik (aka Stanley) was the consummate politician as he navigated the landscape with utter perfection. Emperor Cornelius was quite impressed with the way Duke Ravik handled himself but had no idea the level of Princess Lì Alìgrāwná's manipulations. She knew as well as any the importance of first impression and substance an actor had to play to codify the behavior in ways to cement the perception of who this new Duke Ravik was. Princess Lì Alìgrāwná also knew how important it was to not fully disclose everything at once and ruin the attractiveness by exposing too much too soon. Hence Stanley did not divulge too much and merely answered inquiries while being very pleasant about it.

It did not take long for the emperor to detect Stanley and Princess Lì Alìgrāwná were joined at the hip. They had an operendus vivendi fully developed. With Drákōlìné secret INTEL reports the emperor knew far more than he let on and kept his poker face through the evening. One thing that gave the emperor a lot of interest was trying to figure out exactly how this Earth person captivated his daughter as much as he did.

Princess Lì Alìgrāwná was very articulate and intelligent. She didn't suffer fools, nor did she accept the many numerous suitors who pressed their desires to be a part of her life. The emperor thought it would be fifty to one hundred years before his daughter would ever think about doing what she had now done. It was also a foregone conclusion they had consummated this relationship and the princess was most likely pregnant and that fact would come to bear in about a month when doctors checked her condition.

Emperor Cornelius knew the way she wrapped her wings around this mere mortal she was fully engaged in her emotional transcendence. The fact he saw her in tears a couple of times truly gave the emperor an insight into how this love had magically materialized. He also knew Stanley was not the purveyor of that transcendence. It in fact was his daughter who developed those emotions into a physical embrace that ultimately manifested the cross over to a point of no return.

Hence there was nothing Emperor Cornelius could fault Duke Ravik as this was all the princess doings. That knowledge made this relationship even far more concrete, and the emperor distinctly knew with Princess Lì Alìgrāwná's forbearance it was permanent and final. He understood his daughter quite well and once she decided; it was final. Princess Lì Alìgrāwná's had zero flexibility. Hell has no mercy for anyone that gets in her way. The emperor liked this quality in his daughter as he distinctly knew her mannerisms would lead to a more reliable future monarchy especially if he grew ill and unexpectedly departed the throne.

Emperor Cornelius also saw the dynamics between his daughter and Stanley (aka Duke Ravik). He had some ability to intercept some of their private telepathy. The emperor knew quite well Duke Ravik would accommodate Princess Lì Alìgrāwná his special love always. Stanley had an extensive emotional bond to Princess Lì Alìgrāwná. Their love for each other was very strong and intense. They knew each better than anyone could imagine. The love was golden, and it was real. Their worlds orbited around each other.

Stanley (aka Duke Ravik) gave off good vibes and the emperor felt Stanley was pleasant to be around. Duke Ravik's very reserved personality made him very easy to accept. Princess Lì Alìgrāwná's demeaner and interactions with Duke Ravik further expanded his persona in the eyes of the Royal Court.

Emperor Cornelius steadily grew happier observing his daughter and Duke Ravik in their private telepathic communiques. As the emperor continued to re-evaluate the situation, it now appeared clearer than ever that Princess Lì Alìgrāwná was deeply in love with Stanley. But more so, Stanley was also emotionally attached to Princess Lì Alìgrāwná the love of his life.

Emperor Cornelius was unaware the heart break Stanley left behind as Ami was devastated. Those thoughts and emotions were buried deep into Stanley's psyche. Princess Lì Alìgrāwná knew the implications if the public became aware Stanley left Ami behind. She did an incredible job of bleaching Stanleys memories of Ami and Drákōlìné the Lìsztbrùnést Royal Space Yacht's Captain knew they would be executed if they ever uttered a word about Ami. Ami was now in Stanley's past.

Entertainment from an orchestra created a subtle ambience and the splendor of the event transformed everyone to a happy experience that lingered on throughout the evening as the joyous occasion elevated the spirits of everyone attending.

Like all good things, the dinner party slowly ended, and the guests were slowly escorted out of the palace to their waiting skycars to take them to their homes and mansions, far away from the palace.

When the last guest departed, the emperor excused himself as the orchestra was leaving and the Valet Octavrator said, "Princess Lì Alìgrāwná, may I escort you to your rooms?"

Princess Lì Alìgrāwná thought that was an odd remark and when the valet took them to a guest room for Stanley, the princess interjected: "Duke Ravik and I will be going to my suite."

"I'm sorry your highness but the emperor has directed we give Duke Ravik his private quarters."

"Listen, I have reason to fear for his assassination and other security situations since Duke Ravik is from a very distant planet. I must protect him and shield him. He will stay with me for my security concerns, but you can announce he has his private suite if it makes it more palatable to the Royal Court," Princess Lì Alìgrāwná elucidated in a mild angry voice.

"I'm sorry your highness, the emperor has stated he has his own quarters to avoid the appearance of a scandal associated with the princess sleeping with her lover before the wedding." Valet Octavrator said.

"Sure, he has his private suite. You can advertise it and promulgate that perception all you want. But tonight, Duke Ravik will remain with me for the night so I can be sure he is protected. I would be very angry if something happened to him, and I would have you executed if he was harmed. It's in your best interest you do not interfere with my plans. Go put out all the propaganda you wish. Stanley will always be with me from now and into the future."

The Valet Octavrator knew he was trapped, and the princess was not going to make any changes to her plans. He would soon be having indigestion as he reported back to the emperor who gave him his marching orders.

The princess was very familiar with her suite and grabbed Stanleys hands and led him to the door of her private suite. If the Valet Octavrator did not open the door for the couple, his night would get even more negative as she would then march directly to her father and ask that he be removed from the mansion immediately.

The Valet Octavrator knew he was in serious trouble. He certainly would not have a confrontation with Princess Lì Alìgrāwná. He took the better course of valor (self-preservation) and opened the door for the princess and duke and bowed and asked, "Is there anything I can do for the two of you?"

"Yes, put a guard outside this door tonight with orders that we not be disturbed for any reason. I will visit father first thing in the morning to discuss upcoming plans which I want carried out immediately. I'm sure my father will concur with my request."

"As you wish your highness. I will make sure one of the most capable security men to be posted here tonight."

"Thank you. We do not know yet how principal parties in the power structure of this Empire is settled on Duke Ravik and me entering this lifetime arrangement. We know from lessons learned of my mother not to be complacent because we have no idea what's in store for us."

"Your Highness, I assure you that I'm very concerned about your personal security, and I would gladly give my life to protect you and Duke Ravik."

"Thank you. Perhaps why my father chose you, he understands what kind of a person you are."

"Good night your Highness. The security man will be here momentarily. Don't hesitate to contact me if you need anything."

"Of course, I will do whatever is required."

"Good night Your Highness and Duke Ravik."

Valet Octavrator bowed then turned around and walked out of the suite a short distance and closed the door and locked it as he departed. Thanks to his special communicator, the very capable security man arrived carrying two stands with placards that stated: "Security Zone. Please do not Enter."

Anyone foolish enough to walk past those security boundaries would likely be instantly fried via a very powerful laser pistol as the security man was authorized to apply lethal force to anyone entering the exclusion zone.

The princess suite had two chamber maids there to take care of all her needs and could call in additional support if something else was required.

Drákōlìné was parked in the next room and there was an access that Princess Lì Aligrāwná could order opened if she had any desire to converse with Drákōlìné for any reason. Drákōlìné had special security protocol measures and surveillance abilities and had ample fire power if assassins penetrated the security boundary for any reason such as an attempted coup.

Drákōlìné's current posture was neutral waiting for any event that required her intervention. But she knew the obvious, the princess would soon want to feel the flesh of Duke Ravik pouring out the love to her and experiencing the great affection they had for each other. Drákōlìné knew to an extent how much Princess Lì Aligrāwná manipulated Duke Ravik as this was her focus in her life. Much was at stake including the monarchy and she would protect it to her best abilities.

The chambermaids swung into action and helped undress the royal couple from their ceremonial clothes that were slightly uncomfortable, but the glitz and the ornaments were essential for the dignity of the Royals to convey their majestic qualities and represented the source of their power that was immense.

"Princess Lì, would you like to take a bath," the first chambermaid asked using the term directed to be used in their privacy.

"Yes, I would love a nice bath and I would like Duke Ravik to be with me in the bath."

The chambermaids swung into action and took the couple into the large bathroom with a huge bathtub large enough to hold several people. They carefully escorted the couple into the tub and seated them next to each other where they predicted one day the princess would sit with her significant other.

The computer-controlled temperature of the water was perfect, and the two chambermaids disrobed so they could get into the water with the couple and shampoo their hair and clean them in any manner required. The two ladies were exceptionally pretty and had glorious appearing wings. If the princess requested, they would make Duke Ravik satisfied in a variety of ways, but that was not in the cards. The princess did not share. Duke Ravik was her most important person in her life now. And she knew sometime soon, he would also help bring another life into this world that would one day be the most powerful man in the galaxy.

Their hair was shampooed, and their bodies were messaged which helped them feel much better from the long time they existed on the Lìsztbrùnést Royal Space Yacht. Afterwards they simply enjoyed the nice water laced with emotional enhancements. Soon the princess was ready to get out of the water and dry off and get dressed for her sleep period she knew was coming soon with her great satisfaction being held in Duke Ravik's arms. Just like on the Royal Space Yacht, she would feel the Duke Ravik's great affection during this transcendence into the dream world. She would fully penetrate Stanley's mind as she slowly evolved into that dream state.

Princess Lì Alìgrāwná's well-being then engulfed a state of mind that was quite unique because as part of her dream world, she had numerous bird conversations in her mind. The power of the love the Ski Beach birds had for Stanley was incredible. However, the princess also knew she gave those birds great sadness when she took Stanley away from them. *Would they ever meet another human like Stanley again?*

The princess already planned for another visit back to Ski Beach when her son had grown to the age he could interact with the birds and learn the magic of their relationship with his father.

The two lovers didn't need blankets as Stanley's wings were wrapped around Princess Lì and her wings added an inner layer covering much of Duke Ravik. Duke Ravik (aka Stanley) started his journey to the subconscious travels to times and places that would never be known with silent meditation. He learned to do this during tumultuous times during his life. Princess Lì detected the meditation and explored it during her own transcendence to an alternative mental state. She was always intending to discuss it with Stanley, but soon forgot it and when they awoke in the morning it was forgotten until the next evening when it suddenly reappeared.

The two felt refreshed and rejuvenated when they started stirring in the morning. The two chamber maids were currently in an adjacent room waiting to give the two love birds some privacy in the event they wanted to explore the physical nature of their relationship with joyous lovemaking.

Thanks to the dinner party and the need to rest, the lover's tryst didn't manifest during the night. But now as they lay with their eyes opening and looking into each other's faces, the psychophysical reactions slowly erupted in the pleasure centers of their brains, and Princess Lì telepathically signaled to Stanley she wanted the physical love making intercourse.

In just a few moments that savoring of passions flowed seamlessly and the covalence precipitated a rather strong passionate release as the gratification flowed like a river out to sea, and an endless stream of time created that grandeur and modulation of romantic physical responses. Splendid euphoria slowly ebbed and dissipated ushering in the living holographs of Stanley and Princess Lì's minds that replaced the temporal anomaly of the love making that produced quantities of neurohormones dopamine, oxytocin, and vasopressin during the peak of gratification.

Princess Lì didn't like laying in a pool of sweat created by their fantastic physical covalence and suggested telepathically they get up, use the bathroom, and take a nice refreshing bath.

The bathroom had two personal booths facilitating the princess and her significant other as it was understood this day would one day come and the staff would take care of two of them. Inside those personal booths they could take care of their morning business, come out cleaned well and ready to enter the bath water. By then the chambermaids were alerted by artificial intelligence of what was transpiring in the princess suite, and they were ready for when the two exited their personal use booths ready for the bathing and pampering.

~~~~~
~~~~~

CHAPTER FOUR

UNIFICATION AND REALIZATION

The couple awoke earlier than the emperor predicted and even with the love making and bathing they were still ahead in the timeline for the day's activities, the first being a meeting with the emperor to lay out their major plans that would certainly impact the Lìsztbrùnést Empire because events were now moving along unexpectedly and rapidly.

Neflatraceous, the capital of the Lìsztbrùnést Empire would soon be hosting unanticipated pomp and celebrations. Events were moving along at a frightening pace. The emperor's staff knew the princess but was not fully ready for how she swiftly came of age. Now she was charting her own destiny.

Princess Lì Alìgrāwná moved far more aggressively than the staff could imagine. She left nothing to chance and understood vividly the sooner Stanley and she had the Official Unification the less likelihood unforeseen circumstances would come along and rip him out of her web.

Stanley was Princess Lì Alìgrāwná's ultimate conquest. This was her greatest purpose in life as she felt the slight pangs of pregnancy, she knew was now going to soon take command of her body and redirect her life's energies in more ways than one.

No man had ever made Princess Lì Alìgrāwná cry like Stanley did. Princess Lì's emotions had been fully captured by Stanley. It wasn't something Stanley planned, it was an accident he slid into without the appreciation of the new reality he created for himself, simply because he had made all the birds at Ski Beach love him, minus the hawks he was at war with over killing the lovely pigeons.

Princess Lì Alìgrāwná continued her indoctrination of Stanley with strong doses of telepathic penetrations to remove all traces of remorse Stanley felt for Ami. At this moment he had no thoughts of Ami. His past was bleached, and Ami was the biggest victim of the bleaching process. It was highly doubtful Stanley would ever recall Ami in his thoughts the rest of his life. This was like a new beginning with a person not remembering his past.

It did not take long for the chambermaids to get the couple dressed in Royal Clothing. A makeup artist and hair designer were promptly brought in to put the finishing touches on Princess Lì Alìgrāwná.

This was the first time that Stanley saw Princess Lì Alìgrāwná made up to these high standards. Her makeover was rather astonishing. She was now more desirable than Stanley ever experienced before. *Were they putting on a show for me to seal the deal?*

The couple was then escorted by the Valet named Lucas down to the Royal Dining Hall with three place settings with placards. It was still early for the emperor, but the staff proceeded to give the couple drinks and a few snacks to hold them over for the main event that would start when the emperor arrived.

In due course Emperor Cornelius arrived slightly perturbed because of Princess Lì Alìgrāwná's actions in the night, not accepting the emperor's instructions to have the couple separated to avoid a scandalous appearance. Even though he would like to brow beat her, they had too much work to do to dwell on something that really didn't matter afterall since the two were already effectively a couple and possibly the princess impregnated.

While the food was being served and Emperor Cornelius was starting to enjoy his meal, Princess Lì Alìgrāwná started the discourse in a rather astounding fashion:

"Father, I know all of this is probably putting a strain on you, but I have a proposal to make that I think you will agree that will help simplify a lot of your concerns."

"What exactly is it that you wish to do Lì?"

"Father this will be a good plan for both of us as I understand how you are nervous about my situation being non-unified with an out-worlder living with us here in the mansion."

"Yes, that is a concern of course."

"Father, you have the means to do what I'm requesting as its within your preview as the emperor to do such things."

"What precisely are you referring to?"

"I want you to give us an Official Unification this morning and at a later date we can plan a public reception for your Royal Court and a few individuals you wish to invite."

The emperor with a poker face looked at Stanley and asked, "How do you feel all about this Duke Ravik?"

"I think Princess Lì makes perfect sense because if we are Unified, nobody can create scandals or rumors. I would be happy to have a reception later since I know a reception undoubtedly would require planning and execution."

"Stanley, I will consider this, but I must first warn you, that under no circumstances would you ever be permitted to leave the princess."

"Nor would I want to."

"Even twenty years from now when multitudes of young women throw themselves at your feet?"

"Your Excellency, I think in twenty years, I will have a different focus on life. The distractions will less likely effect my conduct."

"How can, you be sure?"

"Nobody knows for certain what their future will bring. But I know I have a lot to learn about the universe."

"It's quite apparent that you already have discovered far more than any Earth person."

"I realize I'm kind of in a unique situation, but I would not discount what some of our ancient civilizations experienced."

"Our knowledge of ancient Earth is kind of sketchy, but our researchers believe Earth wiped itself out four times in the past."

"Were they advanced societies?"

"Certainly, Atlantis was as advanced as we are now."

"How did Atlantis get wiped out?"

"There was a terrible nuclear war."

"Do you know what caused that nuclear war?"

"There were two groups of aliens who instigated the conflict. One of them sided with Earth's Atlantis and the other aliens supplied sophisticated weapons to the Zerorus Government located in the Martian City Cydonia. When one of those aliens was losing, they decided that neither side should benefit from winning the conflict, so they unleashed dooms day weapons."

"No survivors?"

"There were a few survivors that lived in remote areas that slowly rebuilt the species on Earth, but Mars was completely annihilated. The great city states of Atlantis and Cydonia no longer existed because their destruction was complete."

The emperor recognized that Stanley was showing signs of severe distress and decided to alter the direction of the conversation.

"I've decided that Princess Lì has the best way to proceed with the arrangement in how the two of you will live. Since you are already dressed rather appropriately for any type of ceremony, I will have my Valet Octavrator contact a few members of the Royal Court to be witness to the ceremony and we shall do the Unification sometime later in the morning.

"Thank you, Your Excellency, for your advocating this unification," Stanley responded.

"What I want you two to do is immediately after the unification, is you two travel to a dozen of Empire planets and show yourselves to the public."

"We would be most happy to do that," Princess Lì responded.

I will send along ample security and publicity agents to make sure it's a well recorded event," Emperor Cornelius explained.

"I'm sure it will be a memorable time for Princess Lì." Stanley said.

The emperor looked at his daughter who was just about to burst into tears of joy. He knew this was quite an emotional moment for her. The sad part was her mother would not be here to watch all this unfold.

The emperor then informed Stanley the critical role soon to be bestowed upon him:

"During these exhibits for the sake of the public, it would do your measurable benefit if you spread your wings a few times."

"Why may I ask?"

"If society sees that you have wings and if you can arrange to do some minor flying with Princess Lì at some of these locations it will help increase your popularity among the masses."

"I will do whatever you think is best for the Empire."

"I have already figured that out. Its clear to me why Princess Lì picked you when she could have had any man in the galaxy. The fact she picked you demonstrates there is something very special about you."

Princess Lì could not hold back. Her emotional spike was now reaching the point of criticality and she lunged at the emperor and threw her arms around him and started crying profusely. The emperor was so touched with his daughter's conduct his eyes watered up slightly and it did not go unnoticed by him to see Stanley's eyes water up conveying what was truly in his heart.

Emperor Cornelius hugged Princess Lì while she was crying. It now became ever clear to the emperor that Princess Lì made several astute judgements in moving this unification forward in a rapid pace to get ahead of the news cycle which created an appearance of her brilliance.

In due time everyone calmed down a few notches and Emperor Cornelius then knew he had to do something critical and said, "Lì, I want you to go back to your suite. You have spoiled your makeup and your face with all these tears. Your assistants will fix you up. Also, as a special gift to me I'm going to request you change your dress. The fashion designers will be there shortly with a dress that would make me very happy if you wore it."

"Yes father, you know I would wear anything for you."

"Good." The emperor then nodded at Valet Octavrator who knew to take Princess Lì back to her suite to get her ready. After they were gone, the emperor looked at Stanley and said, "Because of the delicacy of the fabric of the Lìsztbrùnést Empire, in public I cannot call you Stanley. I must refer to you as the Duke Ravik."

"I understand, your Excellency."

"Stanley, I want you to do me a personal favor."

"Yes sir, what would you like me to do?"

"Come with me to my private quarters, I also want you to change into something special."

"I would be most honored."

The emperor stood and he led Stanley and his second Valet Lucas to his private suite and into a walk-in closet where a couple complicated garment storage cubes existed with a pulsating light on a hemisphere locking control mechanism.

The emperor put his hand on the first cube hemisphere and the device then opened after it detected Emperor Cornelius palm print. He reached inside the cubical storage device and grabbed what appeared to be a fabulous white dress and turned to Valet Lucas and said, "Take this to Princess Lì and inform her she will make my heart feel really good if she wears this for the Unification Ceremony."

"As you wish, your Excellency." Valet Lucas said then soon left the suite with the beautiful white dress in a clear garment carrier.

Right after the Valet departed on the urgent assignment, the emperor then placed his hand on the second cubical storage hemisphere locking device which it quickly recognized his handprint and opened. The emperor then took the attire out of the cube and handed it to Stanley and said, "I want you to wear this. I think our sizes are about the same. I can have a tailor alter it, if necessary, but us try it on, I think it will fit the way it is."

The emperor helped Stanley out of his very colorful royal clothes and assisted him putting on the wonderful and immaculate suit that exemplified the essence of Stanley and was designed to allow his wings to be exposed. Soon Stanley was dressed, and the emperor was very happy it fit so well.

"I wore this when I unified with Princess Li's mother. Thank you for wearing this. It will help bring back the precious memories of the woman I loved more than anyone in my life."

"I feel privileged to wear this, your Excellency."

"Stanley, from this day forward, you are now part of my family. You are now my adopted son. In private I want you to call me father."

"I will be very happy to do so father."

"Thank you."

I have some special shoes I want you to now put on. The emperor reached into the garment cube and pulled out gold plated shoes that were shiny as if they were polished that morning. The glitzy suite and the golden shoes now encapsulated Stanley in an unforgettable image. The images of the Unification would be broadcasted to the Empire. Every planet would see this before the day was over thanks to high-speed neutrino communications links. Those neutrino links sent messages and images almost two hundred times faster than the speed of light.

The Valets were quickly contacting the members of the Royal Court the emperor preferred as he wanted his best friends to experience the most important day in his daughter's life.

Princess Li had extraordinary makeup and hair design. Her exquisite beauty now fully illustrated her incredible genetics. When the Valet gave her the garment to put on, she quickly recognized it was her mother's wedding dress based on pictures she saw and soon broke down and started crying which screwed up her makeup.

One of the makeup artists quickly confided with the princess and soothed her and explained, "It is essential you come to grips because the empire would soon be seeing you and you need to be smiling and to let the sadness all go away."

One statement set her keel in the perfect position when the makeup artist said, "All you need to do is think about the love of your life is waiting for you and will spend the rest of his life with you sharing his love. You have reason to be happy and keep smiling."

The statement had an incredible psychological impact on Princess Lì who now felt completely different as happiness pervaded her every essence.

The tears didn't do terrible damage and was easy to repair and soon the living princess was ready to go to the main event of her life.

The Valet Lucas came into the room when artificial intelligence informed him Princess Lì was dressed and ready for the event. He then said, "please wait here and I will go inform the emperor you are ready to proceed with the Unification."

"Thank you."

Out in the courtyard the manifestation of pomp and celebration quickly unfolded. The orchestra was always at arm's reach and were soon in the hastily laid out stage near the Unification platform wearing their very best performance apparel. The luster was as expected to such an important event. Having performed for other important unifications such as for the emperor's relatives and high standing members of the court, they knew what compositions to perform.

For an Earth person, the brilliance of Beethoven, Brahms, Saint Saens, Tchaikovsky, Rachmaninoff, Liszt, Dvorak, and others seemed to be connected to the music. As the court members were showing up some were upset, they were not given adaquate time to be pampered with spectacular designs and preparations, strolled in, and were escorted by security detail members dressed in ornate suits, to their reserved seating assignments. Nothing was left to chance. Having two good Valets helped to streamline the process quite effectively.

The emperor escorted Stanley to the unification platform where a high priest stood ready to anoint the two in a grand royal unification that would soon grip the empire with the sudden surprise.

Most of the court members present had not seen Stanley unfurl his wings, and most of the empire had not as well. This would be a huge surprise to all of them. Thanks to Princess Lì's grooming of Stanley and some of the cosmetic modifications she did to change the appearance of his age and increase his handsome looks, he now stood in awe by the women sitting in the guest chairs. Everyone of them knew they would melt in his arms and allow him to have his way with them. They knew vividly the princess had a keen eye for beauty and his looks bestowed an element of charisma that was entirely uncommon.

The emperor nodded at Valet Lucas who then knew it was time to get the princess and bring her out to the ceremony. The emperor leaving Stanley alone on the unification stage with the high priest followed by Valet Octavrator to the princess suite and thanks to artificial intelligence the other Valet, Lucas then opened the door and led Princess Lì Alìgrāwná out to the hallway to meet up with her father who was smiling and very happy.

"Are you all set?"

"Yes father. Thank you for giving me the best day of my life."

The emperor held out his hand to the princess and together they walked down that hallway that led out to the courtyard.

The musicians played the Royal Lìsztbrùnést March reserved for the emperor and his most special events. Stanley listening to the Military March music thought it had a characteristic to it like Franz von Suppé's "Light Cavalry Overture" several minutes into the piece when the French Horns and Trumpets gave the melody first followed by the entire orchestra in a majestic sense.

Emperor Cornelius giving his daughter away to Unification

was one of those most appropriate times to play such military march music.

Emperor Cornelius led Princess Lì Alìgrāwná down the red carpet and the crowd was mystified by her splendid beauty and the dress captivated their attention. People on Earth would certainly be utterly stunned observing a princess in her wedding dress with wings behind her that she could unfurl at the most appropriate moment.

All the way up to the unification platform, Princess Lì Alìgrāwná looked directly into Stanley's eyes feeling the love she could easily find with her deep penetration into his thoughts with her powerful telepathic ability. She almost wanted to cry a few times but the words the makeup artist bolstered her resolve to keep smiling and giving the love of her life the quintessential transcendence to a new universe he now experienced.

There were a few steps up to the Unification platform. The emperor took his daughter directly up to Stanley and took her hand and placed it into Stanley's hand and did something NOBODY in the crowd had ever witnessed before. The emperor took a long bow to Stanley, who copied him in a similar bow. The emperor then stood erect and bowed at his daughter signifying his great respect for her decisions. The emperor then stepped back and to the side of his daughter facing Princess Lì Alìgrāwná, Duke Ravik (Stanley), and the high priest who then proceeded in a short dissertation on the fabric of life manifested by Unification. Then with a broad smile and utter charm the priest then declared:

"I now pronounce the legal Unification between Duke Ravik and Princess Lì Alìgrāwná."

The two were now officially Unified. It was done. There was no turning back for the *man of birds* from Ski Beach. He was now unified with the most powerful woman in the galaxy.

Oddly at that precise time on planet Earth, Ami felt a strong pain go through her heart. It was as if she received a spiritual signal from somewhere. She broke down crying as she missed Stanley so terribly and knew vividly, you don't know what you have lost until a special moment occurs. She had taken Stanley for granted many years and wished there was something she could do to bring him back. She had no idea where Stanley went as their worlds were now far apart. She would never see Stanley again and after handling all the financial matters moved back to her hometown Hamamatsu Japan where she could be close to her brother's family.

Immediately after the pronouncement of the Unification, the two lovers embraced in a very delicate manner. The love poured through their hearts. Princess Lì knew there was something she now had to do for the sake of the monarchy, because it wasn't all just about them. They had serious social responsibilities and knew lots of video recordings of them was ongoing and soon would be shown to the Empire worlds.

Through her telepathic abilities Princess Lì said to Stanley, "We must now turn and face the crowd and unfurl our wings. This is very important to our civilization. Do it just like we did at the reception."

"Alright." Stanley responded telepathically.

The two then maneuvered their bodies to allow this impressive display of two extremely beautiful people unfurled their wings, showing an incredible majestic pose that would resonate around the empire in just a few hours.

Upon observance of their wings now showing the incredible luster of the two individuals, the emperor then facing the crowd said, "Ladies and Gentlemen, please let me introduce to you my daughter Princess Lì Alìgrāwná and Duke Ravik."

The princess finally had her prince and the majestic unfurling of their wings put an exclamation point on it! The two spread wings created a sensational image captured on video and in the eyes of all those present.

The crowd had been very quiet and respectful up until this moment. The excitement of the moment could no longer be contained as the crowd suddenly erupted in enthusiastic applause.

Several women were crying and even a few men had watery eyes. The special moment had come for the couple that would soon be the central figures in the banquet that would soon spring upon everyone after the couple passed through the guest line personally addressing each guest in a warm and friendly manner. A dozen waiters now arrived with trays of elixirs that were much like champagne with added psychoactive drugs to enhance the moment and multiply the wondrous emotions. These elixirs would also increase their hunger and help create the desire to eat the fabulous meal the chefs prepared knowing it was well an hour before most of their mealtimes.

The 24-course meal that would soon appear as workers efficiently set up tables and chairs and laid out the placemats with ornate tableware's. By the time the newly unified couple traversed through the reception line, the choreography of the great feast was well in hand and the guests were encouraged to take their seats all identified with placards so everyone would know where to sit. Valet's and waiters with electronic AI assistance escorted most of them to their correct seats and the others located them on their own with very little need for assistance as their friends and relatives called out to them knowing the placards identified their locations.

Emperor Cornelius and his family sat next to each other, and the pecking order then laid out the locations for everyone else. The closer a citizen sat near the emperor meant their significance in life mattered more.

As soon as everyone was seated and Valet Octavrator nodded at the emperor, the emperor rose and said, "Ladies and Gentlemen, I want to thank you for being here today to see the Unification of my lovely daughter Princess Lì Alìgrāwná to Duke Ravik. I would like to make a toast to this couple and wish them forever happiness."

As the emperor lifted his glass and then moved it down to his lips, he took a sip of the very expensive elixir saved for a special moment like this. The crowd followed suit and soon they were tapping their elixir glasses with golden tableware created a cacophony of chimes like oscillations depending on how full their glasses were.

It was a happy and joyous occasion for all despite a mystery man was the central figure in all this. It would not be the first time the royalty brought in a complete stranger. But the nature of this, a person coming from a solar system far away from any Empire worlds did create quite a lot of curiosity. Had Stanley not had the wing surgery, the population would be seriously alarmed.

Stanley with his new Royal Identity, Duke Ravik, showing up with wings did a lot to comfort the public as his imagery now purveyed plausible acceptance. His cosmetic reformation which added significantly to Stanley's luster, and left quite a few women spellbound. Stanley had a pleasant-sounding voice. His enhanced IQ and his secret and quiet telepathic guidance Princess Lì interjected during conversations created a surreal appraisal of Duke Ravik (aka Stanley). Princess Lì knew that with minimal assistance Stanley was ready for prime time and would conduct himself in the most impecable fashion. Duke Ravik elucidated poignant information when those closest to him fired away questions and comments.

The Emperor's Royal Court quickly assessed the princess had astutely picked a mate. They didn't quite know the circumstances of how that all manifested, nor would they ever be allowed to know because her most precious moments of her life were highly guarded secrets that only Drákōlìné, the Captain of the Lìsztbrùnést Royal Space Yacht, and the emperor would ever know. It was assured none of them would ever divulge those private details, especially the emperor who knew his daughter would get very angry if she ever discovered the details Drákōlìné gave to him which might cost her life. The emperor was quite savvy and would be the last to ever reveal what he knew as he was the consummate chess master and knew better than to show his hand in anything.

The reception lingered as many members as possible of the Royal Court wanted to rub elbows with the Royal Couple and elevate their status in doing so.

Princess Lì was extremely intelligent and sensitive. Her telepathic prowess was immense and grew slowly. The only person with the ability to intercept her secret communiques to Stanley was her father who kept on his poker face throughout the event. Stanley knew this event wasn't for them, it was for the public and now that he was a Royal member of the family, he had the responsibility to represent Emperor Cornelius in the best of light. The emperor was taken back when he detected the telepathic interchange with the couple:

"I'm glad you are handling yourself so well and giving the members of the Royal Court such charming responses."

"It's important for the Empire. These are the emperor's most trusted friends. We need to be sensitive to their needs and give them our best on such an important day of our lives."

"Thank you for all you are doing, you make me proud."

"Thank you for filling my heart with love."

The emperor saw Princess Lì's eyes water up a bit. It also had and effect on him. It was this very moment he knew the essence of Stanley. Emperor Cornelius actually felt humbled his daughter was able to make such an astute selection for a mate.

Princess Lì waited a long time for this day and turned down so many men the emperor wondered if she would ever *Unify*.

Stanley's presence resolved a lot of questions Emperor Cornelius had in his mind about the future of his daughter. One of the biggest revelations the emperor recognized as a significance, was Princess Lì's amazing selection. It seemed almost like a miracle.

The final arbeiter in Princess Lì's decision was of course the mental connection all those birds had to Stanley. Such a relationship had never existed anywhere in the galaxy that Princess Lì was aware of. She quickly figured out, every single one of those birds truly loved Stanley. The affection was enormous. Princess Lì had a detailed roadmap to Stanleys heart and his soul. She knew no other person to this level. And now Stanley was an extension to her own psyche. She found true love. Stanley gave up his life for Princess Lì. His past was now severed with no possibility of ever going back.

The orchestra played on. The music set the mood. Even though many orchestra members were hungry, they played their hearts out for Princess Lì knowing this was the most important day of her life. The music was exquisite and low enough in volume to allow conversations without destroying the detailed sound and harmonics.

Emperor Cornelius' Royal Court had great understanding of decorum and knew when enough of their presence had satisfied the requirements of their invitations and slowly started thinning out to the emperor's great happiness the event would not linger too long so that other preparations could be made. Soon all the guests were gone, and the emperor nodded to Valet Octavrator who then approached where he could direct him: "Take the orchestra to the dining room and feed them lavishly. As soon as they are all seated and drinking some refreshments waiting for their meals come get us. The Royal Couple and I will pass around their tables and thank them for this performance."

"It will be my distinct pleasure, your Excellency." Valet Octavrator then bowed and approached the conductor of the orchestra.

The conductor instinctively knew Valet Octavrator had something important to relay to him and stopped the performance to hear what he had to say.

"Dear conductor, please inform the orchestra that you are to follow me into the dining hall where your meals are being prepared."

The conductor smiled and turned to the orchestra and said, "Everyone, we are going to the dining hall now. Leave your instruments here. We'll come back after our lunch is served and prepare the instruments to be shipped back to the studio."

The orchestra now feeling hunger pains was more than happy to comply and followed the Valet Octavrator and the Conductor into the fabulous dining hall, where all their place settings had placards laid out almost identical to where they sat in the orchestra.

Within moments the orchestra was enjoying the best and most expensive elixirs of the galaxy! Anticipation was gripping the members of the orchestra as they speculated on the wonderful meal that would soon be served to them. After enough time had passed where most of the orchestra had enjoyed some of the elixirs the next surprise happened.

~~~~~~

As soon as the orchestra was gone, the only people left was the Royal Couple, Emperor Cornelius, Drákōlìné, the Valet Lucas, and several security men protecting the emperor.

"In a few moments, we are going into the dining hall to greet the members of the orchestra and thank them for their fabulous performance," Emperor Cornelius stated.

"Of course, father. Their performance was exceptionally good."

"Since we are alone now, I wanted to now inform you what I want you to do tomorrow."
~~~~~~

"What is that father?" Princess Lì asked with a serious look on her face.

"I want you and Duke Ravik to travel to Azorloma tomorrow."

Princess Lì had a sudden emotional spike. Her eyes watered. Stanley with his mental probing of Princess Lì knew this was a sensitive moment and sat there in a quiet posture waiting it all to unfold.

Princess Lì loved her mother dearly. Her mother grew up on Azorloma and by a freak of nature, Emperor Cornelius accidently met her there and quickly was captivated and quickly fell in love and asked Princess Lì's mother to return to Neflatraceous, the capital of the Lìsztbrùnést Empire with him and share their lives together. Their love seemed ideal, and her mother was attracted to the emperor and easily fell in love with the wonderful gentleman who had impecable manners and a sweetness that transcended everything in her life.

When the Empress life was eventually stamped out in the tragedy, the emperor knew it would be her wish to be buried at Azorloma near her family roots. The last time Princess Lì traveled to Azorloma was to watch her mother be buried there. It ripped her heart out and was the saddest moment in her life. The emperor knew this would not be a good trip for Princess Lì, but her mother's relatives were all there. It would be an act of showing respect for her mother to travel there and introduce Duke Ravik to her family.

Princess Lì could not hold back the emotion. The dam quickly broke, and the floodgate of tears erupted while she quickly embraced her father and cried like she hadn't since that strange episode on Earth where she discovered the essence of Stanley in the most bizarre event in her life. As Princess Lì cried burying her face into her father's shoulder, he felt that he somehow had done something very bad to spoil his daughter's most important day of her life. His eyes too watered and now wished he had not done what he just did.

Stanley sat there in a most somber manner. It was a very delicate moment. Drákōlìné was also affected quite seriously as she was present during the demise of Princess Lì Alìgrāwná's mother and knew how terribly Princess Lì Alìgrāwná took it. It took Princess Lì Alìgrāwná a long time to heal from the loss of her wonderful mother whom she loved dearly. Drákōlìné's eyes were also watery and knew to be patient and let Princess Lì Alìgrāwná to come to terms with her grief and then she would suggest she take her back to her suite to fix her makeup before she went into the dining hall to greet the orchestra members.

In due time, Princess Lì Alìgrāwná got control of her emotions. One thing and one thing only snapped her out of it. Amid her outburst of sadness, Princess Lì Alìgrāwná heard several times telepathically, "I love you, please don't cry." But it wasn't just one voice. It was the entire flock back on Earth somehow was communicating with her. And above all she knew her prince Stanley's voice was the prounounced sound mixed in with all those he cherished. She pulled her face away from her father's chest and looked directly at Stanley. Everyone there saw she had a strange look on her face, and she telepathically said to Stanley, "I love you too. Thank you for helping me in this precious moment."

Stanley smiled, Princess Lì Alìgrāwná smiled, and Drákōlìné knew this was a critical moment to salvage the day and interceded, "Princess Lì, let me take you back to your suite so you can freshen up and we can fix your makeup before we go see the orchestra."

"Thank you. I'm ready. Let's go take care of it."

When the women were gone, the emperor knew he needed to explain a few things to Stanley of what just happened.

"Stanley, I felt it would be important for you to visit her mother's family. I didn't know any other way to do this. But to show her mother's family the proper respect, I felt it would be important to visit them first."

"Father, I think you did the right thing. I will do what I can to help Princess Lì during the trip."

Hearing Stanley call him 'Father' had a huge impact on Emperor Cornelius at that moment. He looked at Stanley with utter astonishment now realizing the extraordinary scenario in how the *man of birds* evolved into this relationship with his daughter.

"I know you will. When Lì stopped crying and looked at you that was her closure. I think you are now as important to her as her mother was."

"I felt her sorrow. It felt like a bird with a broken wing."

"There is no better way to describe it. I can't tell you how badly my wings felt when her mother was taken from me."

Emperor Cornelius eyes were watery now. It was a good thing they had the orchestra to go visit to cheer themselves up, otherwise it would have turned into a dreadful day.

Time passed and Emperor Cornelius and Stanley then had a friendly conversation. The emperor was a great judge of character and had his own telepathic abilities and probed Stanley just as deep as Princess Lì had done. He quickly surmised Stanley was well rounded and a supreme foundation to build his future on. It was now crystal clear why his daughter selected this wonderful man. Even though it was a sad day because of the necessity of conducting Royal affairs like they must, at least there was one positive takeaway: Duke Ravik would be a tremendous asset to Princess Lì Alìgrāwná. Duke Ravik's only motivation seemed to celebrate his love for Princess Lì Alìgrāwná and take that life journey with her to where it must take them.

Drákōlìné knew time was at the essence and they needed to get the makeup fixed and get to the orchestra before it was too late to give the orchestra the proper accolades for their performance.

"I know you went through a very emotional situation when

your father discussed your travel plans. You need to pull yourself together for the sake of the emperor and your significant other and be that wonderful woman and show happiness to the orchestra who just played their hearts out for you."

"I'll be okay now. Stanley helped me snap out of it. As long as I'm with Stanley today, I will be ok."

"Good. You look stunningly beautiful again. Us keep it that way to make Stanley and your father feel great today."

"I'll be fine now. I'm ready."

The two women left the princess suite and walked out to the courtyard and approached the emperor and Duke Ravik.

"We are ready to go see the orchestra now," Princess Li said with a beautiful smile and no signs of sadness.

The emperor and the duke stood up and the group followed Valet Lucas into the dining hall that was currently boisterous with dozens of conversations going on at the same time. The Royal couple were only a few feet away from the first table before the orchestra members were aware of their presence.

The Royal Couple went down one side of the table together and the emperor the other side greeting each individual and thanking them for their performance.

The orchestra members were halfway through their first entrée and fortified by elixirs spiked with psychology enhancers. Everyone was happy and the princess smile added to their ambience. The orchestra enjoyed the pleasant royal couple and appreciated them even more now for greeting them in this manner during the most important days of their lives.

It was almost like a fairytale setting, the princess with her prince charming, full of happiness and love. Several female musicians were emotionally struck by it all. One could feel the love and satisfaction flowing. The moment was filled with a spontaneous eruption of gratification.

The emperor knew one day this would come. He now instinctively understood the implications of a future decedent who would replace him on the throne when the time came. This was an auspicious moment for the emperor who now had a greater appreciation for his daughter who was far wiser than he would have known otherwise.

After the Royals all worked their way down through the tables and intermingled with the musicians the emperor standing at the very end of the table next to the conductor looked at his primary Valet Octavrator and said, "Please get the Royal Couple and myself a glass of Gumonaclaris Elixir so that we can toast the orchestra."

"Right away Your excellency," Valet Octavrator said with a genuine smile.

Valet Octavrator walked a dozen yards to where several bartenders and waiters stood diligently waiting for any drink requirements. Valet Octavrator directed one of the waiters to provide the Emperor and the Royal Couple the glasses of Gumonaclaris Elixir. As soon as the waiter was ready, Valet Octavrator pulled out of his pocket a special scanner that would detect any poisons or foreign matter in the Royals Drinks. Should a poisonous substance be detected, the drinks would then be immediately taken to the laboratory for further testing and the waiters and bartenders would all go through neurotic examination to discover the source of the possible poison and then receive appropriate punishment once they were identified. If such an act was part of a coup, all those involved would be immediately executed after they were identified.

Today, there was no traces of foreign substances in the elixir and the waiter walked very carefully and deliberately to the emperor, never placing his hands over the drinks. Out of protocol, the emperor and the Royal Couple would pick the drinks off the golden tray preventing any possible contamination.

As soon as the three royals had their glasses, the emperor raised his glass and said, "A toast to your very wonderful performance today. I'm very proud of your excellent music you provided for the most important day of my daughter's life. From the bottom of my heart, thank you all for your efforts."

The three royals then raised their glasses and consumed some of the content. The emperor banged glasses with the conductor and said, "Maestro, thank you for your great leadership and the wonderful music provided today."

The conductor stood up and said, "Thank you your Excellency, I am blessed that you provided me with such an outstanding orchestra to work with."

The conductor took a sip of his drink then turned and faced all his musicians and said, "This is to you. Thank you for your wonderful performance."

The conductor then raised his glass and quickly drank its contents, feeling the wonderful effects that soon gave him a pleasant psychophysical response which caused the dopamine flowing nicely through his brain.

The emperor was astute on timing of all events and knew he needed to end this real soon and send the newlyweds to their suite so they could have some exquisite moments of privacy. He knew tomorrow would be a tough day for his daughter. But it was necessary. Even though tragedy had struck the Royal family and taken a key member away from them and shattered several hearts in the process, the emperor loved his daughter, Princess Lì Alìgrāwná beyond words.

Emperor Cornelius had to do this for his own closure. What better way to celebrate the empress life than to take her illustrious daughter back to her home planet and demonstrate his vast affection for her family. Furthermore, Princess Lì Alìgrāwná had a striking resemblance to her mother. The Empress family would see her through her daughters looks and her voice was also very similar in nature.

The emperor said then, "We are going to leave you now so you can enjoy your meals and socialize with one another. I'm looking forward to performances you will conduct in the future. Thank you all." He then did a deep bow and marched off smartly with the Valet in tow and the princess and duke behind.

As they arrived in the main hallway that had a circular path through the mansion, the emperor turned and looked at the Royal Couple and said, "I want the two of you to enjoy yourselves for the rest of the day. If you wish to go for a walk or a swim or any other activity, please enjoy yourselves. Tomorrow afternoon we'll leave for Azorloma."

The emperor then turned and walked towards his private suite where loneliness pervaded his ever waken moment as the death of the Empress left a gaping hole in his heart and his happiness.

Valet Octavrator then took the newlywed couple to their suite that would no longer be a possible source of scandal since several billion Empire Citizens had watched the Unification and were quite amazed over the sudden news that caught absolutely everyone by surprise and the mainstream media flat footed.

The couple arrived at their suite and the couple then freshened up. They were still satisfied from their earlier love making and now just the companionship is all that mattered.

The princess knowing how Stanley loved walking and seeing the birds thought it might please him if they went for a walk in the elaborate parklike surroundings of the emperor's mansion and suggested, "Would you like to go for a little walk so we can work off a few calories?"

"Yes, that would be really nice to do."

"Alright, I'll have the staff bring us a change of clothes and we can then go for a walk."

With the precision of Empire excellence, the staff soon had the Royal Couple dressed in the most appropriate clothes to walk out in the surrounding parklike area which allowed their wings to be exposed to allow them flight if they desired.

A few moments later they were escorted to the park by a security detail that kept their distances but with great concentration on their security requirements.

As the newlyweds walked through the park there were multitudes of birds flying around and enjoying life. Colorful birds unlike anything Stanley had ever seen. At one point Stanley stopped and looked at a bird that was eyeballing him. He gave the bird his strange whistle sound. The bird was amused with the sound. Princess Lì didn't let the moment escape as she telepathically communicated to the bird in a very rare fashion. Nobody knew what she was doing. Her tightly coupled telepathic entry into the bird's thoughts was not interceptable by anyone. The bird was one of the more intelligent species and soon acknowledged Princess Lì who convinced it that Stanley would be forever his friend and not to fear him. The bird felt so good about the mental telepathic influence, it then followed Stanley, just like Rascal would. Unfortunately, they would be leaving the mansion for a period of days. Would the bird remember them?

The two came upon a nice clearing with the bird following them close behind. Suddenly Stanley had the urge to fly and asked, "Would it be okay if we flew around this area for a few minutes?"

"If that's what you want to do, my love, sure we can."

The couple unfurled their wings and the security detachment got to see something they never witnessed before. The security members thought the wings were ceremonial and had no real function. Then the couple took to the air, with their bird friend following them growing emotionally closer to them by the moment.

The bird now had a significant attraction to the Royal Couple and could not understand why. It just knew it wanted to be near them.

After flying around in circles for about fifteen minutes the Royal Couple landed, and the security detail seemed completely overwhelmed observing the Royals flying in formation with the wild bird. But the security detail all knew security activity quite well and knew discussions of this observation to others was strictly forbidden. Only the security detail and nobody else would know the Royal Couple were flying around with a bird. But at the same time, the security team members now had a completely different appraisal of the Royal Couple that gave them new purpose in life. They felt special being a part in all this.

Satisfied from their physical workout the couple went back to the mansion where Princess Lì decided she wanted to bathe to remove the sweat and residue from the workout.

Their new friend, the bird flew to a tree near the entrance of the mansion and watched the couple go inside. He would come back from time to time looking for them.

The newlyweds were soon in the large bath together soaking in utter delight. Princess Lì Alìgrāwná felt total love for Stanley and he was completely satisfied with his new bearing in life. Already Stanley was feeling the effects of age reversal on his body as his sexual prowess seemed multiplied and he recognized in the mirror his wrinkles were almost gone. He felt invigorated but he also was not a fool and understood the incredible dynamics now at play. He knew that with Princess Lì Alìgrāwná's coaching and indoctrination he was easily fitting into this new society. Today observing that friendly bird seemed to help him adjust to his new world. There was now gold at the end of the rainbow.

~~~~~~
~~~~~~

CHAPTER FIVE

AZORLOMA, REMEMBRANCES AND LEGACY

The Royal Couple achieved a really good night rest. The Royal Couple's new lives would seem like Camelot during ancient times back on Earth that the new Duke of Ravik (aka Stanley) understood quite well as one of his leaders lived the fairy tale the public misjudged then tragedy struck.

This would be a long day for the couple, but they would be able to rest later aboard the Lìsztbrùnést Royal Space Yacht.

Princess Lì Alìgrāwná's chambermaids were instructed the night before by the head Valet, Octavrator on the actions they were to take in the morning. They would awake the couple and get them moving and prepare them for the trip. While Duke Ravik slept his clothes were checked and double checked for sizing including video examinations to tweak the tailoring to precision as they prepared his wardrobe for the journey to the planet Azorloma.

Duke Ravik was now a central partner in the monarchy. The emperor now had complete confidence in him as Stanley had gone through more vetting and mental probing than probably anyone in history. The stakes were that high.

Princess Lì Alìgrāwná's heart was a major concern for her father. In all appearances and probing, the emperor had quickly developed trust in Stanley and now as Duke Ravik, he would place more and more responsibilities on him. Emperor Cornelius knew he would give Duke Ravik as much help as possible. There was no need for the emperor to really have two Valet's now, so he did the most logical action. He summoned Octavrator, his longest lasting and most trusted Valet into his private quarters with a very important mission.

"Your Excellency, what can I do for you?"

"Octavrator, you are my most trusted and faithful assistant. Nobody has served me as long and as distinguished as you have. I owe my life to you when you saved me."

"Your Excellency, I feel like I failed you because the Empress is no longer with us."

"Octavrator, the odds were against you. For the sake of the empire, you did the most noble deed. Had I been the one killed and not the Empress, I'm afraid it would have been a matter of time before they assassinated the empress, and the empire would no longer exist."

"Your Excellency, I still feel I failed you."

"Octavrator, I wish the outcome could have been different, but unfortunately you did all you could. There is nothing more that you could have done."

"What is it that you want me to do, your Excellency."

"This new assignment for you is because I need to be assured the very best person is looking out for my interest. At first you might feel slanted in what I'm going to have you do, but you need to understand this is the most important decision I've had to make since I lost my lovely Empress."

"Alright sir, you know you can count on me."

"Octavrator, I'm assigning you to be the Duke of Ravik's personal Valet. You need to understand that very soon he will be the father of my successor. That's why its critical he be protected equally as well as you have protected me."

"Your excellency, I will always do as you request."

"Thank you Octavrator. On this day forward I want you to realize that by protecting Duke Ravik, you are also protecting the throne, because his son will be the person, I turn the empire over too."

"I swear on my life to protect him."

"That's not all."

Octavrator looked at the emperor with great curiosity waiting to hear the big surprise that was coming next.

"Part of your responsibility will be to prepare the heir to the throne so that when I step down, he'll be able to conduct all activities necessary to maintain the Empire."

"He will have his father; I'm sure Duke Ravik will want a hand in raising his child."

"This will be no different that parents sending their children to school. The big difference is you are the school. I have complete faith in you know what needs to be done and how to properly indoctrinate the future emperor so that our longevity is maintained."

"How soon do you expect this child to be born?"

"Very soon. Based on covert examination I know my daughter is already pregnant."

"The timing of the Unification then was very auspicious."

"It was."

"I understand what I must do."

"I have complete faith in you. You are the backbone of the Empire, and we are growing older, and the day will come when we must hand over the future of the empire to my descendants. Your assignment is thus the critical role of ensuring the continuity of the monarchy which directly affects the survival of the empire and the happiness and wellbeing of our citizens."

"My divine emperor, I fully understand the significance of this assignment and I take great pleasure in knowing that I will be beneficial to the empire."

"Octavrator, please continue with your preparations for the trip."

"Will you be on the Lìsztbrùnést Royal Space Yacht with the Royal Couple?"

"No, there is only one sleeping quarters on the Yacht that is worthy of a Royal. I want the Royal Couple to travel on the Royal Space Yacht for the obvious political and social reasons. I will travel on one of the two fast frigates sent along for their protection. Also, from this day forward I cannot travel on the same transport as the Royal Couple to ensure continuity of government. Once the child is born, he will travel with his father and my daughter will trave separately. I want to make sure one or both survives in case we must deal with some unpredictable circumstances."

"I understand all your highness, and I will now leave you and go conduct my responsibilities you have directed me. Is there anything I can do for you before I depart?"

"That will be all Octavrator, go take care of your charges and I will be seeing you in the passing days. Also, if something comes up that you think I need to know about please send me an urgent notification and I'll request your attendance to a private meeting."

"Yes sir, your Excellency, I will make sure you are always well informed about your family members."

"Thank you."

Valet Octavrator did a deep bow to the emperor's satisfaction then turned one hundred and eighty degrees and walked over to the entrance and departed the emperor's private suite.

Lesser men would have been displeased with the apparent demotion and the other Valet would now have exclusive access to the emperor. Nevertheless, one of Octavrator's charges was to raise the new emperor. What that really meant was Octavrator would be deciding the future of the Empire. The emperor had ever reason to place such awesome responsibility on him. Octavrator was now the progenitor of the monarchy. Thus, such an assignment was just as important the day he saved the emperor's life. He took this assignment with ample concern and care to be conducted at the very best of his ability because of the consequences of his actions.

A father is often his son's worst teacher. Not in all but in many cases, there is a psychological barrier that cannot be penetrated, especially if there were two strong egos involved. The wise emperor understood the fundamentals of life as he had been solely responsible for the direction the Empire took. And no matter how hard he tried there were always going to be issues.

The fact his dearly departed Empress was not around to spend their golden years together demonstrated the harsh realities of life, that there really isn't any guarantees, even for a heart broken emperor. But at least he was given the satisfaction of observing his wonderful daughter pick and chose her partner in life that now had an idealistic aura surrounding it. And furthermore, through the security camera's observing the two newlyweds on their walk around the parklike areas surrounding the emperor's mansion and the impact Stanley had on that bird that followed him ever since, demonstrated there were obscure qualities this person had which set him apart from his peers and influenced his daughter's selection.

By the time the Valet Octavrator reached the newlywed's suite, the couple was dressed and ready to go wherever they were required. Octavrator then summoned the chambermaids to open the door for him and announce to the couple he was arriving to help provide for their needs and alert them on their status and arrangements that were now ongoing.

"Princess Lì and Duke Ravik, the Valet Octavrator is here to see you and brief you on upcoming events," the chambermaid said.

"Please invite him in," Princess Lì quickly responded knowing this man would now brief them on what was in store for them.

The chambermaids promptly marched over to the entrance, and one opened the door and bowed very respectfully coincidentally with the other and Octavrator marched in smartly as if he were in total control.

"Princess Lì and Duke Ravik, it will be about two hours before you go aboard the Lìsztbrùnést Royal Space Yacht. I recommend you eat something now so that you are well adjusted when you begin your travels to Azorloma."

"That sounds good to me," Princess Lì responded, and Duke Ravik acknowledged with a nod.

"Would you like room service, or would you like to eat out in the courtyard with fresh air and a nice view?"

"Since we have two hours to enjoy our time, why not the courtyard," Princess Lì responded, and Duke Ravik nodded in complete agreement.

"Alright then please follow me and I will get you situated."

"Thank you."

"It's my pleasure, madam."

The Royal couple dutily followed Octavrator to an area semi

laid out for the morning ambience in expectation of one of the Royals wanting to have a morning drink or snack.

Octavrator slid a chair out for Princess Lì Alìgrāwná simultaneously with another assistant who did the same for Duke Ravik's chair.

Thanks to artificial intelligence the staff was poised to respond to the Royal Couple and their placemats already sitting with a full service of exquisite gold tableware and the finest crystal in the galaxy. Fresh cut flowers in the middle of the table oblique to the two Royals created an ornate atmosphere. The scents of the flowers were evident, creating a spring like scent.

Fruit juices and caffeinated drinks were provided, and the chef's assistants approached their table and quizzed the couple, "What would you like to eat?"

Princess Lì was still adjusting to her surroundings leaving behind the fog of a deep sleep and said, "I need to sip on this drink for a bit and think about it. Could you come back in a while?"

"Yes, madam."

"Sir, is there something I can get for you?"

"I would like to try what the chef would like to make."

"It will be my distinct pleasure to inform the chef whom I'm sure knows how to create something you will enjoy."

"Thank you."

The chef's assistant then turned and walked back to his kitchen.

Several of the waiters stood by in anticipation of any requests. Meanwhile Octavrator, left to take care of business and reappeared every few minutes sizing up the situation in case he needed to intervene in some manner.

The Royal Couple were not fully alert to their surroundings

and the way the security apparatus flowed around the mansion in a manner to minimize their appearance but forever vigilant did not expose the fact a lot of firepower was nearby to ensure the safety of the Royals.

Thanks to AI, the chef was advised the princess had finished her caffeinated drink and now might be a good time to reapproach her and get a readout on what she might like to eat.

The chef's assistant understood manners and decorum and would serve the two Royals at the same time. He sincerely hoped the princess had come to a decision as he approached her in his impeccably clean and pressed assistant chef's uniform.

The princess didn't quite know it yet, but her body was already changing as inception had occurred and surprisingly, she felt a tinge of appetite and knew it would be best to order something now as their time would quickly slip away and they would be ushered out front of the mansion to get on their transportation for their trip.

The Lìsztbrùnést Royal Space Yacht and the two Frigates going on this journey were already in orbit above the planet fueled and ready for the trip. They would be shuttled up in space around departure time.

The Chef's assistant came to the table all smiles, in full anticipation the transaction would get done this time.

"Madam is there anything I can prepare for you?"

"Just make me what you are making for Duke Ravik, I'm sure it will be fine."

"It will be my upmost pleasure, your Highness."

"Thank you."

"You are welcome, your Highness."

The chef's assistant then departed fully glad this was turning into such a simple arrangement.

Princess Lì appeared quite beautiful this morning. Princess Lì exhibited an unnatural sheen. Pregnant Lìsztbrùnést women go through a metamorphism during childbirth. Their skin is rejuvenated slowly in the process. Almost like a butterfly coming out of cocoon they appear to have age reversal and their skin becomes more youthful and beautiful.

Stanley didn't know this was happening to Princess Lì because he had no real experience with this civilization. But he was clearly amused she seemed to be getting prettier every single day. This morning with the soft light of the sun's reflections off adjacent buildings, Princess Lì was bathed with the solar radiation in a manner that highlighted and illustrated her flawless beautiful skin.

Thanks to Princess Lì choosing a meal the chef had already crafted, the two Royals were soon served with very little wait time. With a galactic sensational chef preparing a meal, it is always exquisite, and the Royal Couple was not disappointed in any manner as it hit the spot perfectly.

Octavrator gave the couple the precious moments to lounge there and enjoy each other's company in the very comfortable morning. He could read the satisfaction all over Princess Lì's face and knew how deep her feelings for Duke Ravik had developed. Since Octavrator was the chief of security for the palace, he was also the defacto controller of security for the empire. The emperor did all his work through Octavrator in the past.

Nobody else in the Empire knew Valet Octavrator's assistant Lucas would now be the principal in charge of the emperor's personal security and carry out orders like Octavrator had done in the past. Lucas was a humanoid robot that appeared like a person. He worked exclusively for Octavrator and was his dedicated assistant well versed and motivated to serve Octavrator who had impecable ethics and moral values. In reality, nothing changed as the Robot Lucas had a wireless capability and fully updated

Octavrator on all matters deemed important.

With the synergism of a well-organized support staff, Lucas had prepared the emperor for his trip and while the Royal Couple were eating their breakfast, Lucas escorted the emperor out the front door of the mansion to the waiting atmospheric shuttle to take him up to one of the Fast Frigates that would be part of the escort to the Lìsztbrùnést Royal Space Yacht.

Emperor Cornelius wanted to arrive early on the Fast Frigate and get an operational briefing as he would eventually escort his daughter to several planets. He planned to return to the palace and let the Royal Couple show their faces around Azorloma and in the weeks into the future they would take additional trips around more of the Empire and expose themselves in ways to emphasize their relevance.

As soon as it appeared the Royal Couple had sufficiently finished their meal and had lounged long enough to enjoy themselves, there was one more item to accomplish and that was to allow them to freshen up in their suite before putting them on the shuttle to the Lìsztbrùnést Royal Space Yacht.

Octavrator synchronizing the days events with great precision had been alerted via his earbud that Lucas had taken the emperor up to the Fast Frigate and was standing by to depart as soon as the Royal Couple were ready. He then approached the Royal Couple and asked, "Would you like to go back to your suite and freshen up before the trip?"

"Yes, that sounds like a good idea," Princess Lì responded.

The Royal Couple was led to their suite and the chambermaids swung into action to help the couple get comfortable and take care of business. If there was any last-minute love making to be done, they would also facilitate that in the most appropriate manner. But today, the sensual awareness of the trip precluded any thoughts of exploring a celestial feast for the couple was simply bypassed as the couple prepared for the trip.

In due time thanks to artificial intelligence and the astute leadership that Octavrator performed, the couple was alerted by one of the Chambermaids, "Octavrator is arriving to escort you to the Royal Space Yacht."

Princess Lì had not experienced such "hands on" supervision since she was a child and it struck her there was now a great fuss about her. When Octavrator arrived and escorted them to the front entrance, Princess Lì who had such strong telepathic ability probed Octavrator to get an understanding what his motives were, and she discovered her father's machinations and his directives to Octavrator who would leave nothing to chance. The survival of the future emperor that Princess Lì now had growing inside her was the paramount interest of the emperor.

The sudden loss of freedom of movement was now presented to Princess Lì who slowly felt she was becoming more of a prisoner than the emperor's daughter. But now she understood why. The stakes were high. The emperor had ever right to be concerned after losing his mate and he would do everything in his power to prevent it again. She also knew that Octavrator took the loss of her mother with great pain. She also detected Octavrator deep thoughts he had considered committing suicide but only snapped out of that mental derangement simply because the emperor needed protection and he had no confidence anyone else around would go the extra mile to do so.

Octavrator now had three lives to protect as well as the emperor. His biggest challenge since the loss of the empress was now standing before him. There would never be a second failure, and if there was, then he would not be able to live with himself and would perform the Hari-Kari, but after he punished those who might want to hurt the emperor and his family.

The five individuals including the two chambermaids, the princess, the duke, and Octavrator made their way out to the front of the mansion for the waiting Lìsztbrùnést Royal Space. Princess Lì Alìgrāwná was surprised all of them were going to the Lìsztbrùnést Royal Space Yacht shuttle. Inside the shuttle, Drákōlìné sat in her designated seat. Other than Duke Ravik, Drákōlìné was the only person allowed to be alone with the princess. That included Octavrator and his assistant Lucas.

The five were immediately seated and the door shut, and the shuttle lifted off and in a brief period of time canted up at an angle and increased speed rapidly without making discomfort to the passengers, thanks to the anti-gravity machine. It did not take long before looking out the observation windows the darkness of space appeared as they escaped the light from the planet.

The time it took for docking in the Lìsztbrùnést Royal Space Yacht seemed to be rather quick. Stanley understood the reality and the dynamics of an advanced society with space travel ability like the Lìsztbrùnésts had demonstrated to him on his initial voyage to the Empire.

As soon as the shuttle docked and the hanger sealed and pressurized, the Lìsztbrùnést Royal Space Yacht began its acceleration in formation with the two Fast Frigates. These were three of the fastest ships in the galaxy. They could ostensibly outrun any of their enemies and get to safety where they could be protected by space defense forces. Any Pirate dumb enough to attempt to attack them would quickly be dispatched with the best beam weapons in the galaxy.

Due to concern about the princess safety and her family, the self defense capability of the Lìsztbrùnést Royal Space Yacht and the two fast frigates would quickly annihilate any possible attackers and they would maneuver towards friendly forces scattered around the Empire. Hence it would be counter productive to attempt such foolishness so it seemed except for the Trilaterals who had other ideas.

The people delivered to the Royal Space Yacht were escorted

to the control room to meet the captain who was very happy to see the Royal Couple since they were now the official Royal Couple and completely immune from scandal.

"Hello Captain," Stanley stated in a very positive manner.

"Glad to see you back Stanley."

"Captain, I think its best you refer me as Duke or Duke Ravik."

"Certainly Duke Ravik. I should not have been so clumsy in my speech."

"Not to worry Captain, when we are alone in private, please call me Stanley."

"Your Excellency, Duke Ravik, it will be my distinct pleasure. I've never traveled with a non Lìsztbrùnést as far as I have with you."

"Those were incredible moments of my life. To some extent the only reason why I'm here with you today is what you facilitated in the past. I would not have the company of the princess without your help."

"My dear Duke Ravik, I'm very pleased it worked out for you. I must confess, I was rather moved to see how all the abundance of birds befriended you. We've never seen anything like it before."

"Well captain I think it gets down to the birds discovered what was in my heart and I cared deeply for them."

"That I know, your excellency. I feel privileged to be in your company."

In a brief period, Octavrator repositioned the chambermaids to the Royal Couple's private quarters to wait on them. He went to his familiar study that had a bunk he always stayed in while on trips with the emperor.

Drákōlìné remained with the Ship's Captain to have discussions with him privately after everyone else left the control room. The ship was accelerating to hypervelocity and soon it would start to feel uncomfortable. Instinctively Princess Lì Alìgrāwná suggested, my dear, lets go to our space cabin and get comfortable and I think we'll feel better during the transition to hypervelocity."

"Great idea," Stanley said recalling what it felt like when they left Earth. Laying horizontal to the artificial gravity made it far more comfortable than remaining upright where the tensor stresses twisted the bodies microscopically, but enough to add to an unpleasant sensation. Laying down offered a reduction of this unpleasantness as the stress forces were far less dynamic and much easier to withstand.

In a few brief moments they were in the space cabin undressing and putting on garments to improve their comfort during the flight. As soon as they were dressed in those rest clothes, they reclined in the nice bed and the two chambermaids went through a door to the adjacent room they were stationed at waiting for artificial intelligence to alert them their presence was needed with the princess and the duke.

Once the two Royals reclined with the safety net merely a foot above them for emergencies, they enveloped into a loving embrace as Stanley wanted to hold the princess in his arms and cherish her for a period that helped the hours peel away on this journey.

The three ships reached astonishing speeds. By morning they would enter orbit around Azorloma and shuttle down to the planet in three waves. Only one royal at a time would descend under heavy guard in case there was some nefarious activity going on that would place them at risk.

The day and night passed uneventful as the Newlyweds simply enjoyed each other's company holding each other in splendid love. It felt so good to be in each other's arms. The strange telepathic harmony seemed to comfort each of them quite nicely. It was a strong bond that few would understand nor would anyone but Princess Lì ever have vast memory of bird voices from Ski Beach. Mother nature was reaching out of Princess Lì to ensure she protected Stanley as his sudden demise would break the hearts of a lot of birds.

In the morning the chambermaids took one of the Royals into the special room at a time to prepare them and allow them to freshen up. There were no baths, but a special space shower worked well and left them feeling invigorated.

This was a special occasion, so the wardrobes included Royal Textiles and designs. The Royal Couple didn't quite know what to expect, but assumed the choreography was well laid out by Drákōlìné and the added help she didn't desire nor require, from Octavrator. It would not be the first time nor the last time Octavrator and Drákōlìné rubbed each other the wrong way.

As the Royal Couple, Octavrator and Drákōlìné gathered in the control room with the captain just before departure from the Lìsztbrùnést Royal Space Yacht, Octavrator explained, "Since we are not at Neflatraceous, where our Lìsztbrùnést Empire space defense is more robust, we do not have the full scope of security measures available, we will be doing special procedures."

Drákōlìné had not received the special briefing and was slightly emotionally bruised that Octavrator was keeping secrets from her and asked in a cynical tone, "Just what is that special procedures, Octavrator?"

"By order of the emperor only one Royal at a time will be allowed to travel down to the planet."

"Alright and how are we going to accomplish that?"

"Princess Lì Alìgrāwná will go down first in the company of you, Drákōlìné. When our support group on the ground reports they are ready to receive Duke Ravik, I will accompany him to the planet, and we will all meet the emperor whose already there."

Drákōlìné stood there totally stunned by these revelations.

The Royal Couple was somewhat astonished by the plan, but like all good foot soldiers they were ready to proceed. The shuttle was loaded up with the first group that included the chambermaids dressed up in official court uniforms that would not reveal their real purpose in life. Nobody except the Royals would know their function. Besides being simple chambermaids, they were also martial artists capable of killing quickly to defend the princess and the duke.

The shuttle came down on a city street that had been barricaded. Security was everywhere. This street is where Princess Lì Alìgrāwná's deceased mother only living brother lived. Most of her mother's family had been gathered quietly for this visit.

There was another shuttle parked on the abandoned street with Royal Markings on it that Emperor Cornelius arrived in.

Princess Lì Alìgrāwná was quickly ushered into the nice-looking home that had an eight-foot steel gate around the property and usually dedicated security men since it was the home of Princess Lì Alìgrāwná's uncle.

Inside the home all the relatives had gathered and in the middle of them was Emperor Cornelius himself.

Princess Lì Alìgrāwná had not seen many of them for quite a few years and some of them not since her mother's funeral. They were of course all thrilled to see the lovely princess who was always kind and sweet around them. The hugs and conversations were significant and then a few minutes later, the Valet Octavrator led Stanley through the uncle's home, front entrance and Drákōlìné announced, "Ladies and Gentlemen, I would like to introduce you to Duke Ravik."

The group was captivated by the way Duke Ravik appeared.

His cosmetic makeover was superb, and his dress was impecable.

Princess Lì promptly walked over to Stanley and put her arm around one of his and said, "Uncle let me introduce you to my significant other, Duke Ravik."

Emperor Cornelius was standing back adjacent to the concentration of people now grouped into almost a huddle consuming nearly all the large room. Princess Lì's uncle was given an open area and approached Stanley. The men bowed very solemnly and deliberate.

Princess Lì Alìgrāwná had compartmentalized her emotions and holding on to Stanley seemed to bolster her emotions. She somehow knew she wasn't going to break down and cry even though she worried she might. Stanley was giving her the inner strength to carry on and put the best face forward. This was to be a joyous occasion and in their private telepathic communiques Stanley said to Princess Lì, "Your mother's spirit is with us today. I can feel her. She wants you to have a joyous day with all her relatives. Remember you are not only representing yourself, the emperor, and myself, you are also representing your mother and it's important that you carry out her wishes that today you have a joyous and happy event. In doing so you are celebrating your mother's life."

Princess Lì Alìgrāwná was often amazed at how mature and clear-headed Stanley appeared. This may have been a consequence of his interaction with mother nature through the numerous birds.

Princess Lì's uncle knew the travelers had been cooped up on a spaceship for a while and outdoors might feel more comfortable to them, plus there was considerably more room in the park like back yard that featured impecable landscaping, sculptures, and colorful flora that would leave an impression on Stanley.

"Let's all go out to the back yard where we can be more comfortable," the uncle stated.

There were numerous shaded areas, and the comfort was excellent as the guests all wondered through the home and out the back door into this beautifully landscaped area.

In anticipation of todays events, the emperor sent ahead chefs' waiters, and supplies to make this a very festive event. The best catered party on the planet would probably not measure up to what all now unfolded.

With Stanley's arm in tow, Princess Lì Alìgrāwná systematically introduced him to all her relatives. There were at least a dozen pretty ladies of beauty and grandeur. They were all very friendly and respectful and knew this was Princess Lì's love of her life. They also felt so wonderful that after her tragedy of losing her mother that she was able to go out into the universe and find her prince charming who was slowly being molded into the ideal figure that she and her father would cherish. But more importantly, time was coming when Duke Ravik would be instrumental in producing the next emperor to ensure continuity of the monarchy.

Stanley was happy he had not eaten anything this morning to make room for all the nice smelling delicacies that were now prepped for such an auspicious occasion.

There had been some filming of the event for the consumption of the empire as public curiosity grew by volumes. The Royal Couple was quickly capturing the interest of a large sector of the population. Duke Ravik would be the center of attraction for quite some time as curiosity overflowed and people attempted to learn more about him.

The trip to Azorloma had not turned out to be as dreadful as the emperor feared it might have been if his daughter got emotional from the memories.

Nobody really paid much attention to the emperor other than Lucas, Octavrator, and Drákōlìné who were constantly maintaining vigilance including receiving multitudes of reports via their ear buds from the security apparatus in the event they needed to evacuate the Royal Family and leave the planet abruptly with the security of the two fast frigates and the firepower the Lìsztbrùnést Royal Space Yacht had built in to provide additional security and the means to escape elaborate traps by potential coups or traditional enemies.

As the emperor wondered around engaging in small talk from time to time, he made it a point to remain close enough to detect the telepathic communiques between his daughter and Duke Ravik. It did not take him long to figure out how and why the princess was maintaining her chipper demeaner thanks to Duke Ravik's constant involvement with her. The emperor was deeply touched by some of those communiques. Duke Ravik was far more sophisticated than Emperor Cornelius could ever have bargained for. And to discover his daughter found him on her own was one of her greatest achievements. *He wondered; how did I affect the empress in such a manner that allowed her to be successfully selective?*

The emperor had a rough day as his brother-in-law's home brought back a lot of memories of his Empress. For the sake of his daughter as well as himself he had to constrain his own emotions. The hard part was his daughter looked so much like her mother at this age, it was as if he had traveled back in time and saw her again.

At a convenient time, the emperor nodded at Octavrator which out of their modus operendus meant to follow him for a private discussion.

Not far behind was Lucas and Drákōlìné to make sure nobody approached the two while they talked.

The front of the home had a long-covered porch the full width of the home where a dozen people could sit in chairs in the evening and have great discussions. The two walked out in the middle of the open area and the men faced each other.

"Thank you for all your preparations. You pulled this off very well in such a short period of time."

"My pleasure your excellency."

"I assume you have it all planned out well for the next few days?"

"Yes, your excellency, based on your comments, we have included those stops on the way around the planet you wanted them to visit."

"I'm sure you are aware I had a couple additional Fast Frigates arrive here today?"

"Yes sir, I'm aware they are in orbit now."

"We have a change in plans. I do not want to be the focus off this event. I want my daughter and Duke Ravik to be in the limelight. The reason why I had the two Fast Frigates come here is to take me home to Neflatraceous. I want the other two Fast Frigates to remain here and be able to protect the Royal Couple."

"When do you anticipate leaving, your Excellency?"

"As soon as this party winds down, I'll be taken directly up to the Fast Frigate I'll be riding on."

"Any special messages you want me to give your daughter?"

"Yes, please inform her the reason why I left is I want this to be about them. I'm leaving because I do not want to be a center of attraction when this is their special time. Also, by me being gone everything will be focused on them so that the public is more attuned to the fact my daughter has a growing role in empire matters."

"You have been a good father to her. She appreciates everything you have done and the fact you accepted Duke Ravik means a lot to her."

"Duke Ravik turned out a lot more than what I expected."

"He seems to definitely have a major effect on Princess Lì."

"I see a lot of myself in him when I met her mother. I know I was in love with the Empress, and I know he's in love with Princess Lì."

"But how can you really know?"

"When I'm old and on my death bed I'll tell you how I know."

"Your excellency, you don't have to explain it to me because of my time with you, I've determined that when you know something, I can trust it to be very accurate."

"It's that obvious?"

"It certainly is."

"Alright we'll go back and enjoy the festivities. But before we go back to the party, I want to remind you that you have the most important assignment in the Empire to assure my descendent ascends to the throne after I'm gone and is well prepared for the challenges that lay ahead."

"Your excellency, I know how critically important that is and I promise to always carry out that assignment with the best of my ability."

"Thank you Octavrator, this means a lot to me."

"You are most welcome my emperor."

The men walked back into the house and enjoyed the rest of the carefree day. One thing that made the emperor smile was Princess Lì did not leave the side of Duke Ravik even for a minute.

Princess Lì's uncle and his wife had raised their children and they had all left home and now had their own lives and their own families. The house was fairly empty as a result with plenty of room.

Hence at the request of the Princess she wanted to spend the night at her uncle's home. As the evening wound down and the guests slowly evaporated soon it was just the emperor, the Royal Couple, the uncle and his wife, and the security apparatus. At this time the emperor approached the couple that were still seemingly clinging to each other.

"We have several things for you to do here at Azorloma. I'm going back to Neflatraceous and the palace tonight. I want you two to enjoy yourselves seeing the sights of Azorloma. In a few days when you are all done here, you will come back to the palace to rest up for a few days, then I want to send you to some other planets to meet dignitaries there and be my spokesman and attend some formal affairs."

"Alright father. We will be glad to help."

"Enjoy yourselves and I'm looking forward to seeing you in a few days."

The emperor turned and walked out the door followed by Lucas and a couple other security men and walked briskly to the waiting shuttle that lifted off within less than a minute later, traveled up to the Fast Frigate.

~~~~~
~~~~~

CHAPTER SIX

THE BATTLE OF AZORLOMA

The Gromulites killed the Lìsztbrùnést Empress and came very close to killing the emperor himself. On that very fateful day many years ago Octavrator had to make an instant decision, save the Emperor or the Empress. The decision had to be made immediately and effectively. It tore his heart apart watching the Empress die, but he managed to save the emperor.

The Gromulites were not done. Only one person stood in their way of Galactic Hegemony, Cornelius the Emperor of Lìsztbrùnést. Gromulite spies on Azorloma were reporting the whereabouts of the Royals. The Gromulites were unaware Emperor Cornelius left Azorloma and went back to Neflatraceous, in the center of the Lìsztbrùnést Empire and was now back in the mansion contemplating the future and getting reports of the Royal Couple and their public relations activities that were well received by the masses.

Hectozar the Gromulite despot Dictator was running out of patience. He could not afford a direct confrontation with the Lìsztbrùnést Emperor who had a formidable force but also because the Lìsztbrùnést Emperor Cornelius was an extraordinary tactician and led many successful space battles.

Emperor Cornelius's father plucked him out of the space force and planted him in the mansion, not so much to preserve his life than to ensure continuity of the Monarch. The Prince of Lìsztbrùnést Cornelius back in those days had already achieved enough victories over the Trilaterals which included the Gromulites to where his tactical brilliance was deemed no longer necessary. It was now time for him to produce an offspring and an heir to the throne when he departed life.

But now the Royals were all on Azorloma an easy target and if they could wipe them out, the Lìsztbrùnésts would be leaderless making them easy prey for the Trilaterals to come in and finally take them out.

The Gromulites had a good handle on the location of the Royal Couple who were out in the open and easy targets, but the emperor was hiding in the shadows and INTEL had not been able to figure out how he was moving around but estimated he would be in close proximity of the Royal Couple to make sure they were protected and coach them in their extraordinary behavior that included very astute communications to the public.

The head of Gromulites INTEL estimated the emperor was spoon feeding the Royal Couple everything they said in public because the delivery was so sophisticated that only a brilliant mind like Emperor Cornelius could conjure up the essence of those poignant details and elucidate them with the precision displayed.

Upon arrival to Neflatraceous, the capital of the Lìsztbrùnést Empire, Emperor Cornelius immediately sent the two fast frigates back to Azorloma to bolster the two that were already there protecting the Lìsztbrùnést Royal Space Yacht.

Six hours after they departed, Lucas approached Emperor Cornelius and said, "Your Highness, we have detected Trilaterals near Azorloma. Recommend you send additional backup in the event they decide to strike and make an attempt on the Royal Couple."

Emperor Cornelius was immediately agitated because even though he had no direct evidence it was the Gromulites who killed the Empress, there was enough circumstantial evidence to suggest so. Had he had just a slight amount of INTEL to prove that to be the case, he would have raised the Gromulites home worlds.

"Alright, deploy our Alpha Force right away. Put the other forces on alert and form up space wings and project Tango in case we are faced with the beginnings of hostilities."

"Yes Sir, right away."

"Also evacuate the Royal Couple immediately and send the Royal Couple back on the Frigates and not on the same one. I want at least one of them to survive an attack."

"What about the Royal Yacht?"

"If my guess is right, the Gromulites will make a bee line to the Royal Yacht and destroy it thinking I'm aboard."

"I agree, the Gromulites will no doubt attempt to destroy the Royal Yacht," Lucas responded.

"We can always build another Yacht. We can't replace my daughter nor Duke Ravik."

"It will take high speed neutrino communications about five minutes to get the message there."

"Send it now in the rough, no editing required."

"Understand sir, I will come back in a few minutes with the receipt."

~~~~~~

The couple was enjoying their time at the uncle's residence for the evening and unexpectedly military men came into the home and approached Stanley.
~~~~~~

"I'm sorry to interrupt your evening your Excellency, but you two must depart immediately."

Stanley whose mental telepathy was growing daily quickly analyzed the officer and validated al his concerns and turned to Princess Lì Alìgrāwná and said, "We must leave immediately." He grabbed her hand and followed the officer out to the waiting two shuttles.

"I'm sorry your Excellency, Emperor Cornelius orders are the two of you will travel separately, you get in this shuttle, and she will go in the other."

Within a minute the shuttles were airborne.

Soon planetary defenses spotted a fleet of spacecraft approaching long distances. Alerts were flying. The cusp of war was among them.

Emperor Cornelius' astute decisions now started to bear fruit. The home they were staying at was evacuated just in case.

Just like he figured the high-speed Trilateral Force came in and slowly gained on the three Lìsztbrùnést ships. The captain of the Lìsztbrùnést Royal Space Yacht was ordered to go to flank speed heading for Neflatraceous, the capital of the Lìsztbrùnést Empire. He knew he would be the sacrificial lamb, but to save the Royal Couple was more important than his life.

The Royal Yacht outrunning the Fast Frigates made it a target. The Royal Yacht Captain knew his odds were not good and he was going to make those chasing him waste precious time with sophisticated maneuvers so that by the time they figured out they were chasing the wrong ships it was too late, the two additional Frigates soon arrived on the scene providing substantially more fire power and a short distance behind them was the Alpha Force that would chase the culprits back to Gromulite and Trilateral worlds. The Royal Yacht Captain had a significantly reduced crew since none of the chambermaids, Octavrator, nor Drákōlìné was onboard.

The captain and the small crew gathered into the emergency escape pod that would fly extremely fast to Neflatraceous, the capital of the Lìsztbrùnést Empire.

The Royal Yacht took quite a few damaging hits by the Trilaterals who were semi jubilant they were wiping out the Lìsztbrùnést Emperor and his Royal Couple. They knew their fleet was approaching Azorloma where defenses there would be wiped out then they would soon be in position to attack Neflatraceous knowing they didn't have to worry about their flanks.

Hectozar was convinced he had wiped out the Royals and a leaderless Empire would be able to be taken down piece by piece.

Phase-One was complete his raiding force showed the video of the Royal Yacht exploding.

Phase-Two the home they were staying at was bombed in case any of the Royals were hiding there.

The Trilateral attackers did not observe the emergency escape pod leave the Royal Yacht since it was ejected at the same time of the explosion and hidden in the massive sparkling debris.

Two of the Fast Frigates ignored the enemy and continued flying at flank speed towards Neflatraceous but suddenly two fast frigates appeared, not necessarily a major concern for the Trilaterals, though they would inflict some casualties before they were also destroyed.

Unfortuantely for the Trilateral attackers, they were not facing ordinary Fast Frigates with limited offensive capabilities. These were Royal Escorts. They were loaded with far more elaborate weapons and beam technology.

The real battle now started and the Trilaterals paid dearly for their blunder.

Hectozar observed the initial reports on his high-speed communications network and saw the force sent after the Royal Yacht suddenly confronted by two Fast Frigates, he thought they would swat like flies, then rapidly all reports and video extinguished. Due to Hectozar's arrogance there were no probes in this area since he had the Trilateral Force, so they had no idea what was coming.

"Why hasn't the Force reported results of destroying those two fast frigates?" Hectozar asked.

"Maybe they are busy mopping up the battlefield," The Trilateral Officer responded.

"Send them an immediate message to make reports now."

"Message being sent sir."

The Space Defenses of Azorloma was starting to be an irritant and they had the audacity to refuse surrender. They of course knew the Alpha Force was on the way and surrender was not required.

"Arm our fighter bombers with planetary offensive weapons." Hectozar ordered as he wanted to make the Azorloma military regret not surrendering."

Work was in progress loading planetary attack weapons in the launcher tubes when suddenly Hectozar was informed, "Sir, we have detected a major force approaching us?"

"How can that be? Neflatraceous is at least twelve hours away to get a force here?"

"Sir we have a major force quickly approaching and we have the wrong types of weapons in our launcher tubes. Recommend an emergency retreat."

"This can't be, deploy the planetary attack weapons."

"Sir, this force has just penetrated our trip wires. We are now in a serious situation, recommend an emergency retreat maneuver."

Hectozar stood there frozen for a few minutes when suddenly, he was being screamed at.

"We have to do something fast; we are under attack!"

When the first Trilateral ship blew up in sparkling debris not far from the command ship, Hectozar finally reacted and ordered, "Reverse Course, begin emergency evasive maneuvers!"

The Trilateral Ships began their twists and turns, and the fighting began in earnest. Since Hectozar ordered rearming with weapons to damage the planet, all they had at their disposal for the early moments of the battler were lasers and beam weapons. Those weapons were lethal, but since the Alpha Strike Task Force didn't have to maneuver to avoid space defense weapons, they could lay on the attacks far more efficiently.

The loop back in the course reversal took several minutes to get the fleet turned around and put the attackers in their rears. Their only saving grace was no flanking forces to fight.

Continuing this course heading back to the safety of the Trilateral controlled zone allowed Hectozar to reload the missile tubes with space defense weapons. Unfortunately to Hectozar the thirty minutes to rearm with space defense weapons took its toll on the fleet. One by one ships were exploding because the Lìsztbrùnést Alpha Strike Task Force had all the right weapons and didn't have to rely on laser and beam weapons requiring close ranges to be effective.

By the time the remainder of the fleet was rearmed it was too late. The damage was done, and enough ships had been destroyed the numerical advantage had been squandered. Now they had no choice but to keep running to safety. Their launches of space defense weapons now only provided harassment because they could not deploy them in the numbers they could have, had they not blundered into the fast reaction force with the wrong weapons tube loaded.

The combination of loss of surprise and having the wrong weapons in the missile tubes created a serious misstep for Hectozar.

Hectozar's Trilateral Invasion Fleet was now decimated as the fighting raged on like he never witnessed before.

The Trilaterals had no choice but to continuing transit at flank speed and point their home worlds. The battle lasted while they were increasing speed but at some point, when they were a very long distance away from Azorloma, the chase was no longer going to be profitable for the Lìsztbrùnést Space Forces. Going in a straight line at flank speed quickly covered a great distance and it soon became apparent to Lìsztbrùnést Admiral Timons, it was time to break off the attack and maneuvered and turned back towards Azorloma.

<p style="text-align:center">~~~~~~</p>

The Fast Frigates transporting the Royal Couple arrived at Neflatraceous and were sent down to the emperor's mansion. Drákōlìné arrived with Stanley and Octavrator arrived with Princess Lì Alìgrāwná. The emperor was at the entrance to the mansion to greet them as they arrived.

Emperor Cornelius had a concern on his face. He now was able to figure out who killed the love of his life. Hectozar was likely the person behind the assassination, and now he just attempted it a second time. He would not get a third attempt.

One thing was clear to the Emperor Cornelius: Hectozar had spies on Azorloma who almost got his daughter killed. He would soon have a new mission for Lucas and Octavrator. He needed to capture those spies and subject them to neurotic sonification's to make them wish they were dead and get the final evidence to the demise of the Empress. Then he would make his life's effort for the brutal destruction of Hectozar and his cronies.

Now it was starting to become a clear picture. It was a shame a billion people would have to die. But eliminating Hectozar would soon be the principal modus of operendus for Emperor Cornelius.

~~~~~

billion people would have to die. But eliminating Hectozar would soon be the principal modus of operendus for Emperor Cornelius.
~~~~~

CHAPTER SEVEN
THE HUNT FOR SPIES

Drákōlìné who was lethal in martial arts and a good spy herself became agitated when Emperor Cornelius informed her, "You will remain here with the Royal Couple. Octavrator and Lucas are being sent to Azorloma to locate and capture the Gromulite Spies.

"Your excellency I wish to assist in the matter. As a female I think I can penetrate the spy ring more effectively than Octavrator and Lucas."

"Drákōlìné, you have a task that is far more critical than finding these spies. I expect my daughter to start having discomfort soon as its quite apparent to me she is now an expecting mother."

"What can I do the doctors can't do? She will be just fine?"

"You know the history. We thought the Empress was safe and without much warning she was assassinated by my enemies. I need to have you be near Princess Lì to ensure her safety as well as the safety of the unborn child. If need be Octavrator and Lucas are expendable in case their task turns out negatively, you are not expendable. Your presence near Princess Lì makes me feel more comfortable, because I know I can depend on your high fidelity and devotion."

Drákōlìné was not happy sitting on the sidelines. Especially if these rotten bastards were behind killing the precious Empress. She wanted blood revenge. But she also was a pragmatist and knew it was senseless to argue with Emperor Cornelius who was a brilliant man and decisive. Once he made up his mind on something, that was the end of it. There would be no fruitful purpose in arguing or continuing further discussions.

Octavrator and Lucas were dressed in ordinary clothes, and they were wired as well as armed with very powerful weapons should a shootout manifest.

The emperor walked the two men out the entrance of the mansion and walked with them to the waiting shuttle.

"I hate to send the two of you at the same time. You are irreplaceable. But we are up against some tough agents that I think will require the two of you. Remember I do not want to kill them. I want them taken live as prisoners and brought back here where interrogators can get the details out of them, I need before I make my next move."

"Your excellency, I think they showed their hand already. Hectozar underestimated you and flew into a blunder thanks to your tactical thinking. No doubt the Gromulites were behind the assassination of the Empress."

"I believe you are right, but I want to get the details out of these spies and its possible they might have been involved in her death. If that's the case, I want them to feel the pain I felt for so many years from the loss of my lovely Empress."

"We will make every effort to bring them here alive, but you know spies do not give up willingly. They know their fate and would rather die fighting than surrender."

"I agree, they are not going to willingly surrender, that's why you have your special tools and procedures."

"We will make every effort to bring them in alive, but if they are in a position to fight to their deaths, we may not have any other options but to kill them."

"I know that bringing them in alive puts you at increased risk. That's why I'm sending the two of you in hopes that you can protect each other and apprehend the spies so our interrogators can bring closure to the Empress death, and I can then have full justification to go after Hectozar. Once we know he ordered the death of the Empress, I want to personally have the satisfaction of taking his life from him.

"We will do our best, your Highness," Lucas said.

The men then entered into the shuttle and a minute later it was airborne heading out to space for a disguised black marketeer's *Cosmic Cutter* to arrive incognito on Azorloma.

A *Cosmic Cutter* could make it to Azorloma in twelve hours, but to get to the planet without raising suspicion or giving an appearance of connection to the government would take them a couple days. A Lìsztbrùnést INTEL official in deep undercover would provide them transportation to a safe house when they arrived. There would be no other interface to government forces on Azorloma and their contact would not approach the safe house again until the mission reached its milestone to facilitate prisoner transport.

Octavrator had an ear bud that appeared like the average hearing aid. He also had a telepathic wireless interface surgically installed that allowed him to telepathically communicate to Lucas wireless system allowing them constant unobstructed communications. Lucas had access via his wireless to a Azorloma security directorate channel for data mining purposes. Ever since the Trilaterals attack all security camera video recorded anywhere the Royal Couple traveled was sifted through with a fine mesh screening apparatus.

Due to the nature of the crowds and vast numbers of citizens wanting to get a view of the Royal Couple, finding leads was like trying to find a needle in a haystack. After hours of grueling efforts and sleepless nights by security officials, only one needle in one haystack emerged as a lead.

Facial recognition software eventually identified the woman named Christine through searches of official police records. Christine had an occupation working as a call girl. Women for hire do not mind doing other tasks if the money is sizeable.

This was the only Azorloman who was spotted at most of the Royal Couple functions. Christine was always dressed impecable and in modest and respectable attire. No doubt Christine was picked by her handlers because she didn't stand out. Christine was slightly more than a plane Jane, but for a business arrangement with a well-paying client, it was obvious she could get a makeover and elevate several stratums in looks. Christine's figure was compelling and her ability to be seductive would soon be discovered by Octavrator and Lucas.

At one-point planetary security was about to approach Christine and interview her since she was the only lead. All the other conspirators were invisible. It would not be the first time that spies applied synthetic masks that allowed them to change their facial recognition to defeat security monitoring.

Octavrator knew they were running against the clock because the possibility existed the conspirators would soon silence Christine as she was probably the only way they could be identified. The biggest challenge now was to keep Christine alive without tipping her off the amount of surveillance focused on her.

As reality set in and the fear of insiders possibly involved with the assassins, any backup would have to come directly from Neflatraceous because if there were insiders involved the conspirators would be tipped off and vanish before they could be apprehended. To protect Christine, six hand-picked agents were flown in from Neflatraceous. This time Lucas made contact with them and brought them to the safe house to avoid anyone on the planet from knowing they arrived and who they were. This was now a super clandestine effort without any authorities on Azorloma aware such an operation existed.

Christine's activities were soon determined by the surveillance the extra help was able to accomplish.

Like most expendables, Christine was not contacted unless they had a task for her. Christine didn't know what kind of plot she was involved in but the fact they requested her to make reports on the Royals eventually led her to believe she was involved in some type of nefarious activity. As time went by Christine became nervous and almost paranoid because some of the recent activity including bombing of the home of Royal's relatives became public information.

Christine was now considering fleeing but didn't quite know where to go or how to hide out. Every day grew more and more dreadful. The men Christine worked for had not contacted her since the day of the event. She knew she was going to be extremely nervous the next time they contacted her. Christine also feared if she didn't show up, they would probably find her and make her regret her decision. She was in over her head and almost to the point of panic.

Octavrator knew vividly how a scared animal acted, especially if they were cornered by savage animals ready to attack. This woman displayed all those characteristics. If they could get to her before her handlers and reassure her, she would be protected, she might consider cooperating. She had to remain in place, or her handlers would suspect their identity could be blown.

Due to the nature of the sloppiness of the way the Trilaterals mission was executed with poor planning because Hectozar's arrogance overruled his common sense, the woman had been exposed to them in more ways than the conspirators desired. They too kept an eye on her and if she wasn't acting strange, they didn't have the need to immediately silence her, and they might actually need her services again soon as other activities were being developed as Hectozar wasn't finished. He simply was regrouping, and replanning and this time would not be so sloppy and arrogant and listen to some of his military for a change and let the professionals figure out a more cohesive approach.

While observing Christine with superior technological means, Valet Octavrator determined the day finally came when she could no longer take the pressure. Christine realized what kind of trouble she was in and left her home with no belongings as if she simply was going shopping. After making a swing through several retail establishments, Christine finally got into a sky taxi and went in a circulator route to the intergalactic space port to escape the planet. Christine had no idea she was being trailed by one of the best spies in the galaxy, Lucas who determined immediately what her intentions were as she got out of the Sky Taxi at the interplanetary departure gates.

Lucas could see Christine had panic all over her face and as soon as the Sky Taxi departed and she approached the entrance to the departure lobby, Lucas and his assistants grabbed her and with blinding speed and quickly had Christine inside a sky car heading out to the countryside to a safe house.

Christine was severely agitated assuming the bad guys had her and were simply going to kill her. The game was up, and she was sobbing.

Once they got her into the safe house, Lucas sat Christine down and asked her if she was thirsty?

The woman was ready for anything and had no idea who these men were. They certainly were not her handlers of her recent activities.

Christine nodded as she slowly became placid just like a lamb would knowing the lion was about to eat it.

The task force had some Gumonaclaris Elixir that was laced with psychoactive drugs. The taste was pleasant, and the effects were stronger than being injected with sodium pentothal.

Lucas who had built in sensors could tell Christine quickly

eased after taking a couple sips of the drink.

Christine knew the three men that stood around could be brutal if they had too. She almost wanted to cry just knowing the cruelty and possibly a murder was soon to be bestowed upon her.

Lucas gentle approach and soft-spoken words influenced Christine such that her nerves finally calmed to the point Lucas could effectively communicate with her and give her the quid pro quo.

"I know you are scared, and you are wondering why we brought you here. We have no intentions of harming you. After we talk to you and give you some information and some choices, we think you will be able to deal with your situation a lot better and not be so frightened."

"Any woman would be scared by being grabbed by several men and forced into a skycar and flown away to some obscure location."

"We had no choice. You attempting to run caused us to have to modify our plans. We would have met with you and talked with you in a more leisurely manner, but your sudden flight created an urgent matter for us, so we had to grab you," Lucas said.

"Who are you?" Christine asked.

"Christine, it's best you do not know who we are. If we told you then you would certainly be frightened and not be able to carry out the tasks, we are going to give you."

"I already did what you asked me to do. You had no reason to grab me."

"Christine, it was not us who asked you to do those activities. But if you cooperate with us, we'll make sure they will not hurt you."

Christine now suddenly knew she was in serious trouble because these men knew her real name and not the alias she went by as a call girl. Her misery now grew exponentially as she felt she was way in over her head to something really bad.

Christine knew it would be best if she got down to business right away because afterall she was a businesswoman who made deals all the time.

"All right, what is it you want me to do?" Christine asked.

"Before we get into all that, I want to say a few things, so you understand the landscape a little. You had a lot of surveillance on you and didn't know to the extent that you were followed by our men," Lucas said.

"What if I decide I do not want to cooperate and run away?"

"Christine, you will never be able to escape from us. You have no idea what we can bring to bear. So, any thought of running is out of the question. You will not get very far before we bring you back here and must administer you some special re-education," Lucas said in a way that sent shivers down Christine's spine.

Fear now gripped Christine because she knew re-education would not be very pleasant.

"You also must be aware that your former handlers do not have the fire power at their disposal that we have. They are operating in enemy territory. One bad move on their part could quickly cost all their lives."

Christine now stared at Lucas with utter curiosity.

"When the people you worked for tried to assassinate the Royal Couple, they forfeited any rights to humane treatment. And since the Emperor now knows they were involved in killing his Empress, their deaths will be very painful. You can be assured that we would kill them before they could harm you in any way."

The woman looked at Lucas with sheer wonder. She also knew that by mentioning the empress death, this man exposed he worked for a powerful entity, and she was really trapped.

"Christine, do you understand now the seriousness of this situation and what we are willing to do to solve the case?"

"Yes, I think I understand."

"If you assist us your past behavior including aiding enemies engaged in an assassination plot against the Royal Family will be forgiven. You will be given your life back and if you help us apprehend these people, we'll make sure you have the financial resources so that you never have to work as a call girl again."

"I do not suppose I have any other options," Christine replied.

"No, you do not because since you were involved with the attempted assassination, it would be the death penalty for you. We are sparing your life and treating you well for your cooperation."

"How do I know you can protect me from those bad guys?" Christine asked with a very serious look on her face.

"Rest assured, they do not have the firepower that we have. Plus, we can call in any additional help we want and those assigned to us will know they are serving at the pleasure of the emperor and understand the seriousness of it."

"Alright, I will assist you, but I have to tell you I'm very frightened."

"Christine, we would not think otherwise. We know you will have a lot of stress for a few days and soon this will be all over, and you will be a free woman with a normal life and a chance to have a family."

"I will do what you ask me to," Christine said knowing she had no choices.

"Good. We are now going to ask you a few questions and brief you on how we want you to do things," Lucas said.

"Alright, I've done a lot of things for money in the past I'm not very proud of, but out of necessity I did it. I'm sure I can do what you ask me to do." Christine responded.

Christine drank some more of her drink and liked the way it felt. The interrogators would keep her glass full because the psychoactive drugs acted as a truth serum which streamlined the interrogation to a great extent.

In an hours' time they knew the process of how the spies contacted Christine. They also knew she interfaced with at least four of them of the Gromulite spies which gave an idea the size and scope of the footprint involved.

After giving Christine directions on how she was to communicate with them via a very special communications device the Gromulite spies would never know existed, Christine was taken to a shoe shop to buy a pair of shoes to have an article to bring back the spies would observe as an innocuous package in line with what a woman might do on an outing like today. Lucas and the team had no doubt Christine was under observation by the Gromulite spies and viewed as a collateral person who was easily disposable.

There was no further activity for a few weeks then unexpectedly Christine was contacted by one of her handlers. She was to meet him at a park and given a task.

Lucas gave Christine a special drug. He explained, "This will help keep you calm and suppress fear. It's identical to an invincibility drug we give to shock troops during major combat scenarios. It will heighten your awareness and at the same time keep you completely fearless to allow you perform this task without any indication of anxiety."

Christine took the drug and got out of the sky taxi which gave all appearances Lucas was just the driver. The sky taxi then left the area and headed back to the busy part of the city where the appearances made the Gromulite spies believe the skycar was legitimate and would wait until they got their next ride request.

The Gromulite spies were well trained at detecting surveillance, and they had to be loosely followed or they would simply bug out knowing their cover was blown. New spies would then be sent in to take over the operation.

A spy doesn't know he's being watched from a sophisticated satellite. One thing a lot of spies fail to realize is that when the stakes are very high, governments will dedicate an entire satellite for an operation. If the spy uses clandestine travel methods to avoid being followed, the satellite can often track his movements and his whereabouts.

The Gromulite observed from a far, saw the woman get out of the sky taxi and it flew off heading straight for the center city like any normal sky taxi would behave after dropping off a ride.

The woman walked over and sat down at a park bench waiting to be approached. There was nobody else around or any transportation anywhere visible nearby. The spy and his assistants secured the area, and he approached the woman at the park bench.

The spy went through the anti-surveillance measures before he approached the woman at the park. The woman stood up and they quickly embraced like they always did, and the man felt her clothing she was asked to wear to make it easy to find a wire in case she was wearing devices planted by authorities.

The call girl was a trained pick pocket as well as other unique capabilities and during their encounter when the Gromulite spy would greet her and hug her to feel her body to make sure she wasn't wired, she would slip a very small tracker onto his clothing. He would then easily be tracked back to his safe house where other spies operated out of. Between the satellite and the tracker there would be no way the Gromulite spy could evade surveillance.

The Gromulite Spy handed the woman an envelope and inside it was some pictures and instructions. After she looked at the picture and read the instructions the little device attached to it would silently destroy the contents so that none of the information could be captured in the event they had to bug out.

The woman's task was to seduce a space defense coordinator and lure him somewhere the spies could steal his identity through three-dimensional biological scanning and printing. He would of course be tortured and possibly killed after they coerced a series of passwords out of him. The Gromulites planned to turn this space defense coordinator just before they were going to make another attempt on taking out Azorloma. The woman didn't know that's what they were planning but Octavrator and Lucas quickly surmised that was the essence of the espionage a denial of service at a critical moment.

"Let's sit down here," the Gromulite said then handed her the envelope with the instructions.

The spy was pleased the woman acted like she had no care in the world, she obviously had no fear, nor did she have any appraisal of what they planned on doing with her after she completed this mission as they would be getting rid of her since she could help identify a couple of them.

After the transaction the man walked away not knowing the level of surveillance on him.

The woman pulled her communicator out of her purse and requested a sky taxi that arrived a couple minutes later which took her home.

Once the space defense coordinator was identified by the woman, Octavrator swung into action and the coordinator was obtained and taken to a secret location where he was biologically three dimensionally scanned. Lucas was then modified with the coordinator's biological identity. The three-dimensional biological printing was a lot quicker for Lucas since he was a robot and didn't need time to recover. He was ready for his part of the mission that would happen the following evening.

Thanks to the tracker device that Christine planted on the Gromulite spy, he soon revealed two of their safe houses as he first went to one and met with several agents to brief them on their mission the following evening, then he went to the defacto headquarters where the big boss was and a traitor among them.

Without Christine's help they would never have discovered the insider who was a high-ranking defense person with a champagne diet and the need to have a lot of young women routinely to satisfy his libido.

This spy ring had operated so successfully even before the Empress was killed; their arrogance undid them. They had no fear because the insider always kept them informed well enough to relocate to another safe house before they were apprehended. Every time they moved into another safe house the next one was being identified.

The next night was going to get tricky. Octavrator and Lucas would have to work overtime on Christine to get her psychological posture poised for mission success. The invincibility drugs would go a long way to quell her fear, but she was informed she would not be in any harm because they had a special plan to take down the spies very rapidly and make the arrests and transport them off the planet. The defense coordinator was sequestered and guarded. He would not be getting near any controls and *Operation Tango* was in effect now.

The Gromulite fleet would pay heavily because they would arrive in anticipation of a soft landing but find out it to be an extremely rough arrival.

Lucas disguised as the space defense coordinator was at the club for the arranged party. He was a guest and had an innocuous invitation from a socialite who had no idea she was just a pawn in the overall game of five-dimensional space chess.

The net was now closing in on the safe houses and any auxiliary agents that were getting paid to participate in this nefarious activity. They conducted treason by helping the enemy so they would soon receive punishment they would quickly regret taking bribes and assisting. Some of them were partially responsible for the Empress death so they would be shoved out of an airlock in space and die from asphyxiation for their crimes.

Lucas who had an element of backup was at the club and Christine arrived to seduce him back to her apartment. The night slowly passed as all the activities now blossomed as planned. Shortly after arrival a half dozen Gromulites arrived at Christine's apartment where they would subdue the space defense coordinator. They injected Lucas with a knockout drug and laid him on top a temporary table and started setting up the biological scanner. They thought Lucas was a human and comatose. He was in self hibernation mode and as soon as they began the biological scanning suddenly a purple fog started flowing out of Lucas side. Just as the Gromulite was pointing his blaster at Christine to kill her and remove evidence he was hit with the purple substance. The spies quickly understood they were being gassed but didn't understand how and within a minute all of them including Christine were unconscious.

The safe houses were then raided very quickly and the watchers in the skycars parked nearby for collateral assistance discovered the skycars were rendered inoperative as the government skycar administration deactivated them. The entire spy ring was caught including the traitor.

Twelve hours later the Gromulite spies were at Neflatraceous getting interrogated. Thanks to Lucas hacking skills they knew the signals to send to the Trilaterals indicating to them the defense grids would be shut down just as soon as they were entering the atmosphere for attack. Again, armed with planet busting weapons in their missile tubes, the Trilaterals were not poised to deal with a set piece space battle when the trap was sprung.

Just as the Trilateral Armada entered the atmosphere at a velocity exceeding 50,000 miles per hour thinking they could simply drop their eggs on military establishments and knock them out of action, they were met with the unexpected volley. Aside from the Trilaterals getting butchered from the well prepared and alerted space defense forces on the ground, project Tango also now pounced on then from their rears. They had nowhere to escape as the carnage piled on with ship after ship blowing up into sparkling debris on the dark side of the planet.

Hectozar was less arrogant this trip and stood off at a distance observing the battle that quickly turned out not to be in his favor. Hectozar's command ship and its escorts were soon under attack by project Tango formations and immediately performed a tactical retreat at flank speed.

The results were devastating to the Trilaterals and soon there wasn't much left to do but surrender or be blown up. Hectozar survived with a few escorts and fled to Gromulite worlds realizing his plan had failed and now he would soon receive the wrath of Emperor Cornelius. He would of course plead for mercy and beg forgiveness, but he was not aware his entire spy network had been rounded up and, in a few hours, Emperor Cornelius would know Hectozar was responsible for the Empress death. There would be no quarter for Hectozar. The war would not end before Hectozar met the grim reaper.

The traitor was the first that Emperor Cornelius dealt with as one of the spies was already singing like a canary to save their own lives.

The Traitor still had on his uniform. From the looks of his medals and awards one would conclude he was a significant asset to the Empire. The emperor knew otherwise. The man was semi cocky and had lived a good life thanks to the large, augmented income from espionage.

"According to some of the confessions, you were a traitor when the Empress was killed. That means you are subject to the death penalty for conspiring with the enemy resulting in the death of a Royal."

The man looked at the emperor with a funny look on his face and figured he was dead anyway so why engage with him.

"Do you know how much you hurt me by the loss of my loved one?"

The man looked on as if he didn't care, he was a dead man anyway so why bother?

"Since you are not willing to show any remorse, I have no choice but to place judgement on you."

There still was no response out of the man who looked at the emperor as if he could care less.

It was now time for a demonstration. The emperor nodded at Octavrator who already knew what the plan was and said to his assistants, "Take him to the shuttle."

Two big bruisers lifted the man who was arm and leg cuffed and virtually carried him to the front entrance to the waiting shuttle. The shuttle departed and made its way up to space to the waiting Fast Frigate.

Once inside the Frigate they were soon through the airlock and waiting the next action. The shuttle was flown out of the hanger bay leaving ample room. The man in his illustrious uniform was brought back into the hanger after it was pressurized. Two men with space suits held him facing the video recording equipment. At the proper moment the hanger bay was depressurized, and the hanger door opened abruptly causing a quick equalization to space. The man was going into asphyxiation and the two big guys grabbed him and shoved him out of the hanger into space still alive but becoming unconscious very quickly. The sentence was passed. Since they were in low orbit his body would soon plunge into the atmosphere and burn up going through the ionosphere at 25,000 miles per hour. The hanger access was then closed, and the men went through the airlock back inside the Fast Frigate control room and took off their space suits.

During the remaining debriefings after showed the film of the execution of the traitor, the spies all confessed and hoped for leniency. But to be granted leniency, they had to fully support the investigation into the Empress death. At the conclusion of the investigation several of the spies who had operated in Azorloma stretching back to the days of the Empress assassination were identified. They also were shoved out of the hanger bay into space and died from asphyxiation just like the traitor.

The remaining spies had to cooperate to save their lives. The ground rules laid out was that if they concealed something and did not report what they knew, they too would get similar treatment up in space.

Now it was time to deal with Hectozar without much of a space force left. Once Hectozar was out of the picture, the Trilaterals would fall apart because none of their leaders had the audacity of Hectozar and they feared reprisals.

<center>~~~~~~</center>

Chapter Eight
Back with Rascal

As the days went by, Princess Lì Alìgrāwná slowly evolved as her partnership and Unification with Stanley produced an offspring. Her body was slowly changing, and Emperor Cornelius suspected Princess Lì was now carrying a child because all the symptoms were almost identical to how he observed the Empress in her days giving birth.

The Royal couple who enjoyed having their mornings out in the open courtyard as usual. The princess didn't look too well, and the past few days had been irritable. Stanley couldn't quite figure out Princess Lì's changes. It was almost as if she was falling out of love with him. That's when the emperor intervened.

The Royal Couple were there trying to make the best of it. Princess Lì was tossing and turning and in the middle of the night got sick and went into the bathroom and threw up her dinner. The chambermaids were alarmed and almost panicked first thinking food poisoning, but Duke Ravik showed no signs of illness, and they ate the same food.

The next morning Emperor Cornelius approached the couple with Valet Octavrator and two surgeons dressed in suits that would not expose the fact they were medical professionals.

Princess Lì was still feeling ill and put on her best face for her father Emperor Cornelius who suspected he knew exactly what her problem was and felt sorry for poor Stanley who would soon be going through some tumultuous periods ahead.

"Good morning father."

"Lì, the chambermaids reported you got sick last night."

"I wasn't feeling too well but I feel a little better after having some juice."

"Lì, these two men are our Royal Surgeons. They either perform all the necessary medical procedures on us or they supervise those doctors who do the work."

"Please to meet you." Princess Lì said but didn't quite feel well enough to stand and properly greet them and bow.

The two doctors nodded in perfect choreography and smiled at Princess Lì.

"The reason why these men are here with you now is to do an examination. I've turned one of the guest suites into a medical examination and operating room in anticipation you would one day soon have children."

"Alright father."

"If you are finished with your breakfast, I would like you to go with them for a medical examination."

"I'm fine father."

"Yes, you are my lovely daughter, but you also might be pregnant."

Lì looked at her father with total disbelief and asked, "You can't be serious, father."

"Lì, I am very serious and if you are not pregnant, we need to know why you got sick last night."

"Alright father if that makes you feel better, I'll let them do the examination, but I want Stanley to come with me."

At first the emperor was negative about Stanley's involvement when suddenly one of the doctors said, "It's always good if we have the father with us during the examination so that he can see the procreation and we like to advise both parents at that time of the precautions and activities we think would be essential for the health of the unborn."

The emperor was being slightly overpowering when the other doctor said, "Your excellency, we swear on our lives to take good care of your daughter. We would like her and her husband and nobody else in the examining room."

The Valet Octavrator smiled because he knew the emperor intended to march his daughter to the examining room and personally supervise matters, however the doctors just put him in his place.

Octavrator then offered, "Your excellency, may I suggest you and I wait here and enjoy the morning and a drink while the good doctors do their examinations."

It was clear to Stanley that Octavrator had a lot of influence over the emperor who relented and sat down at the long table and looked up to Lucas and said, "Could you please go get Octavrator and me a morning stimulant?"

"It would be my pleasure, your Highness," Lucas responded and turned around and walked directly for the nearby Kitchen.

The doctors led Princess Lì and Duke Ravik to their fully equipped examination and operating room. Every possible instrument or piece of equipment they needed was there including a staff nurse who managed the room and brought in additional support if required.

Once inside the examination room the doctors asked the nurse to take Princess Lì into the adjacent change room and fit her with an examination gown and slippers.

In due time the princess was laying on a special examination table that had devices that suspended from the overhead that could come down and do non-invasive checks of Princess Lì abdomen using ultrasound to create three-dimensional imagery. One doctor was on each side of the patient as the opened her examination robe to allow placement of the transducers over the belly and being the measurements. In a few minutes the doctors confirmed what the emperor suspected and said, "Our measurements are now being stitched together with computer software that will soon produce a three-dimensional holograph of the child."

Within five minutes the lead doctor said, "We are ready now to show what we measured."

The three-dimensional holograph of the baby reorientated vertically to be able to observe and analyze easier was impressive. The image had a degree of magnification, but the resolution was so fantastic it looked surreal.

"The fetus is probably two and a half to three months old," the lead doctor said, and his assistant replied, "I concur."

Princess Lì was now super emotional. She was now holding Stanley's (aka Duke Ravik's) hand and squeezing it very strongly. The unborn child had perfectly formed lips, eye sockets and body easily exposed the fact the child was a male with testicles and a penis. The very most important attribute for the child born as a Royal was his small wings. The wings were from shoulders down to his midsection already. This would go a long way to ease the emperor's fears the child would be born wingless and viewed as a freak due to the mixing of the DNA. But thanks to dominant genes, the child appeared as a healthy looking unborn Lìsztbrùnést. The public would never be allowed to know Stanleys wings were transplanted, and his body modified. The public would now assume that Duke Ravik was a normal bird man especially since that's how his offspring appeared.

The doctors then started in on the preparations that needed

to be made and the lifestyle changes the couple would now be forced to make to accommodate a healthy born child. Even though Princess Lì had not been in the mood for sexual contact lately, the doctors then gave the statistics on improving the birth rate by abstaining from sex until the baby was born. Also due to morning sickness and irritable nights the princess would have to ensure, they recommended Stanley be moved out of the princess suite and allow her to be alone with the nurse during those episodes she would feel noxious for a few more months.

Within an hour after the examination, the emperor was privately taken to the examination and operating room and shown the holographic presentation of the baby. When he saw how perfectly the boy was formed and how majestic his wings appeared even though he was still just a fetus, the emperor got seriously emotional, and a few tears flowed. It was heart breaking to him that his beloved Empress was not here to see this holograph. And in the back of his mind, he still was designing a method of dealing with Hectozar without causing a terrible blood bath killing billions.

During the days when the princess was feeling bad, they would arrange things to keep Stanley preoccupied. One thing he seemed to like was spending time walking out into the parklike estate of the mansion with Rascal following his ever movements.

Rascal was good therapy for Stanley during the depths of Princess Lì's very unpleasant episodes. Stanley liked exercising but he also had a new method: flying. He would do a combination of walking then in the open field in the middle of the property fly around doing laps. Rascal would fly in formation with Stanley just like he was a dog running with his master.

After their workout together, one of the aids sent out with Stanley had his package that had some treats for Rascal.

In due time, the Royal Aide was quite taken back because Rascal would hop up on Stanleys leg as he set down on a portable chair and slowly fed Rascal. Water for birds is always a problem, so Stanley always brought a small bottle of water and a clear short dish to pour the water into. Rascal learned to drink the water and he would sometimes take his snacks and dip them in the water and let them soak a bit to soften them up before he ate them.

They had their routine worked out. The security staff was advised that Rascal was Duke Ravik's pet bird and to look out for it and not let anyone disturb it as it sat up on the tree across the road from the main entrance to the mansion waiting for Stanley.

Stanley an inquisitive person was not the type of person to stay idle. He did a lot of self-studies and learned a lot about the galaxy. Nobody on planet Earth had the exposure Stanley received and because of his interest in various matters, the emperor who was appraised of Stanley's day to day routines and what he was reading this week would sometimes invite experts in to visit with Stanley and give him an added jolt of discovery. One of those visits led to a mountain top observatory where Stanley got to see a phased array image of a planet in the Andromeda solar system with the dark side of the planet lit up by night lights like most advanced civilizations.

Stanley had several types of field trips to get him out of the mansion and away from the tension of dealing with Princess Lì who was becoming more and more irritable on every passing day.

Because of the importance of the heir to the throne when the doctors determined the child had reached the proper level of development in the mother's womb she was taken to the operating room where the two surgeons would remove the child and do all the necessary surgery to sew the mother back up and make sure she maintained her health.

The operating room turned into the recovery suite with around the clock presence of a nurse and a doctor. In the event something negative occurred they didn't want Stanley in the room until an evaluation was made the mother and child were in a stable condition.

Stanley was dressed in an adjacent room with surgical clothes and disinfected and brought in to see his lovely creation. And there he was, his winged baby with the woman he loved. They brought a chair next to the bed so Stanley could be close to the mother and child.

Princess Lì was on pain reducers and the bird child would receive all his nourishment from the mother for a while. It was at this time that Octavrator's role became more and more apparent as Stanley started seeing more of him than anyone else. It felt like they had their own personal Valet. In a way they did, but it was for the young prince.

Stanley spent so much time with Princess Lì and the child that Rascal started crowing calling out for Stanley. When reports circulated up to Octavrator, he pulled Stanley aside and said, "Princess Lì has plenty of help. You do not need to be there every second of the day. Come with me I want to show you something."

Nobody would have believed the sight had there not been several eyewitnesses. Octavrator led Stanley outside the mansion and pointed up at the squawking bird and said, for your own sake you need to spend some time with your friend. Your princess and son will be here when you get back from your daily routine. About that time Rascal flew down and landed on Stanley's shoulder. This type of bird normally did not get near people. Rascal stopped squawking the minute he was riding on Stanleys shoulder. Stanly felt a little pain with the claws digging into his skin a bit and figured this might happen again and planned to have shoulder pads from now on when he was to be outside with Rascal.

For those who watched Rascal fly to land on Duke Ravik's shoulder it was an omen. They now knew in their hearts; Stanley was a *man of birds*. Nobody ever interacted with birds in this fashion before. In another hour after Octavrator showed Emperor Cornelius the security video. The emperor was significantly moved. This man had changed his empire. He brought his daughter home to a new reality, bore him a grandson, and now the *man of birds* was really with the birds. This of course caused the emperor to take an even more level of interest in Stanley and was soon getting videos to observe of Stanley flying in formation with Rascal just like two of the best friends in the world. At times a few other birds would attempt to join the flock and Rascal would chase them off. He was very territorial and didn't want any other birds near Stanley.

After a few months the doctors indicated to Princess Lì it would be healthy for the young prince to go outdoors and breath the fresh air and get a little sunlight. Their first trip outdoors was now planned, and a cart would be nearby to carry the princess if she felt faint. The baby had its beautiful carriage which Stanley gladly pushed. Rascal immediately came up to Stanly and landed on his shoulder which he now did routinely. Rascal knew something was up he hadn't seen the princess in a while. He knew the princess was Stanleys mate and now there was the little guy. Rascal was of course intrigued at the site of the young prince.

Princess Lì didn't know how Stanley and Rascal had evolved. She tested her mental telepathy with Rascal again which seemed to be as strong as ever. And she planted in Rascal's mind *that was Stanley's baby chick*. Rascal now knew the prince was part of Stanleys family which Rascal felt a part of which meant the young prince was Rascal's brother. Rascal would give his life to protect the prince if necessary. The group stopped at Stanley's location where he and Rascal did their exercises then the treats.

Princess Lì did not feel her body was ready to fly again but nevertheless was anticipating enjoying observing Stanley and Rascal flying together.

The two took off and began their laps for the morning workout. Stanley was slowly working up his miles. He asked for help in measuring his flight distances and the emperor's men set up measurements and fitted Stanley with a wristband that transmitted telemetry so they could very accurately measure distance flown.

Stanley had worked up to ten miles and could handle that every day. Then on one day he did fourteen miles and after lunch and a nap decided to go back out and see how far he could go. At the twenty-one-mile mark he decided he proved the point and quit for the day. Though the next day he did feel the pain.

Today Stanley would only do ten miles which seemed to happen very quickly and probably in just three quarters of an hour. They went back to their landing zone and Stanley sat down in the folding chair like normal with Rascal on his leg being fed.

Princess Lì was holding the young prince in her arms after feeding him and was standing beside Stanley watching his interactions with Rascal.

Rascal was watching the young prince with utter fascination. Then the unbelievable happened.

Princess Lì carefully put the young prince down on Stanley's other leg. Rascal then started making strange sounds unlike they had ever heard before. He then jumped over on the other leg and got very close to the baby and rested his head on the baby's shoulder and did not budge. Stanley looked up at Princess Lì and saw she had a lot of tears.

Stanley asked, "What's wrong?"

Princess Lì responded, "Rascal said he loves his brother."

They just set there for a while not disturbing the serenity that flowed between rascal and the young prince.

Stanley realizing this was a special moment, but they needed to be going back to the palace soon said, "Rascal come over here so I can feed you. You can visit with your brother tomorrow."

Rascal as if he understood everything Stanley said, hopped over on his other leg and made some strange sounds which they didn't understand, and Stanley fed him his treats and then his water and the baby was back in its stroller ready to move on.

Soon the event was over, and the group walked back to the palace entrance. Princess Lì telepathically said to Stanley, "I don't know how to describe it but it's as if I feel refreshed and more energetic."

"That's how I felt after I spent time with the Mallard ducks on Ski Beach. It's something Rascal did."

The Royal Couple entered the mansion and Rascal went up to his tree branch where he waited very patiently. The staff was happy he wasn't squawking and making a lot of noise now.

Per Princess Lì's request they brought another bed into her suite so that Stanley could be in a bed next to her and the young prince. The prince had a bassinet designed to be put on a bed next to the mother and he slept next to his mother the princess who was always there to feed him or comfort him.

Princess Lì knew that Stanley was lonely the past few months and when it appeared the baby was sound to sleep, she crawled into bed with Stanley so he could hold her in his arms and receive all her love.

The chambermaids had cameras mounted always observing the baby and microphones to pick up his noise if necessary. One of them was on duty and always awake if necessary to summon the nurse or a doctor right away for any exigencies.

Over the next few weeks there was a couple times the princess was woken by the chambermaid monitoring the baby so that the princess could do the feeding and attend to him. All in all, the baby slept well and seemed cheerful and happy.

As expected, the boy grew and became more aware of his surroundings including his awareness of Rascal. The boy took a liking to Rascal who reciprocated the emotions. Their bonding was inseparable. When Rascal observed the young tyke first deploy his wings and fan them out, it created great happiness to Rascal who loved his adopted family. Rascal and the family grew together. Rascal was a type of bird that could live up to one hundred years or longer. Since Rascal and Stanley first met when Rascal was a young bird that meant Rascal would possibly outlive Stanley.

Stanley was sent on more and more adventures as the emperor wanted to enrich his life and help advance his learning by associating with the best minds in the Empire.

Because the young Prince slowly turned into a young toddler the trips out to visit and feed Rascal while Stanley was away helped fill in some of the day with a form of enrichment and development of his mind.

~~~~~~
~~~~~~

Chapter Nine

Attempted Kidnapping

Hectozar the Gromulite despot Dictator knew the axe was going to fall soon and it was only a matter of time before Emperor Cornelius came for him and extracted ten pounds of flesh for killing his Empress put together an elaborate plan to kidnap one of the Royals and use that person as a hostage to keep Emperor Cornelius from attacking him.

The team was slowly infiltrated, and it took almost two years to plan it and execute it.

By now the young prince a full toddler loved his day with Rascal. The two were almost inseparable. Mentally they were brothers and the young prince with growing mental telepathy reached a point he could communicate with Rascal.

Rascal had fantastic vision and great hearing. He was always sensitive to his surroundings even though he had a vast and wonderful relationship with humans. Before the princess came out that morning Rascal detected some sounds and movement off into the horizon and took to flight.

To the kidnappers it was just another bird flying around and nothing to be concerned with. They knew the princess had the means to fly and they had a special web netting to capture her and quickly leave the planet with her and or the young prince and set up the stalemate to stop Emperor Cornelius from his ultimate actions they knew would be coming soon.

They were all in place almost 100 of them to make sure the kidnappers could get away with the prize.

That morning as soon as the princess arrived where they normally met up with Rascal, he quickly informed her *danger was present and to get back to the mansion as quickly as possible with her son*. Rascal would do what ever was possible to delay them. He suggested she fly away, and it might be the only way she could get to the mansion in time to save her life.

Princess Lì grabbed her son, informed the assistant to sound the alarm and went airborne. Rascal went airborne at the same time and saw the humans had some sort of device he assumed they were going to use on the princess and possibly harm her.

The mansion was alerted there was an emergency, security was responding, and aerial support was moments away, but may not get there quickly enough to save the princess as they didn't know what the attackers' intentions were, which may include killing her and the young prince.

Carrying the young prince in her arms and flying as hard as she ever did in her lifetime, she was making good progress to get back to the safety of the emperor's mansion.

The Gromulite military technician with the netting device was just about to hit the launch button which would have nailed the princess and allow their plan to work.

Rascal understood what was going on this person was going to hurt the princess, so he dove like a bird of prey and attacked the man just before he pulled the trigger. With claws in one eye and a beak poking out the other eye, the netting device didn't get launched in time and the princess escaped. Unfortunately for Rascal, the troops on the ground killed him with laser fire.

The emperor's forces closed in on the possible kidnappers with precision and within a few moments many of them were getting killed and the remaining few surrendered. The evidence was damning.

Hectozar the Gromulite despot Dictator had pressed his luck and had one or two years of peace to enjoy but this attack directly on the emperor sealed the deal the war would start a lot sooner than Hectozar planned for.

When the emperor personally interrogated those who surrendered and promised he would have them shoved out of an airlock in space today if they didn't cooperate, he got the vivid details quickly. He would immediately start to mobilize his forces and prepare for an eventual attack on Gromulite planets and wipe out Hectozar. Emperor Cornelius special forces had already done sufficient planning and they could indeed launch the attack very soon in the very near future. The big showdown was now a few weeks away.

In clearing the debris out of the battlefield, they found the dead bird. The grounds keepers immediately informed the emperor that Rascal had been killed. As soon as Princess Lì discovered Rascal was dead, she informed her father Rascal had warned them, and she only got away in time thanks to Rascal. Some of the prisoners were asked about the bird and they confessed it had been killed by laser weapons.

A few hours later when Stanley arrived shook up when he learned his wife and child almost were kidnapped by Hectozar's men, he was pulled aside by the emperor himself and informed that Rascal was dead and saved his wife and son from being kidnapped. Stanley of course was very upset and angry and immediately flew out to where rascal lay in the open area next to the webbing launcher.

Stanley picked up Rascal and held him in his arms and wheeped.

Princess Lì was informed where Stanley was heading and soon flew after him and landed near him and slowly approached watching Stanley in his sad state. She walked over and put her arms around him and softly consoled him and held him for a while until Stanley slowly came out of it. He had lost his friend who he loved who had given up his life to save his wife and son. There could never be a friend as good as this for anyone.

Stanley looked around and saw there was a lot of debris including empty boxes used to carry some of the equipment the kidnappers brought with them. Without dropping Rascal, he picked up one of the boxes and put Rascal in it and said, "Let's go back to the Palace. Tomorrow when I'm feeling better, I want to bury Rascal someplace special so that I will never forget him."

The next day after Octavrator made the appropriate arrangements, Rascal was laid to rest next to the tree where he always waited diligently for Stanley to appear to spend their day together.

That night Stanley cried almost half the night, then fell into a deep sleep, something strange happened in the middle of the night that helped Stanley cope with the loss of Rascal. It was as if the bird spirit had reached out to Stanley and informed him, "It's okay Stanley. Rascal is now in a better place and his love for you is eternal."

In the morning Stanley was refreshed and happy that his wife and son were still intact, and life goes on.

Emperor Cornelius knew he would find the Royal Couple at their favorite place in the morning and was going to inform Stanley, "Very soon the fleet will fly to the Gromulite worlds and demand Hectozar's head on a silver platter or we will start destroying the Gromulite Empire."

"I want to go on the mission."

"It's not safe for you to go, I can't let you go."

"I want to be there to personally witness Hectozar pay for his crimes and the death of Rascal and attempted attack on my wife and child."

The discussion wasn't going anywhere and finally Octavrator snapped the king out of his negative thoughts by saying, "The young prince and his mother will be here and safe. Continuity of the Empire will be preserved. If Duke Ravik is killed in the battles, your legacy will continue through your daughter and your grandson."

"Yes, but I do not want Princess Lì to be miserable the rest of her life if something goes wrong and we cannot protect Duke Ravik."

Octavrator turned towards Stanley and said, "I will discuss this with the emperor privately and see what we can come up with. May I suggest you take some time and go exercise and spend time with Princess Lì and your son."

Stanley knew it was pointless to continue arguing with the emperor who was vastly intelligent and had his agenda and responded, "I think exercise would help me blow off some steam and improve my disposition. Thank you for the suggestion."

Stanley went back to their combined suite and changed into his exercise clothes and had Princess Lì get their son ready to go out. He knew he would be sulking a while but knew flying around the field would help him clear his head.

Another consequence of the Gromulites penetration of the emperor's mansion estate included a significantly stepped-up perimeter and sky surveillance. The Royal Couple would be very safe today because anyone coming close to the mansion without an invitation would be immediately detained and interrogated using advanced methods that were not conducive to physical wellbeing. The princess knew she could fly again, but did not want to leave her son's side, so the two of them sat there and watched Stanley make the laps to get in his ten miles.

Around Stanley's five mile mark several birds that were identical to Rascal started flying in formation with Stanley. They continued flying with him until he landed at the ten-mile mark next to Princess Lì and the young prince.

The half dozen birds landed nearby and simply stared at Stanley.

"It's too bad I didn't bring any treats or water," Stanley said.

"We can bring that tomorrow."

"Good idea, these birds seem rather friendly."

"There is a reason."

"What is that?"

"They are Rascal's brothers and sisters."

"They know who I am?"

"Yes, birds communicate and your relationship with Rascal intrigued them."

"I suppose now that Rascal is gone, I could use a few new friends."

"They are already your friends. They think very fondly of you and know how much Rascal meant to you. They also observed the demise of Rascal and it saddened them as much as it did you."

"Tell them I will see them here tomorrow."

"They said they will be waiting for you."

The group left and went back to the mansion and prepared for dinner. Reports had filtered back to the emperor on how the Royal Couple and the young prince enjoyed the day and that already Stanley had new bird friends. The emperor was glad knowing this distraction would help keep Stanleys mind off Hectozar the

Gromulite despot Dictator.

That night at dinner the emperor said, "The prince is now at the age he needs to be named and get used to be called by that name. You two need to pick a name for him."

Princess Li looked at Stanley and asked, "Do you have any ideas about a name for the prince?"

Stanley responded, "I do but I'm not sure you would like it."

"Let me hear it, I'll be the one to decide if I like it or not."

"Alright, I like the name Lacsar."

"Is that the name of someone you know?"

"No, it's Rascal spelled backwards."

"You can't be serious?"

"If you think about it, the kidnappers would have taken you and our son and the two of you might have gotten killed had Rascal not saved your lives."

"The name sounds alright. We can't let people know what it means because nobody names their children after animals."

"It will be our secret."

"Alright then, welcome to the world Prince Lacsar."

~~~~~~
~~~~~~

CHAPTER TEN

RASCAL II MEETS LACSAR

The following day, the Royal Couple went out to exercise and brought along some treats and water just like before. Stanley began his workout, and the flock was immediately following in formation. At the ten-mile mark, Stanley landed near Princess Li and Prince Lacsar.

Stanley suspected there would be more birds today, so he brought along extra treats. And put down the water next to where he deposited the treats on a cloth sheet a few square feet in diameter.

The birds cautiously approached and with Princess Lì applying telepathic communiques to the birds, their anxiety was quickly eliminated, and they went after the treats and drank the clean water.

One of the birds walked towards Prince Lacsar close enough for him to grab the bird. The boy pulled the bird next to him and held it the best he could. Princess Lì telepathically communicated to the bird and informed it that in honor of their dearly departed Rascal, she would now name this brother of Rascal with the name Rascal II.

"I gave the bird the name Rascal II."

"Think he will like that name?" Stanley asked.

"Yes, he likes it and is honored to be named after Rascal who protected me and Prince Lacsar."

Princess Lì didn't know Lacsar was developing telepathic ability at a remarkable rate. His telepathic ability exceeded his language skills and as he grew past three years old, he and Rascal II had bonded completely. They were now defacto *bird brothers*. The entire flock looked upon these winged humans as extra special in their lives. Every bird around had a sense of the Royals.

~~~~~~

Time had passed and the big showdown with Hectozar the Gromulite despot Dictator was going to happen soon. There was no conversations or news about any activity. If there was anything going on it was super quiet.

Octavrator was always pervasive. His hand existed in every element of the empire politics and even though Lucas was now always with the emperor, there was no doubt in Octavrator that his robot Lucas would diligently carry out every task he gave him. Lucas was simply Octavrator's extra set of eyes and ears along with a robot body to do his bidding.

Lucas was highly developed and was continuously going through metamorphism. His artificial intelligence was spellbinding because his equivalente IQ measured 100,000 more than any Lìsztbrùnést. His moral and ethical values were impecable and rules for robots were not necessary for him because his advanced philosophy prohibited him from divergence from the expected fabric of life surrounding his tasking.

Lucas had constant communications via his wireless to Octavrator a real living person and the two often discussed matters to determine the best path forward. Octavrator was not always able to resolve all the issues and sometimes would ask Lucas for his input on those matters. The synergism that Lucas provided
~~~~~~

multiplied Octavrator's abilities by several magnitudes because of his often-astute advice.

The mission that would attempt to nab Hectozar was about ready to begin. The nagging question of how to deal with Stanley existed and even though Octavrator and Lucas were widely separated in different parts of the mansion they could communicate efficiently as if they were standing next to each other.

It was Octavrator's contention that by allowing Stanley to participate in this dangerous mission he felt confident would work, that Duke Ravik would have a sense of duty and achievement. Up to now his truly only accomplishment, even though very important in itself, was creating the emperor's grandson.

Lucas who had huge psychological reservoirs from the greatest minds in the galaxy as well as the best artificial intelligence ever constructed fully analyzed everything Octavrator stated and concluded he was spot on with his insights of how to build a greater sense of achievement in the future Emperor's father. In essence they would be building a legacy that the young prince Lacsar could build his own assessment towards his father knowing he had done something important for the Empire.

"How do we get him away from the palace without tipping off the emperor who would demand his immediate recall?"

"That's simple you have already paved the way?"

"And how is that?"

"The perfect alibi is another one of those scientific journeys."

"What do you have in mind?"

"We know he has exceptional abilities with those birds he has made a family out of."

"That's true."

"Those birds proved to be excellent lookouts and saved the princess and the baby prince from being kidnapped. We can bring them along on the mission to assist us. The enemy would never expect them or consider them to be any form of danger."

"Just exactly how will we use them?"

"They will make it easier for us to snatch and grab Hectozar. They are capable of carrying considerable amount of weight for their body size. Through Stanley we can request they deploy weapons for us to assist in our egress and get away before they can react."

"What do we tell Stanley?"

"I think we can level with him. He already wants to participate, and I know how angry he is knowing Hectozar killed his wife's mother, and tried to kidnap his wife and son, he will do whatever we ask him to do."

"How do we get him and his birds away from the emperor's private park?"

"The ruse will be we are taking him and his most favored flock to a special planet where they will discover birds exist that are more intelligent than primates."

"We only have a couple days now to do all the arrangements."

"I will make sure it all happens. Tomorrow, we'll get Stanley to round up all his birds and we'll take them out into space and head for the planet Ollytrene. Of course, we'll divert and join the task force once out of scanner range."

"When will we alert him to the mission?"

"I will let him know today. If he choses not to go, then he made the decision for us, and we'll simply do it without him."

"What kind of weapons can we use with the birds?"

"I've been thinking about this plan for a while, and I've already had a technologist design them for us. The birds will be given latitude on how they want to deploy them. They will be told to save themselves first, but something tells me they will do extraordinary measures to assist Duke Ravik.

Octavrator had already sent Princess Lì and Prince Lacsar with the emperor to a function where she would meet up with other young mothers with their toddlers for some social engagement with the emperor in attendance. Stanley was left alone at the palace where he could have that discussion away from prying ears.

Octavrator went to the Royal Couples suite when he was informed by the chambermaids that Duke Ravik had bathed from his earlier workout and was now dressed and ready to participate in the activity Octavrator had planned for him.

Stanley was notified by one of the Chambermaids the Valet Octavrator arrived at the door to his suite to escort him to his next activity. He then walked to the door.

The Chambermaid opened the door for Stanley who met Valet Octavrator.

Octavrator bowed to Stanley and said, "Good afternoon, Duke Ravik. Please come with me."

Octavrator then escorted Duke Ravik to the Royal elevator that only the Royal Family was allowed in. They got inside and the elevator did not stop at the ground floor as it was programmed to continue down to the secret chamber a good distance underground below the mansion where a lot of the INTEL apparatus had special services and equipment existed that was ready to deal with several contingencies including escaping a coup.

Stanley had never been here and didn't know it even existed. Octavrator took Stanley into a conference room that had holographic technology for war planning and defense strategies insitu.

"Please have a seat, Duke Ravik."

Stanley sat down wondering what was going on. This was a great revelation to him. He didn't know what to expect and knew the best thing to do is just listen and find out what this was all about.

"The reason why I brought you here is its secure and nobody can hear our conversation. It is completely private and confidential."

"Alright."

"A while back when we were having discussions with the emperor about you participating in an operation against Hectozar you were rather emotional that you wanted to be involved and the emperor who is concerned about your safety flatly rejected that idea."

"Yes, I was not happy he prohibited me from participating."

"Lucas and I have had a lot of discussions about you and how we feel it would be important for you to participate. We have a plan and will invite you to come with us and help. This will be your legacy and after the emperor expires from old age, we'll make sure your son knows what you contributed so he will feel better about your legacy."

"Why should he be told?"

"Since he will one day be the important person to keep this Empire held together, we believe that he would have a better evaluation of you and the respect he will develop knowing what you do, may help him cope with future exigencies he may be faced with."

"What is it you want from me?"

"Do you want to participate in this mission?"

"Of course, you know I do."

"Alright if you agree to go, I'm now going to brief you on how we are going to pull this off without the emperor ever finding out about it."

"I will do whatever it takes."

"You must never mention any of this to anyone including the princess."

"I understand the complications involved. You can be assured of my silence."

"In the event something happens to you before Lacsar grows into a man, I assure you that Lucas and I will make sure your son knows everything about your participation so that later in life he can be proud of you."

"Thank you. I appreciate that."

Stanley now was fully briefed on the entire plan. He didn't flinch a bit and was ready to carry out his assignment as the *birdman* in the operation.

The following morning after breakfast, Stanley informed Princess Lì, "I'm going away for a few days on a scientific study on the planet Ollytrene."

"What about all your bird friends? They will not be happy that you will be gone."

"I'm taking them with me. Part of this study is to expose them to birds very similar to them that have a much higher I.Q. on Ollytrene. I've been told those birds on Ollytrene have a higher I.Q. than primates on primative worlds.

"Lacsar is too young to be going on such a trip, he could get an infection as his immune system is not fully developed."

"You and Lacsar will remain here. With all the possibilities of unexpected activities that Hectozar might attempt, I think the emperor would prefer you stay some place where he can protect the two of you."

"How soon will you be leaving?"

"In a short while I expect my escort will be here to take me to the birds where we have some transportation devices to put them in for the trip."

"You think you can get those wild birds to get in a transportation device?"

"Yes, I'm sure they will do anything for me."

"This I got to see."

"Be my guest."

Just like clockwork, Lucas was at the door within fifteen minutes.

"Princess Lì wants to go with us to see if the birds will willingly get into the transportation devices."

"That's not a problem, we have plenty of room for riders."

Within fifteen minutes they were all gathered at the exercise location and the flock of birds flew in expecting to fly. Stanley's mental telepathy with the birds was now stronger than what Princess Lì exhibited. She was rather perplexed when she observed all this. She also knew Stanley was blocking her penetration of his mind. He was hiding something from her, and it irritated her.

To Princess Lì shocking surprise, every single member of the flock entered the transportation devices. They drove around to the front of the mansion where several shuttles had landed to accommodate all the bird transporters.

While Stanley and Princess Lì were saying goodbye, the princess was disturbed because Stanley's actions were highly unusual as she normally had free rein in Stanley's mind. And his powerful telepathic interchange with the birds astonished her. She didn't know what to think. But part of their goodbye Stanley said, "I love you with all my heart. You mean more to me than anything. I could never live without you."

This was one element of his psyche he could not shield or hide from Princess Lì in any manner. She felt his immense love for her. His love was golden and his affection to her and the young prince was unmistakable.

But Princess Lì knew Stanley needed to explore the galaxy to grow and later to advise his son. Experience begats experience. She reluctantly let him go and soon afterwards regretted that decision.

The shuttles launched and went up to the waiting Fast Frigates. The emperor wasn't taking any chances. The Duke of Ravik would have ample protection. At least that's what he believed to be the case. Unfortunately, the snatch and grab would require far more covert methods and arrival on a Fast Frigate would not be feasible.

The birds were in a way a good plan in case they were stopped. Black Marketers with cages of exotic birds would give the appearance of a legitimate money-making scheme as these birds were delicacies in the Trilateral Worlds that would fetch a big number of credits. But there was no intention of ever allow any of them to end up with butcher's knife in his hand.

The tables were now turned. Instead of a large force coming down to kidnap the princess and her son. The chief instigator was just about to be removed from power in ways he never dreamed possible.

At a rendezvous out in deep space, Stanley, Lucas, and Octavrator with the birds transferred over to a *Cosmic Cutter* type of spacecraft, the task force traveled to Gromula launched shuttles down upon a world that had severely overestimated their space defense.

Stanley now gave Octavrator some extravagant information he was not aware of:

"I have the means to communicate to these birds very effectively. They are the best scouts you will ever have."

"You can talk to them with great precision?"

"Yes, I can, just as if they are human. They will be our spies and tell us everything we need to know when we arrive on the planet."

"And you are sure they can deploy those weapons accurately?"

"Yes. The Gromulites do not know they are sitting ducks."

~~~~~~

The moment of truth now unfolded as the shuttles left the *Cosmic Cutter* planet bound. Thanks to all the planning and INTEL they would be able to land in thick triple canopy forested area that would have a small landing zone prepared for their arrival after dark. In the morning after the heist as security forces flew over the area, they would quickly get curious as to why there were two squares cut out in the forest the night before by a couple teams of special forces who were also perimeter defense to insure, the special operations team could get away but these individuals would also willingly take a wound to protect Stanley if required. They all had their egress plans as well and hopefully this would be a quiet heist and come morning the despot dictator would be missing.

Within ten minutes of the special forces team arrival on Gromula, the silent removal of trees was complete and per plan two infrared shots up into the sky toward the position of the *Cosmic Cutter* marking exact positions that would be hard to detect from the ground confirmed the landing zone locations for the shuttles.

The men arrived and left the bird transporters in the shuttles and Stanley asked the birds to fly around and Hectozar's palace
~~~~~~

and do reconnaissance for the snatch an grab team. The birds left in waves and cycled back making reports to Stanley who then updated a detailed map for Octavrator and Lucas. They now had a complete picture of where all the guards and security were located throughout Hectozar's mansion complex.

Explosives were not the only thing available for the birds. Each bird could drop special darts with very powerful poisons that only took a slight penetration of the skin, and that guard would either be dead or incapacitated for hours. Octavrator explained to Stanley his role of interfacing with the birds was so crucial he had to stay with the shuttles. Some of the special force's men were to put him in a shuttle and launch it immediately if given the bug out signal in case the mission was compromised.

Octavrator and Lucas made their way to Hectozar's palace. Special Forces men systematically deactivated all the perimeter sensors. Now the birds started dropping darts on guards they could find and when they used up all their darts flew back to the shuttle to get more.

By the time Octavrator and Lucas got to the palace almost the entire staff was dead. Hectozar was fornicating with members of his harem slightly drugged up and oblivious to bad things were about to happen.

Thanks to Lucas very capable sensors the few remaining staff members not killed by the birds were easily dispatched.

The door to the harem was open and the group in there was carrying on drugged up and semi crazy when Lucas threw in several of the devices that gave off a thick purple cloud.

Octavrator had on his mask that protected him and would not have any effect. Within moments there was silence in the room as everyone was unconscious and would remain that way for several hours. Octavrator then informed the special forces guys assisting to come in and pick up Hectozar and carry him out to the front entrance. Since the security system was now fully disabled, the team simply flew the shuttles to the front entrance and carried Hectozar to one of the shuttles and bound him up. Stanley directed the birds to get back in their transporters, as they were leaving.

None of the explosives were required as the heist worked in perfect silence. All the birds were accounted for, and the shuttles took off and made their way to the *Cosmic Cutter* that veered off away from the planet and made a high speed run out into open space where hey rendezvoused with two Fast Frigates that took Stanley on board with his birds so he could get to his tropical paradise at Ollytrene and enjoy the strange intelligent birds and have plausible deniability.

The *Cosmic Cutter* continued to Neflatraceous. There the precious cargo was offloaded and delivered to Emperor Cornelius who was in for a huge surprise having no idea Octavrator and Lucas had pulled off this amazing heist.

Emperor Cornelius had his special security detachment deliver Hectozar to an underground area reserved for execution of enemies of the state.

Hectozar was still unconscious from the drugging in transit. He was then placed on a chair fully bound and upright.

Emperor Cornelius then ordered the medical technician, "Administer the drugs to bring Hectozar back to conciousness."

Hectozar slowly came to and saw the person sitting in front of him wearing ornate clothes. He didn't recognize who he was. But realized he was tied up and probably not in a safe condition.

There were ten men behind the emperor who would soon be dealing with Hectozar after the emperor had his final words with him.

"You killed my wife, then you tried to kidnap my daughter and grandson. No person in my lifetime has ever taken so much from me. Had you harmed my daughter and grandson don't you think I would have destroyed all your worlds?"

"I highly doubt you could do that, the Trilaterals would not allow you."

"I have a surprise for you before we execute you."

"And what is that?"

"We lured the Trilaterals into a kill zone to rescue you. You will now see the results of the space battle that is now ongoing. Those images are being relayed to us real time via deep space neutrino communications. I thought you would like to see the results so I can show you how pitiful your space force is and why they will not be missing you."

The emperor stepped aside and on the holographic projection showed the ongoing space battle. Per the emperor's orders, *take no quarter*, complete devastation now showed.

The Trilaterals were boxed in. They had no where to escape. It was like shooting ducks in a barrel. Spaceships blew up into sparkling debris. Pleas for surrender were ignored. This was the final showdown. Trilaterals would pay the price for being aligned with the despot Gromulite dictator Hectozar.

Whatever fragile treaty the Trilaterals had with the Gromulites ended this day and they had no desire to ever engage them in the future under any circumstances.

In a while after watching several spaceships blown up, in what would go down in the history books as the *Battle of Cystanokar*, the Lìsztbrùnést task force commander, Admiral Timons reported:

"Emperor Cornelius, the entire Trilateral Fleet has been destroyed. We are returning to Neflatraceous."

Emperor Cornelius turned towards his military attache and said, "Inform Admiral Timons, job well done and I'm looking forward to having dinner with him at the mansion when he returns."

The holograph display now went blank.

"It appears the Gromulites no longer will be enjoying the support of the Trilaterals since we just destroyed their space force," Emperor Cornelius said looking at the pitiful excuse of a person.

Hectozar looked at Emperor Cornelius realizing bad things were just about to happen.

"You are such a poor tactical commander; I could have easily simply gone to Gromula and destroyed the planet to get to you. But I decided that even though you took something precious from me by assassinating my Empress, I felt it would be unfair to destroy all the Gromula people just because of you. That's why I arranged to bring you here to face justice."

"The Gromula people will continue attacking you. What you do to me doesn't matter."

"I have a lot of videos that will now be shown to the Gromulites and the evidence you murdered my Empress. They will also have the pleasure of watching your execution."

"I still have my cadres back on Gromula that will reform and soon you will have to deal with them."

"Gromula will be given a list of your operatives that were involved in the death of my Empress and if they do not hand them over within 24 hours, Gromula will be destroyed. Now that the Trilaterals are out of the way your forces are no longer able to stop me."

"Go ahead and kill me. I don't care."

"You are not going to die today. I'm sure your collaborators will soon be handed over and you will get the opportunity to watch every one of them die from asphyxiation as we shove them out of airlocks in space. Those involved in my Empress death will get to see you die and they too will die from laser firing squad."

"My people are not going to hand over my assistants. By now I'm sure they left the planet."

"Nobody has left the planet because we have it surrounded. Any ship leaving is boarded and people interrogated with neurotic sonification. As the hour draws close and the entire population knows they will be wiped out, your cronies will be handed over to us."

The emperor then stood up and left the room.

Hectozar was vain, he knew none of his hand-picked men would be handed over. He was wrong.

Members of the Gromulite military had their own INTEL apparatus and knew based on the Battle of Cystanokar, the Lìsztbrùnést were not bluffing, and General Kwang of the Gromulite Joint Chiefs issued the orders to arrest all Hectozar's cronies on the list provided by Emperor Cornelius. He then sent messages up to the Lìsztbrùnést Fleet Commander Admiral Timons they were in the process of arresting everyone on the list and please be patient as they would send them up on Shuttles as they apprehended them.

Most of Hectozar's cronies had no where to go and hide out so they made the biggest blunder by going to Hectozar's palace filtering in one by one and to their surprise the butlers and the staff there were well armed military people that arrested them soon after they arrived. In a brief matter of hours, the 45 men on the list were apprehended and taken in shackles up to the waiting Lìsztbrùnést Fleet.

The Hectozar's men thought they would go off to a prison some place and as each one of them were led off to interrogation they had neurotic sonification's applied and soon screamed with agony until they gave full confessions of their involvement in assassinating the Empress, but they pleaded they were not trying to kill her, they were after the Emperor and she took the kill shot instead of the intended victim, partly thanks to Octavrator saving the emperors life.

Some of those that were hard to crack were given the opportunity of watching prisoners thrown out into space from an airlock. The toughest bastards in the bunch were easily broken when confronted with the airlock departure with no breathing apparatus.

It didn't take that long to interrogate all 45 men and get their confessions. The emperor only wanted a dozen of them, the rest were shoved out of the air lock into space and quickly died from asphyxiation.

The dozen men were then taken to the palace where they got to see Hectozar not in a good mental condition because Emperor Cornelius had showed him the executions of his cronies.

The men were directed to stand in a straight line and were handcuffed and had leg shackles on.

Now it was show time. Emperor Cornelius said, "You men get to witness what I'm going to do to Hectozar for killing the love of my life and soon you will receive your judgement."

The emperor nodded and Octavrator on one side and Lucas on the other carried Hectozar tied to his chair to the back of the execution chamber.

Hectozar sat there stunned not believing this was happening to him and knew most of his cronies were dead and the last 12 Amigos were there watching his execution.

The moment of truth happened now. Hectozar's world ended and soon the twelve others were given similar treatment.

The only thing left to do now was too welcome Lìsztbrùnést Fleet Admiral Timons to the palace for an ornate celebration.

~~~~~~
~~~~~~

CHAPTER ELEVEN

BIRDMAN IN PARADISE

As planning went forward on the celebration at the emperor's mansion, and the news could not be contained because there were numerous Fleet Personnel involved. Word spread fast they had dealt with Hectozar who was missing, and the Trilateral Fleet was shattered and would not be a threat for many generations if ever.

Princess Lì was very smart and intuitive and feared that somehow Stanley had gotten involved in these current events. The fact she had not heard from him gave her incredible anxiety, so she immediately went to her father and asked, "Do you know where Stanley really went?"

The princess probed her father deeply and could not find a trace of anything that deviated from the common knowledge of where he went.

"He's at Ollytrene and will be coming home in a few days."

"I want to go there and see him now."

"Lì, there is no reason for you to go there."

"Father, I have to go."

"If I let you go, you will have to leave Prince Lacsar here. I will not risk the heir to my throne in case something bad happens because space travel is dangerous."

"He gets along well with the chambermaids, I'm sure they would take good care of him."

"Alright, how soon do you want to go?"

"Right this moment."

"You are not ready to go on a trip."

"That's okay I'm willing to travel roughly to get there. I want to see Stanley."

"Alright, let me have Lucas make plans for you."

Soon Lucas arrived and after their exchange informed the emperor, "It will take a couple hours to get the two Fast Frigates here to take the princess to Ollytrene."

That statement was a distortion because the emperor wanted the princess properly packed for the journey with everything she might need.

In due time Princess Lì Alìgrāwná was off chasing after Stanley almost in panic because something didn't add up. They just had a major space battle at the same time Stanley departed. Her heart would be shattered if something happened to Stanley. Princess Lì would never forgive her father if he allowed Stanley to go on that mission.

Thanks to neutrino communications Stanley's handlers were warned Princess Lì Alìgrāwná was on her way. Stanley was lucky he was enjoying his time in Ollytrene to make it look plausible.

The birds were not happy being cooped up on a spaceship so long and were joyous they were able to get off the ship with Stanley who cared for them with uncommon concern. This mission bonded the birds even more with Stanley because they were able to mentally determine they had just fought a battle with Stanley, the adopted member of their bird family.

As Stanley promised they soon met the intelligent Ollytrene birds that only existed on Ollytrene and nowhere else known in the galaxy.

Stanley had a couple days of introduction of his family birds to the smart Ollytrene flocks.

Stanley got in a couple days of flying with his flock and the intelligent birds joined them and flew in formation totally mesmerized at the interactions with the human and these birds he brought with him.

The smart Ollytrene birds could not communicate with the birds from Neflatraceous, but they were keen observers and attempted to find ways to communicate. However, they enjoyed their company and felt these visiting birds were extremely polite and then were even more startled as they discovered by observing, Stanley some how communicated with them without making any noise.

The interactions with the local Ollytrene birds were in progress when suddenly Princess Lì arrived. The entire Neflatraceous flock was happy to see the princess and it appeared like a celebration upon her arrival.

Stanley had asked the birds not to inform Princess Lì Alìgrāwná anything about the mission. But there were cracks in the flock's veneer. The birds were so excited to see the princess, they didn't realize she was reading all their minds, nor did Stanley realize it.

Stanley was somewhat bewildered when he observed Princess Lì Alìgrāwná sobbing.

"Is there something wrong?"

"Of course, there is, and you know it."

"Is everything ok with Lacsar?"

"He's fine but can you imagine what it would be like for him to grow up without a father."

"What are you getting at?"

"Stanley, you have never hidden anything from me before in my life and I'm heart broken you hid this from me."

"What are you talking about?"

"I know what you did."

"What was that?"

"I hope you realized the emperor is going to be extremely upset with you when he finds out you went to Gromula."

"How do you know about that?"

"Do you honestly think your lovely bird friends here can keep a secret from me?"

"I'm very sorry I had to do this. I was aggravated these people killed your mother and they almost kidnapped you and my son. I felt like I had to do something."

"Father explicitly forbidden you from participating in any of that."

"I will beg forgiveness if the emperor finds out. But I would prefer he is not made aware."

"Stanley, you can't keep secrets like this from my father for long. The emperor is a very smart man, and he will figure it out."

"I'll apologize and promise not to ever do something so foolish again."

"Stanley, do you realize what you would have done to me if I lost you?"

"I'm very sorry. I thought you would never know."

Stanley grabbed Princess Lì and held her as she sobbed some more. The birds were all watching and observing and feeling sad because the princess was sad.

"I love you and I'm very sorry I did this to you," Stanley said, and it started having and affect on the princess in ways she couldn't realize. The flock was jointly telepathing her and they were also affecting the local intelligent birds who added their own emotional cloud to the orbit of the princess.

"Alright dear, I'll keep your secret, but please never do something like this again unless we talk about it."

"I'll probably never volunteer to go on another mission like this again as I now realize how dangerous and foolish it was. We probably got lucky this time."

"Plus, you have a son to raise that would be very sad if he lost you."

The two gently held each other with the intensity of the flocks in close observation.

Everyone learned a lot that day and Octavrator knew that one day he would have to level with the emperor. But he felt his explanation would eventually be recognized as quite a development experience for Duke Ravik, plus he was with the emperor during his younger years where the emperor conducted far more dangerous operations despite his father's fears.

Octavrator's number one charge was now the emperor's grandson for the continuity of the Empire. The day would come when the grandson would learn it was his father using the birds to take over Hectozar's mansion to prevent the deaths of billions of people due to one despot.

This turned out to be a mini honeymoon for the Royal Couple. The emperor's spies sent back word on how the couple was getting along. Some of the video showed the Princess looking haggardly when she arrived almost appearing as if her life was being sucked out of her. The secret videos for the next few days showed how her luster grew exponentially when she was back together with the man she loved.

The emperor was obviously curious as to why his daughter's behavior seemed so bizarre to the point, she was almost in a panic to go see Stanley. But he was happy the joyfulness seemed strong.

With the birds to guide them around and the ability to fly themselves, Stanley, and Princess Lì were able to fly around the area near their camp and see all the majestic sights from beautiful white sandy beaches to waterfalls, mountains, lakes, and streams untouched by human activity.

Only one side of the planet was inhabited by humanoids that would be considered hunter gatherers. The intelligent birds of Ollytrene avoided those populated areas because the Ollytrene intelligent birds were considered a delicacy and they would be hunted and killed if they entered anywhere near those hunter gatherer settlements.

The hunter gatherers of Ollytrene had been exposed to spacemen and became aware of the galactic situation and even though they were a primitive society living with the basic necessities. The hunter gatherers of Ollytrene had been informed many generations ago they were a protectorate and normally the Lìsztbrùnést Empire would keep out non-essential travelers and usually only allowed scientific research parties to visit the planet with strict guidelines to avoid the eastern hemisphere and the indigenous people.

Now and then indigenous tribal members went on long trips exploring their planet and looking for more fertile lands to exploit. It was during such an outing they spotted the birdman and woman flying with several flocks of birds. From a distance they observed this activity and witnessed the closeness of the birds to the humanoids with wings.

It was a surreal moment for the indigenous explorers who for several days observed all this from a safe distance. But eventually they were spotted by Rascal-II who warned Stanley, who in turn avoided flying in that direction not knowing what the intentions of the indigenous people were.

The next few days passed rapidly, and Stanley knew they needed to go home because their son may not be happy.

They loaded up all their birds after saying goodbye to all their new friends, the intelligent Ollytrene birds and they departed the planet. As they were passing out into the sky heading for the stars, the indigenous explorers observed their ships and their way back to their distant villages to report everything they saw. Unlike other primative hunter gatherers, these tribesmen would advance at a much faster rate an when they eventually discovered the intelligent birds their lives were changed even more.

<div style="text-align:center">~~~~~~</div>

Arrival at the mansion could not have happened at a more auspicious moment. The young Prince Lacsar was starting to get fussy wanting his mother and father. The chambermaids were at their wits end because it seemed there wasn't much, they could do to help the young prince overcome his increasingly bad behavior, sleepless nights, and a few times crying.

When the chambermaids informed the young toddler, his parents were back, he ran out of the suite and to the front entrance where the door was open and out to his parents as fast as he could with the two chambermaids in hot pursuit. Princess Lì Alìgrāwná and Stanley had just exited one of the shuttles together as Lacsar darted right up to them and grabbed his mother with tears in his eyes. He was obviously upset, and Princess Lì now felt guilty for abandoning him to go chase after Stanley.

As Prince Lacsar slowly calmed down feeling quite happy his parents were back, Stanley was releasing all the birds out of the transport cases. Those birds knew precisely where they were and they immediately flew to their nests out in the park area, except for Rascal II who remained and observed the small boy holding tightly to his mother and taking it all in. Rascal II flew over to the small boy and landed and walked right up next to him.

Lacsar was moved by the bird and bent down and picked him up and held him. The boy and Rascal II interchanged some mental telepathy and when Rascal asked the boy via mental telepathy "Why have you been crying?"

Lacsar replied, "I'm upset because my parents had left me, and I do not like being left with the chambermaids."

Rascal II informed Lacsar, "Your father had very important work to do. It was a very unusual circumstance that could not be avoided. Your mother was concerned about his safety, so she flew off to meet him and bring him back. When you get older, I will explain it all to you."

Lacsar descended into an appearance of happiness and was all smiles when his grandfather approached the group with the chambermaids not far away observing their charge and Octavrator standing near them waiting for a private moment to address their failure in dealing with the young prince who easily escaped their control and possibly placed him at risk.

When confronted the chambermaids simply said, "The boy is very smart, and he runs to fast. It was impossible to stop him."

New security protocols were then put in place to prevent something like this from happening again.

Life at the mansion soon reached a quiescence. Life was predictable and repetitively constant.

~~~~~~

The next issue brewing was the official title for the future emperor. The Emperor's Court had a lot of influence over Emperor Cornelius and the system was set up they would help guide the emperor along, getting possible dissenting opinions and reflection on serious matters to help make mid-course corrections if necessary.

Unanimously the Emperor's Court did not like the name
~~~~~~

Lacsar even when informed the reason behind it.

One of the most influential members of the Emperor's Court, Madam Steflyrian Micheline brow beat the emperor into submission and the decision was finally made. Based on a unanimous vote after analyzing hundreds of possible distinguished names connected far back to Royals, the name Demetrius Ravik was selected. This would be his official public name from this day forward however to the staff and all the insiders, Lacsar would remain. Lacsar's parents would continue using that name and as he grew older explain to him why he had two names and that Lacsar was his very private name that only staff, and insiders would know or ever be allowed to use. Duke Ravik was pleased the second provision was codified by the emperor because all the bird families loved Lacsar, and it would be terribly confusing to them to hear him called Demetrius Ravik.

The years advanced quicker than people seemed to realize. The lack of intergalactic conflict and this great long period of peace and tranquility allowed everyone to get along with great satisfaction in life.

It was about this time the princess became a mother again to a daughter. Princess Lì probed Stanley for ideas of names that were Earthly in origination.

Stanley had been a road warrior and traveler in his previous life, long before he met Ami. In some of those quintessential sojourns into romantic activity he fell in love with a woman who broke his heart. A lot of lovers remember people by the music they listened to during those special moments where love flowed and the transcendence to emotional splendor resonated the passions.

One such tune was an Italian singer Alessandra Amoroso, and the song was *Mi Sei Venuto A Cercare Tu.*

The brain records sound in the prevailing holographs that make up our memories. Sometimes for unexplained reasons, the fidelity of the memory is significantly better than many other memories, especially some that fade with time. But due to circumstances at

the time the music is imprinted indelibly in the mind. Alessandra Amoroso song *Mi Sei Venuto A Cercare Tu* was very strong. Stanley didn't take that heart breaking relationship into the future, and it truncated without his ability to save it and the love. In a way it made Princess Lì sad, but the fidelity of Stanley's memory of the music was rather profound which gave Princess Lì the notion to pick Alessandra as the daughter's name. For Stanley that was alright because he had fond memories of the singer. The woman however in his past had faded long ago and just the music remained.

Not long after Alessandra grew up to a toddler the family was out for the morning exercise and interacting with the birds. Today was a major milestone as Lacsar (aka Demetrius Ravik) asked, "Father can I fly with you?"

"Sure, if you want to try it."

Demetrius had secretly worked his wings and gone airborne a few times in their suite while nobody was paying attention. His wings were getting stronger by the day as he was now in a growth spurt.

Stanley knew not to attempt major flying and would fly at a short height to prevent the boy from receiving injuries in case he fell.

They flew a short distance and in a small circle no more than 100 feet in diameter. Stanley was flying deliberately slow, and the birds were semi amused with Lacsar flying and swooped in formation with them. After a short while Stanley landed near Princess Lì and her daughter Alessandra. The birds were squawking as if this was a major event.

After explaining to Lacsar he did not want him to come on the next set of laps because he would be flying high and hard, Stanley took off with his squadron of birds and did their course completing

10 miles then landed by the family.

It was now time to feed the birds and Lacsar enjoyed that interaction and his private telepathic communiques to all the birds. Every day he bonded more and more with the birds. They truly became his extended family.

On one occasion Lacsar ran away from the chambermaids who took him outside to get fresh air and walk. To their horror, Lacsar took to the air. And he flew high, and the birds all chased after him. Lacsar might have flown completely out of the parklike compound, but the birds flew to Lacsar and talked common sense into him then escorted him back to the front entrance where the chambermaids were in a fit of paranoia and security men were scrambling to go locate the young prince.

Lacsar was soon privately alone with his father for a good talk about what happened and to explain why he could not do these kinds of acts because of security, and he had to be careful because the galaxy was still a dangerous place as peace was not guaranteed.

Stanley knew Lacsar had a free spirit and superior intelligence. Raising him would be a challenge.

Life at the mansion resumed in a normal fashion and when Lacsar didn't attempt to repeat his recent wild adventure into the sky, there grew a sense of relief among the staff. They all fret this boy would one day upset the apple cart.

Stanley did a lot of hands on Lacsar to nurture him and build his intellect. Every day was intellectual development including music, language, history, mathematics, chemistry, science, and astronomy.

Lacsar seemed to be a sponge soaking up all the information and appeared to be eager to spend time with his father. Stanley realized the mansion was too small for Lacsar. He needed to be out exploring the world.

The day came when Stanley made that fateful decision to take Lacsar to Ollytrene where there was wide open area and smart birds to help keep track of the young prince. As an added measure, Stanley would ask several members of Rascal's flock to come with him to assist in monitoring Lacsar. Rascal-II was readily available and interested in going along. Some of the other birds volunteered as they felt a kinship with the intelligent birds on Ollytrene.

To Princess Lì this seemed like a good event to allow Lacsar to bond more with his father and she decided it would be best if the two went alone, plus she would be busy taking care of Alessandra who was now reaching the age where she wanted to get into everything and required constant supervision.

Shortly after gathering up all the birds who wanted to go, they were at the front entrance of the mansion ready to leave. Stanley and Lacsar were dressed in clothes that would appear to be safari outfits like Hemingway wore and depicted in his fantastic Novel, "Truth at First Light."

The big difference is their wings were outside the safari jackets allowing them to fly if required.

As Princess Lì looked at Stanley and Lacsar (aka Demetrius Ravik) she felt proud. Princess Lì's private briefings by scholars observing Lacsar's academic development had articulated the level of success they observed in the non-traditional methods had accelerated his IQ phenomenally. They were unaware of the significant mental telepathy Stanley now possessed and utilized in the nurturing process.

Some experts believe environment is one of the biggest factors in IQ development. Stanley was proving this theory hands down. Another group believe the interactive approach is far more efficient than traditional education methods where a teacher is at the blackboard. Hence Stanley's interactive non-traditional approach had surpassed traditional Lìsztbrùnést educational standards for a child at Lacsar's age.

Lacsar had a million questions every day. He was a very inquisitive and smart kid and wanted to know everything. He wanted to know where his mother and father came from. When Stanley explained he came from planet Earth in a solar system a long distance away from Neflatraceous, Lacsar wanted to hear everything about planet Earth and with his robotic teachers drilled down deeply into Earth's history. The first major discovery that rocked Lacsar's world was Earth people did not have wings!

The huge mystery was, how did his father end up with wings and why did the birds all love him just like he was part of their family?

Lacsar knew the level of love the birds felt toward his father because his own incredible telepathic abilities. Lacsar matured years ahead of his peers. His IQ rocketed and his awareness and intellect became astonishing.

In a few times when Lacsar's grandfather the emperor wanted to spend time with his grandson at about this age, he was captivated by how much the little boy knew and how well he communicated. This was also at the point the emperor became aware that Lacsar had telepathic abilities. It was a tumultuous time now at the mansion because young Lacsar was learning too much too quickly and would not take "no" for an answer. Lacsar was a sponge for information and had the drive in him like nobody had ever seen in a person before. The one positive aspect that Emperor Cornelius detected in his mental probing was the extent Lacsar loved his sister and his parents. The family was hence very close, and it left the emperor with a sense of relief that Lacsar's attitude would diminish the typical Court intrigues that often erupted in a monarch over the lust for power.

Now as Princess Lì looked at the two most important men in her life, she was grateful her intuition led her to solidify her emotions and her future around Stanley. Seeing these two people go off together on a journey to explore the planet of Ollytrene together gave her a sense of happiness that despite what happened in the past with the very dangerous periods in their lives, the future seemed brighter and happier.

There wasn't much more to do. The birds were loaded and wanted to get to their destinations so they could get out of the transporters and fly around. Lacsar was quite animated and fully excited to go off with his dad to experience this strange planet that had intelligent birds. Their flock was also happy to see their friends again, but only for a visit. They would not want to be stuck with birds that didn't have significant telepathic abilities.

With Fast Frigate delivery because the emperor was hesitant to use the new Lìsztbrùnést Royal Space Yacht which he feared could put the two lives at risk, they traveled to Ollytrene in what seemed a short time.

Lacsar spent most of his time in the control room with the Frigate's captain asking multitudes of questions. Appearing years ahead of his age, Lacsar's intelligence really impressed the crew. And most of them had no idea Lacsar was exploiting them with telepathic trespassing into their minds. In doing so he found some answers, but he also discovered interesting questions that at times astonished the control room. By the time they arrived at Ollytrene, young Lacsar had seen every sensor display and asked poignant questions about their efficacy. He even questioned some of their weapons and capabilities. No kid had ever shown this mastery or understanding. The crew now knew this was a special kid and to take him seriously because his intellect was up there with adults.

Shortly after landing at a Ollytrene location prepared for their stay which had all the amenities a Royal Family would like the birds were all let out of the transporters. They soon started flying around and getting a take on their surroundings.

It was a tranquil evening and based on his memories of Ski Beach where there were several fire pits at night for people to roast hot dogs and marshmallows, Stanley arranged for a nice campfire they could all hang around and talk. This was a joyous moment for Lacsar, and all the birds were perched in the trees surrounding them keeping the ever vigilance.

The birds were much better than any guard dogs. With a sizeable security detachment and two Fast Frigates orbiting directly overhead the Royals were seemingly safe to go about their business and enjoy the wildlife.

It took around midnight before Lacsar showed signs of sleepfullness and as he slowly succumbed to that state laying in his fathers' arms, Stanley asked several of the servants to help him get Lacsar to his bed without awakening him. He would not be bathed and cleaned until in the morning and the bedding would be replaced.

Inside the very sturdy huts they went to sleep with the campfire kept burning all night long with a watch routine set up by the security staff working shiftwork.

Morning came and Lacsar was awakened and cleaned up like a Royal should be. Then they all sat at the outside breakfast table soon enjoying the delicacies the fabulous chef made for them.

"What's in store for us today papa?" Lacsar asked.

"We are going to walk in the direction I think we will find the Ollytrene intelligent birds so we can meet up with them again."

"What are they like?"

"They look just like our bird family, but they are very intelligent and do not have the ability to talk telepathically with our birds."

"What makes them so intelligent?"

"We really do not know but they are very smart birds. Almost as smart as humans."

Soon the Royals were sporting a new clean set of safari clothes and special boots and began their walk towards the area they thought they would find their friends. The Neflatraceous flock of birds, flew out ahead working as scouts.

It was around noon when several of the birds came back and said they found the intelligent Ollytrene birds who would be arriving soon.

In the matter of fifteen minutes a flock of intelligent Ollytrene birds arrived and just like birds have facial recognition and knew who Stanley was, he also knew who a few of them were as well.

Very few people knew Stanley had developed telepathic communications with the intelligent Ollytrene birds. Soon they were in full discussion and conveying they were happy Stanley, and the group were here for a short visit.

The smart birds were very happy to see the Neflatraceous flock.

The birds were invited to have lunch with them as Stanley had enough treats for all the birds.

After lunch in the discussion Stanley asked if there were any open fields nearby, they could go to and fly around for exercise?

The intelligent Ollytrene bird response indicated a short distance away was such a place, so Stanley suggested to Lacsar they go over there and get some exercise. Lacsar was more than happy to go, and he wanted to fly high today as his wings were getting stronger every day and wanted to feel his strength gliding up to the clouds.

It did not take long for the group to cover the ground to get to the open area and begin flying. Moments later Duke Ravik and Prince Demetrius Ravik were flying in a large circle in an open area. Stanley was impressed that Lacsar was keeping up with him at his normal workout and cruise speed. At around the eight-mile mark Stanley saw Lacsar was struggling so he said to everyone, "Let's land now."

The group all came down together and landed in the middle of the field. Lacsar seemed slightly relieved he could stop for a while as he was starting to feel stressed.

It wasn't that far for them to walk over to the edge of the clearing where a makeshift camp could easily be set up for them. After looking around a bit, Stanley decided and said, "I like this place us set up a camp for here tonight."

One of the support staff asked, "Why don't we go back to camp where we have good accommodations for the night?"

"We can go back there in the morning and freshen up and change our clothes but, I think sleeping around the campfire here tonight will be fun."

"What about your dinner?"

"Ask the chef to barbecue us something over the fire we build."

One of the intelligent Ollytrene birds then spoke up and telepathically said to Stanley, "There are some wild boars not far from here that would make an excellent barbecue for you."

Stanley asked one of the security men to give him a laser pistol and soon flew off with the intelligent Ollytrene birds for their dinner prey.

There were several of the wild boars which were sometimes a menace to the smart birds.

Stanley came down in the middle of all the wild boars and shot the largest wild boars closest to him with the laser blaster which took it out right away. The bright laser light caused the wild boar to start squealing from the laser pistol, but it was soon dead as the wild boar succumbed to the wound and in the process scared the rest of the wild boars deep into the forested area.

Stanley had a communicator with built in navigation and contacted the staff at the camp and directed, "Send an all-terrain vehicle (ATV) to this location to pick up our meal for the night."

In fifteen minutes, the ATV arrived with a couple big guys who could easily lift the wild bore into the back of the vehicle. It then returned to camp with Stanley and the intelligent birds flying back.

Back at the camp the chef had no idea what to do. Stanley had seen some of the equipment they had with them including metallic poles for tents and other requirements and explained to the chef he would show him how to set up a SPIT and barbecue the wild boar over the campfire.

In a brief period, the group built a very capable spit with an improvised handle for turning the spit during the cooking after they gutted the wild boar a distance away from the prospective campfire and buried the residue as to not attract other animals.

Young Lacsar was animated watching all this unfold. It forever molded him and probably made him a much tougher person in the long run.

There were far more security men present than what was required so they had ample volunteers to keep the spit slowly turning as the wild animal cooked over the nice campfire.

The Lìsztbrùnést Chef's had some nice sauces and pastes which Stanley had slowly grown accustomed to and knew what was on site and explained to the chef as they roasted this wild boar, they would move it off the fire a short distance away where they could baste the carcass and help develop the taste and the aroma that would please everyone. Stanley's recommendations proved to be quite excellent and then it was finally determined the meat had been cooked satisfactory long enough to prevent illness and develop the taste, it was taken over to a table set up to carve out servings.

It was a large wild bore and had enough meat on it to provide ample servings to everyone present. It was a joyous occasion for the group to eat sitting around the campfire. The birds were also giving servings and they enjoyed it immensely. The Lìsztbrùnést birds transported to Ollytrene were thoroughly enjoying the adventure and the intelligent Ollytrene bird friends.

Again, Lacsar fell asleep in his fathers' arms enjoying every minute of this adventure. His only aggravation was in the morning getting cleaned up and a fresh set of safari clothes put on.

Today was going to be different. After conversing with the Ollytrene intelligent birds, Stanley was advised there was a place nearby they could look at rock formations and a waterfall and a nice pond.

The group walked along with the intelligent Ollytrene birds guiding them. When they arrived at the sheer cliffs with the incredible rock formations Prince Lacsar was thunderstruck. Lacsar had never seen anything like this sheer cliff with sparkling gems exposed before. Imbedded in the rocks were many types of gems. To the Ollytrene who were primitive people and to many of the Lìsztbrùnésts, the rocks and the gems had no intrinsic value to them. But to Stanley he knew back on Earth people would be quite animated seeing all this.

As part of his outfit, Stanley had a hunting knife. It would provide very basic self defense but against someone packing a laser blaster, it wouldn't do much in the form of self-defense.

Stanley pulled out his hunting knife which at first alarmed the security staff because of the close a proximity to Lacsar, but they quickly stood down as Stanley walked to the cliff and started digging out some gems and handed them to Lacsar who was intrigued.

"Can I try getting a few?" Lacsar asked.

"Sure." Stanley handed Lacsar the hunting knife and the boy started digging.

Lacsar was incredibly happy and the gems he pulled out were

in fact quite beautiful.

Stanley had polished stones when he was a young man and knew these gems would look fabulous after they polished them up. The waterfall a few feet away had a small brook that was one to two feet deep and easy access.

Stanley looked at on of the support staff and asked, "Do we have any empty containers we can use to clean these gems in the water?"

"If we do not, we can certainly empty one for that purpose."

"Good can you get me a small metal container that would hold a dozen of these gems while we clean them?"

"I'll be right back your Excellency and see what I can come up with."

"Thanks."

A few minutes later the aide came back with an empty metal container that was perfect for the job.

Stanley then instructed Lacsar, "Pick out a dozen of the gems you want, and we'll clean them up. Put them in here, I'll hold it for you."

Lacsar dug away and in a few minutes picked a dozen different varieties of gemstones and placed them in the metal container.

Stanley said, "Come over here take off your boots and do what I do."

Stanley took off his boots and socks and put them in his boots then rolled up his pantlegs. Lacsar quickly followed his actions getting more excited by the moment.

Stanley helped Lacsar roll up his pantlegs a little better to keep them dry then he led him into the water with the bucket full of Lacsar's gems.

The Gems were covered with a lot of dirt like debris, but the spring water hand no problem cleaning them up a good extent.

"When we get back to the camp, we can use a little soap to clean them up a little more."

"Alright."

After fifteen minutes of cleaning and changing the water a few times the gems appeared and looked far better than what Stanley or the assistants imagined would be the case.

Lacsar was totally fascinated observing all the gems that were now far more illustrious and vibrant. This was an incredible moment for Lacsar enjoying his time with his dad and inspired every minute of it. And now he has some things to take home and show his mother and sister.

Thinking ahead, Stanley said, "You need to plan to give some to your mother and your sister and your grandfather. Do you have enough, or do you want to get some more?"

"Papa, I don't think I have enough to give gifts. We better get a few more so I can give each of them nice ones."

Alright, I think you can just walk over there without your boots and dig a few more and we'll clean them up."

In another fifteen minutes the container was full of gems of all types of colors and the two were cleaning them up especially good.

When Lacsar felt they were cleaned well enough he said, "Papa, I think they are clean enough for now. We can clean them up better when we get home."

"Alright us get our shoes back on."

They walked back to camp and Lacsar insisted on carrying the metal container. When hey arrived at the camp he walked over to a table sat up for Lacsar's use and sat down and started taking the gems out of the container and looked them over good.

Stanley asked one of the cooks if they had some dish soap to clean the gems up better. The cook came up with a great idea. "We can put the gems in a strainer and put it in the dishwasher, should make it sparkle."

"That sounds great, us try cleaning them in the dish washer."

The metal strainer was loaded with all the gems were in the portable dish washer and after a compete wash and dry cycle, they came out sparkling like the cook imagined.

Lacsar was now animated and took all his gems back to the table and started studying them. He put all the gems into the container except a brilliant red one and put it in his pocket. Stanley closely observing asked, "Lacsar why did you put that gem in your pocket and the rest back in the container?"

"Papa I will share those with my mother and sister and give one to my grandfather, but I like this one and want to keep it. It makes me feel special."

"Alright son if that's what you want to do. I'll have the rest of these stored and ready to leave with us when we return home."

"Thank you, father."

The group was happy, the Lìsztbrùnést flock of birds were all enjoying the company of the intelligent Ollytrene birds. Rascal-II was never far from Lacsar whom he had a great affection for. Nobody talked with Rascal-II the way Lacsar did. This increased their bond considerably. One thing Rascal-II knew was the boy loved him as much as he did any human. The intelligent birds observed this behavior, and it affected their mindsets and cultivated further mental development, accelerating their evolution.

Tonight, the explorers enjoyed conventional food brought along, but they did have the bonfire and the night slowly wound down and everyone except those security men on watch were sleeping. The watch rotation people checked in with the orbiting Fast Frigates every fifteen minutes in the event extra help was suddenly needed or they needed to do an emergency extraction.

The Intelligent Birds all went home to their nests, and the Lìsztbrùnést Flock went to their temporary nests which happened to be the transporter devices.

The night passed without anything out of the ordinary or of concern.

~~~~~
~~~~~

Chapter Twelve

Chief Yuèliàng's Ollytrene Tribe

When the flock of Ollytrene Intelligent Birds arrived in the morning, they informed Stanley, "There are other humans like you near here."

"Do they appear to be dangerous?"

"No, they are wondering hunter gatherers."

"Are they looking for food?"

"They are attempting to catch animals in the water."

"Can you take me to them."

"Yes, they are not far away."

"Let me tell my people we are going and then we'll fly there."

After making all the reports, Stanley took off with all the birds flying in formation and a drone not far behind showing video to the tactical commander on site that looked over the security situation.

Just two miles away in a riverbed were a dozen people including a few children. They looked totally harmless, and Stanley could see they were fishing from the bank of the river.

The people looked up and saw Stanley and the flock of birds.

They had seen him two days before flying with Lacsar and were mystified and here he was back again.

Stanley landed about 100 feet away from the indigenous people.

All the birds landed with him. Stanley gave a friendly wave at them. They starred and Stanley slowly walked towards them with his wings folded back and now looked just like a very well-dressed handsome human wearing luxurious clothes like the indigenous Ollytrene people had never seen before. But more importantly, they had never seen a bird man before and they were extremely stunned.

There were no hostile feelings, just awe. Everyone stared at Stanley with the most inquisitive look. Stanley could not communicate to them in their native toungues, but he could do so via mental telepathy.

Chief Yuèliàng was there with his family out on a vacation like excursion away from the tribe for peace and quiet to get away from the stress of everyday life and tribal politics. This arrival of a magical birdman was completely unexpected. Even a couple days before they didn't know if they should leave and go back to the tribe since some of the family was terrified after seeing a birdman flying.

As Stanley approached them and used his mental telepathy, they slowly disarmed their emotions and let the circumstance flow. Stanley was kind and courteous, smiled and quickly they felt astounded being near him. Chief Yuèliàng's family felt astonished to see the local intelligent Ollytrene birds assembled with the birdman. Those intelligent Ollytrene birds also made the bird man special because no humans ever got near the Ollytrene smart birds.

There were kids about Lacsar's age in the group. After a few minutes Stanley was able to figure out how to fully communicate with them which startled the indigenous people even more. Stanley thought meeting these indigenous people would be a special event for his son Lacsar, so he asked Chief Yuèliàng permission to bring his son to meet his family.

The Chief Yuèliàng was flabbergasted the bird man would ask him for permission and naturally responded favorably because he would like to meet his son.

"Yes, bring him. We all would like to meet your son."

Stanley then informed the Chief, "My name is Stanley and my son's name is Lacsar."

The Chief responded and said, "I'm Chief Yuèliàng, and this is my mate Tonnerre and our daughter Starlight who is standing next to her."

"I'll be back soon with my son."

"We are looking forward to meeting Lacsar, "Chief Yuèliàng responded."

Stanley knew Lacsar could easily fly seven miles so two miles would not be an issue. He took off and the flocks of birds followed him back to their camp.

Soon Stanley returned with Lacsar and several drones along with all the birds.

The two landed near Chief Yuèliàng who was already liking these birdmen who somehow made him feel good and he didn't know why. Part of those happy feelings perpetuating in the pleasure center of his brain were influenced by the telepathic communication that processed next to it in that side of his brain where the pleasure center exists.

"You will have to converse with them in mental telepathy because we do not know their language," Stanley informed Lacsar.

"Alright father."

Young Lacsar had been trained in Emperor's Court in proper

politeness and greetings. When Stanley introduced Lacsar to the Chief Yuèliàng, the Chief of the Ollytrene Tribe, Lacsar did the very respectful Royal Court type bow, and said telepathically, "It is an honor to meet you Chief Yuèliàng."

Chief Yuèliàng felt positive about the young man had such class at such a young age.

Chief Yuèliàng lined up his family and introduced everyone including his daughter Starlight about Lacsar's age, certainly nowhere near as sophisticated but Starlight seemed in awe of these bird people.

Starlight was exceptionally beautiful. Everyone in the tribe knew eventually every young man she met would want this girl. Starlight's beauty was incredible even though she was young and almost starting puberty.

Lacsar was obviously touched by Starlight and felt something special about her and immediately used his mental telepathy to give her a strong sensation. Lacsar then reached in his pocket and pulled out that brilliant red gem he loved so much recently polished to a great luster by one of the Fast Frigate crew members and through mental telepathy informed her, "I think I love you. I want to give this to you."

The young girl looked at Lacsar and smiled and looked down at the red gem he now placed in her hand and then Starlight held out her other hand for Lacsar.

This was unprecedented in Tribal History. The young girl had already been trained that is the signal you give the man you give your heart to. Her mother suddenly had tears flowing down that the young boy with wings had moved her daughter so much.

Stanley was taking this all in and reached a major level of astonishment. The boy was clearly in love.

Love at first site.

The beautiful girl, Starlight, according to Tribal Rituals had just given her heart to young Lacsar and the mental telepathy flowed between them for a short eternity. They held hands and smiled at each other in an undeniable fashion that observers knew was real and animating to them.

The indigenous Ollytrene tribe named Yuèliàng after their Chief Yuèliàng along with Stanley didn't know what to do. It was if the two young people were seemingly in a trance. The adults collectively didn't want to interrupt this mental transcendence that engulfed their children's ever thoughts.

Lacsar informed Starlight via mental telepathy. "I'm Prince Lacsar from the Lìsztbrùnést Empire and I want to come back to visit you in the future. I want us to grow up together and stay together for the rest of our lives."

Rascal-II then hopped on Lacsar's shoulder and started crowing at that very moment. The other birds then chimed in and there was a chorus. Chief Yuèliàng knew this was somehow divine intervention. He felt so wonderful at that time because the intelligent birds had never given them the time of day and here, they were with the bird chorus singing to his daughter.

Stanley knew this moment needed to be truncated because his main purpose of bringing Lacsar here was to introduce him to what the Tribe was doing, fishing. So, he interjected and said, "Lacsar, I would like you to watch Chief Yuèliàng and his family catch the animals in the river."

Lacsar explained to Starlight, "My father wants me to learn how you catch the animals in the water."

Starlight Yuèliàng as her full title given, responded, "Let me show you how," then she turned to her father and said, "I would like to teach Lacsar how to catch the fish."

"How do you know his name."

"He told me."

"How did he tell you that, I didn't hear him say anything."

"Lacsar told me in my mind. We can talk to each other with our thoughts."

Now the Chief was really in a state of shock. This was an incredible experience to the point he didn't know how to respond other than say, "Alright I'm sure you can show him how to catch fish."

Holding hands Starlight said to Lacsar, "Come with me so I can show you."

Starlight then took Lacsar over to where she had a fishing pole and was soon in the process of putting bait on a hook, then throwing the line in the water. She then schooled him after the hook, weight and a wooden bobber landed in the water and hoped they would get lucky.

Within fifteen minutes Starlight who knew what she was doing pulled a two-pound fish out of the water. It was the first catch of the day, and everyone appeared suddenly happy that the young couple caught the very first fish that morning.

Lacsar was utterly astounded and viewing the animal from the water intrigued him greatly. In his near future he would delve into studying aquatics based on this experience.

Family members took Starlight's fish and hung it on a line they had strung across an area for all the fish the caught that day which they would cook and enjoy later that evening during this camping trip.

All day long the two Royals stayed with the indigenous Ollytrene Yuèliàng tribe but soon Stanley informed Chief Yuèliàng, "I need to feed these birds and give them some water."

"We don't really have much here to give the birds."

"That's not a problem, I will have my staff bring them food and water."

Chief Yuèliàng nodded and was curious to see how all that was going to unfold. Since they were two miles away and it would be easier flying over the terrain than walking and carrying heavy amounts, the staff loaded up snacks, water, drinks, and elixirs in a shuttle for everyone including the indigenous tribe and the birds and flew it over to provide the group.

Now Chief Yuèliàng was mesmerized as this activity unfolded. Soon the staff was setting up tables and a full meal for everyone. The Chefs knew precisely how many indigenous people were there thanks to the drones and planned accordingly.

When tables and folding chairs were all set up with servings placemats and tableware, the staff notified Stanley who then said, "Chief Yuèliàng will you please give me the honor of having a meal with me."

"I would be most honored," Chief Yuèliàng said and gave Stanley a warm smile.

Chief Yuèliàng then said to all his family, "We are going to have a meal with our new friends. We will get back to fishing later."

The crowd slowly crept to this table in awe.

Even though they were hunter gatherers, they had tables and chairs and sat down and had their meals in dignity back in their villages.

The group then coalesced around the two young people soon sitting in the middle of the table and who had broadcasted an increíble affection for each other.

Starlight was very intelligent and had been groomed by her mother so that one day she would be the next queen of the tribe when she met the proper suitor. Hence, Starlight was far ahead of girls her age in etiquette as well as social skills. She was also her father's favorite and knew how to tweak him to get what she wanted.

The two youngsters sitting next to each other acted as they were their very best friends in the world. Starlight who was completely aware of how these Aliens ate their meals, but she watched Lacsar very closely and copied his actions with great precision.

After they finished their meal, Starlight pulled out the red gem and looked at Lacsar and said, "Nobody has ever given me such a wonderful gift in my lifetime. I will always cherish this."

"If you allow me, I will come back and see you and bring you more gifts and one day you will go with me to my world where we can live together for the rest of our lives."

"Do you really feel that way."

"Yes. I feel you in my heart."

"I feel you in my heart too."

Stanley violated his own rule not to eavesdrop on Lacsar's thoughts, but this was so strange he could not help it and soon discovered the breath of the transcendence of these two young people into an emotional bond virtually years ahead of their time.

Stanley thought Princess Lì would be extremely agitated when she learned what transpired. But Stanley knew his boy would grow up and one day be his own man and make his own decisions. Stanley also recognized how beautiful Starlight appeared and could easily understand the attraction especially for a boy with an unusual high IQ like Lacsar.

The drones and the probes recorded everything and soon the emperor and Princess Lì were seeing everything. The emperor didn't mind because his own Empress came from a far-off world. The main issue with this girl was she had no wings. The emperor knew the truth that Princess Lì had wings surgically added Stanley's body and modified him to become a *man of birds* so she shouldn't have any philosophical issues with Lacsar doing an identical activity with this beautiful young girl if he chose her to be his Empress. But what if the girl refused to have wings surgically added to her body? That would create a monarchy chrisis.

This was all somewhat speculative because the children were still young and had a long way to go to become adults. Unfortunately for that philosophy, the young prince already had an adult level IQ. No doubt he would also facilitate an education for his bride to be in a few years.

Lacsar was very happy he went on this trip with his *papa*. This was a pivotal moment in his life, and he realized how much his father had impacted him. No other children except maybe his sister would ever experience what his father facilitated for him.

And now Lacsar had a new development as the young Starlight captivated his psyche in ways, he knew was quite pleasing. But the feelings were mutual. In their secret and private mental telepathy Lacsar and Starlight promised each other they would wait for the other for the rest of their lives no matter how long it took. Starlight now knew the power of love, but she also knew something her tribe people did not know. Lacsar had phenomenal telepathic ability and probably knew every thought each of them had. There would be no secrets around Lacsar. But if she was giving her soul to him, why should that matter?

The two groups comingled for a couple more days, then it was time for Chief Yuèliàng to take his family back to the tribe.

After discussions with Stanley, the decision was made to fly everyone including Tribe members to near the Tribe's village. They would then get out of the shuttles and walk into the village so that Chief Yuèliàng could introduce the bird people to his village and inform them, *they were his personal friends and to expect visits from them in the future.*

The Yuèliàng Tribes' people were utterly overwhelmed to see people with wings. More so when they said their final goodbyes, Stanley and Lacsar flew a mile or so out to the shuttles then back to base camp where the remnants of their camping expedition was packed up and they left on shuttles back up to the Fast Frigates to take them home to Neflatraceous.

Chief Yuèliàng knew Starlight's bright red gemstone must have a magical aspect to it, so he said to her, "I want to make a necklace for your gemstone."

"That would please me father."

Together Chief Yuèliàng knew Starlight took some of his gold tailings and hammered and melted and shaped the gold into a very fine necklace with a superior mount to make sure the red gem would never accidentally be lost.

Soon the villagers called Chief Yuèliàng's daughter *Red Starlight* which she did not mind because it was a symbol of her love for Lacsar whom she would wait forever to come back to her.

When Stanley's camping party arrived back at the emperor's mansion, Emperor Cornelius had a special dinner for everyone who had participated to thank them for all they had done. Every one of the staff members that went on the expedition to Ollytrene was invited and enjoyed the company of Emperor Cornelius and he was certainly always respectful and kind to them.

Lacsar had a few interesting moments when Stanley (aka Duke Ravik) explained while the orchestra was playing light music, "Lacsar has a few gifts for special people in his life."

The cooks had worked hard on the gems and a few of the Fast Frigate crew members who were also machinists, had some micron level abrasives to polish the gems down to a glistening appearance. Because Lacsar was so extremely pleased with what the machinists had done with the gemstones, he requested his father invite two machinists that helped the most to the dinner party to personally thank them.

Lacsar requested a table set up to display his gems and before they began their dinner and asked his sister to come up to the table. Alessandra was walking and talking by now and fully coherent and seemed rather bright.

"Alessandra, I want you to pick which Gem you want."

"The young princess picked a very bright blue Gem that if it been cut by artisans; it would no doubt create a luster people would enjoy greatly. Even as an uncut Gem it had very pleasing attributes since it was shined by the micron grit abrasives. Alessandra would fondle this Gem for weeks before she would slowly grow tired of it and switch her attention to other matters.

Next, Lacsar gave two beautiful Gems he selected for his mother and father. Then he had the biggest and most spectacular he pulled out of his pocket and handed it to his grandfather who in turn hugged the boy with great affection. The emperor could feel the love of the boy and could never ask anything more from the heir of his throne.

There were now a few more gems left other than a couple Lacsar kept for himself. Lacsar requested the two machinists to come to the table and then he gave them gemstone gifts as he planned to publicly thank them for their efforts. When the two machinists stepped forward and approached the table, he handed each of them a Gem he selected as gifts for them.

About this time the emperor inserted himself into the conversation and said, "I want those Gem's mounted in a display case for you gentlemen. My grandson will sign the certificate and gemstone we'll mount in the display case in honor of what you have done for him."

He then turned to and nodded at Lucas who then promptly

took the Gems and then said to the two men and said, "We will have you come back tomorrow to receive these Gems mounted in display cases. You may bring a friend or relative with you to observe you receiving the Gems from Prince Demetrius Ravik."

The two machinists were thrilled at the invitation and to come back again tomorrow and bring someone special with them. One said, "Thank you."

Princess Lì Alìgrāwná along with Emperor Cornelius had observed the entire video recording of young Demetrius Ravik (aka Lacsar) on his camping trip with Stanley. Thanks to drones, probes, and a variety of other means, they saw firsthand how Stanley had enriched the boy's life. And now he had experienced his first love, even though Emperor Cornelius considered it was simply a crush among kids.

Princes Lì knew otherwise. Her son Lacsar was intelligent and utterly brilliant. She also knew Lacsar's mental telepathy was getting stronger every day just like his wings. Princes Lì assumed Lacsar had used his mental telepathy on Starlight and the relationship between them was now at the complication stage.

It was quite evident to Princess Lì that she knew all she had to do was look into the mirror to see someone who would go to extremes for love. Thus, Princes Lì realized vividly that her son Lacsar with his growing powerful telepathy would be exactly like her. She also understood the consequences. Princess Lì realized what she would have to do in a few more years. Bring the girl to the mansion and start preparing her for the court. But she suspected one thing by then Alessandra would want a good friend because its lonely in the mansion for Royals and she would most likely be instrumental in helping Starlight develop.

Before Princess Lì would go to that stage, she would personally go to the village and meet with Chief Yuèliàng and explain to him, at some point Starlight would have to come back with her to be prepared to become an empress. And then she would have to explain to Chief Yuèliàng, that part of changing her into the Empress would require them to surgically add wings to her body allowing her to fly.

Chief Yuèliàng would have to make some tough decisions about the daughter he loved very much. And when the day came, he knew the love the daughter had was so great that to deny her would crush her heart and probably kill her. The decision would be made for him, simply his daughter would decide, and he would support her intentions.

The tribe had no financial or political gain in any of this. That added to the luster and the beauty of it because it meant the future Empress was untainted. She was pure, just like the spring water that came down at the waterfall they visited. No Emperor could ever receive the beauty and purity of such a fine young lady.

In over a years' time Princess Lì noticed Lacsar was getting slowly unhappy and almost despondent at times. When they were alone together Princess Lì who was starting to worry about the changes in Lacsar's psyche decided to do some telepathic probing of her son and quickly understood the problem centered around Starlight. She then knew it was time to proceed to deal with the situation and had a secret meeting with her father where such important decisions had to be vetted.

This meeting hence was the decision on the direction the monarchy would take and the strategic planning to ensure success. It would be a team effort and the outcome had to be made successfully because Princess Lì knew Lacsar was slowly growing despondent and emotionally melancholy.

One of the problems facing them as the realization that Lacsar had growing telepathic strengths, it would soon be impossible to hide anything from him.

When Stanley was brought into the discussions probably much later than they should have, he schooled them very quickly and said, "Lacsar is a very intelligent young man. His IQ is up there with anyone in the room. I think the best way forward is to be just honest with him and bring him into the discussion. Tell him what we recommend and get his buy in. Don't underestimate him just because he's still physically young. I'm sure he will respond appropriately if given the facts and the recommendations."

Hence the agonizing would soon be over as the emperor and Princess Lì realized they only had one way forward unless they didn't want to risk disenfranchising Lacsar and creating lingering negative feelings that might be eventually impossible to patch up when he reached manhood.

After a long period of time when Lacsar grew increasingly restless and more and more unhappy as the days passed, the emperor and Lacsar's parents decided they would first send Princess Lì to the tribe to talk with Chief Yuèliàng and then on a subsequent trip, Stanley and Princess Lì would escort Lacsar to Ollytrene and begin formal negotiations with Chief Yuèliàng. If Chief Yuèliàng would entertain the trip, the Royals would bring Chief Yuèliàng, his wife Tonnerre, and Starlight back to Neflatraceous to welcome them into the Royal Family and help them understand how serious they were about this business and a future Unification between Lacsar and Starlight.

When presented with this plan Lacsar suddenly appeared uplifted and his smile returned. The decision gave him hope and happiness for the future. He would do anything to be with Starlight again.

The Ollytrene Tribe was not the only Tribe on the planet. There were several hundred, but they were far removed from the others, which added to their security, but also created that chance encounter between Lacsar and Starlight that would change the destiny of the empire.

Stanley and Princess Lì had private discussions far away from Lacsar and the emperor. One of the points Stanley made was,

"Your safety and your acceptance will be enhanced if you take our bird flock with you." They then got into the methodologies of how to approach them which could create a deadly scenario as these tribe members had deadly weapons such as bow and arrows and spears. The Ollytrene Tribesmen also had martial arts skills and were formidable.

Eventually the day came, and Princess Lì went to Ollytrene with Rascal-II and the flock who would be dedicated to her to do her son's bidding.

In a couple days the Fast Frigates reached Ollytrene, and the Princess and her entourage landed on the planet in shuttles a few miles away from the Tribe early in the morning before anyone was stirring.

Princess Lì had so much body armor, she weighed too much to fly. One of the things Lacsar did was give Starlight images of his mother through mental telepathy. As soon as Starlight saw Princess Lì, she would know exactly who she was.

With drones and probes watching the village, Princess Lì and the support staff patiently waited until the tribe started doing their morning activities. The girls in the village had their chores and went to it including Starlight. As soon as advised by the INTEL people assigned, the flock escorted by the intelligent Ollytrene birds flew into the Tribe and landed and stood in perfect formation.

The tribe was alerted that something was occurring and soon they all appeared looking at the birds and those on the fishing expedition knew exactly who they were. Moments later Princess Lì came out of the clearing into Chief Yuèliàng's Ollytrene Tribal Village and walked down the middle of the birds with her wings fully furled in great majestic fashion.

Starlight immediately said to her father, Chief Yuèliàng, "I think that person is Lacsar's mother."

Chief Yuèliàng holding Starlight's hand approached Princess

Lì Alìgrāwná very slowly and deliberate. At the end of the line of birds, Princess Lì stopped and looked at Chief Yuèliàng and Starlight and saw that beautiful red Gem mounted in a gold ornamentation around her neck and knew instantly her image and who she was. She indeed was incredibly beautiful, and it was no mystery why her son fell in love with her at first sight. The Yuèliàng Tribes watched Chief Yuèliàng approach Princess Lì who brought her wings back to her rear and when the Chief was a few feet away, the princess bowed very respectively.

Before the Chief could say anything, Starlight said, "Father, let me introduce you to Lacsar's mother."

As Princess Lì raised back up, the Chief said, "It's an honor to meet Lacsar's mother."

Princess Lì had mastered the tribe's language and had her extensive mental telepathy responded, "I'm Princess Lì Alìgrāwná and as your daughter indicated, I'm Lacsar's mother."

"It's a pleasure to meet you. Princess Lì Alìgrāwná."

"Thank you. I'm very happy I could come here and meet Starlight and her family. I would like to have a few moments and talk with you on behalf of my son, Lacsar."

"What is it about your son you wish to talk?" Chief Yuèliàng asked.

"In case you do not know it my son is in love with your daughter Starlight."

"He seems a little young to have such emotions."

"My son is very intelligent. His mental abilities match most adults. If he fell in love with your daughter that means he had very astute judgment and looking at her there is no doubt in my mind, why he fell in love with her."

The daughter now had tears going down her eyes because she

knew if the mother of Lacsar came here all the way to meet them and discuss this, it really meant his love for her must be a really strong.

Her father looked down at Starlight for some reason he didn't know why and asked, "Why are you crying Starlight?"

"I'm crying because I know Lacsar loves me. I feel great love and emotions for Lacsar too."

The chief looked at Princess Lì and saw her tears as well and the way the birds lined up gave him an extraordinary feeling.

He didn't know what to do, his world was terribly confused so the best he could think at the time was to say, "Please come into my home and we can talk there."

"Thank you." Princess Lì said and as they were walking towards the Chief's home, she held her hand out to Starlight and they joined hands. Starlight still had tears, but it was the happiest day of her life and Lacsar's mother made her feel so special.

Princess Lì knew these were primative people, but she didn't care. Afterall, she selected a man from the backwards planet Earth, and he has since filled her with joy like she never imagined possible. She saw herself in Starlight for similar reasons. Starlight's mother, Tonnerre was a very attractive woman and had distinguished traits that would easily motivate mature men. Tonnerre was no fool, but at the same time had experienced and observed Lacsar while her daughter and him were together enjoying their fishing vacation.

Tonnerre was taken back by Lacsar's gentleness and kindness. He seemed far more mature than his age. Tonnerre had seen Lacsar fly with his father, and it all seemed rather remarkable to her. She was still coming to grips with all those revelations including the fact these people came from other planets and the stars.

Starlight's mother, Tonnerre felt very comfortable with this winged woman. Tonnerre didn't know Princess Lì was using her mental telepathy as she could not fail. This was a crucial moment for Princess Lì's son, and she would do anything possible to ensure success, even if it might seem unethical to people in higher places.

The conversation was simple, almost subdued but it was pleasant as the Chief Yuèliàng took a liking to this woman who had introduced herself as Princess Lì Alìgrāwná. But during their conversation asked Chief Yuèliàng to just refer to her as Lì.

Now Chief Yuèliàng could see with his own eyes what ingredient was part of the development of such a nice boy Lacsar who he liked.

Meanwhile Lacsar was home with his father in great anticipation of the results of his mother's journey knowing precisely what it was about because they were not going to hide it from him, nor did they think they could.

Thanks to probes and drones, Stanley and Lacsar could see a lot of video and sound of Princess Lì's arrival. They were both pleased it seemed to be working out so well.

Princess Lì spent several hours discussing with Chief Yuèliàng and his wife Tonnerre what the Royal Family viewed as Starlight's future. And now it was apparent that Princess Lì would soon be a part of Starlight's family. There were no objections by Chief Yuèliàng or his wife Tonnerre who knew this would make Starlight's life significantly better. They also knew Lacsar had chosen her for reasons they couldn't imagine. They didn't know exactly why but they knew Lacsar had Starlight in his heart and there would never be any turning back. His mother's unexpected visit brought in extraordinary disclosure and information they never pondered before.

Finally, after a couple hours of discussion on the way forward, Princess Lì who was a fantastic analyst said, "I want to go back to Neflatraceous and in a week or so come back with Duke Ravik and Lacsar. Chief Yuèliàng. we would like to have a meeting then to take you, Tonnerre, and Starlight back with us for a few days. If you agree, we want Starlight to stay with us, and we will educate her in our ways and prepare her for the Royal Marriage when she feels she is ready."

Starlight and her mother were in solid tears now. Chief Yuèliàng was the most somber he had been in his lifetime and responded. "We are willing to go with you. I'm glad you will give us a week because I must explain this to the Tribe so they will know why we are doing this and it's in Starlight's best interest."

Princess Lì knew Starlight's movement to Neflatraceous to become part of the Royal Family was not a done deal, but it looked promising. Princess Lì also understood unequivocally they needed to give Chief Yuèliàng and Tonnerre time to deal with the change in circumstances in their own way and when they came back, to transport Chief Yuèliàng's family to Neflatraceous, the Tribe would be prepared for a short absence of Chief Yuèliàng and his family.

As the discussion reached a point when the future seemed laid out for everyone in agreement, Princess Lì stood up to leave. Starlight approached Princess Lì still with tears in her eyes and threw her arms around Princess Lì, and they hugged for several minutes in a solemn manner.

There was no dry eye in the room. Next Starlight's mother Tonnerre approached Princess Lì and they both hugged and cried as if they were long lost friends. The emotions were strong. Starlight's mother felt very lucky that her beautiful daughter had met a prince far greater than any tribesmen she could possibly ever meet. And at this precise moment, light coming through a window struck Starlight's necklace red Gem at the perfect angle to make Starlight look magical for this great moment to add a moment of magic to the event.

Princess Li shortly walked out of Chief Yuèliàng's home with his family. The birds had remained exactly where they arrived with the village looking on in astonishment.

About this time several of Princess Li's escorts came to the end of the birds, far away from tribe members. Princess Li took off her body armor and handed it to one of the escorts and she turned around and looked at Chief Yuèliàng, Tonnerre and Starlight and said, "I'm looking forward to seeing you again in a week."

"So shall we," Tonnerre responded.

Princess Li spread her wings, then she and all the birds then flew off together in a perfect formation. The escorts turned and walked a short distance and hopped into the shuttle and flew in the direction they knew Princess Lì would soon land with all the birds. After Rascal-II and the flock said goodbye to the intelligent Ollytrene birds, the shuttle crew assisted the flock get into the shipping containers for the journey home.

All the birds were quite happy to see each other again and be part of this wonderful event where the future of the beautiful Ollytrene Starlight was cast in a role that few would ever believe possible.

~~~~~
~~~~~

Chapter Thirteen
The Families Meet

Princess Lì traveled back to the mansion and met with her joyous husband Stanley and son Lacsar who had observed much video and were very happy about the outcome.

Emperor Cornelius was also happy because the young girl had a few years of development left where she could be shaped into a Royal and by the time of the Royal Unification, she would be well prepared to take on her duties and responsibilities as a Royal and a part of the progeny of the future of the monarchy.

There would soon be drastic changes in the mansion as the future empress would have her own suite and several chambermaids as well as a person exactly like Drákōlìné who would watch every move she made and protect her with a promise on her life if something negative happened to the girl.

All the plans were now in earnest including royal clothes for the future empress family. They would not appear like tribal members for long as they would be spoiled and cared for with the ultimate care.

The future Empress parents would have a guest suite normally reserved for the top diplomats of the galaxy.

Quite frankly the emperor didn't care how they appeared or showed up or how they dressed. Because the future Empress would be welcomed as is and the guest list would be very short while they were here.

One week to the day as they had promised to the tribe, Stanley, Princess Lì Alìgrāwná, Lacsar, and Alessandra arrived at the edge of the Village in a group of shuttles with plenty of security. Not that they feared the Villagers, they just could not afford to have the entire Royal Family wiped out by some unknown tragedy. None of the Royals flew in the same Shuttle.

After the shuttles disgorged their passengers, they departed and flew a mile away and parked in a designated area. Probes and Drones flew overhead doing significant surveillance in the event the vast number of security forces need to be called in for a situation.

The Tribe members were all dressed in ceremonial clothes that would seem fashionable in some parts of the Empire. They had master seamstresses and knew how to produce beautiful clothing.

Princess Lì Alìgrāwná was thunderstruck at all the beauty of the Tribe. It touched her heart deeply how beautiful they could make themselves appear very attractive even though they lived in meager and seemingly backwards ways.

The Chief and his family were center and forefront and invited the Royal family into their home. As before Princess Lì and Starlight held hands, but at the same time Alessandra who took an instant liking to Starbright held Starlight's other hand. That did not go unnoticed by Starlight's mother Tonnerre who now had watery eyes. Such a magical journey was in store for them.

Chief Yuèliàng said to Stanley (aka Duke Ravik), "We will have a ceremonial tea before departure." This event was their symbol for two families combining.

Lacsar sat between his father and Chief Yuèliàng in great appreciation what his family was doing for him. Sitting across the ceremonial table from him was the love of his life and he looked deeply into her eyes, and they connected telepathically. The love as flowing between them, and Stanley and Princess Lì detected it and knew how precious it was. *Love at first sight*, strong and genuine.

When the two first saw each other, Starlight was modestly dressed not showing any hint of sophistication. It was love of personality and something they could not figure out. And here she was right at their departure, dressed elegantly like the Chief's daughter would be in a grand celebration.

Lacsar had no idea Starbright could look so beautiful, he was now awestruck, and the mental telepathy flowed through each other. The two young individuals now experienced fantastic love and emotions that close proximity allowed them to now experience.

Chief Yuèliàng was so pleased with the politeness of Lacsar and didn't quite understand why he liked the young man so well. Lacsar was mental telepathically affecting Chief Yuèliàng. Stanley detected it but knew he would cause a disaster if he confronted the boy in this auspicious moment. He had to simply allow things to happen and have a long talk privately with him later when they were flying around together back at the mansion.

It took almost twenty minutes to slowly drink the ceremonial tea and not rush one second of it. During the small talk a few of the special tribal words were said to commemorate the moment, then on cue from Tonnerre official tea ceremony ended.

The Tribe knew Chief Yuèliàng would be away for about a week and not return with his daughter as she would now be part of another tribe in the sky, but her family would double because she still had the tribe here and they were assured she would come back from time to time to visit her parents, and the Tribe. Stanley and Lacsar would love to come back and go fishing with Chief Yuèliàng's family and again enjoy their company around the campfire with the intelligent birds who were growing companions in many ways.

When Chief Yuèliàng stood up, his family followed suit and the Royal family stood up and the Chief Yuèliàng escorted Stanley out of his home and they walked to the waiting shuttles. As explained by the procedure, none of the Royals could be in the same shuttle together and now that the Chief's family was part of the Royal's family, they also were requested to not fly in the same shuttles together.

Chief Yuèliàng got in the shuttle with Stanley. Princess Li went into the same shuttle with the Chief's wife. Alessandra and Starbright went into the same shuttle and Alessandra seemed animated she felt like she had a big sister and was sincerely happy. Lacsar went into the shuttle with Valet Octavrator.

On the flight from Ollytrene to the Fast Frigate, Octavrator asked Lacsar, "Tell me how you feel about Starlight after seeing her today."

"This is one of the happiest days of my life. If I can remain with her the rest of my life, I will be very grateful."

"That's good to know that you can be committed at such an early age, it will make Royal affairs much easier to deal with."

"I feel good about it because since I've already made my selection for my mate for the rest of my life, I can concentrate on learning from Grandfather what I must do when I ascend to the throne."

"Your grandfather is very much interested in your development. By you showing commitment and understanding of how Royals must proceed simplifies it for him and as you stated, your attitude goes a long way towards making that process more efficient."

In a brief period, Chief Yuèliàng's family was on the Royal Space Yacht and the Royals were on Fast Frigates escorting them home.

The trip to Neflatraceous was uneventful other than on the Royal Yacht, Drákōliné spent the travel time to indoctrinate Starlight and her parents about the Royal Court and about many procedures relating to security done at the mansion. She also explained a lot about the people they would deal with and to explain a lot of things appropriate so that when they arrived, they would not be in a complete culture shock.

Chief Yuèliàng's wife Tonnerre was sophisticated in Tribal matters and understood how critical it was for her daughter's future and swallowed any pride necessary to take the full brunt of the quick paced education and indoctrination that was systematically throwing them thousands of years into the future. There were quite a few holographic presentations shown which allowed Starlight and her parents to see a visual of everything Drákōlìné discussed.

Since Drákōlìné had several days to make all the presentations, Starlight and her family slowly developed a keen sense of what like was like for the Royals as well as getting a crash course on Lìsztbrùnést society and the essence of what they would soon see at Neflatraceous the capital of the Lìsztbrùnést Empire, as well as the emperor's mansion where they would be staying.

One thing that was comforting to them is they would never be left alone that someone would always be nearby to assist them with anything they required.

Chief Yuèliàng didn't care one way or the other how the ostentatious living arrangements would be provided. He simply liked the Royal Family and would do whatever was necessary to fit in and please his wife Tonnerre who had significant influence over him.

Tonnerre of course was delighted that the Chief Yuèliàng demonstrated cooperation for Starlight's benefit, and he was more than happy to be a team player and would do the best he could.

Starlight was a very fast learner but wished Alessandra came with her on this ship as they could have enjoyed the companionship together. However, it was probably good that didn't happen because Starbright received significantly better indoctrination than had she been enjoying the company of the young princess who would have gobbled up all her spare time.

Chief Yuèliàng and his family had packed some clothes to bring with them that had been loaded up on the shuttles and delivered to the Royal Space Yacht and had their special Tribal Ceremonial Clothes with them to show a good first appearance. They were warned when they were about one hour away from landing, so Chief Yuèliàng's wife then swung into action and made sure they were all presented the way she intended.

The Lìsztbrùnést Royal Space Yacht landed a couple miles from the mansion along with the shuttles bringing down the Royal Family. They were all indoctrinated this was done for security reasons, but the two families would then get in the Lìsztbrùnést Royal Space Yacht together and fly the remaining distance to the mansion and meet the emperor.

Lacsar was excited he got to sit next to Starlight who was as glamorous as he could ever imagine. He was very proud of her and the way her mother had prepared her put on the exclamation mark. When the Lìsztbrùnést Royal Space Yacht landed near the mansion the emperor would know the Tribal people were the best looking that arrived today.

As soon as the Lìsztbrùnést Royal Space Yacht touched down in the very wide-open area next to the entrance of the emperor's mansion, the emperor walked out the front entrance with color guard on each side and twenty members of his staff behind him to meet the grandson's new family. Emperor Cornelius stood near the Lìsztbrùnést Royal Space Yacht to greet Starlight and her family.

As to not overwhelm Chief Yuèliàng's family, Emperor Cornelius would not be wearing his full decorated uniform and would be more casual and toned down. He would not get into the more formal attire until everyone had a chance to get to meet and get to know each other.

The tribe had master makeup artists and the Chief Yuèliàng's wife was the best among them. She made a point to make a statement not only for her daughter, but also for herself and if it made Chief Yuèliàng jealous when the emperor gazed upon her with with the expected response.

It made Tonnerre happy that that if her makeup seemed to soon get Chief Yuèliàng jealous, it might rekindle some of the fading passion in their marriage.

In great expectation the door opened and as laid out by Drákōlìné, Princess Lì Alìgrāwná escorted the Chief's Wife, Tonnerre to meet her father first.

And just like the Chief Yuèliàng's wife predicted the emperor was stunned. The ancient makeup process was far more exotic and evocative than modern techniques. And moments later when the emperor first gazed up on his future heir's empress, he was entirely proud of his grandson for picking such exquisite beauty.

The entire staff at the mansion felt the same way. Lacsar (aka Demetrius Ravik) completely surprised them with the pick of his future empress. Nobody in the empire could have found him a more beautiful Empress searching 100 solar systems. He did it all on his own in a very unsophisticated manner that was built on emotion, friendship, and love at first sight.

The Tribal members have a ceremonial curtsy reminiscent to Stanley as what an opera singer would do.

Looking at the beautiful mother the emperor knew how the grandson's mistress would appear in 30 or 40 years and to look this beautiful at that age was a significant positive attribute the emperor appreciated. If the Chief suddenly met an early demise the emperor would be happy to take care of his wife from then on.

Next came Chief Yuèliàng and Stanley, the Duke of Ravik for the introduction. The tribal clothes looked inspiring to the emperor who bowed very deeply to Chief Yuèliàng the stood straight and said, "It is my distinct honor to meet you Chief Yuèliàng and if there is anything I can do to make your stay here more enjoyable, please do not hesitate to ask. I want to introduce you to my two

Valet's Lucas and Octavrator who will always be around to assist you in any manner. Don't hesitate to ask them as they are looking forward to your company and making your stay as enjoyable as possible."

"Thank you, your Excellency."

"You are now part of my family so when we are together, please call me Cornelius."

"I shall Cornelius."

"Thank you."

The emperor smiled at Stanley and knew no words were required. Stanley had pulled off a miracle. In one short trip he had completed what the Royal Court normally took twenty to thirty years to achieve.

Behind their parents came Demetrius Ravik (Lacsar) and Starlight holding hands and smiling as if it were the best day of their lives. To some extent it really was.

Looking at the future Empress, Emperor Cornelius knew Starlight's persona was just as glamorous as the bright red gem in the golden artwork that enshrined her beautiful neck.

To some people the young woman with the extensive makeup might seem rather strange, but this was the most important day in the girl's life coming face to face with Emperor Cornelius her future benefactor who now immediately adopted her as his own daughter/granddaughter. Starlight's splendid beauty was unquestioningly beyond anything Emperor Cornelius could ever hope for his grandson.

And here the lovely and beautiful Starlight was in standing in front of Emperor Cornelius the most powerful man in the galaxy holding Lacsar, Demetrius Ravik's hand who presented her to his grandfather:

"Grandfather I would like you to meet Starlight, my future empress and my very good friend."

"Demetrius Ravik, you have excellent taste and intelligence. You have made me very proud today, and I'm very happy to see you and the young Empress Starlight. This is a wonderful day for me. My Empress, who is no longer with us, would no doubt have tears observing the two of you together. This is one of the most joyful moments of my life. Thank you for bringing joy into my life."

The emperor then looked at Starlight and said, "My dear Empress Starlight you are beautiful, and Demetrius Ravik has shared some nice comments about you. I want you to know you are very important to me. If there is anything I can ever do for you don't hesitate to ask. It warms my heart that my grandson will have such a wonderful person to share his life with. From this very moment you are now part of my family. You have now been elevated to Lìsztbrùnést Royalty and the house of Emperor Cornelius. Anyone from this day forward should understand and today I will put out an official declaration you are now part of the family and should be treated as a direct member of the family."

Starlight was taking it all in and understood everything said and looked at Emperor Cornelius with a sense of relief as her reception now seemed very positive.

"Starlight, please be patient with us and we will do everything in our power to help you adjust to your new family and your new world."

Starlight simply smiled full of happiness taking it all in. It was a magical moment and said, "Thank you."

"I also want you to understand your mother, Tonnerre, and your father Chief Yuèliàng the head of your Ollytrene Tribe are now also Royalty and a member of my Royal Court, and you can be certain when you feel homesick you will be taken to visit your mother and father."

"Thank you, I appreciate that."

"I'm quite certain, that Demetrius Ravik who enjoys traveling there will want to go with you and visit your parents as well. If you parents wish to come here to visit you and the Royal Family, they will know they are invited to come whenever it pleases them."

Starlight didn't know how to respond she felt overwhelmed and simply could only think to say, "Thank you."

"We are now going to have a private celebration for you and your family with just a very few guests, who are my most important and trustworthy friends who would like to meet you. Before you parents go home back to Ollytrene, we will have a much larger event because the entire court is looking forward to meeting you and your parents."

"I'm sure my parents will enjoy that."

The emperor astonished everyone there and bowed deeply to Starlight and when he raised up said, "Starlight, I welcome you to our family."

Starbright almost felt like crying but Lacsar was working on her holding up her emotions, being the future partner that he would be this very moment and he helped her tremendously remain her poise which she would always thank him for. Afterall this day was to be a happy day and most important day for Starlight and Lacsar. Starlight felt this greeting could not have started out any better.

On the Royal Yacht, Drákōlìné indoctrinated the Royal Family that everything would be done for them. They no longer had to carry anything or do any physical exertion because the staff was there to do that for them. All their personal belongings and everything would be taken care of for them and put in their private guest suite and all they needed to do was socialize or relax or do just about whatever they wanted as someone would be there to take care of them and help them achieve whatever they wanted.

The emperor then said to his new Ollytrene family, "I would like to introduce you to the main members of my staff who will be always looking out for you. Someone will always be nearby to help you in any manner you need. Please follow me."

Emperor Cornelius then turned and walked through the line of twenty people introducing them to Starlight and her parents. Everyone bowed and greeted in the most respectful and professional manner. It was quite clear to Starlight and her parents these people were sincere and quite affectionate. It was a very pleasant atmosphere, and they were led into the nice courtyard where the orchestra was playing some very nice music of the type, they had listened during entertainment on the flight here. Tribal music has some interesting sound and complexity to it and there were intricate Tribal instruments that made just as beautiful sounds as the orchestra. Nevertheless, Chief Yuèliàng and Tonnerre enjoyed the lovely symphonic quality produced by such lavish instruments.

As promised a few higher-ranking court members were there to greet the grandson's new in-laws and future Lìsztbrùnést Empress. One thing the court members knew vividly was in about 30 years, Starlight would be the very most powerful woman in the galaxy and if they crossed her anytime soon, it could be a disaster for them in the future as she gained all that power through her husband.

Hence, the ass kissing started right then and there.

One item a couple of the older ladies who had been court members since the emperor was first Unified focused on the golden artwork and fantastic red gem that Starbright was wearing and made nice comments about it that pleased Starlight.

Starlight viewed her red gem as the foundation to the relationship with Lacsar and informed the ladies, "Prince Demetrius, discovered this gem on my planet and gave it to me as a gift. Craftsmen who work for my father shaped the necklace like artwork and mounted it in a way to make sure it would sustain abuse and not fall off and get lost."

The women then said a few more nice things to Starlight that helped her maintain the nice feelings she felt being with Lacsar.

Knowing that dinner would be served soon, and the emperor would want to sit next to Starlight's parents and that Alessandra would be wanting to be pestering Starlight, Princess Lì Alìgrāwná looked at the seating arrangements and informed Octavrator the changes she wanted made.

Starlight's parents and Starlight sitting next to the emperor at the end of the table, would sit facing Lacsar and his parents. Alessandra would sit next to Starlight. The rest of the guests would be moved around to accommodate and with Lucas help the new seating arrangements would easily be accomplished long before the emperor invited them to join him for dinner.

After a few refreshments and small talk, the emperor invited everyone to the dinner table set up in the most lavish fashion. The dinner was immediately served, and the conversations flourished but the Court Members were upset they didn't get to sit closer to the prospective young future Lìsztbrùnést Empress Starlight. They would privately complain to the emperor later who would have to promise preferred seating assignments and explained to them, "After her parents travel home, you will be able to sit next to me and Starlight often."

Chief Yuèliàng who sat across from Lacsar was impressed with his politeness as well as his conduct at the table. Lacsar smiled a lot and answered a lot of questions and seemed to dedicate his time towards Chief Yuèliàng.

Lacsar and Starlight were relieved they were sitting across from each other and could telepathically communicate, mainly because of Lacsar's ability. The emperor caught on to some of it and had to work hard to keep his poker face.

Stanley also telepathically eavesdropped on the two young people and quickly wished he hadn't. They were discussing their futures telepathically and very much entuned to what they would be doing together. They were dedicated souls to each other, and the enjoyment and fulfillment expanded their passions to create new situations in their life. Stanley now knew the two young people had seriously dedicated their lives to each other. It was an extraordinary revelation to him. He knew his son was ultra-intelligent, but now he knew he eclipsed his own awareness as how fast he was mentally developing. Starlight was a woman in a girl's body. Her wisdom and intelligence dwarfed her age.

Stanley figured that this at least resolved one issue, it was unlikely the two would ever desert each other as the bond was now complete and no turning back.

The music and the ambience created a lot of great feelings. Chief Yuèliàng didn't quite understand why he liked Stanley so much, but there was a friendly attraction there as Chief Yuèliàng could feel the affection and respect. He felt relieved his daughter would marry into such a pleasant family especially with the future groom so positive for them.

The dinner party continued for several hours, and everyone enjoyed the time, then suddenly, Lucas approached Chief Yuèliàng and Tonnerre and asked, "Your Excellency Chief Yuèliàng and your Majesty Tonnerre, would you like to go to your suite and freshen up, then come back when you are ready for some refreshments?

Tonnerre looked kind of nervous, and she was long overdue to freshen up and answered for Chief Yuèliàng and said, "We would love too."

Tonnerre then looked at her precious daughter Starlight and asked, "Starlight would you like to go back with us and freshen up?"

Starbright responded, "I'm okay now, I would like to stay here with Lacsar, and if I need to freshen up, someone will take me to our suite if I need to go there."

"Alright Starlight, we'll see you in a while," Tonnerre responded knowing her daughter and the young prince were a couple now that will grow up together and spend the rest of their lives together. She also recognized that Lacsar was such a decent young polite gentleman she already knew had her daughter in his best interest.

When Chief Yuèliàng and Tonnerre departed so did a lot of the rest of the participants from the wonderful dinner. However, Starlight would always have a chaperone until Starlight's parents and the Royal Couple agreed the Unification could proceed and Lacsar would be allowed to deflower Starlight at that time. Tonnerre had faith in the system the Lìsztbrùnést exposed openly to them because they were now family, and Starlight's future had already been charted.

The next day, Stanley and Lacsar did their normal morning routines and visited the special flock of birds and Rascal-II was there to meet them. Starlight was with them along with her chaperone who happened to be Drákōlìné.

Tonnerre had been briefed on the trip to the mansion that until unification Starlight would never be allowed to be alone with Lacsar until the Official Unification. They were very strict about this which Tonnerre was most in favor of. She fully understood the Royal family viewed her daughter as part of their family now even though Official Unification not occurred, and her daughter would be protected at the same level as the emperor himself. Anyone who hurt Starlight would quickly be executed. She was now Royalty and her Royal Certification by the emperor happened the following morning. The entire Royal Court as well as all the staff knew the implications of the Royal Certification. She's a Royal and if something bad happened to her it would be viewed as negligence on the part of those assigned to protect Starlight, which usually had a serious punishment attached.

Starlight had seen Lacsar fly with the birds before and today as he flew with his father in the long circle around the open area in the park like open area, Lacsar made it up to eight miles before Stanley decided he had enough, and they landed and spent their precious time with Rascal-II.

Starlight observed the interaction between Rascal-II and Stanley and felt a great sense of admiration. To her surprise Rascal-II walked directly up to her and stared at Starbright then squawked some bird words, then flew away.

Through mental telepathy Starlight asked Lacsar, "What that was all about?"

The response really intrigued Starlight as Lacsar responded, "Rascal-II welcomed you to the family and said the flock would look out for you."

"How do you know what he said?"

"My father and I communicate with Rascal-II telepathically."

"Just like you do with me?"

"Yes."

"That's incredible."

"We love Rascal-II like a brother. His father saved me and my mother's life. The birds have always protected us."

Lacsar noticed Starlight was rubbing her red gem which he figured out was one of her emotional reactions when she received bewildering information. It was as if rubbing that red gem somehow rarefied her emotions and clarified many things for her. See seemed to grow strong afterwards.

One thing that Starlight had evolved to be the realization she and Lacsar now had a permanent relationship. She also knew for a fact Lacsar would always look out for her. Starlight knew Lacsar loved her dearly. In their mental telepathy where they thought they could communicate in total privacy, they could express their feelings, unfortunately there were three people who could intercept part of it, the emperor, his daughter Princess Lì Alìgrāwná and Duke Ravik (aka Stanley).

Lacsar and Starlight's secrets were not so secret, but a lot of it was hidden because there was no way the three who could intercept the telepathy all the time nor would they always be in position to detect all the telepathic ensembles.

Often out of simply the nature of the relationship Lacsar and Starlight didn't express themselves to each other in the degree they sometimes did while they were around their parents or the emperor, so a lot of their telepathy was never discovered. But some of the sweetest telepathy occurred while one of the three was close enough to detect it. Since they were designated a couple now, the transmission of love between them was expected and it eventually became muted in the dichotomy of prevailing events.

Starlight enjoyed being with Lacsar all the time and especially when he was with the birds in the morning. It touched her most positively that wild animals loved her prince.

When Lacsar and Starlight walked back to the mansion, they were informed that Chief Yuèliàng, Tonnerre, and Starlight would be given a tour of the planet, stopping at a dozen places to see what life was like on Neflatraceous. This added to the steep learning curve for the parents of the future Empress, but they were good soldiers and simply took the indoctrination in the best manner possible and were enlightened in many ways.

What struck Tonnerre was how much she was treated like royalty and fussed over. She knew it was all genuine and Lìsztbrùnést culture was explicit in many ways. She felt the affection of the Lìsztbrùnésts who treated her with such grand mannerisms. She also felt the warmth of the emperor who seemed to have a special interest in her. The entire experience was uplifting as it didn't take long to realize they had transcended into a new family who looked strongly out for their best interests.

Drákōlìné spent a lot of time with Tonnerre indoctrinating her on a vast array of information. Tonnerre learned the emperor would be setting up a communication link to the tribe as so Tonnerre could routinely communicate with her daughter even though the response was usually delayed a day due to distance.

Tonnerre didn't know why, every time she got near the emperor, she had some strange feelings. They were pleasant feelings, and she took a liking to him. The emperor felt great joy when Tonnerre was in his presence and his compassion for the beautiful woman leaked and radiated unintentionally telepathic emotional reverberations that struck Tonnerre that caused those strange feelings.

All Lacsar's scheduled training ended for this week deemed a Royal Holiday because the future Empress family was visiting the mansion. Each day they did a little of the same, including visiting with Rascal-II and his flock. The future empress and her family with Lacsar traveling with them were also taken around the planet showing them the highlights of Neflatraceous. It was mild culture shock to Starlight's family, but they quickly evolved into a new mindset. No matter how glorious this futuristic Neflatraceous seemed, Chief Yuèliàng and Tonnerre wanted to go home to their tribe and ancient lifestyle living off the grid.

The Ollytrene practical methods mitigated every technological challenge, and they had every issue covered to facilitate living in an ideal world where there was no crime, disease, or social unrest. But for their daughter Starlight's happiness, this trip was an essential part of her development and her future happiness. The way they analyzed it; tribes sometimes had members go off to other tribes when they were unified by the other tribes' members. Chief Yuèliàng simply looked at the Lìsztbrùnést as a different tribe that required travel to space which they had perfected so it would be no different than having to walk 100 miles to visit a daughter at another tribe.

In a very short time, Chief Yuèliàng and Tonnerre got to see firsthand how the treatment of their daughter would be since she had elevated to a Royal Level and only one event stood in the way of her becoming the Empress and the most powerful woman in the Galaxy, the unification with Lacsar.

In many ways it was good Starlight and Lacsar would grow up together as best friends before the official unification occurred. In addition, Alessandra was a very lonely girl and having Court members children over to visit Alessandra wasn't the same as having a best friend living with you. Over time Alessandra and Starlight became very close friends and sister like. It did not surprise Starlight that Alessandra also had growing mental telepathy like her brother.

Starlight was in for a big shock herself. In the years to come, being around telepathic individuals had an impact on her own telepathic ability she didn't know she had. All humanoids who came from the bread of life, all mighty, have photoreceptors in the center of their brain that facilitates telepathic communication. How humans on earth lost the ability to be telepathic was unknown because of the stretch of time, but the physical ability remained to be utilized if their minds were somehow rewired to utilize that capability. Starlight eventually had the revelation she had telepathic ability when she initiated the interchange with Alessandra.

It seemed like a spiritual awakening realizing the telepathic ability existed. And a few days later as the three young people were enjoying their time with Rascal-II, Starlight initiated a telepathic communique with the bird who immediately came to her. Lacsar and Alessandra watched this interaction play out and they both knew that Rascal-II said *he was very happy that Lacsar and Alessandra had her as a friend, because they were lonely, and she brightened up their lives.*

The final day before Chief Yuèliàng and Tonnerre were scheduled to depart to Ollytrene, a dinner party for the Court was scheduled. This would include Court Members of various stratums. These are the only individuals the Royals would ever deal with except for the staff and possibly the military.

Drákōlìné explained to Tonnerre that since Starlight was now an official member of the Royal Family, that meant her parents were direct and extended members of the Royal Family and that this type of official dinner meant they all must wear Royal Attire. The entire Royal Family would be dressed alike and nobody else would ever be allowed to wear such attire since it was restricted to the Royals. Drákōlìné asked Tonnerre to help prepare Chief Yuèliàng and explain to him why it was important as Royals they were dressed as such for this very important event.

Tonnerre was a team player, and she took matters into her own hands so that when the Taylors arrived to fit them, Chief Yuèliàng who didn't want to remove his Tribal Gear was ready to comply with whatever was required because he knew if he didn't Tonnerre would make his life hell for years when they got home.

Later when Chief Yuèliàng saw how the fashion designers changed Tonnerre's hair and applied ingenious types of makeup that made her look twenty years younger and extremely beautiful, he suddenly didn't mind at all extra fuss doing this public event.

The baths they gave Chief Yuèliàng and Tonnerre had pleasurizers and psychoactive drugs in them to improve their personal psychology for the evening events as to not suffer stress that such an event could place on anyone, especially when you are being scrutinized by the most powerful people in the galaxy.

When everyone was prepared to be seen by the Royal Court, all those invited to attend were in the courtyard patiently waiting to see the family of the future Empress. None of them knew anything about Ollytrene, and the only thing permitted for them to know is the future Empress father was a Chief ruler on Ollytrene.

As part of the parade to the first exposure, the Royals were all arranged for the grand entry. There would be galactic wide filming and within hours billions of people would see this. The emperor because he didn't have a woman in his life was lined up with Chief Yuèliàng and Tonnerre who was in the middle of the two distinguished looking men. Directly behind Starlight's parents and Emperor Cornelius was Lacsar and Starlight holding hands and smiling. Lacsar was helping Starlight all throughout the event and was politically smart and through their private telepathic abilities kept reminding her to smile now matter how painful it was. It was now part of her responsibility to illuminate the essence of who Starlight was.

Starlight and Lacsar's clothing were the same but slightly different than the other Royals to accentuate who they were.

Behind Starlight and Lacsar, Duke of Ravik (aka Stanley) and Princess Lì Alìgrāwná came with Alessandra between the two carrying a beautiful bouquet of flowers perfect for her size. She would be soon part of the introduction as this all unfolded.

Emperor Cornelius and Starlight's parents stepped up on the short podium to one side of it facing the crowd. Lacsar and Starlight came up to the very middle and based on the two yellow circles on the platform they stepped slightly forward almost a foot in front of the emperor and Starlight's parents. Then came the Duke of Ravik, Princess Lì Alìgrāwná, and their daughter Alessandra stand slightly back and on the other side of the lovely young couple. Right on cue when Princess Lì directed telepathically, Alessandra walked forward and turned and walked directly to Starlight and handed her the bouquet of flowers in a powerful display of respect and admiration. Giving the flowers to Starlight was all that was required, but Alessandra had special feelings for her new adopted sister and said, *I love you and I'm very happy that Lacsar discovered such a lovely princess to spend his life with.*

People that were close to the platform heard the comment and saw tears forming on both Starlight and Lacsar. Alessandra had unintentionally pushed them over an emotional cliff. Those persons who could hear the comment were equally affected. As soon as Starlight took the flowers, Alessandra hugged her then stepped back and bowed then walked back to her position between her parents.

It seemed the young couple got over their emotional spike rather quickly and not knowing the cameras were capturing it all which had a very positive impact on the public opinion in general, the emperor stepped forward and down the other side of the platform which faced the Royal Court members and in front of the Royals began speaking.

"Thank you all for coming here tonight to meet my family. As you probably know from my official proclamation of a few days ago, we now have a new member to our family, the young Empress Starlight."

Emperor Cornelius then turned around and raised his hand towards Starlight who was telepathically told five times by Lacsar, "Keep smiling."

Starlight then did as Drákōlìné trained her, a perfect curtsy towards Emperor Cornelius.

"And next to the lovely future Empress is my Grandson most of you know, Demetrius Ravik, the heir to the throne."

Emperor Cornelius then turned back towards the Royal Court members and said, "We are very lucky tonight we have Empress Starlight's parents here with us to celebrate this most auspicious occasion. I would like to introduce to you the Duke and Duchess of Ollytrene."

Emperor Cornelius then turned towards Starlight's parents and again raised his hand in salute to them then he bowed. Tonnerre did her own curtsy and Chief Yuèliàng did a long respectful bow.

Tonnerre looking twenty years younger with her makeover and her elaborate beautiful hair was unquestioningly probably the most beautiful woman present. The Royal Court members were astonished. And they also knew the Empress would grow into a very beautiful woman like her mother. The court was happy the family looked so stunningly attractive. One thing they knew for sure was to never underestimate Emperor Cornelius and now here he was with a daughter who unified with an *off-worlder* and his grandson's future Empress also an *off-worlder*. Emperor Cornelius had reached out to the far stretches of space to fine such exquisite additions to his family.

None of the Royal Court knew Stanley had participated in a very highly risky mission that could have got himself killed. All that mattered to Stanley was that Lucas and Octavrator knew Stanley was the real deal and extremely brave, though they did receive some harsh treatment by Emperor Cornelius who stated most emphatically, "Never put Stanley into a situation like that again, because I do not want to see my daughter's heart broken in case something goes wrong."

Lucas and Octavrator knew they would never plan for such a future event, but they also knew one thing, one can never predict the future and bad situations that could arise, and Stanley would be willing to go to hell and back to protect his family. They also knew something the Royal Court didn't. Stanley could talk to birds, and he was a member of their flock which gave him some unusual capabilities.

Before dinner the Royals were now meeting members of the court they had not met before, but Drákōlìné hustled Starlight back to their suite to fix her makeup she ruined crying. It only took a couple minutes, but the fix was essential as she would soon be meeting a bunch of snobs and had to be picture perfect. Drákōlìné took the time to reinforce to Starlight to hold back her emotions. "No more crying, no matter how wonderful it feels!"

"I promise I will not. But Alessandra really touched my heart."

"If I were in your shoes, I would have done the exact same thing. But now we are past that. Go smile for your future emperor who loves you dearly."

"I know he loves me, and the feelings are quite mutual."

The two ladies went back to the reception going through lines meeting people. Drákōlìné took Starlight right up to Lacsar and admonished him telepathically: "Do not leave her side for a second."

"I promise I will stay with her." Lacsar responded telepathically.

Lacsar then grabbed Starlight's hand and said, "We need to meet a lot of people now."

Lacsar many years ahead of his peers and a brilliant genius walked through the crowd with several security men right behind the couple and introduced Starlight to everyone who stepped forward to the greeting.

It was slightly stressful to Starlight but now and then Lacsar would telepathically say to her, "You look beautiful, keep smiling."

It was a joyous occasion and the Royal Court all wanted to meet Starlight's mother. She was an exotic creature and could capture the heart of any man present very easily.

Because of the language barrier, Lucas was with Chief Yuèliàng and Tonnerre doing all the translations and as such the couple had a supercomputer figuring out on a nanosecond rate the appropriate response to questions or comments, they should say in response to Royal Court Members comments. As such the Royal Court very quickly determined the future Empress parents were extremely sophisticated. And in many ways Starlight's parents were sophisticated because as the head of a tribe, Chief Yuèliàng had to deal with some very powerful politics, especially negotiating treaties with other Tribes and intervening sometimes in strife that developed. He in a sense was an emperor on a smaller scale, but the scenarios he experienced were quite similar.

When Starlight came upon some of the picky women present who wanted to throw out a mine field for her to step on, the genius of Lacsar intervened and telepathically guided Starlight through the maze these ungracious women attempted. Lacsar had a semi-photographic memory and would soon privately tell the emperor the disgust those women made him feel. Since every inch of the courtyard was recorded, in the days to come, the emperor invited those particular women to the mansion for private meetings where he replayed the audio and warned them, "If you know what's good for you, you don't want to cross my grandson's empress because one day she will be the most powerful woman in the galaxy and you will then have to deal with her."

Those women left the mansion fully calibrated for any future events and instead of attempting to lay psychological mine fields they were kissing the future empress ass.

Thanks to Lacsar handling matters and doing as he promised never leaving Starlight's side that evening, it turned out to be a very joyous event.

Tonnerre was feeling exquisite as all the men who approached her had twinkles in their eyes. Her own attitudes helped the process along because when a lovely woman responds to a man in such a lovingly fashion it multiplies the effect.

By the end of the dinner and as all the guests were slowly filing out and saying their personal goodbyes to the young royals, the Court was convinced the emperor who had proven may times before how successful he was in all his endeavors, was impressed by the way he facilitated his grandson's future empress. There would never be any questions about her beauty and after engaging with her in conversation they discovered Starlight was a lovely person and that red gem she wore seemed to accentuate her and when the lighting reflected the thousands of streams of beams from it, it gave her a sense of magic as she clearly touched all their hearts in the most positive manner.

Another factor the Royal Court perceived, such a gracious and beautiful young lady had been raised by extraordinary parents. Her poise and her demure was superior in every way. And then when the husbands of many of the Court women looked at Tonnerre and saw her exquisite beauty, they knew this young lady would blossom into a spectacular empress they would all cherish.

The security men were at first a little irked because the flock of birds showed up for the event. But they stayed in the back and simply watched. When one of the security men approached Emperor Cornelius and asked what they should do about the birds, he responded, "Leave them alone. They are here because Lacsar and Starlight are part of their family. You will observe they will be very behaved. Rascal-II will make sure of that."

"Whose Rascal-II?"

"See the bird on the far right over the entrance to the guest rooms?"

"Yes."

"That's Rascal-II."

"What's so special about Rascal-II?"

"Rascal-II is the son of Rascal who prevented Hectozar the Gromulite despot Dictator from kidnapping my daughter and grandson."

"How did a bird do that?"

Emperor Cornelius saw Lucas nearby and signaled him and he came right over.

"Yes, your Excellency, what can I do for you?"

"I want you to take our head of security to my special chamber and give him a special briefing on how Rascal saved my daughter and grandson."

"It will be my pleasure." Lucas then turned to the man and said, "Please follow me."

The emperor continued circulating among the guests and fifteen minutes later, Lucas and the security manager returned. The security official was quite perplexed at how compartmentalized information was in the mansion. That event also showcased how security had failed their mission and almost got the princess and her son kidnapped and possibly killed.

The security manager walked up the emperor and said, "I feel privileged to know what happened. Thank you."

"Now you know why Duke Ravik and the flock are so very close."

"Your excellency, I learn something from you every day. You are the best teacher I've had in my lifetime."

"I'm pleased to know that."

The security manager bowed and continued with his duties and later as he approached Rascal-II he smiled at him and nodded his head. Rascal nodded back. That movement sent chills down the security manager's spine.

The following morning there was a breakfast and a final meeting for an important discussion with Emperor Cornelius and Starlight's parents.

"As you know Duke Ravik did not have wings before he met my daughter. We have the ability to transplant wings onto people giving them the ability to fly just like Duke Ravik. We want your daughter to have wings."

Tonnerre suspected something like this would come up and knew the safest and most proper response would be, "We can't make that decision for Starlight. She must make that decision on her own. We will accept whatever decision she wishes."

At this time Lacsar was doing some serious telepathic communiques to Starlight and they had discussed the wings. He wanted Starlight to agree to it in front of her mother so there would never be a question as to the Royal family coercing her into the decision.

Starlight already knew one thing which was the most important part of her life. She would be with Lacsar the rest of her life because she was in love with him completely and she also with her growing telepathic ability knew she had Lacsar's heart completely. They were a couple even though they had not entered an Official Unification.

Starlight knew as a Royal she had responsibilities and she was far more sophisticated than girls her age because she had grown up in the midst of a chief's family where he had to do constant interventions for various reasons. Starlight realized receiving a pair of wings would simply be a necessity of life in fulfilling her future responsibilities and decided it would be best to get it over with and get the wings so nobody would have any doubts about her.

"Mother, I've made the decision on my own. I do not feel pressured in any way to make the decision. I know I must receive the wings and want to proceed with the medical procedures as soon as the doctors are ready to proceed."

"Alright my dear, I'm happy you made that decision and informed us before we left."

Starlight stood up and walked over to her mother and hugged her very strongly. The mother and daughter feelings were strong. Tonnerre could never ask for a better daughter even though this incredible journey made her feel like she was living a fairytale.

After breakfast and some last-minute socializing, it was time for Chief Yuèliàng and Tonnerre to leave and go back to Ollytrene.

They all walked out the front entrance together where the Royal Space Yacht was parked to take them home with two Fast

Frigate escorts, loaded with extra capabilities.

The Duke and Duchess of Ollytrene were escorted to the spacecraft by the entire Royal Family.

Tonnerre looked at her daughter knowing she would not be the same person when they met again. But the thought of watching her and Lacsar flying together gave her a sense of surreal satisfaction.

They said their goodbyes and the emperor did something few people ever seen him do before as he first walked up to Chief Yuèliàng and held out his two hands which the Chief grabbed for reasons he didn't quite understand as the emperor was giving his brain some subtle suggestions.

"Your daughter is one of the most important persons of the empire now. I will personally look after her and make sure she remains healthy and happy. We will communicate from time to time and one day I would like to come visit you."

"You will always be welcome."

"Thank you. I looked at the video taken from my daughter and grandson's visit to you, and I want you to know it warmed my heart. You and your daughter have made a huge impression on my grandson, which I will be forever in debt of gratitude to you. You have created significant happiness to my family. Thank you for doing what you have done for me. I will always be grateful."

"You are most welcome."

The emperor let go of the chief's hand then he approached Tonnerre and said, "You are an extremely beautiful woman. It gives my heart great thanks because I know my grandson's empress will be beautiful like you. Your daughter is more than I could ever hope for as the future Empress of this empire. I will always hold your family in my highest regards. You are now part of my family for the rest of my life. I wish the best for you."

"Thank you for your kind words," Tonnerre said feeling glad they were leaving because the emperor gave her such good vibrations, she could easily lose her self-control and create a scandal that would wreck her daughter's future. She knew for reasons she could not quite understand, the emperor lusted for her like no man before. It was an intense pleasure and if conditions were different, she would act upon her intuition.

Starlight hugged her parents then they entered the space craft and the door shut and the emperor asked everyone, "Please step back and come with me to the steps of the palace."

As soon as the pilot saw all was clear and the emperor gave him the thumbs up, the Royal Space Yacht went airborne and was on its way to Ollytrene.

~~~~~
~~~~~

CHAPTER FOURTEEN

GROWING UP TOGETHER

The following week things were back to normal at the mansion. The vacation was over, and the young royal couple were now subjected to the routine nurturing required for heads of state and someone given the awesome responsibility to ensure peace and tranquility existed in the empire.

Educational experts were brought in because the future empress would have to jump up centuries of evolution as well as be taught the history of the Lìsztbrùnést Empire.

Lacsar didn't need most of what Starlight was being taught, but he insisted on attending all her classes with her and anytime she had any issues or troubles with the curriculum, he was instantly interested in helping her. Starlight determined young Lacsar was by far her best teacher, and she absorbed it quickly. In the span of months Starlight moved ahead 20,000 years in technology. She handled it quite well mainly because her Tribal Heritage believed in spacemen and spaceships. The arrival of the Lìsztbrùnést proved their history and theories about the universe right on the mark.

~~~~~

After a year it was time for Starlight to visit her parents. She was asked by Drákōlìné if she would feel better going alone, and
~~~~~

she surprised Drákōlìné, "I do not wish to go anywhere without Lacsar."

Soon planning and discussions started. In short order, Duke Ravik, and Princess Lì Alìgrāwná immediately stated they wanted to go along if possible. And shortly afterwards Emperor Cornelius surprised everyone when he said he wanted to go to Ollytrene as well.

This created a conundrum for the planners and security. The fleet going to Ollytrene would have to be much larger because the emperor stated, "None of the Royals will travel together. I want everyone on separate ships."

For this trip since the emperor himself would be going, a couple large battle cruisers would be sent along with a tactical ready group of Fast Frigates. The emperor would travel on one of the battle cruisers and young Lacsar the other. Empress Starlight would travel with Drákōlìné on the Lìsztbrùnést Royal Space Yacht.

Young Lacsar would travel aboard the cruiser with Lìsztbrùnést Admiral Timons. In private meetings with Admiral Timons, Emperor Cornelius gave Admiral Timons instructions he felt would be important for the development of Lacsar.

"Admiral Timons, while in route to Ollytrene I want you to give detailed briefings to Lacsar on the Battle of Cystanokar."

"It would be a pleasure to brief Prince Lacsar," Admiral Timons responded and smiled.

Emperor Cornelius then in a very focused manner said, "Lacsar is at a very impressionable age where this would help him nurture him in the most positive manner."

"Understand, your Excellency."

"The Valet Octavrator will escort and protect Lacsar during the trip."

"Alright."

"I want a special briefing conducted by Octavrator around mid-point to Ollytrene to brief you and Lacsar on what his father did with Hectozar the Gromulite despot Dictator and how the birds were involved in the battle."

"Your excellency, I will make sure that happens."

"Octavrator will ensure the space you obtain his briefing, most probably your state room, will be bug searched by his intelligence team and you and Lacsar will understand you can never reveal this information."

"I understand your Excellency."

"It's important he know his father risked his life for the sake of the empire going behind enemy lines."

"Sounds intriguing."

"When you hear the details, you will understand it was a very risky operation which I did not know about until its conclusion, and I was very agitated to learn Octavrator put my daughter's love of her life in such tremendous risk."

"Octavrator is still with you, so you must have worked out that problem."

"He will never make that mistake again; I assure you. I cannot risk losing Stanley because it would cause my daughter extreme grief. She loves him so much she might even attempt suicide if she lost him."

"I understand the importance."

"I need her to make sure there is a peaceful transition of power when my grandson becomes the next emperor. I believe my daughter is the only person who can ensure my desire that my grandson be place upon the throne upon my death."

"Your Excellency, we have a lot of information concerning the Battle of Cystanokar recorded as we routinely discover new tactical methods by reviewing this information. I believe I have enough spectacular sensor and visual data to put together a briefing that will last a couple hours to show Prince Lacsar the entire battle and if necessary, I can bring in some commanders to explain aspects that will enhance your grandson's knowledge of the battle."

"Thank you. I know I can count on you. You have never let me down before."

"And nor shall I."

During the planning, it was decided to send the Valet Lucas in an advance party to Ollytrene to meet with Chief Yuèliàng and Tonnerre about the circus that would soon descend upon their doorstep and offer any kind of help they might need to help manage things such a personal servants, chefs, and chambermaids as to not over burden the Chief and his family.

Tonnerre a very shrewd woman responded by simply saying, "Send as many as you wish, we'll figure out a way to accommodate everyone."

As the plan came together the only hitch quickly evolved when Stanley said, "We must bring the birds with us."

In due time that was all worked out and the flock was happy they would get to visit with the smart birds on Ollytrene.

Everyone didn't depart at the same time. For security reasons the transiting ships left with one Royal at a time except for the Royal Yacht which had a cruiser and fast frigate escort with the emperor on the cruiser.

The fleet was on alert and several groups of combatants were staged between their solar systems to allow prompt arrival if they needed help. Any detection of foreign warships would immediately send them to the area.

Lucas was sent down first to announce the Empress and the Emperor would be arriving shortly in a couple days so her parents would have sufficient time to get themselves and the tribe poised for the reception. Already traveling with Lucas was chefs, servants, and chambermaids to assist in any manner possible. The tribe took them in and cooperated fully and together performed any necessary tasks to ensure everyone's comfort.

Emperor Cornelius and Starlight were the first to arrive. The next arrival would be his grandson Lacsar on Admiral Timon's cruiser that would be in geosynchronous orbit the entire stay to ensure their safety and to send in reserves if an enemy force approached.

The moment of truth was now. The emperor's shuttle landed on the Royal Yacht and delivered him there so he could escort the grandson's empress to the planet.

The emperor's Royal Yacht came down adjacent to the village that Lucas and Tribe members had roped off as a makeshift landing pad.

The majestic ship landed, and all the tribe members were in awe. They all knew the lovely Starlight quite well. She was very popular in the village because she was always kind and polite, a well-polished kid. It was no mystery to tribe members whey Lacsar fell in love with Starlight at first sight and when he gave her the red gemstone he loved and carried in his pocket she knew it was something special and displayed his intentions with his heart.

The door to the Royal Yacht opened which was sufficiently wide for Emperor Cornelius and Starlight to exit the spacecraft holding hands. The emperor was very proud of Starlight. She had advanced very quickly in a years' time, and she had grown quite a bit and was already showing the development of breasts of a young woman. Starlight was dressed up as a Royal Princess with the full glamor associated.

Starlight had something her parents knew she had but the tribe was not aware. Starlight now had wings and had already learned how to fly with Lacsar, her greatest joy in the world with Rascal-II's flock flying in formation with them.

Lacsar could easily fly twenty miles now and Starlight was already flying over eight miles each day with her wings getting stronger daily. The emperor and Starlight had planned the revelation to the tribe and after the initial greetings to her parents looking upon her in total awe. The emperor disconnected her cape and she spread her wings. Besides the new breasts and the wings, the tribe was utterly shocked at the transformation of Starlight.

The arrivals were all staged and after Chief Yuèliàng introduced Emperor Cornelius to the tribe, the next arrival in a shuttle was Lacsar who grew fast like a weed the past year. His frequent exercise flying and his stretch pants as part of his Royal attire and his abdomen gave an incredible image to the women of the tribe. This bird man had a body that could possibly not be on a boy they saw just the year before.

Lacsar walked up to Chief Yuèliàng and Tonnerre who was feeling very great vibes from the emperor at the moment and gave a very long and purposeful bow and greetings:

"I'm very honored to be here today in the company of your daughter whom I love with all my heart."

Tonnerre's eyes were watering up a bit and some of the tribe members saw that and it affected them as well.

"What would you like to do while you are here?" Chief Yuèliàng asked.

"Sir, if you can find the extra time, I would love to go fishing with you."

"For you son I will find the time."

"Thank you. That is one item I'm really looking forward to doing."

After a moment or two of discussion, the next shuttle landed and Duke Ravik (Stanley), Princess Lì Alìgrāwná, and Alessandra exited the shuttle and approached Chief Yuèliàng.

Alessandra also grew fast in a years' time and looked totally different. She was also far more sophisticated by hanging around with her best friend Starlight.

These three Royals approached Chief Yuèliàng and Tonnerre and all three as planned did a long bow. Then they stepped aside slightly and all three spread their wings astonishing the crowd.

Just as if on cue, the emperor, Lacsar and Starlight moved behind these three Royals and spread their wings. About that time their flock of birds they brought with them also arrived and lined up behind them and in a perfect semi-circle spread their wings exactly in the same manner. The tribe was animated and felt the magic they gave.

The Duke of Ravik then gave the short speech and said, "Duke and Duchess of Ollytrene, Chief Yuèliàng and Tonnerre we are blessed that we have your daughter in our family. She brings love and joy to us every day. We are also very happy we have this opportunity to visit with you and catch up on our lives and spend this special time here with you and your daughter our empress.

Chief Yuèliàng and Tonnerre felt the telepathic stroking. The emotions were running high, and it was time for the families to now join and enjoy each other.

Chief Yuèliàng then said, "Duke Ravik, will you please give me the honor and come with me to my home where we can all enjoy a ceremonial tea."

"It will be my greatest pleasure Chief Yuèliàng."

Chief Yuèliàng led the Royals into his home where they had ceremonial cushions laid around the Japanese like short table and soon, tribal members began serving all of them tea. Starlight was sitting directly across from her parents next to her special love Lacsar on one side and Alessandra on her other side.

Tonnerre had been informed by Lucas during his planning visit how much Alessandra had improved because Starlight was there every day for her. She was a very lonely girl and unhappy and seldom smiled and after Starlight and she met and became best friends, Alessandra smiled and showed true happiness every day.

The emperor sat next to Tonnerre. To him it was almost love at first site and he wished he had a beautiful woman like her to share his life. He unconsciously flooded her brain with telepathic transmissions that impacted her demeaner and she felt a strange valance in the vicinity of the emperor and knew it could get very dangerous for her if they were ever alone. She didn't think she could control herself.

Stanley observed Lacsar looking at him strangely like never before. Lacsar now knew what his father was made of. The briefing he received from the Valet Octavrator had a huge impact on his feelings towards his father. He wondered why that was arranged and asked Octavrator in front of Lìsztbrùnést Admiral Timons.

"Lacsar, we never know what could happen in life. All this activity is a very guarded secret as it could cause some repercussions for your father's safety in the future if our enemies knew his role in all this. But your grandfather wanted you to know your father is very special and put his life at risk behind enemy lines for the sake of the empire. He also wanted you to know the story behind Rascal so that you would know why your father has such strong feelings towards the flock." Octavrator stated during the briefing.

"Thank you for telling me all this, it means a lot to me."

"I hope you also understand why we must protect this

information."

"Yes, I know, and I promise to never reveal it in my father's lifetime."

As Stanley caught a few more gazes from Lacsar he wondered what that was about and decided to probe his mind and discovered great love the boy had for his father. He didn't know why but it made him feel really good because he loved his son as well as his daughter and to feel the affection from his son was quite a pleasant notion.

The staff brought down bird perches for the flock and stationed them next to the shuttles that would remain there with the Royal Space Yacht in the event they had to do an emergency extraction because danger was approaching. The birds were directed as part of the plan to fly back to their perches when the Royals went into the Chiefs home.

Rascal-II decided he wanted to let the Ollytrene smart birds know they were back, so he flew away and a half an hour later came back with an entire flock of the intelligent Ollytrene birds who joined them on their perches. The tribe members saw this and knew those were the intelligent Ollytrene birds who never got near humanoids. Here the Ollytrene smart birds were with the Alien birds acting as if they were all one big family.

Chief Yuèliàng's Ollytrene tribe had sufficient food to feed themselves, but they did not have the added quantity for the large contingent of Lìsztbrùnést Royal's and their staff. The emperor knew this and had several shuttles brought down with all the items they needed including a portable generator, refrigerant unit portable cooking stoves used for Space Marines and various other items and a series of tents with temporary wooden floors designed to support Space Marines in a landing or amphibious operations. The tents were camouflaged for combat situations which the Ollytrene tribe thought was simply elaborate artwork.

A long line of tents without sides, just the tops for shade were set up with wooden floors to create an outdoors dinning area. Cooks and chefs from the fleet and the Royal Yacht were provided to create a feast, working with several tribe women. After the ceremonial tea and a nice conversation, one of the staff members approached Chief Yuèliàng's home and informed the emperor, the feast would be ready in about fifteen minutes to give them time to go mingle with members of the tribe before they went to their meal.

The place settings at this impromptu dining hall were made with ornate Royal table clothes and gold table-wear. Since this trip was all about the visit and homecoming for Starlight, she and Lacsar were seated at the head of the table together. Starlight's parents were seated on one side of the young Royals. Duke Ravik and Princess Lì Alìgrāwná were seated on the opposite side facing Chief Yuèliàng and Tonnerre. The emperor was seated next to Alessandra who was next to Tonnerre giving her good vibrations and allowing conversation between the two.

In a few days most of the Lìsztbrùnést would be gone but Alessandra had requested to stay with her best friend Starlight and return with her when she would depart on the Royal Yacht with a couple Fast Frigate escorts.

The dinner party was very nice and several musicians from the fleet were brought down to the planet to play soft music during the feast. The violin like instruments gave off pleasing music and everyone enjoyed it.

Chief Yuèliàng had a sense that his wife, Tonnerre had subtle attractions towards the emperor and was relieved to discover the emperor didn't plan on staying and would depart and go back to his mansion at Neflatraceous, the capital of the Lìsztbrùnést Empire later in the day. He didn't need to remain because all the drones and probes would send back a complete video record of this vacation.

Since Alessandra would be staying with Starlight during her entire stay, the Valet Octavrator and Drákōlìné would remain until prince Lacsar and the future empress returned to Neflatraceous. Since they were not allowed to travel together, Lacsar would return with the birds after about a week stay to enjoy fishing, digging for gemstones, and other recreational activities the tribe arranged for him.

Duke Ravik (Stanley), and Princess Lì Alìgrāwná spent the night sleeping in the Royal Yacht with Lacsar and Alessandra in their private cabins. The following day they would leave on a shuttle up to separate Fast Frigates and transit back to Neflatraceous, the capital of the Lìsztbrùnést Empire. The birds would stay to add as an extra layer of protection for the young Royals and return when Alessandra and Starlight came back later via the Royal Yacht.

Octavrator would not leave Lacsar's side and Drákōlìné would always be near Starlight and Alessandra. Drákolìné was packing some heavy-duty laser weapons as well as being an expert in martial arts would be the wrong person to mess with if something negative were to occur. The three young people were the emperor's greatest concern since they were the progeny to the monarchy.

It would be a couple days before Chief Yuèliàng arranged the fishing expedition for young Lacsar. In the meantime, Lacsar wanted to go hunting for gems again. He approached Rascal-II on his perch and through telepathic communication asked him to locate the waterfall and the rock cliff where he dug his gems in the past.

Rascal-II and some of his scouts took off and flew with the intelligent Ollytrene birds flying as escorts and easily found the waterfall and rock cliff, then returned and made the report to Lacsar and distance which was easily within he and Starlight's flight range. It was possibly too far away for Alessandra who soon indicated she wanted to attempt the flight.

Lacsar turned to the Valet Octavrator and said, "We are going to a waterfall and rock cliff nearby to hunt for gems. We'll need three metal containers to clean and hold the gems at the waterfall.

After a brief discussion on how the young people would be escorted to the site by a couple shuttles, Octavrator went to the cooks requesting small metal containers for the gem hunters.

A lot of the food stuffs brought to Ollytrene were shipped in metal containers to protect the contents from possible damage by cosmic rays and provide physical strength when stored in the cargo bays. They had several metal containers that would be discarded when they gathered up all the trash and refuse to remove any possible pollution to the planet and tribal lands.

Valet Octavrator indicated to Lacsar (aka Demetrius Ravik), "We will carry these containers to the waterfall for you as to make sure nothing affects your flight."

"Thank you."

When everyone was ready to commence the flight, the three-bird people took off first flapping their wings and soon escorted by the flocks of birds from the two planets flying directly to the waterfall almost five miles away. Lacsar kept a close eye on Alessandra and if she started exhibiting any problems keeping up, they would then land and give her a rest.

Closely following behind was two shuttles while drones and probes were overhead filming and watching the young people and always on the outlook for trouble. On the horizontal after reaching almost 100 feet into the air, the bird people achieved sixty miles per hour in level flight. Just when Alessandra was starting to experience some longevity issues they arrived at their destination. She was happy she made it the entire way without having to stop. Her wings were getting stronger every day.

Knowing the prince and future empress would be digging for gems, the Valet Octavrator brought along some digging tools Chief Yuèliàng provided making it easier to dislodge the gems when they discovered them. Each of the three Royals had a tool to use to find gems on this cliff near the waterfall.

In due time the Royals were digging away and each one had a metal container to put their gems in. It only took an hour to completely fill the three metal containers. Lacsar took Starlight and Alessandra over to the shallow pool of the waterfall and showed them how to clean the gems. In about another hour they were sufficiently cleaned off enough to show the luster each gem exhibited.

They were ready to go back to the village and work on the gems. Lacsar knew how Alessandra struggled near the end of the flight to the waterfall suggested, "Alessandra, I think you are tired from flying here. Would you please ride the shuttle back to the village?"

At first Alessandra pitched a fit and then Starlight intervened and said, "Alessandra, I will ride with you in the shuttle."

Starlight always had an influence on Alessandra who considered her a sister and best friend, suddenly had a change in aspiration and attitude because she would be with Starlight.

The metal containers were loaded up in the shuttles and then Lacsar flew into the air with his bird escorts heading back to Chief Yuèliàng's Ollytrene village.

The shuttles, drones and probes were in formation as well.

The drones were very capable and had far more weapons than the shuttles that had basic self-defense. If any enemy now attacked, they would discover the drones to be quite dangerous.

When they arrived back at the village all the birds went back to the perches set up for them. Today however there were a few more installed to reduce crowding the birds.

The distinguished Valet Octavrator had a table set up for the Royals to work on their morning gem findings. The Royals were in for a treat because based on video recordings of Lacsar's last gem activities a year before, two machinists from the fleet were brought down with some tools and equipment to help them polish their gems. One of the machinists had a big surprise. They brought along a gem cutting machine that could turn them into multi-faceted objects acting as prisms sending light reflections out in multitudes of angles.

They could cut only one gem at a time. The future emperor Lacsar was of course the senior member of the Royals and got to pick the first gem of his to be cut. The machinist gave Lacsar some images with a portable holographer of the different types of cuts that could be made.

Lacsar picked a circular cut pattern which the machinist immediately went to work on. This was an expensive piece of equipment, electrically operated requiring a portable generator for energy. The first gem took almost an hour to complete, and the measurements done down to microns revealed the cuts were absolutely perfect and matched the programming of the machine doing the cutting.

Normally a gem cutter down on the micron level leaves a serrated edge because the cuts are not absolutely perfect. With laser trimming, all the serrated edges were removed leaving a highly polished surface for each facet. The results for the blue gem were rather astonishing and the growing crowd looking at the results were mystified.

This circular cut gem was the most beautiful object Starlight had seen in her lifetime. Lacsar probing her mind discovered Starlight's great attraction to it, so he said, "I want you to have this. I love you."

Starlight was immediately consumed in emotion and threw her arms around Lacsar and cried on his shoulder for a bit while Lacsar tenderly held her.

Tonnerre observed all this, and it added to her positive valence for Lacsar who had won her over as she knew as a mother her precious daughter was in good hands by a kindhearted person who would always hold Starlight in high esteem. Tonnerre's eyes also watered up a bit and she fought off the tendency to copy her daughters' actions.

Lacsar holding Starlight in the most affectionate manner helped her quickly overcome her emotions, primarily because she felt so good touching his body and feeling his soul. In a few minutes her chipper self was back and now it was time for one of the other Royals to pick a gem to cut.

Starlight said, "Alessandra, you get to choose the next gem to be cut."

Alessandra fully ensconced with what she just witnessed replied, "Starlight, I want you to pick the next one because I know Lacsar created special feelings in you."

That comment struck Starbright as she was realizing every day how much Alessandra was changing into a more mature person. She never showed any selfish traits and was happy just to be with Starlight, who took away a lot of her loneliness. She was like a sister and best friend all in one.

"Alright," Starlight replied and felt satisfaction from the nice words Alessandra had stated.

Perhaps it was the red gem she was currently wearing that Lacsar gave her the year before, drove her to pull out her red gem and handed it to the machinist that would now do a cut on it. The young people had no idea what these gems consisted of, and it would soon take an expert gemologist to inform them what they obtained.

The large red gem Starlight picked was a sapphire gemstone eighteen by twenty-two millimeters. After looking at the gem and the possible cuts, the machinist had the computer do a calculation and soon advised Starlight, "If you have it cut pear shaped you can preserve most of the material and it will polish at approximately fourteen by eighteen millimeters when all the facets are created.

"Alright let's do the pear shape."

The machinist and the computer slowly cut the gem and laser trimmed it with perfection after one hour. The machinist took the gem out of the machine, and it was still somewhat warm and handed it to Starlight.

Starlight peered into Lacsar's eyes and said, "Lacsar, I love you with all my heart, I give you this gem as a sign of my love to you."

Tonnerre right behind Starlight hearing every word suddenly had tears streaming down her face because she knew that Lacsar's behavior towards Starbright who a well-disciplined and practical girl and nobody's fool, had achieved this wonderful attachment.

The ubiquitous Valet Octavrator was also struck at the magic between the two who were in love growing up together. By the time of their Official Unification there would be no mysteries between them as they were already soul mates and their valences had utter attraction that nobody could possibly break. Octavrator also observed Tonnerre in a very respectful manner knowing silence now was essential to allow this moment created the transcendence people observing the Royal Couple glorious activity for moments. And now the strangest reaction of all occurred as the young Lacsar's eyes also watered. His emotional transcendence was unmistakable.

The following day the emperor sent a coded message to the omnipresent Valet Octavrator, "You did a superb job of filming the Royal Couple at the table with the gems. I will confess to you my dear friend, that I felt very touched observing the dialog between the future emperor and empress. Well done. You never cease to amaze me. I'm very pleased by you."

Octavrator felt uplifted receiving such kudos from the emperor. Those words were seldom spoken by the emperor to his staff. In fact, no such utterances ever happened before. Octavrator would like to serve Lacsar through his reign, but knew the obvious, his days were numbered, his longevity would soon come to pass. But one thing he knew he could count on was his robot Lucas being there. In the meantime, he would slowly find someone trustworthy to fill in when he departed this life that would be dedicated to the new emperor.

~~~~~~

Finally, Lacsar was able to do what he was looking forward to the most during this trip, going fishing with Chief Yuèliàng and enjoying time around a bonfire at night hearing stories and talking with his close friends and relatives.

Because there were not many places for the birds to perch by the river where they would be fishing, shuttles delivered all the perches near where the bonfire would be set so they could be part of the festivities. Lacsar explained to Rascal-II what the plan was.

Soon they walked to the fishing site in a group with full escorts of birds, shuttles, drones, and probes. It was a good hike, but it wasn't terribly taxing. Everyone was happy, especially Lacsar looking forward to all this as he held Starlight's hand during their walk.

Tonnerre walked behind the Royal Couple holding Alessandra's hand who wanted to be side by side with Starlight. But Tonnerre explained it to her, "You need to allow them to have these precious moments together. When you get back to the mansion Starlight will be there for you all the time."

"I know what you mean."

Alessandra didn't make any further fuss in the matter and she kind of enjoyed the company of Tonnerre who was so gracious and
~~~~~~

kind.

It took most of the morning with a small army to set up the camp site and dig a pit and bring in small boulders to rim the fire pit.

They all had a snack around lunch time to fortify them for their hours of fishing that would soon start.

Eventually what Lacsar was waiting for commenced as he finally got his fishing line into the water and patiently waited for the magic of hooking one of those great catches.

Lacsar would look back on these as some of the best days of his life when he was with his princess who had a heart of gold and a smile that pierced his heart.

Chief Yuèliàng had a good sense of people as he had to arbitrate many issues and deal with a variety of tribe members, some who may not have the best in mind for other tribe members. Lacsar wore his personality on his sleeve. What you see is what you get. For an arbiter such as Chief Yuèliàng, it was apparent that Lacsar had no avarice in his heart. He was practical and kindhearted and Starlight took to him with great affection. Every time they were together, she was smiling and full of life.

The fishing trip lasted several days and on the first night when the kids were getting sleepy, Lacsar laying on a portable mattress with something like a sleeping bag was drowsy and then Starlight laid down with him and he put his arms around her and the two were soon sleeping. Rascal-II was on a perch directly above Lacsar keeping an ever vigilance. If any intruder got close Rascal-II and his army of birds would create such a cacophony of sound, there possible intruders would lose the element of surprise. The drones and probes were ever present, and their infrared capabilities were the best in the galaxy. The fishing party was safe but knowing Rascal-II was there gave Lacsar a sense of security and satisfaction.

Laying in Lacsar's arms, Starlight felt wonderful. She cherished this moment and was glad her mother didn't wake her up to move her and instead simply put a blanket over the two of them so they would not get cold.

Alessandra was not in the mood to sleep. She was wide awake and enjoying the bonfire and as the fire burned down one of the staff would put on more wood to keep it burning through the night. The fire would be a beacon to people that might want to do them harm, but the perimeter defenses were just too great. Any entity that tried something foolish would quickly discover the results of high technology thwarting their attempts.

Eventually Alessandra grew sleepy and Tonnerre laid her down on a cot with her to be able to protect her if necessary.

<center>~~~~~</center>

Drákōlìné had been awake for several hours as she was awakened suddenly during the watch turnover by the security people who didn't make much noise. However, Drákōlìné as a trained spy and could be aroused by the slightest sounds and could trigger a response if her situational awareness discovered danger approaching. Once awoken and her adrenalin rush hitting her, it would be impossible for her to go back to sleep so she casually just watched over everyone knowing sunrise would be soon.

In the morning when the first rays of sunlight were slowly breaking above the far-off distance when Starlight first awoke and felt she was in someone's arms and slowly turned and saw Lacsar sleeping. She had the most wonderful rest and sleep. Nobody else seemed to be awake so she took the opportunity and kissed Lacsar who then stirred feeling the kiss and he kissed her back and they embraced in a loving fashion.

Tonnerre was suddenly awoken by powers she didn't understand. What was occurring is she was close enough to detect the mental telepathy going on between the young couple and she saw the morning kiss. She very carefully played like she was sleeping and only observed Starlight finish the kiss then turned around putting her back to Lacsar and the two simply embraced full of love and happiness with a glorious smile on her face. This observation cemented her notions of how her daughter truly felt for Lacsar. It was in fact divine love, a commitment to a lifelong relationship she hoped would last.

Tonnerre wasn't the only person who saw the kiss. Drákōlìné saw it as well and decided it would be best for everyone if she acted like she didn't see it. But she knew the obvious. The drones and the probe probably caught it. It was one of those issues where she wasn't in position to prevent it and while it was occurring, it would be extremely difficult to intervene without creating a bigger issue.

Another day of fishing and wading in shallow water was in store for the day. The three young people were very happy and cherishing every moment of it.

Chief Yuèliàng and Tonnerre were very happy because they never saw Starlight smile so often. She was full of happiness and Tonnerre knew to the extent her daughter was willing to go based on that morning kiss she knew Starlight instigated.

Drákōlìné had chief responsibility for the future empress. She knew the emperor was quite capable of dishing out severe penalties for failures, especially if something bad happened to Starlight, the chosen one to be the next empress. She also knew the emperor got all the infrared imagery and had analysts pull out all the golden nuggets for him to personally observe. She wondered if the emperor would view her negatively for allowing that kiss too happen. Drákōlìné thought she had probably screwed up terribly by allowing the situation to occur where Starlight was in position to administer that very affectionate kiss to the future emperor.

In some way Drákōlìné was frightened because she knew how Valets Lucas and Octavrator were admonished when Emperor Cornelius discovered they took Stanley behind enemy lines where he could have been killed. She was ready for her fait that morning and just as she expected a shuttle arrived and Lìsztbrùnést Admiral Timons himself arrived in full official uniform and nodded at Drákōlìné which meant he had some words for her.

Drákōlìné approached Admiral Timons and asked, "What can I do for you Admiral."

"Please step into the shuttle we need to talk." He then asked everyone in the shuttle to step outside so he and Drákōlìné could have a private discussion.

Inside the shuttle, the Admiral asked, "I suppose you want to know what this is all about."

"I think I know."

"I suspected you did."

"Am I in trouble?"

"This is of course highly confidential. Stanley and Princess Lì are not to be briefed on this matter. This is solely between you and the emperor."

"Alright, go ahead and give me it I'm a big girl and can handle it."

"The emperor contacted me privately using the ultra-high speed Royal Purple Code that only I have the decipher Crypto that is usually reserved for war time use only. That's how serious this matter is to him."

"I understand sir."

"He knows you were awake during the incident and for the better part of valor or some other reason you remained calm and did not interfere with the romance between the Royal Couple."

"Did I screw up really badly?"

"Emperor Cornelius was pleased to see the girl initiate the kiss

Lacsar. He knows what is in her heart now and wants to keep it that way. Your actions were consistent with what he wants, a growing and permanent relationship. But as to not screw it up, he does not want you to inform Lacsar's parents. He also knows that Tonnerre was awake and observed it, but he has faith that she will keep her silence for the benefit of her daughter."

"I'm not in any kind of trouble?"

"No, you did well."

"That's a huge relief."

"The only thing that Emperor Cornelius asks is that when you get a chance and you are alone with Starlight, to let her know others saw her kiss Lacsar and she needs to be very careful but more discrete. Also, let her know the emperor supports her relationship with Lacsar completely and wants her to be Empress."

"What is the purpose behind me telling her this?"

"Emperor Cornelius doesn't want Starlight to have any difficulties if any of this ever gets exposed to the public. She could quickly find herself in a position she doesn't want to be in especially since she already has a huge visibility and a lot of eyes on her. He certainly doesn't want Princess Lì interfering and spoiling things."

Alright Admiral, I think I understand, but based on what happened, I want to make a recommendation to the emperor I want you to send back to him in Royal Purple Code."

"What is it you wish to convey to the emperor?"

"Let Lacsar stay here another day or two then send him back to Neflatraceous. Emperor Cornelius can have a private meeting with Lacsar to inform him he is doing this to make Starlight miss him and want to come home to be with him. When she requests to go home early, it will show Lacsar, the love is stronger than he realizes."

"I think that's a great recommendation. What will be your cover story to tell Starlight about the change in Lacsar's schedule?"

"That's very simple and Alessandra will love to hear this: The emperor has decided he wants the two girls to spend time together and bond more as sisters which they have become."

"Drákōlìné, I must say you are one of the most brilliant women I've ever met."

"Perhaps one day you can tell me that again while we are enjoying a nice elixir together next to a fireplace at a winter resort."

"I'll make every effort to arrange that."

Drákōlìné then exited the shuttle and informed the crew members they could re-enter.

As soon as the crew was back onboard, the door closed, and the shuttle flew back out into space and in a short period docked on the battle cruiser that was now waiting to take Lacsar home within a couple days.

Currently, Lacsar was reaching puberty. Time had flown. It was also known at Starlight's age she was already in puberty, meaning she could get pregnant. Vigilance was required especially knowing the two were in total love with each other and if they decided to copulate there would be little that could be done to stop them, especially if they flew off one day to somewhere they could do it without anyone stopping them.

Everyone was curious as to what that shuttle business was all about but when Drákōlìné came from it smiling and appearing happy, they let their guard down thinking there was nothing to be concerned about.

Lacsar was brilliant and a genius. The pathways in his brain were wired like few others. He was a brilliant analyst, and his telepathic ability was along the line of his mother now and there were no defenses from him.

When Drákōlìné came back to the campfire, Lacsar swung into action to discover what the conversation between Drákōliné Admiral Timons was all about. He didn't need to ask any questions, as his telepathic intrusions into Drákōlìné's thoughts easily derived the entire conversation with Admiral Timons.

A young person at Lacsar's age would probably pitch a fit now and complain he didn't want to leave. But Lacsar, brilliant beyond his years and constantly learning at the highest levels possible in politics, espionage, warfare, Court Politics, the monarchy, and everything else around him had already taught him some powerful techniques. He looked to the future outcomes he would manifest by his future activities.

Lacsar having a brilliant analyst mind at an early age and determined the emperor had made some good decisions on his behalf, always gave him some new insights on how to deal with the love of his life. He calmly realized what Drákōlìné recommended made perfect sense and he could wait for gratification because he understood vividly the big picture and doing things at appropriate times.

Lacsar would certainly make use of every moment he had left with Starlight before he had to depart in a couple days. He would also inform Rascal-II the change of plans and ask him to personally look out for Starlight.

Rascal-II responded, "Brother, I will keep a vigilance for your mate."

"Thank you, I do really appreciate what you do for me."

"Lacsar the feelings are mutual what you do for us we could never ask for more. We are your flock and your family."

"Thank you."

Lacsar and Starlight did a lot of fishing and flying together in formation with the two flocks. Alessandra enjoyed flying with them and felt her wings getting stronger along with her endurance.

In a few moments that day knowing the big revelation would come tomorrow and the tribe would be informed Lacsar was leaving, he approached Rascal-II and asked, "Tomorrow can you quietly wake me up just before the sun comes up?"

"Certainly brother."

It was a repeat around the campfire, and nobody complained when Starlight ended up in Lacsar's arms as the two fell asleep.

Just as Rascal-II promised just before the sun started coming up, he hopped off his perch and quietly walked over to Lacsar and tapped him on his neck a couple times with his beak. Lacsar awoke and said to Rascal-II telepathically. "Thank you for the wakeup."

"My pleasure, brother."

"Rascal flew back up on his perch and observed everything from up there."

Lacsar, using telepathic communiques stirred Starlight who slowly awakened.

Starlight asked telepathically, "Why did you want to wake me up?"

Lacsar telepathically said, "Turn around and face me."

Starlight turned on her side and faced Lacsar and he said telepathically, "I want you to know I love you."

He then kissed her.

Drákōlìné observed Lacsar initiating the kiss. She also knew it was being recorded by the infrared sensors of the probes overhead and the emperor would likely soon be viewing it.

Tonnerre thought she was hearing Lacsar talking to Starlight. What she didn't know she was receiving telepathic communiques between the two. The conversation was very clear as if they were talking but Tonnerre knew she wasn't hearing it because there was no sound. She was puzzled and she watched Lacsar kiss her daughter and tell her he loved her. She suddenly had tears flowing because she knew the love was genuine and strong. She also heard her daughter's voice, but there was no sound. What her daughter said to Lacsar made her tears flow even more in abundance.

The kiss was very long and strong. If it wasn't for the fact, there were many people around they probably might have made love.

Morning came too early, and they were all stirred and fed the most wonderful breakfast.

Tonnerre was acutely observing Lacsar this morning as she knew the relationship with her daughter had evolved considerably. In her observations she detected a sadness in Lacsar and wondered what that was all about. Later when the shuttle appeared and Lacsar's eyes watered up a bit, she realized Lacsar knew something none of the rest of them knew. She also knew the shuttle came down the day before and there was that strange meeting between Drákōlìné and Lìsztbrùnést Admiral Timons wearing his dress uniform.

Today Admiral Timons was back. Lacsar already knew his fate. Drákōlìné walking side by side with the Valet Octavrator went over and talked to Admiral Timons outside of hearing range. After the conversation ended it was now time for Lacsar to depart.

Since Octavrator was Lacsar's official escort he approached Lacsar and said, "I'm sorry to inform you, but the emperor has requested you return to the palace. He has a task for you."

"Alright, let me go say goodbye to Starlight."

In front of everyone, Lacsar walked up to Starlight and

telepathically said, "I've been summoned back to the emperor's mansion. My grandfather has a task for me. Alessandra will remain here with you for the rest of your vacation as the emperor wants you two enjoy your friendship and you spend some quality time with your parents."

Starlight's eyes started watering up as if she was going to start crying and Lacsar knew that it hit him in the heart as well. He never wanted to be separated from Starlight the rest of his life. His next move completely moved everyone observing. He put his two hands on the side of Starlight's head and pulled her face to his and gave her the most romantic kiss any of them had ever seen before while saying telepathically, "never forget how much I love you."

The tears were streaming down Starlight's face. Lacsar also had developed a few tears and said as he released Starlight's face. "I'll see you when you get back to the palace."

Lacsar didn't want to breakdown and cry in front of everyone and did a good job of keeping his composure and walked briskly over to the shuttle and got onboard with Admiral Timons and his Valet Octavrator. The shuttle lifted off and went into space and docked on the cruiser that immediately headed to Neflatraceous, the capital of the Lìsztbrùnést Empire.

Starlight would have broken down and cried uncontrollably over this extremely sad moment of having her lover ripped away from her and taken away, but Rascal-II was there reminding her:

"Lacsar loves you very deeply. I know because he has told me. You will be back together soon. All this is necessary as the emperor must deal with Lacsar since he is the heir to the throne. You would have gone back too, but the Royal family wants you to spend time with your family who misses you terribly while you are away. Your sister and friend Alessandra will be here with you so you can enjoy girl stuff together. Alessandra needs you as her big sister. She loves you more than you can imagine."

Tonnerre approached her daughter and saw the tears and was still reacting to the astonishing kiss Lacsar did to put an exclamation point on it. She held Starlight for a while who seemed to regain her composure quickly. Then she informed her mother what was happening before Drákōlìné could interject herself and the two of them walked away from the campsite leaving everyone behind so they could have a mother to daughter talk. They of course were under full observation by the drones and probes including audio recordings and Drákōlìné received real time recordings of their conversation.

Drákōlìné was happy with the conversation as it continued. Instead of Tonnerre trying to reassure Starlight the conversation ended going in the opposite direction. Drákōlìné was quite surprised at the poise the young lady exhibited. She knew all the details even though Drákōlìné had not informed them of any of this. That's when Drákōlìné discovered the sophistication that Lacsar already attained. He was light years ahead of his age. A human sponge soaking up every bit of INTEL. His grandfather will be proud when he discovers the extent to which Lacsar had grown in stature.

Later when the mother and daughter returned everyone was smiling again and Starlight seemed to be happy. Drákōlìné knew why. Starlight's telepathic abilities were growing stronger each day and she and Lacsar often communicated without anyone knowing, except for Rascal-II. Drákōlìné looked at Rascal-II and he turned towards her and said a couple things telepathically that sent chills down her spine. Rascal-II knew everything!

~~~~~~
~~~~~~

CHAPTER FIFTEEN
CARVLESIS CLOSE CALL

The Cruiser did not transit as fast back to Neflatraceous, the capital of the Lìsztbrùnést Empire as it did while traveling to Ollytrene. Emperor Cornelius wanted ample time for Lacsar to calm down before they had their meeting. Ripping someone away from their lover is about the dastardliest deed anyone could do especially at such an impressionable age.

After reviewing the magnificent kiss that Lacsar did in front of the Tribe and his sister left a great impression on Emperor Cornelius. The initial reports back from Drákōlìné and Lacsar's dedicated Valet Octavrator were promising the young prince was not coming home with a chip on his shoulder. He was acting perfectly normal and chipper and spent most of his time in the wardroom with the officers eating or engaging in conversation or in the control room with Admiral Timons who was there not because he needed to be, since the crew was fully trained and capable. Admiral Timons was there under orders by the emperor to spend a lot of time with Lacsar and to elucidate military doctrine and history to the young prince. That was one of the reasons for the slower transit speed.

Various battles were discussed in detail including the Battle of Cystanokar since his father had a great impact on it by the removal of the Gromulite despot Dictator Hectozar. Once the Gromulites leadership was decapitated it had a material impact on the Trilaterals who were far less aggressive once they knew Hectozar was gone and out of the picture.

Lacsar understood vividly the implications that espionage and sabotage had in shaping of the battles. Admiral Timons had no idea the extensive telepathic abilities that Lacsar had developed. These extra days gave Lacsar the opportunity to read Admiral Timons mind and learn vast amounts of information about the Space Force, his personal Valet Octavrator, Lucas, and how his father fit into all this epic battle. Also, through Admiral Timons, Lacsar now knew how the birds played a huge role in taking down Hectozar's security force to enable an easy access and abduction. Even though his heart was aching for Starlight, he was also glad in a way this all happened to give him precious training and briefing in the way the Empire was ran.

Eventually the cruiser sent Lacsar down to the mansion in a shuttle, then were ready to transit back to Ollytrene to be in position to assist the Royals who remained.

Emperor Cornelius was at the front door of the mansion with Lacsar's parents to receive him home. Lacsar was dressed up in official Royal apparel on par with the grand uniform Admiral Timons was wearing.

When the door to the shuttle opened Lacsar said to his personal Valet Octavrator, "I want Admiral Timons to escort me to the emperor."

Octavrator turned to Admiral Timons with an apprehensive look on his face, but Admiral Timons nodded as he understood the request was genuinely sensible.

The three walked side by side to Emperor Cornelius and a couple feet away simultaneously did a very long and steep and respectful bow. Then they raised and the emperor was smiling because after reviewing all the video and the secret purple code transcripts, he felt this reception for his grandson would be quite positive and not the dreary negative he feared by ripping him out of the arms of his lover and bringing him back early.

"Grandfather the reason why I asked Admiral Timons to escort me to meet you is I wanted to say some things to you in front of him, so he knew exactly what I said."

"Alright Lacsar, please speak freely."

"Your excellency, I learned a lot from Admiral Timons, and I feel privileged to have been with him and learn from him. In a short period of time, Admiral Timons gave me a lot of information and I will always remember how much effort Admiral Timons put into indoctrinating me and educating me in a lot of military affairs and history. He is a great teacher."

Unexpectedly the young prince turned toward Admiral Timons and bowed very deep and respectfully and then stood tall and said, "Admiral, thank you for everything you taught me. I am proud to have been on your cruiser with you for this journey."

Admiral Timons knew the emperor would allow him to respond and he did, "Lacsar, it is always easier to teach when you have a willing student as eager as you are. The report I got from the wardroom is your time with the officers was full of good questions and they were willing to teach you because of your behavior is quite impressive to them."

"Thank you, Admiral."

"Prince Demetrius Ravik, when my entire wardroom starts liking someone, that means you made a positive impression on them."

"They were great teachers as well."

"I salute you for your efforts and the attempt you made to gain as much knowledge as you could in such a short period of time. I also know you gave up a lot of sleep and a few mealtimes to be in the control room or the wardroom to learn and study. We were privileged to have someone that was willing to put forth such great effort like you exhibited."

The emperor wanted to have an immediate private talk with Lacsar, so he curtailed the discussion by saying, "Admiral I'm going to have to ask you to leave right away, I want you to get back to Ollytrene quickly and be there to support the future empress and my granddaughter the princess."

"Your excellency I will leave immediately."

"Thank you."

Admiral Timons then held out his hand to Lacsar and the two shook and Lacsar knew thanks to his mental telepathy that Admiral Timons was most sincere in his remarks.

Emperor Cornelius then said, "Come with Lacsar, me I want to talk to your privately."

Princess Lì and Stanley followed the emperor, his Valets Lacsar, and Octavrator down the hallway to the emperor's private suite as they got to the door. Emperor Cornelius turned to Princess Lì and Stanley and said, "I will talk with Lacsar privately for a few minutes, then you and him can get together in the courtyard where I've planned a nice meal for Lacsar because I know he has not had much to eat in a days' time."

The two went inside the emperor's suite and Octavrator shut the door and stood there looking at the astonished parents slightly agitated the emperor would not talk to Lacsar in front of them. They were extremely curious about all the secrecy, and it upset them a little.

Inside the suite the emperor asked Lacsar, "Please sit down." He then pointed to the chair he would soon be facing him in another chair with a small table between them for the discussion.

"Are you angry at me for bringing you home early?"

"Grandfather I know you did what you thought was best for me. Even though I miss Starlight, I know we'll be back together soon. I enjoyed my time with Admiral Timons and all the briefings I received."

"I thought it was important that you understood some things your father has done. As you have been briefed that information needs to be kept quite confidential because of what it could cause if our enemies discover it."

"Yes grandfather, I understand fully. I've studied espionage and sabotage and understand how it plays into the outcome of major battles. I'm also quite pleased to know my father utilized the flock of birds to assist in this extraordinary operation."

"You also know I didn't send him and was quite upset when I discovered Lucas and Octavrator took him behind enemy lines in a very risky operation without my permission."

"I understand how important it is for people to always follow the emperors' decisions, otherwise we will have chaos. But to be honest I can't help but to feel grateful to Lucas and Octavrator they gave my father a chance to prove his manhood and his bravery."

"In the beginning I was very upset but as I rationalized the operation, I come to terms along the lines of what you just stated. But I did direct them too never do it again!"

"Grandfather, my dad does not need to prove multiple times he is brave and committed to you. We know what kind of a person he is and that's all that's necessary."

"What do you view your role with your father in the future, especially after you become emperor?"

"I love my father dearly. He is very insightful in many ways. I know I can trust his opinion and he will always look out for what's best for me."

"What do you think about Lucas and Octavrator?"

"You can have no better people assisting you. You are very lucky as they are dedicated to you and will do anything for you."

"Octavrator saved my life, but at the same time the Empress was killed. It's a mixture of feelings."

"Grandfather I know his motive, as painful to you as it was losing your Empress, Octavrator knew he had to preserve your life at all costs because the Empire would have crumbled if you had been killed. I think the Empress would have preferred you live to save the empire."

"I believe you are right, but I still can't get over the sadness."

"Grandfather you need to let it go. Bury the past and in the future, you might have the opportunity to meet another woman and fall in love."

That statement made the emperor think about Tonnerre. If something ever happened to Chief Yuèliàng, Tonnerre would quickly become a permanent fixture in the mansion. Lacsar caught his grandfather's thoughts and smiled."

"One last thing before we go out to the courtyard to be with your parents, I'm going to start taking you a few places to meet people in our Empire. When you become emperor, you will have to deal with them to keep the Empire running smoothly."

"Grandfather, I will always be ready to travel with you."

"What if you have to leave Starlight behind?"

"She has Alessandra to keep her company while I'm gone."

"You don't feel bad being away from Starlight now?"

"I miss her but like you said, we'll be back together soon and I'm willing to wait for her."

"Do you really love that girl?"

"With all my heart."

"Alright, thanks for this discussion and the comments I got back from Admiral Timons privately were exactly what he said to you at the front entrance. You made me very proud by your conduct aboard the cruiser."

"Thank you, grandfather, I enjoyed the experience."

"Us go join your parents."

Stanley and Princess Lì were sitting at a lovely table waiting for Emperor Cornelius and Lacsar. They knew they would now get to the bottom of what that was about. But they were first relieved the emperor and Lacsar were both smiling and appearing happy.

One of the reasons why the emperor was smiling is he discovered his grandson was far more versatile than he imagined and way ahead of his years in analytical power and insights. He was learning at a meteoric pace.

He now had confidence in his heir apparent who would be able to step in at his death and take over and keep things running. All he needed now was a little more grooming.

Stanley and Princess Lì stood and bowed at the emperor as he arrived with Lacsar and then sat down at the table with them.

Lacsar seemed rather at ease with no care in the world, which surprised them.

The emperor now exposed his plan to Lacsar's parents now. It quickly become obvious for the private meeting.

"One of the reasons why I had Lacsar come home early from his vacation to Ollytrene, is its time I start introducing him to important people, so they get to know him. In a couple days we will leave here and travel to several planets including Empire planets and non-Empire planets."

"Why would you go to non-Empire planets?"

"You never know when you might have to negotiate with those people for various reasons."

Later in a private setting, the emperor changed his mind and decided he would show Stanley and Princess Lì the confidential video of Lacsar kissing Starlight out in the open in public in the most romantic fashion that startled everyone including Alessandra who was fascinated with the interrelationship between them.

Princess Lì was moved entirely by what she saw. After spending a year with Starlight and observing how sweet she is, it touched her heart that Lacsar had found such strong love in Starlight. It was more than an attraction. Princess Lì knew her son quite well. She also knew Lacsar orchestrated this kiss for a reason. Why? Was it because he was upset about suddenly being recalled?

In exploring her fathers' thoughts and the emperor knew she was doing it, she discovered the emperor was pleased with that display of passion as it gave more assurance Lacsar fell in love with a very beautiful lady that would grow into the luster of her mother, whom the emperor would love to enjoy. Princess Lì was shocked and almost wished she had not probed her father.

Unfortunately, now she knew. The emperor had lust for Starlight's mother. If he ever acted on that lust, it would create a tumultuous disaster that frightened Princess Lì because she knew the power of her father and if he wanted that woman bad enough, nobody could stop him. It was no longer her son that caused her concern. It was her father!

<p style="text-align:center">~~~~~~</p>

Over the next few days Alessandra would pester Starlight for details about Lacsar kissing her and not get the answers she expected. It was much simpler than Alessandra realized. Love was a passion that was incredibly strong and once a couple realized they were in love that bond becomes very strong.

But Alessandra wanted to know is *why Lacsar picked that time and place to do it where everyone could see.* Then she got a big surprise answer.

"That wasn't the first time he kissed me. He did it in private and I kissed him too."

"But why did he choose this particular time to kiss you in front of your parents?"

"Lacsar and I both knew a secret he was leaving and going back to the emperor's palace early for a meeting. He wanted to make sure I knew when he left, he loved me dearly."

"But why did you cry?"

"Because his kiss and his words touched my heart."

"I didn't hear him say anything."

"He said everything to me telepathically so we could have our private conversation."

"You really love Lacsar?"

"Yes, with all my heart."

"When did you know that?"

"When he gave me this red gemstone, he telepathically said he loved me. I felt love for him too right then."

~~~~~~

The girls enjoyed their friendship back in the village since the fishing expedition was over. The birds kept a vigil going looking out for the two girls. Any man who attempted to touch Starlight would soon discover two large bird flocks attacking them and
~~~~~~

poking his eyes out before they killed the person. Being attacked by two hundred powerful birds that had 350-foot pounds of bite down force could shred a human a lot quicker than they realized.

Rascal-II was in effect Lacsar's brother emotionally. Rascal-II's ties to Lacsar were through his father who gave his life to save him. Ever since Lacsar was greatly attuned to Rascal-II who would do anything possible for him. Rascal-II took his responsibility to protect Starlight with his life if necessary.

The days slowly passed, and the two girls slowly grew restless and bored with tribal life. The arts and crafts and all the other things the tribal women did for them to attempt giving them something to fill their time with was slowly wearing thin. It was none other than Starlight who wanted to truncate the visit and travel back to the mansion where she knew her happiness would thrive in the company of Lacsar.

At the same time Starlight was informing Drákōlìné she wanted to truncate the visit and go back to the emperor's mansion; a response came back abruptly to Drákōlìné.

"Emperor Cornelius has taken Lacsar on a trip to several solar systems to meet government officials there for future dealings. He does not want Starlight and Alessandra brought back to the palace for three more days. You will have to inform them, the earliest we can get the escorts there is three days. The emperor does not want Starlight to come back to the palace until Lacsar is back to receive her."

The two girls had to suffer for a few more days until finally the escorts arrived to take them back to the emperor's palace at Neflatraceous, the capital of the Lìsztbrùnést Empire.

~~~~~~

Everywhere the emperor took his grandson they were impressed. He caught on fast and was a natural diplomat and caring person.
~~~~~~

The biggest surprise to the public when on one trip Lacsar said to the emperor during the planning meeting, "Grandfather, I want to take Rascal-II with me on this trip."

Lacsar then explained how he could wear a shoulder pad for Rascal-II to perch on. The emperor decided that since his grandson had turned into a great team player and took his diplomatic instructions quite well and acted on them like a professional, he would accommodate him on this trip. Part of his rationale was to minimize the sadness Lacsar was showing in a growing manner day by day because Starlight was gone.

With several shoulder pads quickly assembled and demonstrated, they were ready to travel. Per Lacsar's instructions the staff put a perch and a basket in his space cabin on the Royal Space Yacht. Rascal-II and Lacsar were almost inseparable. They had transcended to a strong relationship. Lacsar knew most emphatically Rascal-II would give his life if necessary to protect him.

One of the Frigates sent a shuttle down to the surface of planet Ollytrene and Drákōlìné was called to the shuttle to receive instructions.

"What do you want?"

"From the emperor himself, get Rascal-II and bring him here and let him know we are taking him to Prince Demetrius Ravik who has requested him. Rascal-II is to inform the other birds he's leaving and to continue their vigilance protecting the young empress, Starlight."

Starlight telepathically detected the shuttle pilot's conversation with Drákōlìné and walked over to bird perches where Rascal-II already knew what she wanted to say before she spoke her telepathic sentence.

"It's all been arranged; I must leave now." Rascal-II said then flew over to the shuttle and hopped inside ready to go to his brother Lacsar's need.

~~~~~

Rascal-II was transferred via a shuttle to the Royal Yacht that had a transporter for the bird and everything he needed.

The Royal Yacht with a small Armada of two Cruisers and four Fast Frigates transited to the Flavian Solar system where the planet Carvlesis existed. This planet was the home of the green skinned Carvlesis civilization.

The Carvlesis people were quite unusual in appearance with purple eyes and reddish-brown hair. Carvlesis women were admired by men throughout the galaxy as the sexiest creatures that ever existed since physical contact with them gave a plain humanoid enhanced sexual desires. The chemicals female Carvlesis women excreted during copulation was a strong aphrodisiac more powerful than any other known substance.

Carvlesis diplomats who received the Lìsztbrùnést Royals were not enthused and were merely being polite for galactic politics. Carvlesis people didn't particularly care for plain skin people as they felt an utter lack of attraction in any manner. When Lacsar showed up with Rascal-II on his shoulder the Carvlesis diplomats were taken back a few notches as this unexpected behavior caught them completely off guard and the King's daughter just a couple years older than Lacsar immediately showed great fascination.

The Carvlesis diplomatic corps set up a reception and a meeting and it appeared very simple since only four Lìsztbrùnést arrived in the shuttle including Emperor Cornelius, Lacsar and his Valet Octavrator, and Admiral Timons.

Due to the strange brain patterns of the Carvlesis, the Emperor
~~~~~

and Lacsar were unable to penetrate their minds to determine what their motives really were. Perhaps it was because of the unique wiring of the Carvlesis brains, Rascal-II was able to penetrate Carvlesis minds and data mine their thoughts and understand their intentions.

In the negotiations, Rascal-II was telepathically briefing Lacsar who seemed to be able to ask very poignant questions to Carvlesis diplomats.

Emperor Cornelius was extremely impressed with the way Lacsar presented himself and seemed to force a lot of discussion out into the open, including some items Carvlesis diplomats hoped to not come up during the discussions.

The strenuous negotiations went on for an hour and in cases in this manner, both sides expect a quid pro quo. Emperor Cornelius planned to not fall into that quid pro quo trap because it always becomes counter productive in the end. It was Lacsar who suggested a modus vivendi and set down the conditions. Emperor Cornelius looked at Lacsar and Rascal-II and seriously wondered how his grandson came up with the idea.

Since they were not making any progress in the negotiations because the Carvlesis were extremely good and tough negotiators, and no headway seemed possible, Emperor Cornelius then presented the modus vivendi precisely the way Lacsar had suggested.

The lead Carvlesis negotiator was completely taken off guard and felt a strange inducement and then said, "We will take into serious consideration this modus vivendi and present it to the King Carlatar. We will have an answer for you later before the dinner King Carlatar is arranging for you."

"We'll be looking forward to hear the King's response."

The meeting was then adjourned and the Carvlesis princess approached Lacsar and had some strange feelings for him with the bird perched on his shoulder.

Nobody in the room had ever seen the princess approach a male before. She was thought to be completely hypoactive in sexual desire and frigid. King Carlatar was advised his daughter was most likely a nonlibidoist, which put his monarchy at risk with nobody to inherit his throne.

"You have a very beautiful bird," princess Arabella said when she got near Lacsar.

"His name is Rascal-II and is one of my best friends."

"Would it be possible to touch him and pet him?"

"Yes, I think he would like your touch."

Rascal-II was penetrating Arabella's mind giving her pleasure in ways she seldom felt. If it wasn't for the fact, Lacsar was in love with Starlight, Arabella could easily have seduced the young man and would then be part of two monarchies.

Arabella had a couple pet birds that were caged up now because she was away from them.

"I have a couple pet birds; would you like to see them?"

"Sure."

The Carvlesis princess Arabella led Lacsar toward a hallway that would take them to the princess private quarters. She saw Lacsar's Valet Octavrator who had been standing by Lacsar stopped and asked Lacsar, "Why is he following you?"

"It's a requirement, he's part of my security detail."

"Don't be ridiculous you are perfectly safe with me."

"I prefer him to stay with me."

"What if I decide to have romance with you in privacy, would you want him watching?"

"That's probably not going to happen today since I barely know you."

"Well, I've already decided I like you and would let you do anything to me you desired."

"My desire is to get to know you and become friends before we would ever consider something beyond that."

"That statement just made me more attracted to you. I've never met a male person before that ever gave me the vibrations you give me."

"I'm flattered to hear that, but I know I do not deserve such comments."

"You do, don't underestimate yourself."

The three people turned into five people as Arabella suddenly had increased security and the group followed her into her private quarters where she walked over to a couple bird cages, she put the birds in when she was out of the room.

Arabella opened the cages and the birds hopped on her arms as she carried them over to a perch, she had for them that had been installed with sanitation collectors a foot below the perch to catch all bird droppings including shells for some of their nuts they enjoyed.

The two birds were noticeably calm which was seldom when others entered the room.

Arabella said, "I've never seen these birds act this way when several people are in the room. This is quite extraordinary."

Rascal-II started telepathic communiques with the two birds as soon as they entered the room. The birds were quite surprised to see Rascal-II sitting on top of Lacsar's shoulder pad rig. The birds looked at each other and remained very quiet and calm.

Would you like to sit down? Arabella pointed towards a nice sofa with a coffee table She had a chair on the other side so she could entertain friends and guests.

"Yes, but first I think Rascal-II would like to sit up on that perch with your birds."

"Sure, lets see if they get along."

Lacsar walked near the perch and Rascal-II jumped off his shoulder onto the perch by one of the other two birds.

Arabella's two birds turned and stared at Rascal-II as if they were in a trance. One of Arabella's birds moved closer to Rascal-II and continued studying him. Arabella didn't know that Rascal-II was telepathically communicating to the bird that was responding favorably.

Lacsar walked back and sat down on the sofa next to his Valet Octavrator.

Lacsar and Arabella had on a name tag attached to their clothing as everyone did that was attending this conference so people would know each other's names written in standard Lìsztbrùnést on one line and in Carvlesis on the next line.

The birds seemed content and quiet in their own little world and Lacsar quickly ignored them focusing on Arabella.

"Tell me Lacsar what is your favorite pastime back in your worlds?"

"I like collecting and studying gems."

"That's kind of interesting."

Lacsar brought along a gift in the event he made a new friend and pulled out a Green Tourmaline Gemstone with an oval cut. The 24 surfaces on the upper half of the gemstone gave it a surreal multiplication of light panes that transited through the stone. He handed the stone almost 26 millimeters in width to Arabella and said, "I would like to give this to you. Its one of the gems I found and had cut."

Lacsar handed the gemstone to Arabella who was quickly mesmerized by it and as her two birds saw the reflection and prismed effects, they turned staring at the gemstone.

Arabella took the beautiful Green Tourmaline Gemstone and studied the oval cut. She quickly responded, "Nobody has ever given me such a beautiful gift before."

"It's my pleasure."

While Arabella fondled the gemstone, she continued in her conversation feeling somewhat elevated as Lacsar a few years younger than her seemed light years ahead of young men his age. His sophistication and suave surpassed a lot of grown men.

"We now have two things in common, birds, and I love this gemstone which I will always cherish."

Octavrator sat there in total politeness and quiet observed the young princess slowly melt away at the rapture of Lacsar. He could tell by her body language she was captivated and if she could somehow remove Octavrator from the picture she would have her way with Lacsar even at the risk of a scandal.

It was moments like this Octavrator had to protect Lacsar the most. It would not be the first nor the last time a beautiful princess and daughter of a powerful Kingdom would seek the romance of Lacsar. But the decision had been made and too much had developed already with Starlight to reverse course now. Especially since official proclamations had been published.

Lacsar penetrated Arabella's mind with his strong telepathy and discovered her strong desires. She was still a virgin and wanted to lose her virginity to Lacsar. She was a princess in heat. Lacsar put forth a maximum effort to console Arabella and diminish her flagrant desires. He wished he could accommodate her lust and eagerness and even liked her, but he was a very bright person and realized he had traveled down the path with Starlight too far to change his destiny now. But he could at least extend to Arabella plutonic love which he did, and Arabella didn't understand how she knew that but realized the sophisticated person sitting across from her had affected her like no person ever before. Plus, he was a genuine intriguing person unlike anyone she met before. *Was that why she was so emotionally struck by this handsome young man?*

The two talked for more than an hour including ordering refreshments. As part of that Lacsar requested a small bowl of water for Rascal-II who informed Lacsar via telepathic communication was dehydrated that nobody else could hear.

Arabella was quite curious to observe Lacsar hold the small bowl of water near Rascal-II on the perch, while Rascal-II drank from it. The two other birds were also watching and soon Rascal-II moved to the side and one of the other two birds approached the bowl and drank from it just like Rascal had done.

Lacsar was wearing a cape which hid his wings. Arabella had no idea he was a bird man.

"I would like to take Rascal outside so he can fly and take care of business."

Arabella said, "Of course whatever you would like to do."

Rascal-II immediately flew over and landed on Lacsar's shoulder pad and Octavrator stood up near Lacsar.

"Why don't you bring your two birds with us, they can fly with Rascal-II."

Arabella was afraid to do so and said, "They might fly away."

"Don't worry, Rascal-II will bring them back to you."

Arabella put her two birds into a carrying cage and they

proceeded to walk out to the beautifully landscaped parklike Carvlesis King's castle.

They walked out to some permanent seating where guests could relax and had tables to hold their drinks. Arabella put the bird cage down and said, "If I lose these birds, I will be very sad if they fly away."

"Rascal-II will make sure you will not lose them. Do not fear." Lacsar then applied mental telepathy to reassure Arabella and calm her nerves.

The moment of truth now occurred, she opened the bird cage and the two birds exited and stayed on the tabletop staring at Rascal-II.

Lacsar turned to his Valet Octavrator and said, "Could you please help me take off the cape."

"It will be my honor your Highness."

Arabella was in for a huge surprise as Lacsar unfurled his wings then took to the sky with Rascal-II following in formation and Arabella's two birds following in formation.

The security men didn't know if they should shoot the creature and just as one of them was starting to point a laser rifle at Lacsar, one of the Lìsztbrùnést bodyguards saw the weapon and yelled, "Do not shoot Prince Demetrius Ravik or we'll have a war, and this planet will be wiped out!"

The security man lowered his weapon and with an incredulous look on his face asked, "Is that really Prince Demetrius Ravik?"

"Yes, that is Prince Demetrius Ravik the future emperor and known as Lacsar."

The security man trembled slightly when he realized his actions almost resulted in a tragedy and his King Carlatar would likely severely punish him for what he just did.

"I'm sorry we should have briefed you the prince had wings and could fly," the Lìsztbrùnést security official stated.

The security men watched intently the young prince flying around with the three birds in a circle for a few moments then landed right next to Arabella. The three birds landed on the table next to the cage in perfect alignment.

"You are extraordinary. I want to get to know you a lot more," Arabella stated in the sincerest manner.

"There is no reason why we cannot be friends, but you must know I am a busy person and have a lot of commitments. Our visits will most likely be rare."

"Alright, I will enjoy you when I can."

The security detail shook up a lot of nerves and soon Arabella's governess came out to the outdoors sitting area and said in the most profound manner, "Princess, you and your guests have been ordered back into the castle immediately."

The governess didn't explain what it was about, but Lacsar reading her mind with telepathic investigation determined he had almost been shot by a trigger finger happy security guard who didn't get authorization to brandish his weapon in the direction of the princess and her guests. Lacsar was shaken when he discovered how close he came to being killed. He now had an appreciation for procedures.

Rascal-II directed the two birds to get into their cage which they did immediately to the surprise of the Arabella. The group then followed the governess back into the castle where Lascar was separated from Arabella and immediately taken to Emperor Cornelius who already had the reports. Had the emperor not had the insight to post his security men side by side with Carvlesis security agents, the heir to his throne would now be dead.

Carvlesis King Carlatar said to Emperor Cornelius, "The

security man who pointed the laser rifle at you grandson will be severely punished."

Lacsar standing beside his grandfather intervened.

"Your excellency may I ask you for a favor?"

King Carlatar looked at Lacsar with an inquisitive look and replied, "What would you like Prince Demetrius Ravik?"

"Please do not punish your security man. It's all my fault for assuming I could do what I did not thinking about the possibilities. I will feel terrible if anything bad happens to that man. Perhaps the best thing for him is to bring him to me now to meet me."

King Carlatar didn't know why he felt compelled to respond favorably to Prince Demetrius Ravik but quickly agreed and turned to his personnel valet and directed him, "Bring the security man to us."

Emperor Cornelius caught the manipulations that Lacsar was doing telepathically to King Carlatar and realized his grandson was in fact a master manipulator and wondered, *has he manipulated me?*

The security man appeared like he saw a ghost when he arrived and was in total fright because he thought he would be severely punished if not executed for pointing a very capable laser rifle with computerized targeting at Prince Demetrius Ravik, he didn't know could fly.

Lacsar spoke softly to the man and said, "This incident was not your fault. You were doing what you thought you had to do to protect princess Arabella. I want you to relax and not worry about anything because King Carvlesis has promised me nothing bad will happen to you."

"Thank you, your excellency," the man responded in total fear slowly realizing he might somehow escape torture and possible execution for his terribly dumb actions.

"I want you to do one thing for me now," Lacsar said in a calm soft voice.

"What is that your Excellency?"

"I want you to smile and be happy today because nothing happened. I'm happy that you were thinking about princess Arabella's safety, and I imagine what I did was terribly confusing and frightening to the security detachment."

"Yes sir, I will try to smile."

"Good it will make me feel better if you feel happy today."

Lacsar held out his hand to the security official who now had watery eyes and they shook hands.

The security man bowed then turned and departed promptly not wanting to break down in front of everyone.

King Carvlesis was struck at the sophistication of how Lacsar handled the situation. This was turning out to be an auspicious visit afterall.

When Arabella returned to her private quarters, she showed the gem that Lacsar gave her earlier to her governess.

"That is very beautiful, and it came from the future Lìsztbrùnést Emperor, so it is extra special," the Governess said in a very pleasant tone.

"I want this mounted on a necklace so I can wear it at dinner tonight," Arabella replied.

The governess replied, "We have a fashion expert on the staff who is standing by to support preparations for the dinner tonight, I'm sure he can have it mounted on a necklace in time."

"Thank you."

The governess left Arabella's quarters carrying the gemstone and went to work promptly on the task of arranging for the mounting in time for the dinner party.

The emperor asked everyone to leave their guest suite except Lacsar.

When the two men were alone, Emperor Cornelius said in telepathic communications, "The room is probably bugged so we need to communicate telepathically for this discussion."

"Yes grandfather, what do you want to talk to me about."

"Lacsar you should know by now every movement you make or anything you say probably has a way of getting back to me. You can't keep secrets from me. I know princess Arabella is attracted to you and is cunning and resourceful. She will do everything in her power to seduce you. I don't know how you touched her heart the way you did, but she is infatuated with you, and showing off your wings and flying only made matters worse.

"I'm sorry if I did something wrong grandfather."

"You didn't do anything wrong but you need to stay close by my side so I can protect you and prevent a scandal from erupting."

"Alright grandfather."

"If you and Arabella transcend into a romantic liaison, it will be impossible to cover it up. King Carvlesis himself would broadcast it around the galaxy because he would view the possibility of Arabella becoming the next Lìsztbrùnést Empress a great achievement for her life."

"Alright grandfather, I understand."

"Also, I want you to know about some other developments."

"Such as what grandfather?"

"Starlight is not doing to well being separated from you. Today she informed her mother and Drákōlìné she can no longer tolerate being away from you and has asked she be returned immediately to Neflatraceous."

Lacsar looked at his grandfather with an amazing look of astonishment. He was suddenly emotional but poised and said, "Thank you grandfather it means a lot to me to be able to see her again real soon."

"Princess Arabella is going to try very hard to seduce you tonight, you need to fight off all the inducements and entanglements because when you meet Starlight in a few days, if you make the wrong move now, it will cripple your relationship.

"Grandfather, may I make a request?"

"What would you like?"

"As soon as the dinner is over can we return to Neflatraceous?"

"We had some diplomatic mumbo jumbo scheduled for tomorrow, but under the circumstances I agree with your request, is quite appropriate under the circumstances."

"Thank you."

"We'll have to give them some excuse such as you are not feeling well."

"Actually, thinking about Starlight, I'm not feeling well."

"Love is sometimes painful. Especially when you can't be with the one you love."

Knowing the room was bugged and they were being monitored, Emperor Cornelius had to speak and give the listeners something to pass on to their handlers.

"I'm going to now tell you something with my voice so those listening to us will think this is the reason for this private meeting."

"Alright grandfather, I understand."

"Lacsar, I wanted to talk to you about today's events before I forgot what I wanted to say to you," Emperor Cornelius said in open voice.

"What is it you want to tell me grandfather?"

"I wanted you to know you did nothing wrong today. We had our checks and balances at work and our security people prevented the disaster."

"Thank you for telling me this."

"Sometimes things happen that are mind boggling and there is no rational explanation to it like why that security man thought he should shoot you. But that's life and explains how accidents sometimes happen when people make the wrong assumptions and do things at the spur of the moment they would regret later."

"I understand grandfather."

"I want you to feel you did nothing wrong but also, I want to congratulate you on how you handled it. You were kind and courteous and protected that man's life. I was very proud of the way you handled yourself today."

"Well, I certainly didn't want something bad happening to that man, that would stain our visit with something that wasn't necessary."

"I'm delighted you think that way."

"Thank you, grandfather."

"Alright, we are going to have to get ready for tonight's event and you will have to let Rascal know that he cannot go to the dinner with us because it might irritate some of the guests."

"I'm sure Rascal will understand."

"Good, I'm going to go meet the King now for some private discussions, Octavrator will be here soon to help you prepare for the dinner."

The emperor departed and Lacsar informed Rascal, "I suppose you know you will remain here during the dinner time."

"I understand, there are many civilizations that are not ready to be near birds."

"We will have a lot of happiness in a few days when Starlight returns."

"I'm sure she really misses you."

"I can't begin to describe to you how much I miss her."

"I will be happy to be flying with you in formation again when we return home."

Preparations were started a while later as the young prince was fitted with his royal uniform already sporting a few medals and decorations commemorating his space patrols he made with Admiral Timons, and the admiral was wearing an identical uniform except with considerably more medals and medallions.

~~~~~~

A while later Emperor Cornelius returned and observed everyone was ready to proceed and nodded at Octavrator who knew to go outside and inform the security personnel.

As soon as Octavrator informed the castle staff, they were ready, an escort of four well dressed military men at the entrance to their suite appeared and led them to the grand dining hall that had over 50 guests from the aristocracy of Carvlesis society. The guests formed a line for introductions to Emperor Cornelius and prince Demetrius Ravik (aka Lacsar). Behind the emperor and prince walked valet Octavrator followed by Admiral Timons.
~~~~~~

After they went down the line and met all the guests they mingled for a while. Lacsar looked around and noticed Arabella was nowhere to be seen. Even though he was going to avoid her spider web, he still was disappointed he had not seen her.

After cocktails and a lot of conversations going on in parallel, the guests were invited to their seats at the tables with placards set out for each guest who was escorted to their seating arrangements by a dozen valets performing due diligence in the matter. Emperor Cornelius and Demetrius Ravik was taken to one of the tables that only had six place settings. The other tables slightly larger had fifteen or more.

A royal valet seated each person including the young prince. The orchestra set up to play soft dinner music suddenly played a military march. At the main entrance came King Carlatar with eight military escorts with his daughter Arabella whose arm had hooked through her father's arm escorting her to the table.

Arabella was wearing a champagne-colored evening gown with a slit down one side revealing a lot of leg and a backless design. The entire ensemble was personified by the extremely beautiful necklace Arabella was wearing with the gem mounted that Lacsar gave her earlier.

After observing how extravagant Arabella appeared, Emperor Cornelius was more than happy to leave the planet after dinner because Lacsar would be the victim of this black widow who would sink her fangs into Lacsar and never let him go.

Arabella's beauty and charisma were utterly astonishing. But Emperor Cornelius knew this was one of many mine fields Lacsar had to navigate carefully as to not wreck his future by making dangerous decisions.

What saved Lacsar that night was his grandfather's news that Starlight would be back in his arms in just a few more days. He found solace in that and even though he was charmed at dinner he avoided the web Arabella placed before him. Lacsar penetrating Arabella's with his telepathic powers discovered her great desires for him and Lascar then understood now why his grandfather had that private meeting with him.

Arabella appeared seductive and tantalizing and her thoughts were unbelievable, as Lacsar discovered every one of her motives. If he didn't already have Starlight, he would easily descend into an expansive expression of emotional bonding and horizontal Tango with Arabella on a theme from Paganini.

To Arabella the meal was insignificant the only thing she wanted to consume was the passions of Lacsar as her motives and intuition developed a great desire that created a spellbinding like environment for Lacsar as he probed her mind and discovered her feelings.

This was a nurturing process for Lacsar, and the emperor was proud of how his grandson was handling the matter. Any other warm-blooded male would have succumbed to the desires of the black widow Arabella.

The dinner went well, the music and the ambience were perfect. Even though Lacsar was not going to give Arabella what she wanted including sexual intercourse, he appreciated the loveliness she directed at him.

The fact Arabella had the gem mounted on the beautiful necklace in time for dinner underscored her growing passions that Lacsar knew would turn to bitter sadness when he departed. Lacsar knew Arabella's feelings included she wanted to spend as much time with him as possible.

Lacsar had other responsibilities now. His first and foremost responsibility was to his grandfather who eventually needed a descendant to maintain the monarchy and ensure the empire did not collapse due to mismanagement. It would be a daunting challenge. It takes character to walk away from love and fulfill responsibilities. Emperor Cornelius was acutely monitoring every moment and had instructed Octavrator how to proceed and not let Lacsar out of his site and informed him their secret plan to leave right after dinner to make sure there were no *accidents*.

The meal went by without a hitch though King Carlatar was concerned his daughter wasn't eating much and consumed all her focus on Lacsar. It was unmistakable what King Carlatar's observation of his daughter's body language wanted. He would assist her to the extent he could, but he also knew Emperor Cornelius had his own agenda and Arabella might not be part of his plans.

In some way, King Carlatar was also glad the Lìsztbrùnést Royals left right after dinner so that Arabella's emotions could be contained in a simpler manner. King Carlatar knew that if the two had crossed over the line and did the unthinkable such as copulating, the consequences would be disastrous because Emperor Cornelius certainly did not want his grandson to be too distracted by outsiders when so much of his empire was at stake. Lacsar (Demetrius Ravik), had a lot of responsibility, and a romance with Arabella now would not be feasible in the near future.

King Carlatar nor did anyone else present except for Emperor Cornelius, Octavrator and Admiral Timons knew Lacsar had already committed to another female. That commitment had gone past the point of no return. It was too late to make other accommodations as Starlight was now his chosen future bride.

Arabella and Lacsar didn't say too much and didn't need to because Lacsar knew all her thoughts and he was polite to her. Arabella was coy and scheming and was calculating the best way to get Lacsar into her bed to deflower her and make the beginning of a relationship. Lacsar knew her sexual desires and had some reflective reinforcement, but his thoughts of Starlight showing up in a couple days slowly consumed his heart, mind, and soul. This was the very first battle in Arabella's life she would lose, but it would not be her last.

The evening slowly came to an end and the Royals went back to their suite and then Emperor Cornelius walked outside the door to the suite and informed the security guards, "My grandson isn't feeling well. We are leaving now. Please escort us to our waiting shuttle outside the castle."

The security informed King Carlatar that Lìsztbrùnést Emperor Cornelius, and his group were at the front entrance as the King approached in great alarm. Hearing the prince was not feeling well disturbed him in his first thoughts were: the prince might have been poisoned by someone involved in nefarious activity. He escorted the emperor and the prince who looked perfectly fine to the waiting shuttle and said goodbye. Arabella heard the reports and ran as fast as she could to the entrance and saw the shuttle leave. She fell to the floor and started weeping.

Shortly after Emperor Cornelius' armada was outside the solar system heading home, King Carvlesis received a communique from Emperor Cornelius thanking him for his hospitality and enjoyed the time spent there.

King Carlatar didn't see much of Arabella the next few days as she was keeping to herself but when she finally was seen walking around the castle, Arabella was wearing that necklace with gem that Lacsar had given her. King Carvlesis asked, "Where did you get that?"

"Prince Demetrius Ravik gave the gem to me as a gift, I had the staff mount it on a necklace for me."

"Did you develop feelings for Prince Demetrius Ravik?"

"Yes, father if he wanted to make love to me, I would have let him do it."

"Is that why you have been depressed lately?"

"It is but I'm getting over it. I know it wasn't his decision to abandon me."

The king now knew more than he wanted and now it became crystal clear why the two had that intensive stare at each other. Then he shuddered thinking the repercussions had the security man shot Lacsar with his laser rifle.

~~~~~
~~~~~

Chapter Sixteen

Home Coming

Lacsar arrived back to the palace a few hours before Starlight and his sister. In his world wind tour of these other planets, he was introduced to green and blue skin women who offered to teach him sex in front of Emperor Cornelius. Lacsar politely declined and simply waited for the love of his life.

Lacsar was slightly emotional as he was waiting for Starlight to return. He was lucky that Rascal-II was with him as he had a companion to be with and take his mind off things. He felt bad that he had to leave Anabella the way he did as he truly liked her. But he also understood fully the possible consequences of remaining near her any longer. Her desires were simply too great, and he wasn't quite sure he could have stopped her advancements before they reached a point of no return. Then he would have to deal with breaking Starlight's heart which would also be a huge negative event in his life. It was now clear to him without his grandfather's help, he might not have been able to avoid that outcome.

The Royals didn't know exactly when Starlight would return and Lacsar was so worked up emotionally, he decided that since he had to take Rascal-II back outdoors so he could return to his natural environment, he might as well get in some exercises and work on his wing strength.

Lacsar and Rascal-II flew around the open area in a brisk manner burning off all the energy he could because the delay in seeing Starlight was agonizingly unpleasant. Right when he was around the ten-mile mark Rascal-II said to Lacsar via mental telepathy, "We need to land, you have a visitor."

Lacsar and Rascal-II flew over to their normal landing zone and there she was. Starlight was standing there alone and had asked Drákōlìné to give her some space. Drákōlìné walked back a healthy distance to allow the two some privacy in their conversation.

Starlight was made up and dressed up in the most extravagant manner. Emperor Cornelius sent a private message to Drákōlìné explaining to her that princess Arabella played for Lacsar's heart and he wanted Starlight made up in the most beautiful manner by the best makeup artist and fashion designer. They fulfilled the emperor's wish and with her natural beauty, the additives strengthened Starlight's image which very easily eliminated and lingering feelings Lacsar had for Arabella.

The two approached each other and the affection was multiplied on each step forward. They embraced and kissed. There was no lingering doubt in anyone's mine the affection between the two.

The emperor was very happy that Starlight returned when she did to erase any possible memory of Arabella who Lacsar reluctantly left behind. Lacsar also realized that based on his intrusion into Arabella's thoughts via mental telepathy, she had never felt that way towards a male before and unlikely she would ever again. Her emotional attraction to Lacsar was too great to allow her to freely give her heart again to anyone without considerable efforts on the part of the male.

Emperor Cornelius understood he could not hide the near tragedy from Lacsar's parents because eventually they would know because of their own mental telepathy so while Lacsar and Starlight were rekindling their fantastic love, Stanley and Princess Lì were shown the surveillance video and given a full explanation of how close it came to their son getting killed. At first, they were horrified, but as reality set in and the knowledge the emperor's security detail was in position to prevent the catastrophe, they realized checks and balances worked out.

The emperor then said, "On all future visits the security detachment would brief the host security apparatus about Lacsar's ability to fly and to be careful in how they reacted if they saw a human with wings flying around. And he also conveyed, "Lacsar will eventually become the emperor, I have no choice but to continue introducing him to other world leaders."

"That stands to reason father," Princess Lì replied.

The emperor then saw no other way than to simply divulge Lacsar's involvement with Arabella.

"Lacsar knew trouble was brewing and he asked that we leave early which led to our early departure."

"What about the future, this is probably not going to be the only time a Royal from another empire attempts the same seduction."

"I have a solution," the emperor offered.

"What is that father?"

"On future trips to other worlds, Lacsar and Starlight will travel together so there would never be another black widow trying to seduce my grandson as he will be preoccupied with Starlight."

Princess Lì knew that Starlight was having her periods and could get pregnant and brought up the point, "What if on one of these trips they have sex and Starlight gets pregnant?"

"There is a simple solution, they simply undergo an immediate unification," the emperor said.

"But they are kind of young for such a situation."

"I've not divulged everything to you, nor do I intend to do so. Lacsar is way beyond his physical age in intellect."

"He still has a lot of growing up before we think he should be fathering children."

"He's done many things which demonstrated to me his intelligence level and common sense is very advanced for a person his age. They will eventually spend the rest of their lives together so if he gets her pregnant, don't worry about it."

"I'm not sure he's ready for all that."

"He is quite capable of fulfilling his requirements and will in due time be well prepared to be the emperor. He doesn't need to be non-unified when he ascends to the throne."

Princess Lì was now very unhappy about Lacsar's situation but realized his manifest destiny was in his own hands and all they could do at this point was to give him good advice and hope he took the prudent course.

In a few days when Starlight communicated to her mother, she explained how she was so relieved to be back with Lacsar and she was now feeling so much better.

Her mother knew that when the two young Royals got back together, Starlight would return to her normal happy self after watching her steadily decline in spirits in her final days visiting Ollytrene.

Lacsar had good advisors and his Valet Octavrator indoctrinated him in why it was necessary for him to abstain from having sex with Starlight because their lives would ultimately be much better off if they waited a few more years. Lacsar being very attuned to his development and demonstrating his calm and intelligent approach to all aspects of his life, knew this important pathway forward was the most appropriate.

Even though Starlight eventually let Lacsar know she would allow him to deflower her any time he wanted, he impressed her by saying, "I want to save that special moment for our official unification and celebrate our unification with our parents before we lose our virginity. But after Unification we will make love as often as you wish."

Starlight was very happy that Lacsar had such a good head on his shoulders, and he was always teaching her many things she would never know, or experience otherwise had Lacsar not discovered her, and she remained on Ollytrene with no such opportunity.

For the next few years, they grew up together as best friends in love and there were many moments they kissed and hugged and lived to enjoy every single day together.

As stipulated by the emperor, they went together on the next stops at planets to meet their leaders. While out in space the three traveled on separate spaceships to ensure the progeny of the empire.

In some of those planetary visits, it turned out to be a safety valve having Starlight with them and with her makeup artists and fashion designers, they made her appear so exquisite that other Kings' daughters were no longer a threat to derail Lacsar and change his future. Some of those young women were very attractive and would do about any scheme possible to hook Lacsar, but he always stayed close to Starlight. And in the few times they slept on the planet, the two slept together without having sex which thwarted all ingenious attempts. It's kind of hard to crawl in bed with a male when he already has a woman in his arms.

~~~~~~

Time crept by and after a few more years the royal couple eventually reached the age when the emperor decided they were old enough to Unify. They were now well educated, completely secure in their relationship and their mental telepathy had grown strong.
~~~~~~

The emperor sitting in his suite having made the decision asked Lucas to bring Lacsar and Starlight to his suite he wanted to have a private talk with them.

The two had just finished working out flying with the flock and cleaned up and dressed in Royal attire that Lucas initiated to prepare them for the meeting with Emperor Cornelius.

Lucas left Lacsar's suite with him and walked the short distance to Starlight's suite where the chambermaids had her prepared and expected Lucas at any moment.

Starlight was a little apprehensive for the sudden unexpected private meeting with Emperor Cornelius. The fact Princess Li and Stanley were invited not to attend added a totally mysterious aspect to it that added to some anxiety that Starlight now felt.

The chambermaids opened Starlight's double door to her suite and bowed. Lucas standing outside bowed towards Starlight and said, "You look quite lovely, the emperor will be very pleased to see you."

Lucas then marched the couple down to the emperor's suite with Octavrator following behind boxing them in and preventing anyone including the parents from interfering.

As soon as Lucas was at the door to the emperor's suite the security man posted outside opened the door and only the couple went inside. Octavrator and Lucas remained outside in a respectful stance to intercept Princess Li and Stanley had they approached.

"Please have a seat," Emperor Cornelius stated and pointed towards the sofa across from the coffee table where the emperor sat in a well-padded throne like chair.

The couple sat down, and Emperor Cornelius was smiling and full of happiness, for this important day.

"I am very pleased with how the two of you have grown and

educated yourselves. Your development has been phenomenal and inspirational. I'm honored to have you as my family. Now its time we chart a new path in your lives."

Lacsar could not conceive of anything further the emperor could throw at them for their development since what they had already experienced was very extensive.

"Grandfather what do you have in mind?" Lacsar asked attempting to probe his grandfather telepathically but was blocked. The emperor was ready for him.

"I believe the two of you are intelligent enough and developed well enough to where now is the time for you to start your Unification."

Lacsar was stunned hearing this from his grandfather!

Lacsar couldn't believe what was now transpiring, and he had no idea when this day would come or what possibly could constitute the trigger point for the emperor to draw this conclusion.

Starlight was tearing up slightly. Emperor Cornelius knew he had emotionally struck her. Just like Lacsar she had no idea when this day would come or what measures would make the determination it was time. Starlight was totally caught off guard and she was now emotional and could not hold it back.

Lacsar saw Starlight's transcendence and grabbed her hand and held it and looked her in the eyes and said telepathically, "Please do not cry and screw up your makeup during this important moment."

"I can't help it. You have no idea what I feel right now."

"Is there anything I can do to put a smile on your face?"

"You already do it every day."

The two lovebirds thought their communications were private, but the emperor overheard every bit of it. But he knew he needed to get Lacsar to ask the question, so he telepathically jolted Lacsar with a telepathic question: "Don't you think you need to ask her the question now?"

Lacsar turned to his grandfather with the most astonishing look on his face and looked into his eyes for a moment then turned towards Starlight and then it started.

"Starlight I love you more than anything, would you please Unify with me."

Starlight then totally lost it and threw her arms around Lacsar and really started crying. She was super emotional now and held onto Lacsar as if it was the end of the world.

Lacsar held Starlight and allowed her to sob for a while.

The emperor was very patient and knew the flood gates had opened and it was only a natural reaction for a woman in love to receive her wish come true. He knew it would be best to allow them to come to terms with the question and act accordingly.

In a few minutes when Starlight calmed herself down, she pulled away from Lacsar and held the side of his face with her hand and said, "That is the most beautiful question you ever asked me. I love you with all my heart and I will give you whatever you ask."

"Does that mean you are willing to go through Unification now?"

"Yes, my dear love."

The crying had totally screwed up Starlight's face. Her makeup was ruined and Lacsar knew that when they left the emperor's suite, she had to look her best because the entire staff would soon descend upon them. Because of his vast intellect and analysis, he said what he had to.

"Grandfather, this is one of the most important decisions of our lives. When we leave here, we will soon be meeting my parents and the staff. This has been a very emotional time for Starlight, and I fully understand she had an emotional spike which was unavoidable. But I think when we leave your suite, Starlight must be looking her best because of everyone will come up to us. Would it be possible for you to have her makeup artists come here and patch her up before we leave and meet everyone?"

"That's not a problem Lacsar."

The emperor's artificial intelligence always listening and looking out for the emperor's needs said softly in the background, "Emperor Cornelius would you like Lucas to come into the room to make those arrangements?"

"Yes, please send Lucas in."

Lucas received via his wireless a moment later instruction and the security man in his ear bud was directed to open the door for Lucas so he could enter.

"Yes, your Excellency, what would you like me to do?"

"Go and get Starlight's makeup artists and bring them down here right away they need to work on Starlight to fix her makeup before the Royal Couple leave here."

"It will be my distinct pleasure, your Excellency."

Lucas then exited the suite to go get the makeup artists who were on hot standby and totally surprised to be summoned by artificial intelligence.

Emperor Cornelius then stood up walked over to a cabinet and pulled out three glasses and sat them on a golden tray and took a bottle that was sitting there he had prepared for himself knowing this would be an emotional time for him as well, and poured three glasses and took them over to the coffee table and sat the tray down and handed one to Starlight then one to Lacsar and said,

"This elixir has some additives that will help us all maintain our emotions better. "

The emperor then raised his glass and said, "This is a toast to the next emperor and empress."

The couple raised their glasses and with perfect etiquette they were trained in copied the emperor's actions and swallowed the content then sat the glasses down on the golden tray and were now smiling. The content hit them with a very pleasant feeling.

Moments later Lacsar returned with two makeup artists and one of them was carrying a folding chair that allowed Starlight to sit higher so they could perform their magic more efficiently.

In due time after Starlight's makeup was fixed, the emperor said, "I think your parents are out in the Courtyard waiting for this meeting to be over, lets go out and give them the news."

The couple dutifully stood up and followed Emperor Cornelius out of his suite and then walked down the hallway leading out to the courtyard where Stanley and Princess Li were waiting with great interest in what that meeting was all about.

They could see the young couple were all smiles and the emperor led them up to Duke Ravik and Princess Lì Alìgrāwná and then said, "Lacsar has an announcement he would like to make."

With Starlight beaming with happiness, Lacsar said, "Mother and Father, a few moments ago I asked Starlight if she would be willing to Unify with me now and she agreed to do so."

Duke Ravik and Princess Lì Alìgrāwná approached Starlight and Princess Lì Alìgrāwná, threw her arms around Starlight, and said, "You have made me so very happy. I love you." The two women hugged, and Starlight fortified with the emperor's magic potion was able to hold back another flood gate of tears and smiled with great happiness showing. She released Starlight then walked a couple steps over and threw her arms around Lacsar and hugged him.

Princess Alessandra was summoned to the courtyard by Octavrator and told her what it was about. Alessandra ran up and threw her arms around Starlight and hugged her and said, "I'm so very happy for you Starlight."

As Starlight reflected on this moment she realized, Lacsar promised this when he first met her many years before. He had been kind to her ever since and they were no doubt the very best friends who grew up together with some rather incredible experiences.

The emperor sent word to Starlight's parents the Unification was to happen, and he personally would arrive to transport them to Neflatraceous so they could be present at the Official Royal Unification.

In less than a week Starlight's parents arrived at the emperor's mansion and Emperor Cornelius was beaming with smiles when Tonnerre and Chief Yuèliàng stepped down out of the Lìsztbrùnést Royal Space Yacht after he went to personally escort them for the Unification ceremony. Emperor Cornelius flew on the Battle Cruiser with Admiral Timons and the empress mother and father traveled aboard the Royal Space Yacht which he boarded on the way down to the planet.

Starlight's parents had their own suite, but Starlight was now a well-developed lady who was well educated, had traveled the galaxy with her true love and had slept with him on numerous occasions. She was not going to stay in her parents' suite as she had her own and wanted her privacy and her lovely princes' frequent visits late at night.

On a few nights before the unification, Tonnerre saw Lacsar depart Starlight's suite early in the morning with his sleeping attire on.

When Tonnerre visited with her daughter in the morning she asked, "Have the two of you been having sex?"

"No mother, we sleep together often but I'm saving my virginity until after the unification."

"Is that true?"

"Absolutely. A long time ago, Lacsar and I decided we wanted to make our unification night extra special. We decided the best way to do that and give our total love to each other would be after the ceremony. We feel it's a gift to ourselves to make that night extra special."

Tonnerre didn't know if she wanted to believe it, but her daughter had never lied to her a single time in her life and she was quite serious about this situation, it became crystal clear the two lovers had managed to do the impossible and showed great respect for each other. Tonnerre's admiration for Lacsar suddenly grew even more than it already was. He truly was an anomaly that comes along once in a lifetime and for many, never.

It surprised Tonnerre that Starlight was not frazzled or overly emotional hours before the unification. Tonnerre asked, "Why are you so calm? I would be on pins and needles."

"Mother, Lacsar, and I have been unified by our souls for many years. This is nothing more than a disclosure to the public we are now a couple."

"And you are not nervous in any manner?"

"No mother, because I already know the man I love, and he knows me. Our emotional transcendence happened over many years because you allowed us to grow up together. There are no surprises for us as we know what is in each other's heart. I'm very fond of Lacsar and you know I love him dearly. His feelings for me are the same. We have had numerous discussions in the past about everything we face and now the public will know we face it together."

Tonnerre hugged her daughter who had grown to be such an

intelligent woman.

Only a small segment of the emperor's court was invited to the unification, but it was recorded for the public. This was on Emperors orders to enhance security in the event some nefarious activity attempted to stop the unification because once completed, Starlight would be given the full honors of a top Royal as the designated future Empress.

Starlight's wedding gown and her makeup were provided by the best talent of the galaxy. Nobody would argue she was extremely beautiful and just as the emperor predicted based on the way her mother looked, she would turn out like her mother who was also an exquisite beauty.

Everyone was dressed and beautiful for the occasion. Tonnerre was a head turner, her natural beauty as well as the fashion designer and makeup artist created trembles in the emperor. Chief Yuèliàng also looked very distinguished, and his makeover made him look almost twenty years younger.

A color guard escorted Demetrius Ravik followed by Duke Ravik and Princess Lì Alìgrāwná to the elevated platform. They stood aside next to their son.

Princess Alessandra carrying a basket of flower petals was escorted next up to the platform and stood beside her parents.

Chief Yuèliàng and Tonnerre were escorted with Starlight that left gasps in the room when those attending saw the exquisite beauty of Mother and Daughter. Starlight stepped up to the platform and faced Lacsar. The calmness the two exhibited seemed almost supernatural. Little did the public know the two were in mental telepathy together saying things to each other that made them happy and they smiled. It wasn't drudgery, it was a relief that they finally could get this past them.

Now that everyone was present and standing where they had practiced and were ready for the ceremony, there were two dozen long trumpets on each side of the isle that blasted an exquisite melodic notification. Then the emperor with a dozen escorts walked up to the elevated platform then turned around facing the guests and the two to be unified. The ceremony was short and sweet. The emperor could declare the unification with one quick sentence and before he did, he looked at Starlight and asked, "Starlight, do you wish to be Unified with Demetrius Ravik?"

"Yes, I do."

Emperor Cornelius then looked at Lacsar and asked, "Demetrius Ravik, do you wish to be Unified with Starlight?"

"Yes, I do."

"Very well, as the emperor with the authority vested in me by Heaven and Neflatraceous, I pronounce you Demetrius Ravik and Starlight Unified."

The trumpets started blasting a tremendous melody. The newly Unified Royal Couple then turned to face the guests.

At the completion of the trumpet music, Princess Alessandra stepped in front of the platform and threw flower petals and slowly walked down the isle towards the main hallway the royal couple would walk and leading them with a walkway full of beautiful flower petals and left the area to go back to their honeymoon suite to change into their dinner clothes as a feast would soon commence. The other Royals and Starlight's parents followed and went to their suites to change clothes. They would all come back wearing Royal Celebration Attire that was the emperor's designated official attire for the most important events in empire activities.

The couple were given an hour to be by themselves to celebrate their unification. Starlight knew exactly what she wanted and didn't care how long it took. She had watched training videos of what she had to do and was more than ready to attempt. Lacsar was more than eager knowing they had complete privacy with guards and Valet Octavrator who would prevent any disturbance. This private hour was well understood as the official deflowering of the future Empress. In a brief period, the two lovers combined in that perfect choreography of tumultuous allegros and created transcendental explosive passions and gratification. The deed was done in the most romantic fashion full of love and kisses and it quickly felt to both the delay until after unification was well worth the wait. For that Starlight would always be grateful because it showed the character of Lacsar which proved his worth to her.

When they finished the deflowering act and love making, it was time to take a bath together and clean up and get ready for the next event. When artificial intelligence notified the chambermaids, they immediately went into the bathroom to assist the newlyweds bathe and get ready for the next event. Lacsar was easy to bathe and prepare, but Starlight required a little more time because it took a while to deal with her deflowering and restore her fabulous makeup to make the couple look distinguished.

When they were ready, the two newly Unified Royals departed their suite holding hands in love knowing one day this would happen.

Tonnerre approached her daughter Starlight and said, "Lacsar, could you please give me a moment with my mother?"

"Of course, my dear mother [as Lacsar often referred to Tonnerre]."

The two walked down the hallway together and mother and daughter faced each other.

"How is everything going?"

"Mother, I'm no longer a virgin and I'm grateful that Lacsar is such a gentleman he saved this for our unification day. I feel so wonderful feeling his love."

"I'm so glad to hear that. You look so beautiful, and you are so intelligent now."

"Lacsar spent many years educating me. I've learned so much with him. He's opened my eyes to a lot of things. He's the most wonderful person I met in my lifetime."

"How do you feel with those wings?"

"My wings are strong now. I can fly with Lacsar anywhere. Also, I'm going to tell you something in total confidence."

"Alright dear."

"Lacsar taught me how to talk with the birds. I'm very close to Rascal-II now who has adopted me as a sister. He's totally dedicated to Lacsar who he feels is his brother. I now know a lot of things I would never know without Rascal-II who looks after us better than the security apparatus here."

"When your father and I go home to Ollytrene how will you be?"

"Mother I will be fine, and we will come and visit you now and then."

"How soon do you think you will visit us?"

"As you probably know, Lacsar misses fishing with daddy and the bonfires."

"I'm glad he likes spending time with us.

"Mother when I get ready to start having babies, I will spend time with you to help me."

"I will always help you."

"I know that, and I know I will probably be having a baby soon, so I will be coming home with you. Lacsar and father can go fishing why you help me with my baby."

"I'm sure your father would enjoy Lacsar's company."

"You need to prepare father because I think the babies are coming soon."

"I will. Now let me take you back to your lovely prince so you can spend a wonderful day with him."

"Thank you, mother, for being here for me."

"It's my pleasure honey. You are a wonderful daughter and I treasure you."

The two women hugged, and Starlight went back to Lacsar and was ready to be escorted out among the emperor's court and face the public.

The Royal Couple and future emperor were escorted out to the crowd and now they had major security like they never experienced before. All the contingencies were planned and executed.

At the request of Starlight, a tall holographic projector was delivered to the Ollytrene tribe with a generator and a communications link from a Fast Frigate in geosynchronous orbit above the tribe to relay the deep space transmission down to the tribe to observe the Royal Unification. By the time they received the time delayed signals it was evening and the lack of sunlight helped to enhance the holographic projection. Tribal members were enthralled to see how beautiful their Starlight had grown into such a fine-looking princess and soon to be the most powerful woman in the galaxy.

The guests lined up along the isle leading from the hallway out to the courtyard, to meet the couple and exchange a few words. As the Royal Couple walked down the line of guests, the Royal Court members were all stunned at how incredibly beautiful Starlight appeared. The Royal Court people in high enough standing with the emperor knew the two had grown up together in special circumstances. The newly unified Royal Couple had been combined in heart soul and mind for many years.

The satisfaction that Starlight felt eclipsed any notion she ever had before and thus her luster shined and with the loving telepathic ensembles she and Lacsar now fed each other gave her the splendid euphoric transcendence as they met each guest. The guests all had an incredible feeling when the Royal Couple stopped in front of them to greet and socialize. They didn't know it, but they were feeling the tumultuous allegros the couple telepathically resonated into each other at the happiest day of their lives.

As the staff set up the tables on one side of the courtyard, they created and interesting layout. Lacsar and Starlight had a table to themselves and what astonished the guests was the staff placed bird perches a close distance behind them. Rascal-II and his flock were fed beforehand as this was to be a visual display for them.

Two tables were situated next to the Royal Couple. One table had settings for the emperor, and the Royal couples' parents. The other table was set up for Alessandra and children that Princess Lì Alìgrāwná wanted her daughter to socialize with for future intelectual growth. Also sitting at the table to supervise the children and add a layer of security was Valets Robot Lucas and Octavrator along with Drákōlìné who would be spending less time looking after Starlight and focus her attention on Alessandra who would soon be her main focus.

Valet Lucas approached Emperor Cornelius to inform him the feast was now ready to invite the guests to their tables.

The emperor nodded at Lucas then made the announcement, "Dear guests and members of my Royal Court, we shall start our wedding celebration now. You will all be escorted to your tables."

All the guests were escorted by a dozen well dressed security men wearing full military dress uniforms. Each had a full set of diagrams for the tables reserved for each guest.

A color guard escorted the newly Unified Couple to their private table with Rascal-II and six other birds from the Flock

Rascal-II invited all now sitting on the perch behind them and observing.

Rascal-II informed the other birds telepathically, "Keep the vigilance as our primary purpose for being here is to enhance security by quickly catching any nefarious activity designed to harm the Royals."

Through mental telepathy Rascal-II informed Lacsar, "All conditions are normal. No sign of anything to be concerned about."

"Thank you for the reassurance."

There was an element of concern that a faction might not accept the prince unifying with an off-worlder.

As soon as everyone was seated, the guests were served an exquisite meal like they had not enjoyed in a long time, with the best elixirs that were very rare and excessively expensive.

Lacsar looked at Starlight and telepathically said to her, "I'm really glad we got the preliminaries completed and made love. Now I don't need to rush this meal."

"I hope you realize I could not wait any longer?" Starlight asked then winked at Lacsar.

Emperor Cornelius who was the closest of anyone to the young couple detected the telepathic communiques between the young Royals and could not help but broke into a big smile. He was glad he was facing away from them, or they would suspect he might have known what they said.

The emperor was sitting between the two sets of parents and Tonnerre was close to him. She had a surreal affect on the emperor who could easily have made arrangements to privately enjoy Tonnerre. But the risk of scandal precluded such actions. The emperor had no doubt that if Chief Yuèliàng had some fatal accident, he would feel obligated to bring Tonnerre to the mansion to console her, then maker her his lover. *Other men as powerful as me would no doubt create that accident if they were in my place, Emperor Cornelius thought.*

Tonnerre didn't understand why she felt like a *bitch in heat* every time she was near the emperor. *Is it because I have lust for him?*

Every movement of any individual in the dinner was under great observation by the birds. Humans have an awareness and a thought process of about twenty Hertz. Even though our brains can process wonderful holographs and produce psychoacoustics that defy imagination. These birds have thought process of about one hundred and eighty hertz which makes them far superior to dogs, that only have the advantage of smell and sometimes hearing depending on the breed.

Just like Rascal who sacrificed himself to prevent Hectozar from kidnapping Princess Lì Alìgrāwná and Demetrius Ravik (Lacsar), Rascal-II would make a similar bold movement if necessary. But unlike Rascal, Rascal-II had six other birds with him that were equally dedicated to Lacsar, and any assassin would quickly discover how fast seven of these birds with powerful beaks that can compress almost 350 pounds of pressure would do to them. If a person brandished a laser pistol by the time, they got it up to an elevation to harm the Royals, the assailant would most likely be missing their eyes and in great pain.

The layout of the tables also added an element of safety because an assailant on the young couple was blocked by the two tables offset and provided a barrier to the young couple. An assailant would have to stand to shoot over the emperor and the parents of the couple. The birds would immediately see someone standing and if they brandished a weapon, would be on that person in about a second, clearly time enough to prevent getting a shot away. Security cameras would also catch the person in the act and that person would soon be pushed out of an air lock in space after dying from asphyxiation.

Lacsar's motive in having Rascal-II present wasn't intended for added security, though that came with it. He wanted him here because he grew up with Rascal-II. They were indeed very close. On many a day especially while Starlight was away and Lacsar was miserable, Rascal-II acted as his personal psychiatrist and helped to calm him and make him feel better and more rational.

The food was excellent, and the elixirs provided an element of great satisfaction. Everyone was happy, even though security was on pins and needles because the power of the empire was closely confined in this dinner party. An enemy could do a lot of damage to the empire by attacking this Unification Dinner Party.

The orchestra played lovely music which had sounds people present had never heard before thanks to Stanley (aka Duke Ravik) had music taken from Earth for this momentous occasion. A grand piano was on the stage, and nobody present had seen one before.

Another one of Stanley's secret operations he, and the Valet's Lucas and Octavrator conducted was obtaining that Steinway, recordings and videos of pianists performing the works. The Unification Dinner Party now heard piano music samples composed by Viktor Kosenko, Rachmaninoff, Tchaikovsky, Kurt Atterberg, Eduard Künneke, Moritz Moszkowski, Xaver Scharwenka, Bortkiewicz, and Saint Saens. To play the full length of the compositions would require far too much time so Stanley working with the music director pulled out portions of the compositions that were the most inspiring and meaningful. What would normally take all day long was compressed down to just a few hours.

Stanley wanted Lacsar to know some of his heritage. The sound fascinated everyone including Lacsar and Starlight. Later the emperor would discover how that music instrument and the music came about. Just about the time the emperor was going to go heavy handed with the Valet's Lucas and Octavrator, Stanley stood up for them and said he forced them to do it because he wanted this music for his son's Unification Dinner Party. It was now hard for the emperor to deal harshly with the Valet's since it was a Royal that forced them to do it.

As the emperor rationalized the event, he realized that they had plucked Stanley out of his civilization and never gave him an opportunity to ever go back, and with that the emperor said privately to the two Valet's, "All is forgiven. I'm sorry I yelled at you."

Emperor Cornelius also was acutely aware of how much Stanley meant to Princess Lì Alìgrāwná who became aware of the secret operation and had not known about Stanley's trip to the Gromulite empire to snatch Hectozar until Lacsar discovered the ordeal the emperor was putting the Valet's Lucas and Octavrator through.

When she approached her father with tears streaming, she asked, "How could you consciously hide this from me?" the emperor realized he caused so much grief in his actions that exposed far more than he wanted, he then squelched the entire event and wished he had never gone there.

After the young Royal's Unification, the emperor had to take the Royal Couple to several planets for receptions and to introduce the future Empress.

This also got messy at one point. King Carvlesis and Arabella were guests of one of the Kingdoms they simultaneously visited. Arabella was of course crushed and very emotional. A lot of unintended disclosure then occurred. This event might have triggered a significant negative trimmer through Starlight who was briefed ahead of time on the situation, but thanks to Lacsar wanting to bring Rascal-II along, Starlight got briefed by Rascal-II who she knew was an honest broker and would never lie.

Even though Arabella came close to getting her claws into

Lacsar and dramatically changing his future, the emperor saved him just at the 11ᵗʰ hour, so no harm was done. In a way this situation gave Starlight a quick education in that she could not take anything for granted for a minute because no doubt, Arabella would not be the only woman wanting to experience Lacsar, especially when it all became apparent his ability to wield massive power was in the not-too-distant future.

One thing was certain, if anything ever happened to Starlight and Arabella discovered that information she would have her father, King Carlatar send immediate requests to meet Lacsar at a future date to fertilize a future relationship.

Emperor Cornelius knew he had maybe twenty good years left to indoctrinate Lacsar and develop him into the future emperor. One thing that pleased the emperor quite well was Princess Lì fully supported everything the emperor did in that regard.

Emperor Cornelius knew that Stanley would do anything for Princess Lì. Stanley's motive was to simply be helpful and encourage his son to learn as much as he could from his grandfather and be grateful, he unified with a beautiful and intelligent woman that with her wings transplanted now had the appearance of the Royals with wings.

But one thing that worried the emperor was Lucas and Octavrator had cooperated and led Stanley on dangerous and risky missions. Even going to Earth to acquire the piano was severely risky. The thought of Stanley being trapped on Earth and handed over to security forces created horrible thoughts, especially if their interrogations broke him and he divulged he came from Earth. They would never see Stanley again. The emperor knew in his heart that if something happened to Stanley, Princess Lì would have a very serious psychological issue and that would interfere with a smooth transition to the next Emperor, Prince Demetrius Ravik.

<center>~~~~~~</center>

CHAPTER SEVENTEEN

STANLEY'S ENHANCED EDUCATION

The intelligence services number one priority was to monitor Stanley's activities and disrupt any possible clandestine activity that Valets Lucas and Octavrator might manifest. However, the two Valet's knew there was a time and place for everything, and it might come down to the fact only Stanley could pull it off with his unique skills and abilities and growing fantastic physical condition with his strenuous daily workouts and constant education.

The two Valet's were also aware that Stanley's telepathic ability had grown very strong over the years thanks to Princess Lì always influencing that sensory perception. What the Valets Lucas and Octavrator understood which the emperor misjudged; Stanley was an ideal person to engage in espionage should the need arise. They also knew that nobody anywhere would ever consider Stanley a spy. He would never be on anyone's radar for clandestine activity.

Lucas being a robot had ability to get at information unlike anyone else in the mansion. He was a trusted authority and the emperor had great confidence in him because of his many years of dedication and always performing any mission or activity the emperor requested of him.

Stanley had a lot of private meetings with Lucas and Octavrator where they honed his espionage and sabotage skills and indoctrinated him in that it may come down to him to save his son's life or the emperor. They explained to Stanley, that no matter how hard they tried to protect the Royal Family, there were avenues of penetration and compromise, and the near kidnapping of Princess Lì and Lacsar underscored the point.

In some of the educational ventures designed to enhance Stanley's social and economic understanding of the empire because after the emperor was out of the picture, Lacsar would need advice from him from time to time. Lucas and Octavrator had a modus operendus to get Stanley off the planet to some location where he could receive martial arts and weapons training.

The INTEL apparatus sent along to make sure Stanley didn't get involved in any riskier engagements were slowly infiltrated and indoctrinated by the two Valets who explained the facts of life to them and made sure no reports made it back to the emperor. It did not take long to win over the INTEL people especially when they were confronted with their failure to detect and prevent the kidnapping. Their asses were saved by Rascal, because if Hectozar got his hands on the Two Royals, they would be human shields the rest of their lives living in a dismal situation with little hope of rescue.

Stanley grew in stature and understanding of the spy business and thanks to Lucas and Octavrator eventually had a good knowledge of galactic level espionage and who all was involved.

One of the dicey moments for the INTEL men that helped Lucas and Octavrator have more influence on them came about when after a few tips they found out there actually was a spy at the Royal Unification sent there to kill Lacsar.

The probable assassin somehow got distracted and it appears the birds might have had a hand as a deterrent saving Lacsar's' life.

In computer analysis of the man who had a cosmetic makeover to steal the identity of a Royal Court member, it was clear the birds distracted him and one bird in particular, Rascal-II.

After that revelation Stanley had a private meeting with Rascal-II to find out why Rascal was focusing on the man?

"I did not detect any motives, but I could feel evil in his heart. I could not understand why a Royal Court member would have such evil thoughts, so I closely observed every move he made. He seemed to react when I stared at him throughout the celebration. He was one of the first to leave and when he was gone, I felt no further evil in the courtyard area."

The actual Royal Court member had been accosted and drugged. He didn't remember going to the celebration even though he had an invitation. The man was taken away and put through heavy hypnosis and administered significant amount of truth serum which ultimately convinced INTEL, he had probably been drugged and soon the toxicology report came back showing he had traces of a drug in his system that takes weeks for the body to fully rid.

In due time thanks to significant investigative techniques that were manifested partially by Stanley's telepathic ability, they slowly located the individual hiding out on some neutral planet waiting to meet his masters and explain why he failed his mission to kill Lacsar, known as Demetrius Ravik.

The Valet's had to get to the man before his handlers did because most likely he would be killed and silenced so that Emperor Cornelius would not know there had been an attempt on his grandson.

This was Stanley's baptism to fire in the espionage business. He would be infiltrated into the planet and facilitate the snatch and grab.

Stanley decided he needed Rascal-II as part of his mission and even though Lucas and Octavrator were against it, Stanley reminded them how Rascal-II and his bird flock had taken down the security apparatus allowing them to snatch Hectozar so efficiently behind enemy lines. Rascal-II would also be equipped with darts in the event he had to take out possible aggressors.

Stanley and Rascal-II got into the stratospheric glider and was soon dropped out of the large shuttle cargo bay to fly down to the landing zone. This stratospheric glider capable of carrying one person brought Stanley and Rascal-II down to the planet. The stratospheric glider was designed to be very stealthily and at the completion of the mission it would self-destruct as to not leave traces of it behind.

Since Stanley would be clothed to minimize his radar cross section, he could fly late at night to the assassin's hideout where he was lavishly drinking, drugging, and whoring around thinking he was safe, and his handlers would simply give him another assignment after he had given them a BS story on why he couldn't get near Lacsar to do the assassination.

By the planning, Stanley landed the stratospheric glider in a wooded area about ten miles from his target. He had drugs and dispensers to disable the assassin including anyone with him.

In the final decision the mission went with the bird and with Stanley taking Rascal-II with him, it seemed rather innocuous as it was something he had done in the past.

Stanley was very fortunate the spy was intoxicated and drugged up. The darts that Rascal-II had with him took out the two others that were in the safe house and the prostitutes had left for the night with a request to come back the next evening which they would be more than happy to do since the financial reward was quite high.

When the assassin discovered Stanley, he attempted to kill him even though he was intoxicated and drugged up, but Stanley injected him fast enough to where his efforts were foiled. The man was now unconscious, and the landing party then descended in a stealth shuttle and restrained the spy and placed him in the shuttle which took Stanley and Rascal-II back up into space with them and soon they were on their way to another planet that was part of the Lìsztbrùnést empire where the man would be interrogated by INTEL and given options he could not refuse.

The assassin was quite good at not revealing who he worked for during the interrogation. INTEL was just about to give up when Stanley asked everyone to leave the room except him and Rascal-II.

Once they were alone with the man and there were no other mental emissions in the room, Stanley with the help of Rascal-II were able to probe the man's mind and discover who sent him. The assassin's handlers were none other than the Trilaterals.

Stanley did an amazing job in convincing the man his pet bird was a mind reader. Stanley then said, "My pet bird here can read minds and he can telepathically communicate to me. He just revealed the Trilaterals sent you to kill my son."

The man started sweating. He didn't know if this was BS and a fishing expedition, and Stanley knew that too, so Stanley started giving the man acute detailed information on how he was able to get to Neflatraceous, the capital of the Lìsztbrùnést Empire, steal the identity of a Royal Court Member with an invitation to the Unification and make it past security with a shielded blaster that sensors could not detect and was the trade craft of assassins.

As the man started to come unglued opening up other pathways into his mind that Stanley and Rascal-II could exploit, Stanley gave the identity of all the living relatives of the man and precisely where they lived and if the man didn't cooperate, the emperor would soon send a task force to that planet and apprehend them and shove them out of an airlock into space where they would all die from asphyxiation. And then Rascal put thoughts into his mind of birds poking out his eyes and eating him and bit the guy with full force of 350 pounds to show him he wasn't playing around.

Stanley and Rascal-II broke the man who now was willing to

sign all the confessions and provide information of his handlers that were due to arrive in a couple days at the safe house. They too were captured by the force the Valet's put together and soon the Trilateral Governments received a special communique with the confessions and a warning the next time they attempt to do nefarious activities the Lìsztbrùnést Empire would consider it an act of war, and to be prepared for very harsh treatment.

The Valet's could not risk the emperor finding out that Stanley was a spy and doing clandestine activities had no choice but to allow the men to die from asphyxiation in space and their bodies burned up when they entered the atmosphere of the planet at a velocity of 30,000 miles per hour.

Stanley and Rascal-II had a private talk where Stanley explained to Rascal-II why he had to hide this information from any human or any bird. They then went bird watching to fill their minds full of bird images and experiences to flush out the espionage business.

Rascal-II was quite intelligent and understood what he was doing protected the life of Lacsar which made him happy.

After a week of bird watching Stanley returned to Neflatraceous with Rascal-II as if nothing happened.

The two Valet's Lucas and Octavrator explained to their INTEL personnel involved in the operation:

"Duke Ravik and we had nothing to do with the operation. We were busy bird watching and doing other logistics support for the bird watching excursion."

"What's our cover story?"

"The Intel Directorate handled the matter with the assassin. Any information surrounding the mission is compartmentalized and the team involved has been disbanded, relocated, and not allowed to discuss any aspects of it with anyone due to the sensitivity and the seriousness of potential Trilateral involvement. "

The INTEL director responded, "We can state whatever is required."

"Your party line is you must protect sensitive sources and methods and all your interactions were remote and you have no means of discovering the identity of those involved in the operation.

"Understand, sir."

"Also, during the operation, you never saw the three of us and we were off somewhere bird watching in case someone asks you and they can refer to Duke Ravik if they have any questions about what he was doing. The case is closed, and the assassin and accomplices are not available for comment.

The Trilaterals on the other hand knew something big happened because they lost quite a few people in the operation and feared treachery from an inside job including the possibility of defectors.

The basic information was an attempt on the prince was foiled and Trilaterals were involved and warned the next time would be considered an act of war.

It was at this time, Valet's Lucas and Octavrator decided it was time to start destabilizing the Trilaterals. The rationale was that keep them off balance while Prince Demetrius Ravik was in the process of ascending to the throne.

The Valet's also knew one element that would prevent Emperor Cornelius from executing them for carrying out such clandestine activities would require Duke Ravik's participation.

To Lucas and Octavrator, placing Prince Demetrius Ravik on the throne unmolested and without huge issues to deal with Trilaterals right away, made Stanley expendable if it came down to it.

The Valet's didn't want Stanley to get killed in the process of setting back the Trilaterals. But by hurting the Trilaterals so badly that Prince Demetrius Ravik would have the empire fully under control before the Trilaterals would be able to reconstitute themselves was worth the risk.

Lucas and Octavrator understood the consequences of the operation they now viewed as the pathway to achieve that objective. Stanley continued training vigorously and his physical being was always improving to the point he not only was a galactic scale spy, but he was also physically as well developed as any of them. Thanks to interacting with Rascal-II assistance Stanley cut his reaction time down measurably and his martial arts skills steadily improved and expanded.

For his own psychological well-being, Stanley would not know what his target was until just before the plan was attempted.

The Trilaterals had a yearly meeting. The leaders of the three waring powers met to plan their next moves. They knew they had to be extremely careful because the Lìsztbrùnésts were agitated to the point they would consider outright warfare if they made the wrong move and got caught in the process. The next attempt had to be successful because it was getting too close for Prince Demetrius Ravik to become the new emperor. For some reason they assumed that killing Prince Demetrius Ravik would cause so much disarray in the Lìsztbrùnést Empire, it would give them a window of opportunity to chip away at the empire and reduce its significance.

A vital piece of INTEL was apparent.

Demetrius Ravik would soon escort the future empress to Ollytrene to visit her parents again. That's when they would strike him down.

What foiled that operation was the good sense of the emperor who was now very concerned about the safety of Demetrius Ravik and the transition of power to the throne.

It was a mere coincidence that Stanley embarked upon his

mission at the same time the Trilaterals had their meetings and launched the attack.

Prince Demetrius Ravik and Starlight traveled to Ollytrene, this time with far more security than they ever experienced before. Traveling in the Royal Yacht would most likely not happen again for a long time. But they didn't mind traveling on Frigates, though they didn't like traveling without each other as the emperor was adamant, they would not be on the same craft especially if Starlight was pregnant, there was still a possible heir to the throne in the event of a disaster.

The Trilaterals allowed the Royals to get to the planet without being molested, then they swung in the plan to kill the Royals.

They Royal Couple was on the planet when the escorts were hit with a heavy force. The best they could do for Demetrius Ravik and Starlight was tell them to go hide and help was on the way.

Demetrius Ravik and Starlight flew out of the village and knew where to go hide out, near the waterfall. Their good shape saved their lives. They were hiding near the waterfall when the Trilaterals hit the village looking for the Royals and killing anyone who would not inform them where they were hiding. The villagers had no idea where the Royal Couple flew too so the violence against them wasted precious time.

Chief Yuèliàng knew help was on the way and he needed to delay the Trilaterals as long as possible to give the two Royals time to escape and hide out. His efforts did work to some extent, but it cost him his life and most of the male tribe members. Before they could start killing the women, help arrived and the Trilaterals were quickly taken down and their spaceships that delivered them were destroyed and any attempts to surrender were rejected. They paid the price for this folly.

Starlight was heart broken when she found her father dead and her mother severely beaten.

Lacsar (aka Demetrius Ravik) exposed his likely leadership skills during these moments when a dozen Trilaterals were captured were brought before him.

Nobody was going to second guess what the prince would do next as he faced the Trilaterals that were bound and could not prevent any type of punishment.

"See what you did to my empress father?" Lacsar said most passionately and pointed the the corpse of his deceased father-in-law.

The Trilateral's men stood there dazed because their plan wasn't so great afterall.

"I want to know who sent you?"

Lacsar walked up to the first Trilateral and said, "Who trained you and who sent you?"

The man refused to talk. Lacsar couldn't quite break into his mind because the man was thinking about his wife and all the other thoughts were blocked out."

Lacsar turned around to one of the security men and said, "Give me your laser pistol."

The security man gave Lacsar the laser pistol. Lacsar then said to the Trilateral hit team member, "This is your last chance to cooperate."

The man refused to talk.

Lacsar placed the laser pistol near the front of the man's face and pulled the trigger. Much of his face was blown away and the man fell dead.

Lacsar walked over to the second prisoner and said, "As you can see, I'm not fooling around. You killed someone special to me and you beat up my wife's mother. You start talking now or you will get the same treatment I just gave to your friend."

This man was a little scared allowing Lacsar to easily penetrate his mind and get all the information. The three leaders of the Trilaterals sent them to kill him.

Lacsar, then said, "I know who sent you. The three leaders of the Trilaterals. I've decided not to kill you right away. My birds like fresh meat sometimes."

Lacsar turned towards the security man and said, "The three leaders of the Trilaterals, sent them here to kill me. Send that report to the Emperor Immediately."

In a short period of time the emperor knew what occurred and directed the security people with Lacsar to bring the Royal Couple and Tonnerre back with them immediately and make sure the surgeons in the fleet give Tonnerre comfort right away. The Chief's body was also brought back for a Royal funeral and a period of mourning.

There wasn't much left of the tribe, so they were also all brought back.

Now it was time to plan for revenge.

What the Emperor was going to learn in the next few hours troubled him greatly.

Stanley and the Valet's Lucas and Octavrator were gone, and it appeared they were on a secret mission.

It was a mere coincidence that Stanley penetrated the security apparatus of the Three Trilaterals at the same time as the Chief was being killed. The Trilaterals were drinking drug laced elixirs and pre-celebrating their extinguishing the young prince to disrupt the Lìsztbrùnést Empire.

This mission was so dangerous that Stanley brought the entire flock with him. Every bird was weaponized. Even though over one hundred security men were present, the birds quietly and seamlessly did their killing with the poison darts. Layer by layer the security apparatus was taken down until all that was left was in the room with the three Trilateral leaders.

Stanley regretted having to kill them, but the plan did not permit a snatch and grab. There wasn't enough time as it would be a razor's edge of timing to bug out after the killing.

In the inner sanctum of the Trilaterals, the fighting got rough, half the birds were killed, but the security was taken down and Stanley did the kill shots and did a second shot to make sure none of the Trilaterals could be saved.

Stanley knew he could not bring all the dead birds back with him and he had some powerful weapons that would create a very large blaze time delayed. He and the living birds flew to the location of the hidden stratospheric glider with more than enough fuel to get them back out in space and picked up by the shuttle that would get them to a fast frigate and out of the solar system.

When the stratospheric glider was near the shuttle, the weapons went off and the Trilaterals were soon incinerated with the birds not leaving behind any trace of how this all manifested.

As soon as the INTEL people divulged to the emperor where Stanley went, he sent his fleet to the Trilateral worlds to intercept Stanley and bring him back right away. The emperor didn't know the mission was almost complete with Stanley and the birds doing their activities.

In due time the Fast Frigate was detected and the Trilaterals went after it with a bone in their teeth, highly agitated because they had struck the planet and destroyed the mansion where the Trilaterals were meeting.

The Fast Frigate was traveling as fast as it could, but the Trilateral ships were slowly gaining and at maximum range started firing self-propelled weapons that could go faster and their explosions came close a few times even with radical maneuvers the captain did.

Stanley looked at Lucas and Octavrator and said, "It doesn't look like we'll make it. I just want you two to know I feel like you like my brothers."

Lucas and Octavrator were somber and the kind words from Stanley uplifted their emotions a notch despite the peril they found themselves in.

Just about the time the three were about to give up hope the Fast Frigate Captain stated, "I have no idea how the hell they found out where we are, but friendly forces are converging on us now. We might make it!

The task force commander directed the Fast frigate Captain to take a specific geometry to enhance their safety and was escorted shortly on an opening course while the two fleets converged into an unholy dogfight.

Spaceships were blowing up right and left and the past skirmishes the Trilaterals had depleted their firepower to some extent, so they were certainly an underdog and as soon as the Trilateral commander realized it was a lost cause and ordered, "Reverse Course! Retreat at maximum speed."

Stanley, Lucas and Octavrator were brought back to the emperor's mansion right away. The emperor was fuming mad, but his sorrow for the future Empress losing her father seemed to cool off his anger a few notches.

The three men met privately with Emperor Cornelius and had not been informed about Chief Yuèliàng's death.

The fast frigate brought back a lot of data. One essential piece was the Trilaterals conference building burning in a horrific fire. Rascal-II made it back which made Stanley very happy because he would have felt very bad if something happened to that bird.

The three men along with a couple INTEL people sat in the inquisition with the emperor. Lucas and Octavrator knew they had crossed over the line this time, but they had their motives and knew the transition of power could now occur without the menace of the Trilaterals.

As they briefed Emperor Cornelius not knowing what their fate would be, they calmly stated all the facts. They were more than ready for whatever punishment Emperor Cornelius was going to be dished out at them.

During this moment, Stanley realized he didn't have anything to lose so he telepathically engaged the emperor and now became aware how close his son came to being killed and the tragedy of Chief Yuèliàng. When the tears started flowing down Stanley, the emperor knew there would be no way he could punish these men for doing what needed to be done. He then said, "Would all you men except for Stanley please leave the room. I need to talk with Stanley alone."

When they were alone with tears still flowing down Stanley's cheeks, the emperor said, "Stanley you never cease to amaze me. My biggest concern of course is how Princess Lì will take all this. And you and I both know we do not have the power to conceal it from her."

"I understand your Excellency."

"Your punishment will be, you will be required to tell Princess Lì everything and explain to her why you did what you did."

"I will."

"Now I want to ask you what punishment you think I should dish out to Lucas and Octavrator?"

"I think the most suitable punishment would be to escort me on future scientific research and discovery trips."

"That sounds reasonable to me. Ask them to come back in here and I want you to go see Princess Lì and confess everything."

"I will."

"Thank you."

CHAPTER EIGHTEEN
THE NEW EMPRESS

The days passed and Tonnerre was devastated emotionally but physically she responded well to medical and psychological treatments and enjoyed being with her daughter.

The emperor was a lonely man. Every time he was near Tonnerre he had wonderful feelings. He knew eventually what he needed to do and that was to make her an Empress before he retired and made his grandson the next emperor. It was going to be an interesting scenario where the current empress would be replaced by her daughter. It had never happened before because it was impossible under normal circumstances.

Slowly but surely Tonnerre's life came back to what someone might considered normal. The emperor made excuses to spend more and more time with Tonnerre, and at all social events always had her seated by him. The staff knew the emperor wanted Tonnerre to be treated like an Empress and dressed accordingly. With the expert makeup artists, Tonnerre appeared like a goddess, she personified incredible beauty. Starlight was so pleased her mother was doing so well and looking so exquisite all the time. Happiness then seemed to slowly comeback especially when it was learned Starlight was an expected mother.

The day of the official acknowledgement of the expected mother, the emperor took Tonnerre on a little trip around the planet showing her the sights including a ride on a train that was part of a museum that preserved their ancient heritage. During the time they were on the museum train traveling only a dozen miles and back to the station, Emperor Cornelius laid out his cards

"Tonnerre, you may not know this, but I've always had warm feelings for you."

"Well, I find myself happy when I'm around you, your Excellency."

"When we are alone, please call me Cornelius."

"Alright Cornelius."

"Tonnerre, there is something I want to ask you now, if I may."

"Cornelius, you are always welcome to ask me questions."

"Good. I want to make you my Empress and spend the rest of my life with you."

Tonnerre was utterly shocked Emperor Cornelius wanted her, but she always felt special around him and responded, "I would love to spend the rest of my life with you."

The big event soon happened. Emperor Cornelius and Empress Tonnerre were Unified. Everyone was happy, especially Starlight who was happy to see her mother slowly recover from the terrible disaster of her father's death which Lacsar felt something responsible because his presence on Ollytrene is why Starlight's father was killed.

Lacsar remained angry about the Trilaterals, and the emperor detected the rage in his grandson who wanted a war and to destroy them. Lacsar didn't know what his father had done.

The day after the emperor's unification with Tonnerre, the emperor informed Lacsar, "I want to take you some place special where we can have a private talk."

The two were flown a great distance to one of the emperor's favorite places when his first empress was still living. The two were alone as security was asked to move a good distance away, then Emperor Cornelius said, "Lacsar, the reason why we have come here for a talk is because I know the personal rage you have towards the Trilaterals."

"Grandfather, I can't help it. I really liked Chief Yuèliàng who taught me a lot of things and spent very special moments with me when I was young."

"What I'm going to tell you now is very confidential."

"Alright, I will not repeat any of it."

"The Trilaterals no longer exist."

"What do you mean by that?"

"Your father killed them."

"He what?"

"Please do not let your father know I'm telling you this, it will upset him but as the future emperor you must know the history so that in the future you will be able to deal with it since you will be aware of what happened."

The emperor who previously read Stanley's mind to capture all the imagery of the battle with the Trilateral's security team and the loss of half the birds were vivid. He then telepathically put those images into Lacsar's mind.

"Why did he do that?"

"He did it for you because he knew they would keep coming for you and one day they might get lucky."

The details of how close he came to getting killed for the sake of his son hit Lacsar in the gut like a ton of bricks.

"Why did you tell me all this grandfather?"

"You are walking around with rage. Your father has already dealt with it. The Trilaterals no longer exist, and their empires are collapsing now and will not be any issue for you probably the rest of your life. I told you this so you can let it go. Chief Yuèliàng's death has been avenged."

Lacsar suddenly feeling the weight of the world removed off his shoulders and his consciousness felt the relief and he responded. "Thank you, grandfather for telling me all this. I feel so much better now."

"Your father receives a lot of anger from your mother all the time for going on this mission. Perhaps you can help her calm down and be gentler with your father. He's gone through a lot, and you know this wasn't the first time he put his life in extreme danger for your well-being."

"I will try my best."

"Alright I hope you liked the view here."

"I do."

"Good us go back to the mansion."

Lacsar noticed his mother wasn't speaking to Stanley much if any. He now saw the anger in his mother who somehow felt violated by Stanley's actions.

Lacsar made it a point to be around his parents as much as possible when they were together enjoying golden silence.

One day when Princess Lì was with Lacsar and Starlight discussing plans for the baby arrival, Lacsar knew this private moment was a perfect time to confront his mother.

"Mother can I ask you a question?"

"Sure."

"Why are you being so mean to father?"

Princess Lì didn't realize it was so obvious to the point her son now confronted her.

"I'm not sure I know what you are talking about."

"Let's take a walk out to visit Rascal-II where we can discuss it."

Lacsar telepathically said to Starlight, "I need to talk to mother privately, we'll discuss the baby matters later."

Princess Lì of course was nervous as to what Lacsar was going to bring up. But she knew she had been very mean to Stanley lately in many ways.

Rascal-II was perched near the spot they always met and soon discovered the mother and son were into a discussion the bird needed to ignore.

"Why did you say I've been mean to your father."

"It's obvious don't you think?"

"I treat him like I usually do."

"Mother you need to let it go."

"What do you mean?"

"You are upset because he dealt with the Trilaterals in complete defiance of emperor's orders."

Princess Lì looked at Lacsar looking stunned. Then she said, "How do you know about this?"

"I know everything, and I know my father has put his life at risk twice now for my behalf, and you are punishing him because of what he did for me."

"He could easily have gotten killed. He didn't consider my future when he went off and did those things."

"Those missions were very complex and dangerous. The only way they could pull them off was by having a very small footprint with very courageous people involved. You need to realize it probably could not have been done any other way short of initiating a major war with lethal adversaries possibly killing billions of people."

The two stood there for a while and soon tears were flowing down Princess Lì because Lacsar had put her in her place in a major way and she should have given more thought to Stanley's emotions. Now Lacsar did what needed to be done. His mother didn't know a lot of the details so Lacsar planted those thoughts into her mind and soon her brain was producing those holographic images of the control room where the Fast Frigate crew thought they were finished and would perish in a few moments to the point Stanley was saying goodbye to Lucas and Octavrator. Had the emperor not sent the fleet out to recall them, within a span of two minutes they would have been dead, it came that close.

The there was the telepathic images of the battle inside the Trilaterals conference room where Stanley fought bravely and without half the birds giving their lives Stanley would have been killed, he was outnumbered so severely.

The tears flowed down as the dam broke. Princess Lì never felt so miserable in all her life for what she had done to the man she loved. Then suddenly there was a mysterious thought. She didn't know why but she looked up at Rascal-II who was staring at her and there was a brief exchange.

Because of the telepathic images that Lacsar gave his mother, Princess Lì knew Rascal-II was there a short distance away from Stanley willing to take a shot to save his life and giving orders to the other birds on how to attack to make sure Stanley survived. She owed Stanley's life to Rascal-II, just like Rascal-II's father had once saved her and her son but had not been so lucky.

She telepathically asked Rascal-II, "So what do I do now?"

"Go to Stanley, he needs you now more than ever. He is heartbroken and only you can fix it," Rascal-II responded telepathically.

After Princess Lì slowly regained her composure she said, "Alright us go back to the mansion."

They entered the mansion and there was the Valet Octavrator waiting for her.

"Where is Stanley?"

"Let me take you to him."

Stanley was out at the far extreme of the courtyard under a nice shade tree sitting on a soft chair with a small table next to him with an elixir glass sitting on it. Stanley didn't look happy. He was disappointed and wondering if he made a big mistake in his life getting on that spaceship many years ago.

Princess Lì had no idea the damage she had inflicted in the relationship. Her reaction and subsequent mean treatment of Stanley left him a lot to think about.

The Valet Octavrator stopped about ten yards away from Stanley who had his back to them. He gestured towards Stanley and turned around and walked away because this was going to be a delicate moment. They needed their utter privacy.

Princess Lì slowly approached and said, "Hello Stanley."

"Hello." There wasn't much emotion in the response.

Princess Lì now fully exercising her mental telepathy discovered Stanley was thinking about going back to Earth and calling it quits. She was almost devastated. She then walked over to Stanley and fell to her knees sobbing uncontrollably because she had no idea the terrible damage she had done to this fine man. She had broken his heart and crushed him.

As she started crying and holding onto Stanley with a very strong grip, she said, "Please don't leave me. I can't live without you."

The emperor was observing all this with his security monitors and had high fidelity audio to hear it all.

Stanley didn't say anything. He felt emotionally dead. The spark had gone out.

The emperor prayed that Princess Lì would do the right thing now as she was perilously close to losing Stanley. She needed to say those magic words and really quick or it was an end game. Stanley would insist on transportation back to Earth and his daughter would be heart broke forever because of her own despicable conduct lately towards Stanley.

Stanley was feeling the effects of his elixir and totally emotionally numb now he wasn't responding too well, and Princess Lì knew she had one shot at it or lose it. She was a razor's edge away from losing the love of her life and she knew it because of what she was finding in Stanley's mind with her mental telepathy. She decided then to lay her cards out on the table and said, "Stanley, I really do love you dearly. You are in my heart."

Those words seemed to take Stanley's mind out of his trance and his misery and reached down and pulled Princess Lì up to him and hugged her while she wept.

Stanley felt something in his emotions and there suddenly was a spark again. He didn't know what was happening, but Princess Lì felt really good to him suddenly. His mind then opened and the love between them flourished and they hugged like it was like it felt back on the spacecraft traveling here from Earth.

The emperor had tears himself and when Stanley said, "Lì, I love you and perhaps you can forgive me. But I did what I did for the sake of our son. He needed protection and I would gladly have given my life to protect him."

Princess Lì then cried like she never felt before over her guilt and her realization what Stanley had been through and when he returned home, she treated him so terribly cruel. She was now ashamed of herself.

The two sat there together in each other's arms while Lucas and Octavrator kept everyone away from them and their tender moment. They stayed like that for a very long time and people were getting anxious but, in his earbud, Octavrator was directed by the emperor to keep everyone away and give them their special moment.

Finally, they stirred. Princess Lì stood up and held her hand out to Stanley and the two of them walked back inside the palace and to their suite where they could continue their private intercourse with no intrusions.

~~~~~~
~~~~~~

CHAPTER NINETEEN
THE BABY IS BORN

Time seemed to pass quickly. Starlight's pregnancy resulted in delivery of a healthy boy. Knowing what his father had done in shaping his destiny and vastly improving his personal safety, Lacsar decided to name him after his father, Stanley II.

The emperor as now reaching a point of complete happiness like he had not felt since he was a young man and first met the empress. He was once again with a woman that that inspired him, and with the birth of his great grandson, his legacy was assured for a long time. Thanks to Stanley's significant bravery his heir to the throne was now a lot more secure.

Thanks to Stanley being a wonderful and decent person, he overcame the dark period in his relationship with his partner Princess Lì.

In due time it was time to transfer power and retire and spend his life enjoying Tonnerre's company. There would be great festivities as that process all materialized.

Lacsar had a good head on his shoulders, and he had a solid foundation with his father. He knew he could trust nobody as much and viewed him as his best advisor.

Lacsar had developed into a very handsome and intelligent man. During his nurturing process, nothing was left to chance. His education was vast and broad. By the time of his ascendency to the throne he had travelled to every solar system in the empire. He was a fair and just man and had the benefit of two intelligent parents and a spouse that had grown up with him. They were lovers and best friends. The bond between the Royals was decisively strong. There were no mysteries or any veiled agendas.

Lacsar was also lucky enough to have the two Valet's that had a few years left and Drákōlìné who looked a lot younger than her real age, to protect their son.

Once the former emperor handed over the reins to the throne, his job was to tell people not to take their concerns and questions to him, but instead to request appointments through one of the Valets to meet the new emperor.

Emperor Cornelius and Empress Tonnerre eased themselves out of the limelight and into joyful retirement. With vast fortune at his disposal, Emperor Cornelius and Empress Tonnerre could go and do just about anything they wanted.

The Tribe from Ollytrene was eventually returned and a few men from other tribes were borrowed to help restore the tribe. Emperor Cornelius and Empress Tonnerre decided living with the Tribe on Ollytrene was where they wanted to be to grow old together in their final voyage of their life. Added security and space defense was set up in case any nefarious activity decided they wanted to bring harm to the former emperor.

Thanks to the former emperor's needs, the tribe slowly evolved into a modern society with all the advances made possible available to them. Reconstruction of the village turned it into a more modern setting with clean water, electricity, and many other conveniences in life. The former toil and hard work to survive had ended. The former emperor and empress would be comfortable for the rest of their lives and enjoyed visits by their descendants.

Stanley and Princess Lì stayed at the mansion and acted as advisors and assistants to the new emperor and empress who had a good head on their shoulders.

~~~~~~
~~~~~~

CHAPTER TWENTY

ALESSANDRA GOES TO LARAFRACEAN

Princess Alessandra had suitable number of men who wanted to be in her good graces and have access to power. But she was a lot like her mother and wanted to explore the universe. So just like her mother she departed the mansion with Drákōlìné like her mother many years before.

Stanley felt uncomfortable with Alessandra departing, but Princess Lì reminded him, "I would not have met you had I not done a similar journey."

Princess Alessandra traveled to several solar systems and eventually met a plain skin person named Charbriel on the Larafracean planetary system in a not much different manner than when her mother first met her father.

Charbriel was not a social climber, just a pleasant person Alessandra slowly grew attracted and slowly psychologically bonded. Charbriel had just completed medical training and was looking forward to the future where he would not have such a grueling schedule with physical and psychological demands.

The meeting with Alessandra happened at the most auspicious time where Charbriel could indulge in romantic proclivities because completing medical school eliminated his seemingly Sapioromantic or Cupioromantistic persona.

The chance meeting and encounter was at a social gathering instigated by Larafracean diplomats who wanted greater exposure to the Lìsztbrùnést to enhance trade and commerce.

Charbriel didn't know much about the Lìsztbrùnést Empire or the significance of Alessandra in the overall scheme of things. His invitation to the event only occurred because his diplomatic relative knew he was very intelligent, attractive, and had a pleasant disposition with no baggage since he had escaped relationships up to now due to the demand and rigor of his medical studies and training. This started out simply as political patronage on the part of the diplomat who had no realistic expectations his relative would in any way enthrall Princess Alessandra. His motive was simply social climbing using his intelligent relative who had accomplished a great deal of intellectual work as a pawn in the game of political intrigue.

During the reception while all the introductions were being made, Charbriel who had an element of curiosity as well as a vast study of biology due to his profession, developed some inquisitive mental tendrils that Alessandra easily detected and explored with her growing mental telepathy. As she probed deeper and deeper into Charbriel's mind she discovered the resplendence of this wonderful Larafracean who was so caring and idealistic wanting to spend his life helping other people recover from ailments.

That evening as Princess Alessandra met and socialized with the selected guests, she gravitated towards Charbriel and initiated conversations with him. While many people present saw Alessandra's charm, she slowly focused on Charbriel and ignored most of the guests creating an atmosphere that allowed her and Charbriel to experience a lot of the evening with each other.

The thoughts of many around them were having a negative effect on Princess Alessandra's ability to fully telepathically investigate Charbriel so she asked, "Would it be possible for us to walk over to the balcony where its quieter where we can hear each other better?"

Charbriel was already starting to have unexplained feelings for Alessandra didn't mind that at all and eagerly agreed and said, "Let me take you there, I see a nice empty area."

Alessandra who was the consummate socialite among the Lìsztbrùnést Royals, fully trained in etiquette and demure projections, held her hand out to Charbriel to grab to guide her along, if nothing else but to convey to others, give us some space and privacy.

The security detail wasn't far behind and when the two arrived at the empty area along the balcony, they positioned themselves to block intruders.

"Thank you for taking time to talk with me," Princess Alessandra said in the humblest fashion.

"It's a great honor for me, plus I've not had much time to socialize the past few years because of my occupation."

"What is your occupation?" Alessandra asked out of politeness but already knew much about Charbriel by her telepathic investigation of his thoughts.

"I just finished all my training requirements for a medical practitioner."

Princess Alessandra Charbriel most likely lived an exhaustive schedule and his premature aging showed signs of the effects.

"That must be challenging."

"It certainly is every single day."

The two enjoyed a very lovely conversation that lasted quite a while until one of Princess Alessandra's female handlers approached and said, "I'm sorry Princess Alessandra, but some of the guests are now departing, I recommend you come back into the room to say goodbye to them."

"Alright, I will be right there, give me a minute."

"Yes, your highness," The handler stated then she walked back into the room towards a group of guests that appeared to be departing.

"Would it be possible to see you again?" Princess Alessandra asked Charbriel and then started manipulating him telepathically to ensure the right answer came out.

"I have a full schedule, but if you would like, meet me at the hospital tomorrow and we can have lunch there and have a chance to talk during my lunch break."

"I would be most happy to meet you there. I'm sorry but duty calls I must go see all these people off. Can I see you one more time before you leave?"

"Sure, I will wait for you. Go do what you need to do."

"Thank you." Princess Alessandra was feeling much better because she had an attraction to this man Charbriel.

After the crowd thinned out, Charbriel thought it was time to say good night to the princess and he approached her.

"Thank you for waiting."

"It's my pleasure."

"I will visit you at your hospital tomorrow at lunch time. My assistants will soon be making all the arrangements, and someone will notify you when I arrive."

"I'm looking forward to it."

Princess Alessandra now digging deeper into the persona of Charbriel knew his emotions, he could not hide them from her telepathic probing. She knew exactly how he really felt, and it was uplifting to her to discover the mutual attraction. Charbriel only had one issue that Alessandra knew how to overcome easily.

Charbriel didn't feel important enough to ever become a significant other to Princess Alessandra. Alessandra was a lot like her brother, very intelligent and astute and knew quite perfectly well she could help Charbriel cross that gap. She now had intentions towards Charbriel who was the very first man to captivate her or to make her feel eager for a relationship.

As soon as the Larafracean diplomat informed his superiors about the interactions with Princess Alessandra and Charbriel, there were slowly changes being done to his schedule to free up time so Alessandra could spend more time socializing with Charbriel. Just like Princess Alessandra said, he would be notified when she arrived at the hospital the next day which turned into a public relations event as well.

The Larafracean Diplomat was not going to waste this special event, he would systematically create a nice public relations event to shine the princess in the best of light including asking her to walk through a ward that had children being treated for cancers and other severe life-threatening medical conditions. Just as if the planets had aligned, Charbriel had worked in this ward for a while under supervision of senior doctors and was the favorite of most of the children who had great affection for him.

The ruse they pulled on Princess Alessandra was he had about 30 minutes left before his relief would be there and asked her if it would be okay if she accompanied him visiting some of the children who would love to meet a living princess?

Princess Alessandra was intelligent and sophisticated and knew she was being used for public relations purposes, but she didn't mind because she kind of wanted to see the interaction between Charbriel and his patients.

Princess Alessandra was escorted to the children's cancer ward and there she was led up to her prince charming who looked good in his medical clothes.

Charbriel was of course slightly emotional but polite. Alessandra was extremely curious because his demeaner had shifted. And she did the one thing she probably should not have done at that moment and probed him telepathically and discovered something she wished she hadn't. One of his young female patients died that morning holding his hand. He was heartbroken. Charbriel tried everything he could to save the beautiful young girl, but when the disease gets too far along there is nothing any doctor can do.

It was a somber walk through the ward and Princess Alessandra was astonished how well Charbriel was holding up with his great sorrow. But as they went into all the rooms and saw all the children, Alessandra quickly felt their emotions and great love for Charbriel. He was their savior and a person they all collectively loved. He wasn't the cold practitioner that many of the doctors were. His social skills were impecable. All the children had great positive emotions for Charbriel which Alessandra picked up on. Her intuition quickly grew along with her desires for this man.

Some of the parents were there visiting their children and as Charbriel walked into their room, the parents were very humble and appreciative, and they unquestioningly felt good about Charbriel for what he had done to save their children's lives that were showing signs of recovery and the efficacy of the treatments were apparent.

Charbriel had dealt with some of them for a few months working through the treatments and in some cases surgery was necessary. Some of the last patients and parents they saw were children who had a very successful outcome of the treatments and were going to be discharged in a few days after some additional tests were done to confirm the effectiveness of the treatments. Those families had vibrations of love and admiration to Charbriel, and Princess Alessandra had to fight strongly to not have an emotional singularity and expose more of herself than she knew was proper in this setting.

~~~~~~

Because of security concerns a small area of the cafeteria was roped off and gave Alessandra and Charbriel a semblance of privacy, even though from a short distance they had 1000 sets of eyes on them and later when worldwide entertainment and news channels showed them, billions would see the couple having lunch and talking.

The lunch hour ended too swiftly for Alessandra's satisfaction, but she understood Charbriel had important business to attend and they said goodbye and Alessandra was soon taken back to the Lìsztbrùnést Royal Space Yacht where she started giving her handlers instructions on maximizing access to Charbriel.

~~~~~~

The Larafracean Diplomat was contacted by Alessandra's handlers and soon was given the most delightful information, that conveyed Princess Alessandra wanted to spend more time with Charbriel. The diplomat was quite happy to accommodate their request and soon began the intergovernmental intrigue that would facilitate the Lìsztbrùnést Princess' apparent bourgeoning sentiments displayed and who also happened to be the sister of the most powerful emperor in the Galaxy.

Because of orders from the chief surgeon who was directed by higherups in the Larafracean government, the hospital was ordered to cut down on Charbriel's hours.

When Charbriel inquired with the chief surgeon why there was reduction of his working hours, the chief surgeon simply lied, "Because of some of the patients passing that you were especially close to and fought inordinately to save the lives, we are worried we have pushed you too far and too fast and you need some of your own recovery time."

During the first free day off periods which Charbriel positively enjoyed to the maximum taking the chief surgeons advice winding down a notch, his Diplomatic Corps relative contacted him:

"Princess Alessandra would like to spend some time with you. Would it be possible for you to take her around the planet and show her some sights?"

"I suppose I could, but it takes a while to travel to places I would think she would like to see."

"All your transportation will be provided by the Lìsztbrùnést who have security concerns for their princess and require special handling of events. They have the means to get your there very quickly."

"Sure, I suppose I could go."

"Since you have the day off, can you be ready to travel in a couple hours?"

"Sure."

"We have a list of places we think would be appropriate plus the security arrangements will be far better there."

"I will be ready in a couple of hours."

Just like clockwork, two hours later Charbriel had visitors. Two Larafracean security men in suits were at his door.

"Charbriel?"

"Yes."

"Your ride is here, please follow us."

Charbriel knew these two bruisers were no doubt very capable people that could take down an assailant very quickly. No doubt they are packing laser weapons.

The two well-dressed security men escorted Charbriel down to the waiting skycar they all got into that immediately went airborne and flew about 10 miles to a military base with high security that sat down, right next to the Lìsztbrùnést Royal Space Yacht. Standing by the door to the Lìsztbrùnést Royal Space Yacht was Princess Alessandra, the ship's captain and a couple chaperones that doubled as chambermaids. Drákōlìné had just been recalled to the emperor's palace to help out with Starlight and Stanley-II.

Princess Alessandra looked spectacular every time Charbriel saw her. But today, she obviously had extra detail to her wardrobe and makeup. She stood there utterly seductive and attractive.

Charbriel had been stewing about his patient dying trying to second guess himself as to what he possibly could have done wrong or what he could have done to get better results. Princess Alessandra discovered these and many more items while she probed Charbriel.

Nevertheless, when it's reported to higher authorities a doctor was taking it really hard about a patient passing, management takes action right away and Charbriel soon found himself sitting in front of the desk of the chief surgeon. Alessandra telepathically probed these memories of Charbriel that were crystal clear as if she were actually present during the events.

The chief surgeon had words with his fine young medical practitioner and explained, "There was nothing more that could be done. The disease had worked its course and all their therapeutics and surgery just couldn't prevent the eventual outcome."

"I just wonder if there is something I could have done."

"Charbriel, let it go. It is over. There was nothing more you could have done."

The chief surgeon was a brilliant man and had a team that analyzed each death for quality control purposes including all the paperwork and processes used. They knew Charbriel had done a heroic job putting in far more time than he was assigned to be bedside with the young patient and look over test results repeatedly.

Unfortunately, the parents brought the child to the hospital to late and Charbriel was fighting a losing battle from day one.

"There are some cases you will not be able to save, and you might as well start understanding it now. That's how life really is," The chief surgeon said feeling empathy towards the struggling doctor.

Charbriel could not get that child's demise off his mind, but when he got out of the skycar and faced Princess Alessandra, he slowly was coming back down to earth and his thoughts and feelings about the patient slowly dissipated. Princess Alessandra was saving Charbriel from himself, and the effects were feeling better moments after greeting Alessandra.

"Hello Alessandra."

"Thank you for visiting me, Charbriel."

"My pleasure."

Because of protocol and security concerns the Larafracean Security team had to travel everywhere with the Royal Alessandra. The Larafracean government wanted their own set of eyes and ears in the vicinity of Charbriel so that if any negative happened, they would get an unfiltered and direct report. The two bruisers that brought Charbriel to the military base followed him and Princess Alessandra up into the Lìsztbrùnést Royal Space Yacht and they were soon on their way to their first stop.

The Lìsztbrùnést Royal Space Yacht a fully graviton ship had exceptional acceleration and deacceleration capabilities without making the passengers sick thanks to the artificial gravity. The Larafracean satellites and military aircraft that acted as escorts had a hard time tracking and keeping up. The Larafraceans knew the Lìsztbrùnést Royal Space Yacht sported spectacular technology. They also knew this was the most powerful Empire in the galaxy. Hence it would be in their best interest to improve relations any way they could.

The Lìsztbrùnést really had no need for a Larafracean relationship. But the specter of a Larafracean citizen involved with a Lìsztbrùnést Royal certainly had a major effect on the Larafracean government. Charbriel's involvement with Princess Alessandra was deemed far more important to society than his efforts at the cancer ward. Politics always override all other elements of life.

The first stop was at a tropical paradise that on a small bridge they could see crystal clear water down forty feet. This was an exclusive zone for the well to do as only the ultra-rich could afford to come to this resort area.

After a short period of time walking on a nice sidewalk next to the beach, Alessandra asked, "Would you like to take a swim with me here at the beach?"

"I didn't come prepared for such activity," Charbriel responded in dismay that it would be impossible for him to please the princess. He was unaware she had wings because they were hidden with her cape and all the materials she had at her disposal.

"Not to worry, I'll ask my valet to give us a change of clothes and we'll be ready to get into the water in a few minutes if you would give me the honor."

"Sure, if we can get accommodations of attire, I would love to."

"Charbriel, before we do that, I want you to know some things about me so that in a while you find out it does not shock you and put you into a negative psychology."

"I'm sure there is nothing you could do that would affect me more than my patient that just died."

"Alright, us find out. We might as well get this out of the way. Let's return to the Royal Yacht so we can change."

To Charbriel's surprise, within five minutes he had swim wear because the Royal Yacht was always prepared for such contingencies such as an unscheduled swim at a beach. Charbriel fit nicely in swimming attire staged for Stanley and Lacsar.

Charbriel was escorted out of the Royal Yacht and informed, "The Princess would be ready in a few minutes."

Charbriel was cooling his heels on the white sandy beach wondering what the princess would look like when she came out.

Princess Alessandra's grand appearance soon occurred.

The princess had on a cape but her revealing swimsuit showed she had very nice breasts and an incredible figure that would even impress any medical practitioner.

The Chaperone walked a short and discrete distance behind the Royal Princess Alessandra as to not interfere with the elegance she wanted to display.

Thanks to her mental telepathy, Princess Alessandra already knew Charbriel was psychologically affected by her appearance. But she knew not to lay her cards on the table quite yet because Charbriel had not been presented with the image of Princess Alessandra's wings, which he might not be able to handle. There were still some unknown elements of this growing emotional bond. But soon Alessandra would do the ultimate test and she would then know if this was a viable relationship for the future.

Princess walked up to Charbriel and held her hand out and said, "Could you take me to the water, I would like to wade in it?"

"Certainly."

Princess Alessandra purposely delayed the huge revelation to Charbriel as they walked down the beach holding hands giving herself time to get her wits together and better properly manage the big revelation that would soon be bestowed upon Charbriel. With all kinds of INTEL people observing the couple with spectacular photonics with great magnification, Alessandra knew this event would expose her essence.

The couple waded aimlessly in the water discussing irrelevant and trivial things, mentioning the marine life, rocks, and seashells they observed.

Princess Alessandra doing her telepathic analysis of Charbriel's thoughts felt he had reached quiescence and his mind was now totally away from the hospital and his patient that had passed. He was feeling a sense of relief and Alessandra knew because of her telepathic probing he was developing a serious attraction to her.

Charbriel's heart was in a very vulnerable state, which sometimes happens after a person experiences grief. And since Charbriel experienced incredible grief about the child passing, Princess Alessandra was happy she was helping him reach this peaceful moment. She knew that as Charbriel came to terms with his grief that now was the time to show Charbriel her attributes. Alessandra would now disclose the essence of herself including her wings and depending on Charbriel's reaction would be the deciding factor if such a relationship had a pathway forward.

"Let's stop for a moment there is something I want you to see so we will know if this is really for you."

Princess Alessandra looked in Charbriel's eyes and hoped her wings would not kill the deal. She had grown fond of Charbriel to almost the point of no return. For her own personal psychology, Princess Alessandra had to get over this revelation or continue searching the universe for someone who would accept her for what she was, a woman with wings.

Princess Alessandra looked back at her chaperone and nodded at her. The Chaperone came directly to her knowing what was next.

"Please remove my cape."

All the INTEL people now had a sight to behold, it was an incredible revelation to the two bruisers who came with Charbriel here.

As soon as the Chaperone removed the cape, she stepped back several feet because she knew this would be a delicate moment and the couple had already experienced powerful emotions together at the hospital where Princess Alessandra was able to peer deeply into Charbriel's soul.

Charbriel was looking at Princess with incredible curiosity. Princess Alessandra then unfurled her wings. It was the most incredible sight that Charbriel had seen in his lifetime. A beautiful woman with a beautiful face and body also had wings.

Emotions suddenly hit Charbriel of how special Princess Alessandra appeared in this majestic image. Princess Alessandra underestimated Charbriel by quite a margin. In no way did Alessandra's wings diminish Charbriel's enthusiasm for her. In his thoughts he was saying "I love you."

Princess Alessandra fully probing Charbriel telepathically understood right away his response. It touched her very positively.

As they stood looking into each other's eyes, Alessandra knew what Charbriel was thinking as she poured her telepathic probes deep into his psyche, every bit of it.

Alessandra knew Charbriel's love, and affection was genuine and strong. Alessandra felt it and she knew that Charbriel had no means to know she had such powerful telepathic ability. Princess Alessandra knew Charbriel's love, and affection was totally legitimate and pure love from heart of a man with a great mind and extraordinary history especially in his dealings treating children with life threatening issues.

Charbriel stood there stunned and in a semi state of shock and didn't know what to do. He was stuck in awe and wonderment, but his emotions were quite strong and when a person has such strong emotions, it is almost blinding to someone like Alessandra who was super sensitive.

Alessandra walked through the glare and approached Charbriel with her wings fully furled and spread in the most majestic fashion and walked up to him. She knew her actions were safe because she knew every thought Charbriel had. She placed her hands on the sides of Charbriel's head and pulled his face towards her and she gave Charbriel the most romantic kiss possible. The tantalizing kiss was mutual and was strong.

There was no doubt in anyone watching the significance of this event. It was an affirmation of the new love between the two. It seemed fresh just like spring green synthesizing scents and thoughts that usually eluded ordinary people living lives lacking such luster.

Charbriel knew he loved Alessandra. His heart poured out to her, and Alessandra knew every bit of it and was pleased her evaluation and anticipation came to be true as she hoped.

Alessandra knew she was in love and would spend the rest of her life with Charbriel no matter what it took. Just like her mother before who stumbled across Stanley, Alessandra found her prince charming in the most unpredictable fashion.

After the long kiss and neutrino messages back to the emperor, the mansion was happy that night because Alessandra whom they feared would wonder fruitlessly around the galaxy had somehow by the grace of God discovered this incredible person who had a magnificent reputation and the charisma and affection of all his patients. Charbriel wasn't an accidental meeting of someone for a brief affection. This was a game changer because Princess Alessandra's brother the current sitting emperor knew his sister was very intelligent and quite articulate and would never avail herself to a simple man. This had to be a special man, or she would never be interested.

Charbriel was suddenly the most investigated person in the galaxy and when the emperor received the reports about this wonderful medical practitioner, including his success as well as his tragedies, he felt happiness for his sister could find such a man.

Emperor Lacsar knew one thing for certain, the only way he could make sure Alessandra would never lose Charbriel was to bring them both back to the mansion and begin the process of bringing Charbriel into the Royal Family including the necessity of a Royal Unification.

Instructions were then sent to the Lìsztbrùnést diplomats to start discussions with the Larafraceans to prepare Charbriel for a journey to the mansion where it would all begin.

Now that the preliminaries were out of the way, Charbriel took Princess Alessandra to other locations to show her his world. This was important especially after a Royal Unification because this world would soon be one of Alessandra's responsibilities as it now would be an important place for her and in the future no doubt there would be many visits.

From mountain tops, to deserts, to tropical rain forests, to majestic landscapes, Princess Alessandra got a fast course on what existed on this planet. Overall, she liked what she saw. But more so, she had the reverberations of emotional resonance from the person who had a quickly building emotion for her. Princess Alessandra knew these feelings because without him knowing, Alessandra pierced every thought Charbriel had because she knew he was in love with her, she reciprocated and started flooding his mind with feelings and emotions he didn't know were a composite from two of them.

What started out as one of the worst days of his life fretting over the loss of a child who essentially died in his arms despite everything he tried, here he was feeling the love of this gorgeous woman that touched his heart in ways he could ever imagine. In a sense Alessandra pulled Charbriel out of his temporal nightmare and gave him new life so he could put behind him the sadness of the recent tragedy with his patient and all the other unpleasant events in his life.

After the future Royal Couple were all done with the sightseeing and visiting special places on the planet it was time to get dressed up for the evening activities.

"Charbriel, would you do me a big favor?" Alessandra asked.

"I'm sure I would be delighted," Charbriel answered fully willing to do anything for the princess.

"We will be having dinner with the leaders of your planet in a while. I feel very special about you. Because I feel you are someone that will always be special in my life, I'm requesting you wear Royal Lìsztbrùnést attire with me to the dinner."

"I suppose I could."

"I know it might seem like I'm rushing things, but I know what is in your heart and I know you love me, and I love you and we will soon be a couple."

"I feel the same way."

"Let's make this special announcement tonight at dinner that we are now a couple by you wearing the Royal uniform we have for you."

"If that would make you feel good, I will be happy to do so."

In front of the security personnel and the chaperone, Alessandra walked over to Charbriel and threw her arms around him and kissed him because she knew what was in his mind and his heart because her telepathic intrusion was very strong.

Alessandra's telepathic probing allowed to sense every thought Charbriel had during the kiss. She knew it was pure love and exactly how Charbriel felt about it. Alessandra knew secretly Charbriel had gone past the point of no return with her in his emotions.

Alessandra's seduction of Charbriel was complete and final. As a powerful woman, Alessandra knew a lot about what went on firsthand especially with her grandfather and her father in recent history, she knew how a person had to be decisive, acting on instinct with superb INTEL to have success. Her *mission* was clearly now *Charbriel.*

After spending quality time with Charbriel over the next couple of weeks and penetrating his mind with her growing telepathic abilities, Alessandra knew what was in his heart and it was time to pitch him her plan.

"I've learned a lot about you in this short period of time and I would like to invite you to Neflatraceous, the capital of the Lìsztbrùnést Empire, to meet my brother the emperor and my parents, and if we can arrange a trip to visit my grandfather."

"I'm concerned about how my absence will affect the hospital."

"If necessary, I will arrange to have a dozen advanced doctors flown in to assist while you are gone."

"Let me go talk with the chief surgeon and see what he has to say about this."

By the time Charbriel made it to the chief surgeon, the spooks and the diplomats had already paid the chief surgeon a visit and convinced him what he needed to do if he knew what was good for himself. This relationship with a powerful woman was too big of a deal now.

The Chief Surgeon would have to figure out how to deal with daily routines without Charbriel who would now experience much more important things to do for the sake of the Larafracean people who would greatly benefit if Charbriel ended up as a Lìsztbrùnést Royal. The stakes were very high.

Charbriel was completely surprised when the Chief Surgeon said, "Take that trip. Because of your excellent work you have done here you deserve some time off. Plus, the strain placed on you with recent events, it would be in your best interest as well as our own for you to go away for a while and enjoy yourself. The hospital will still be here until you get back."

Deep in his thoughts the Chief Surgeon already knew the facts of life. The minute Charbriel got aboard that Lìsztbrùnést Royal Space Yacht, they would likely never see him again based on the discussions with the diplomats and the spooks. He also knew Charbriel would have a chance of a lifetime, he would never otherwise get, and it was in his best interest to get on that spaceship and leave with Princess Alessandra.

The following day the same two bruisers arrived at Charbriel's residence and when he answered the door, they asked, "Are you packed and ready?"

"I suppose I'm as ready as I'll ever be.

The three men walked out to the skycar and got inside. Within a few minutes they arrived at the military base. The Lìsztbrùnést Royal Space Yacht was already in space orbiting the planet where it took on items for their journey back to the Lìsztbrùnést Empire. A shuttle was there and standing beside it was Alessandra in ornate decorated Royal Clothing smiling as if it were one of the happiest days of her life.

Charbriel approached Alessandra with a neutral emotion realizing he was going on a journey that would probably change his life, forever. He didn't know what to expect being with a woman with wings. But every other aspect of her seemed like a normal human. Charbriel did feel he had remarkable emotional attachment to Alessandra now and didn't quite understand how a person such as himself with a scientific mind would transcend into a relationship to a powerful Royal like this.

The spontaneous decisions and abrupt change in the direction of Charbriel's life seemed almost artificial in nature. If it were not for the fact, he had special feelings for Alessandra and deep in his heart he knew he had fallen in love with her, he never would have gotten into that shuttle with her.

There were minimal crew, a pilot, co-pilot and the two passengers. The shuttle was escorted by Larafracean Space Force craft up to the Lìsztbrùnést Royal Space Yacht where it quickly docked, and the future Royal Couple soon exited and made their way into the control room to meet the captain and those who that Alessandra necessary. The Royal Space Yacht then left orbit and headed back towards the Lìsztbrùnést Empire.

A couple days passed and while Princess Alessandra her new love Charbriel were on their way to the emperor's mansion almost halfway to their destination, when they were jumped by an outlaw group operating out of an extremely corrupt world Zorcrarisp that hosted pirates and a nasty band of mercenaries that often relied on nefarious activities such as kidnapping, prostitution, human trafficking, and a variety of other despicable activities to enrich themselves allowing them to contract to build some of the finest spacecraft in the galaxy sporting substantial capabilities.

All during the battle the Fast Frigates sent off Neutrino messages requesting assistance and when one of them blew up the other Fast Frigate and the Lìsztbrùnést Royal Space Yacht sent those terrible images to the empire. The Fast Frigates also continuously sent out emergency distress signals and all three ships launched extremely fast communication drones that easily outran the captors that carried detailed situation reports and INTEL on the makeup of the outlaw mercenaries operating from Zorcrarisp.

The Royal Yacht and the surviving Frigate were able to fight the Pirates and Mercenaries off for a while but eventually they were outnumbered and after the second Frigate blew up the captain of the Lìsztbrùnést Royal Space Yacht realized they were severely outnumbered and surrounded by so many craft, he would risk the princess life if he kept fighting, he decided to surrender the ship and hope her brother would quickly pay the ransom so they would be released.

The Captain of the Royal Yacht heeled too and allowed the pirates and mercenaries to board the Yacht where it was taken to the planet Zorcrarisp as a prize ship. A group of filthy mercenaries that had boarded the Royal Yacht to take custody of it started evaluating what was on board to figure out what their take was.

When the Royal Yacht arrived on the planet Zorcrarisp where all the passengers were removed except the captain kept there to teach them operations of the craft. Charbriel was then severely beaten and dumped into a dungeon with several diseased criminals waiting their fate of crossing the wrong people.

In due time the Zorcrarisp Mercenaries were offering the princess to other worlds for a big price noting she was still a virgin. The young man Charbriel barely clinged to life.

As soon as the young emperor Lacsar was informed about his younger sister's fate, they started emergency planning and Fleet assets were dispatched to the vicinity of Zorcrarisp where the abduction occurred, and Intel immediately started working on hard to figure out where exactly on the planet they were.

There was no resolution by the emperor that night exactly what they would attempt to do, but he did say, he would use brute force if Alessandra has harmed.

In the middle of the night Lucas, Octavrator, and Stanley disappeared, so did the flock of birds. Stanley was not going to go without his family of birds as he knew they had some very big advantages in the art of breaking into well protected compounds.

By morning the three amigos were long gone and in the fast frigates they flew on were loaded up with extra special weapons. The next battle would not go over too well for the Zorcrarisp Pirates and Mercenaries if they engaged in a space battle.

The Fleet took a more conservative approach to planet Zorcrarisp. They flew through other solar systems to hide their approach. Stanley's force did a high-speed direct transit that was highly risky but would get them at the target area at a much quicker time. Because of all the birds and the three spies they had four stratospheric gliders with them to get down to the planet surface and attempt rescue. Part of the plan was to attack the mercenaries' fleet with special weapons as a diversion. A space battle would be going on while the spies along with the birds infiltrated the security apparatus and slowly took it down.

Several communiques were intercepted along the way and deep space communications revealed one of the entities bidding on the Princess was none other than a son of a Trilateral Stanley killed. That only meant one thing the Trilateral wanted the girl for a revenge killing. Time was more pressing than they imagined.

It would not be a clean mission. There would no doubt be casualties this time, especially with the birds. In telepathic discussions between Rascal-II and Stanley their odds of survival were presented, and Rascal-II didn't flinch one bit and responded, "If we must die to save the Princess, we are willing to do whatever it takes to get Princess Alessandra back."

By the time they arrived at planet Zorcrarisp, the Trilateral was already there getting ready to do the transaction and he was currently in the Den of thieves celebrating their big score.

The Trilateral even hinted he might entertain raping the woman in front of the mercenaries for their entertainment. The only thing that delayed him for a while is when one of the women with the lead mercenaries whispered in his ear, "If you let him rape her in front of me, I might kill you in your sleep."

That warning only delayed events for a short while, then the Trilateral eventually ignored the statement to leave her alone and began to prepare to rape her in front of everyone.

Just as he ripped off some of Alessandra's clothes the Trilateral received a dart from one of the birds. Many other mercenaries were intoxicated and almost passed out started receiving deadly darts. In a few minutes it turned into a terrible firefight.

With the outer security layer taken down and telepathic guidance by the birds, Stanley was able to get into the room and quickly did the kill shot on the Trilateral holding his daughter. Mercenaries in the room were shooting at Stanley and unfortunately Stanley received some terrible wounds, but he felt he could fly.

With the birds, Lucas and Octavrator shooting them a way out of an apparent trap, they got to where they could take Alessandra to the air, but Alessandra pitched a fit they were leaving her lover Charbriel behind, and he was beaten badly and taken to the dungeon.

Stanley wounded and bleeding said, "All right I will go back and get him, but you need to follow Rascal-II back to a stratospheric glider and get in it and fly up to one of the Fast Frigates immediately."

Alessandra free from her shackles had no problem keeping up flying with Rascal-II who led her to a camouflaged stratospheric glider and got inside. Once inside the stratospheric glider took off, but Rascal-II flew back carrying another batch darts with him. The stratospheric glider went airborne and thanks to the surprise attack, they wiped out so many Mercenaries spaceships, the Fast Frigates were easily able to stand off at a safe distance and destroyed any mercenary ships brave enough to approach with their special weapons. It did not take long for the Mercenaries to figure out attacking these formidable ships would probably cost them their lives and stood back analyzing the situation.

The Fast Frigate with Alessandra had been ordered to leave immediately but Alessandra using her rank of a Royal directed the captain, "You will not leave my father behind. We are not going anywhere until he comes back."

Thanks to the birds and the use of telepathic assessment, Stanley was able to locate the dungeon and rescue the young man, Charbriel. Stanley was in a lot of pain but carried Charbriel to the surface and was soon met up with a dozen birds to help protect them and soon they found Lucas and Octavrator who had sustained several firefights which resulted in Octavrator seriously injured.

They couldn't fly to the stratospheric gliders because two of them were injured so hey had to walk out of the trap going through several more firefights where Octavrator and Stanley received more injuries. Thanks to his wireless capabilities Lucas was able to get Octavrator and Stanley into stratospheric gliders and send them on their way up to the Fast Frigates. Only one Lìsztbrùnést Special Forces person was left with Lucas at the stratospheric glider. It was going to be a tough going as the mercenaries were getting close. Lucas took the other man's weapons and said, "You go back to the frigate with the birds."

Rascal informed Lucas via telepathic communications, the other birds would leave but he was not going to abandon Lucas. The stratospheric glider blasted off and was on its way. Rascal-II had all the remaining darts, but they were facing a growing squad of mercenaries. When Stanley was informed Lucas was still on the planet, Stanley said, "We can't leave him behind."

Stanley didn't last long on the Fast Frigate before he became unconscious due to the loss of blood, but the doctors were working frantically on him. Octavrator was conscious and severely wounded said to the doctors, don't waste your time on me, take care of Duke Ravik first.

Octavrator almost bled to death to give Stanley a margin of survival because Stanley's wounds were rather serious. The Doctors knew they were making headway on saving Stanley's life and thanks to his blood type any of the crewmembers could and did donate blood, otherwise he would have died from his injuries.

Alessandra's young male friend Charbriel was in serious condition, but the doctors slowly restored him and gave him powerful pain killers for his terrible injuries. It was getting close to sunrise and Lucas had no way off the planet, but he at least had his wireless giving coordinates as to where he was located.

The Fast Frigates sent several weaponized drones down to shoot up a perimeter to give Lucas a chance to survive. Eventually Rascal-II ran out of darts and one of the Mercenaries got lucky with a laser rifle shot and nailed poor Rascal-II. Now it was Lucas all by himself.

The Frigates had done a good job of holding off the Mercenaries but eventually the mercenaries were emboldened by promises of a huge pay day and came after the Frigates again in a massive attack. The Frigates had no choice but to bug out leaving Lucas behind.

Just when the Mercenaries were getting within weapons range to the Frigates, the Lìsztbrùnést Fleet arrived on the scene. With the vast integrated fire control systems of the fleet getting all the intel from the two Fast Frigates, the Mercenaries quickly discovered the error in their way as the most powerful Fleet in the Galaxy was now upon them and smashed them. The surviving Mercenaries were directed to surrender immediately, or they and the planet would be completely destroyed.

The mercenaries were hauled off all their ships that were then destroyed to make sure they would never pose a threat to society again.

Lucas was slowly on the move using his computer brain to out guess his trackers and with nano second response avoid much of their weapons, but after 12 hours of constant combat fatigue was sitting in. Then suddenly fire erupted all around him. Swarms of drones were quickly wiping out the Mercenaries. All the electrical generation capability on the planet was shut down. The planet was now dark and in fear. Once a safe landing zone was established, a shuttle from a cruiser arrived and picked up Lucas who now had some serious injuries to his arms and legs.

To make sure these rats didn't repopulate, the mercenary compound was annihilated. The surviving mercenaries got to see firsthand what a major force could do to them.

~~~~~

The Royals were all shipped back to Neflatraceous where Stanley and Alessandra's young male friend Charbriel could receive the best medical treatment possible.

Stanley barely came back to consciousness after he was resting several days in the hospital room in the mansion. The young Emperor Lacsar, and Princess Lì along with Alessandra were at Stanley's bed side.

When the Royals arrived, Princess Lì was in total outrage, and she was going to tear into Stanley because he had once again crossed her with his *spontaneous mission* without permission from her or the emperor (his son Lacsar – Demetrius Ravik).

Stanley should not have undergone the brutal mental torture like he did upon the return of this mission as Alessandra thought she had schooled her mother and gave her the telepathic images of the Trilateral getting ready to rape her in front of all the Mercenaries.

After visiting her father for a while, Alessandra then took her mother to go see her special love, the young Charbriel who had been beaten unconscious by the evil Mercenary miscreants.

Charbriel's face was cut up terribly and he lost one of his testacies. He was now in a drug induced coma as part of the pain medications as the doctors knew his body needed to heal some before, he was brought back to consciousness because the pain would be terribly agonizing otherwise.

In a few days Charbriel was brought out of his coma still receiving massive opioid pain reducers and Stanley was soon
~~~~~

introduced to him by his daughter Alessandra.

"We finally get to meet," Stanley said.

"Thank you for saving my life."

"Alessandra loves you very much. If something happened to you, she would be miserable for the rest of her life."

"Well, I love her too."

"Nobody has suffered as much pain as you have for members of my family when you took that journey to get here which goes a long way to prove your commitment to Alessandra. I am grateful in how you have changed her and given her new meaning in life."

"Thank you, that means a lot to me," Charbriel said in a very somber manner.

Lacsar standing next to Stanley then decided to insert himself into the conversation: "Charbriel, may I ask you a question?"

"Sure, your Excellency."

"Do you plan on staying with Alessandra for the rest of your life?"

"If she accepts me, I will never leave her."

Alessandra could not hold back and threw herself onto Charbriel weeping.

Lacsar waited and observed Alessandra slowly recovering from her sudden emotional outpour and when she appeared to calm down, he decided now was the time to do his next act.

"Alright then Charbriel, in a short while I will put out an Emperor's Decree making you a Royal, you will now be part of our family."

"Thank you that means a lot to me."

Princess Lì observed all this and knew the condition Charbriel was in when he arrived clinging to life. For some reason observing all this didn't faze Princess Lì one bit. She had pent up anger and was waiting for the proper time to tear into Stanley, because this time he had finally crossed over the line as far as she was concerned.

~~~~~~

Eventually that same day, Stanley and Princess Lì were alone for a private discussion about the secret rescue mission to Planet Zorcrarisp with Lucas and Octavrator to save Alessandra.

"Why did you do this Stanley?"

"My dear, there was no time left. The boy would have died from his injuries and your daughter would have been raped by a dozen wretched scoundrels. We had to attack immediately to save Alessandra's dignity."

Stanley had far more powerful telemetry than Alessandra and he decided it was time that Princess Lì get a little dose of reality. He flooded her mind with all the images of the battle.

Unfortunately for Stanley, those images had no effect on Princess Lì who was extremely agitated feeling Stanley had violated her by sneaking off behind her back in this manner.

When two telepathic individuals argue it can be quite painful because you can't shut out that other person who's in your thoughts. Its like magnifying the sound 100-fold and can almost be destabilizing. People would prefer severe Tinnitus to such experiences

Princess Lì had picked the wrong fight at the wrong time and even with the horrible images she still wanted to punish Stanley. And she tormented Stanley remorselessly to the point she psychologically broke him.

At the peak of Princess Lì's telepathic punishment, Stanley
~~~~~~

softly said, "As soon as I'm healed up, I'm going back to Earth."

Princess Lì who remained heavily agitated ignored the comment and left the room. She didn't want to be around Stanley any longer.

~~~~~

A week later, Stanley went into Lacsar's private study where he was reading the report of what happened and thanks to Lucas' computer memory, he got a full video of the entire event. He also knew Stanley was again having serious issues with his mother. It now had grown out of control and quite serious as his mother seemed to want to torture Stanley in every awaken hour.

"What do you want to talk to me about today, father?"

"I want you to take me back to Earth today."

Lacsar sat there stunned but he knew that based on Stanley's dispute with his mother, that his father had finally reached his limit and a separation was now going to occur.

Lacsar could not turn down his father's request because he knew his father had another option if he wasn't taken back to Earth: suicide. And it was in his thoughts because Lacsar could easily penetrate Stanley's thoughts. The threat to commit suicide wasn't said, it didn't need to be since Lacsar knew what was in Stanley's mind.

Lacsar had no choice but to take his father back to Earth as his father requested, because he certainly did not want his father to kill himself. And that death would be soon because Stanley was now calling it quits for good.

The Royal Yacht had been rescued from the planet as the fleet was able to control it remotely and fly it up into space and return it
~~~~~

to the emperor's mansion.

The former captain had been rescued as he was still aboard as the mercenaries planned on torturing him to give them all the controls so they could use it. The surprise attack prevented that from happening and saved the captain's life. Since returned from the Planet Zorcrarisp incident, the Royal Space Yacht was restocked and reprovisioned with weapons and defense systems in essence it was ready to go.

"What are you going to do about your wings?"

"Your mother told me a long time ago all I must do is wish them away and they will eventually fall off. I'll wear a cape until they are gone."

Lacsar was a genius and a brilliant man who loved his father dearly and it upset him greatly the way his mother was treating his father who was now obviously heart broken over the ordeal, decided perhaps his mother needed a dose of misery to make her feel what she made his father feel. Thus, Lacsar determined the psychological shock his mother would receive by Stanley's departure would change her attitude and hopefully they never had to go through this again.

Stanley was provisioned with money and identity so that upon reaching earth he could survive. He also had something on him he wasn't aware of, a tracker. Lacsar didn't want to lose his father and drones and probes would look out for him. Without saying good by to Princess Lì, who didn't know he was leaving, Stanley boarded the Royal Yacht and was on his way back to Earth, this time for good.

~~~~~~

Towards evening when Princess Lì had not seen or heard of Stanley's whereabouts, she approached the Valet Octavrator and asked, "Where is Stanley?"
~~~~~~

Octavrator knew he couldn't hide his thoughts from Princess Lì knew he had to simply tell her the facts.

"He's gone."

"What do you mean he's gone?"

"You will find out soon enough so I might as well tell you now, he went back to his planet Earth. It's unlikely you will see him again."

Princess Lì suddenly had a psychological tremmors as her rational thoughts suddenly overcome her pent-up anger, then started feeling emotionally crushed then fell to the floor weeping and crying out to the point it got everyone's attention. Princess Alessandra was immediately requested and ran to her mother's side and asked Octavrator to help her take her mother to her suite.

Soon doctors were brought into Princess Lì's suite to sedate Princess Lì to help her get over this terrible psychological meltdown. She was soon comfortably sleeping and dreaming of Stanley, the love of her life. Doctors were ordered to remain with her around the clock and to inform the emperor as soon as his mother became conscious again.

~~~~~~
~~~~~~

Chapter Twenty-One

Life is Great Again at Ski Beach

Stanley had checked into a cheap hotel in Pacific Beach and stopped by his favorite grocery store where he met up with his friend from many years ago, Duff who worked there.

"Where you been? Have not seen you in a long time?"

"I went on a long trip."

Stanley was wearing a cape because he still had wings and he was lucky it was wintertime and cold and people were wearing jackets. Stanley purchased a few items to give to the birds at Ski Beach. The Uber driver had waited for Stanley who then gave him a business card and was available to give him a ride any time to Ski Beach.

The uber driver dropped off Stanley in the parking lot and then Stanley started walking around the park in a clockwise direction like he often did in the past.

As Stanley walked around the park, he wondered if any of the birds he knew were still here and if any remembered him.

Strangely one of the black birds flew up to Stanley and landed a short distance away and seemed to remember him. But now Stanley had great mental telepathy and could communicate to the black birds This happened to be the bird Stanley named Rascal many years ago had thoughts that appeared to telepathically transmit to Stanley, "We missed you. We feared we might never see you again."

"I'm back my friend. It's good to see you again."

"How is it you are able to talk to me."

"It's a long story and I got plenty of time and I'll tell you all about it."

~~~~~~

Finally, when Princess Lì awakened, Lacsar and Alessandra were at her bedside. She looked at them and knew this was a difficult moment for all of them.

"I really screwed up this time. I can't believe what I did," Princess Lì said after a few minutes.

Lacsar and Alessandra didn't say anything because they were afraid, they could cause their mother to have another serious negative mental episode.

"Lacsar, I want to ask a big favor of you."

"What is it you would like me to do Mother?"

"Take me to Earth right away so I can tell Stanley I love him more than anything and I'm very sorry the way I treated him."

"I don't think father is ready for you, what's to assure him you will not do this again?"

"This time I know I was wrong, and he was right. I want to tell him face to face I apologize for being so terribly wrong and that I love him with all my heart and will do anything to be back with him again."
~~~~~~

"It's kind of interesting how things happen the way they do. The Royal Yacht did a high-speed transit back here and could be reprovisioned in a few hours," Lacsar said.

"That's wonderful, send me right away."

"Mother this time you did a lot of damage and do not know you almost drove my father to suicide. Had I not agreed to take him to Earth, he would have killed himself that day."

The tears started flowing down Princess Lì who now was fearful she had lost the love of her life over her stupid attitude and her brutal behavior.

"I think there is only one way we can get him to come back."

"What's that?"

"I know someone available whose very influential with my father."

"Who is that?"

"Your father. I think he can convince father to come back. But I seriously recommend you let him talk to father first. Then we'll take you to the planet to face him."

"Alright, I'm willing to do that. How soon can father be ready to go?"

"For something this important I think he is ready to go now. Let me go speak with him."

The former emperor Cornelius was brought back to the palace when princess Alessandra was captured as Lacsar thought he would provide valuable advice, especially after it became known Stanley was gone and Lacsar had a notion where he might have gone.

Lacsar was naive to think he could ever hide something from his grandfather who made it his point to know everything just in case he had to use his wisdom to intervene.

Lacsar walked to his grandfather's suite, and he was waiting for his arrival knowing what was coming because he just finished observing and hearing the surveillance video and audio.

"Grandfather I need your help in a matter."

"Sure Lacsar, you know you can count on me."

They discussed the situation and the emperor asked, "How soon will the Royal Yacht be ready?"

"Latest reports I received is one to two hours."

"Alright. I think Tonnerre might like to see planet Earth, this will be a good trip for her."

In a while with Princess Lì full of fear and regret, and most of the Royals left for planet Earth with the fleet. The Royals were split up on Frigates, Cruisers, and the Royal Yacht to make sure they all didn't perish in a dreadful unexpected disaster.

The fleet enjoyed going fast and they seldom had the opportunity, so this trip to Earth made Admiral Timons quite happy.

Once again Lacsar was with Admiral Timons. Starlight was left home at the mansion because the little tyke didn't need to travel. He was now the most guarded person on the planet. Charbriel was still in his hospital bed slowly recovering and feeling better every day. Alessandra who remained with Charbriel was growing more and more happy because the Doctors indicated after his successful surgery dealing with testicular damage, he would soon be able to get out of his bed and start walking again and he would be able to procreate their children in the future after the Unification once her father Stanley, Duke of Ravik came home.

But Alessandra knew it would be terrible times in the mansion if her father chose not to come home to the point, she and Charbriel might consider returning to the Larafracean world to live for a while and be Unified there.

Drákōlìné was sent along to help Princess Lì deal with all exigencies, especially if Stanley said he would not come back.

There would be no point in kidnapping him and bringing him back because he would simply commit suicide and because of his vast martial arts training it would be in a spectacular way and its unlikely it could be prevented.

The tracker Stanley was wearing in his cape made him easy to find. There he was walking around Ski Beach exercising and discussing with his new Psychiatrist he renamed Rascal-III all the circumstances and events that happened.

Rascal-III decided it was time to advise his good friend and said, "Stanley, I know that Princess Lì loves you more than anything, why don't you go back to her?"

That's kind of hard since I have no way of getting there. Rascal-III saw the shuttle land behind Stanley who didn't know it was there yet. A few beach goers saw the UFO start taking pictures and posting it on Facebook.

"Rascal-III said, "Stanley, I know how you can get back to Princess Lì?"

"How would that be possible?"

"Look behind you."

Stanley turned around and there was Emperor Cornelius with Tonnerre exiting the shuttle. Emperor Cornelius suggested to Princess Lì, "I don't want you to screw this up. Stanley's heart is severely wounded. Let me talk to him first."

In his royal garb, Emperor Cornelius appeared like something right out of a movie. More and more people at Ski Beach were approaching and completely overwhelmed because they now knew for a fact *there are Aliens*!

Stanley stood there until Rascal-III said, "In your heart you know you want to talk with them. Go to them."

"Okay only if you hop on my shoulder."

"It will be my pleasure, Stanley."

The growing crowd saw the blackbird fly over and hop onto Stanleys' shoulder and he approached Emperor Cornelius walking towards him. They met up and stopped a few feet apart. Stanleys eyes were watering up. So were the emperor's and Tonnerre's eyes. This was quite an emotional moment for Stanley.

"Stanley, I want to talk to you for a few minutes."

"I'm always willing to talk to you, Your Excellency. I always liked you and I always will."

"I feel the same way about you, Stanley."

There was too much noise by the growing crowd yelling and making noise, so Emperor Cornelius swung into mental telepathy, and said, "Princess Lì loves you more than anything else."

"I love her too."

"Then come back with us Stanley, her heart will be shattered if you don't come back."

The tears were rolling down Stanley's cheeks and he said, "I suppose I could come back, but would it be okay if I bring this bird with me."

"You might want to ask him if he's willing to go."

By now Stanley had developed a serious protocol with Rascal-III and the bird answered the emperor in telepathic voice which surprised him, "I would be very happy to go with Stanley. I know all about his life."

When the three of them with the bird Rascal-III started walking toward the shuttle, Princess Lì could not hold back and jumped out of the shuttle and flew to Stanley halfway across the park area where the Lìsztbrùnést Royal Space Yacht had landed when Princess Lì Aligrāwná first met Stanley many years ago.

Now the crowd was super animated seeing this bird woman fly up and embrace Stanley, crying and so relieved because her father was smiling which meant he made progress with Stanley.

"Come home with me Stanley, I need you."

"Alright, I'll go but first we need to give these people something to see." Stanley took off his cape and handed it to Emperor Cornelius and said, "I want to fly around the park one time then I will get in the shuttle with you."

Stanley held out his hand to Princess Lì and said, "Come fly with me, just a short trip around the park."

The two leapt up into the air and flew around the park which put everyone there into a state of wonder. Rascal-III flew in formation with them, and they made the two-mile lap and came back and landed next to the shuttle. Everyone including Rascal-III got into the shuttle and it took off and went back into space and landed on the Cruiser where Lacsar and Admiral Timons were waiting.

With tears in his eyes, Stanley approached Lacsar and threw his arms around him and hugged him and said, "Thank you for rescuing me."

"With everything you have done for me and my sister, it's the least I could do for you."

They held each other as Lacsar felt his father weeping. It was post-traumatic stress at its finest. Stanley needed some down time to heal himself.

Princess Lì knew the Royal Yacht was just off their starboard side and asked Lacsar, "Would it be possible for Stanley, and I go to the Royal Yacht and spend some private time together?"

"Those were my thoughts exactly."

Stanley then said, "If its okay I would like Rascal-III to come with me."

"That's not a problem a shuttle is ready to take you there."

This book is dedicated to my *mother*.

It's also in honor of her heroic brother Francis Jordan who died in Vietnam.

Paul D. Escudero

保罗·道格拉斯·埃斯库德罗

Bǎoluó ·Dàogélāsī ·Āisīkùdéluó

July 19, 2020

San Diego, California

GLOSSARY

Name	As know as	Additional information
Emperor Cornelius		Lìsztbrùnést Emperor
Stanley	Duke Ravik	From Earth (Ski Beach)
Princess Lì Alìgrāwná	Princess Lì	Stanley's spouse & lover Emperor Cornelius daughter
Zerorus Government		Government located in the Martian City Cydonia
Lacsar	Demetrius Ravik	Stanley and Princess Lì's son
Princess Alessandra		Lacsar's sister
King Carlatar		Carvlesis Planet King
Princess Arabella		King Carlatar's daughter
Charbriel		Princess Alessandra's lover
Larafracean		Charbriel's planet
Planet Zorcrarisp		Where evil mercenaries exist that boarded the Royal Yacht
Planet Ollytrene		Where princess Starlight came from
Chief Yuèliàng	Moon 月亮	Tribal Chief from Ollytrene

Starlight	Starlight 星光	Lacsar's Empress and daughter of Chief Yuèliàng
Tonnerre		Chief Yuèliàng's wife,
Lìsztbrùnést Admiral Timons,		Supreme commander
Hectozar		the Gromulite despot Dictator
Valet Robot Lucas		
Valet Octavrator		
Azorloma		Planet where Princess Li's mother came from
Astronomical Units		The distance from the sun to Earth that takes light eight minutes to travel.
Gumonaclaris Elixir		A very expensive elixir that has psychoactive drugs in it.
The Battle of Cystanokar		One of the pivotal battles between the Trilaterals and Lìsztbrùnést
Lìsztbrùnést		Main civilization in the drama
Ami		Stanley's mate on Earth
Drákōlìné		Princess Lì Aligrãwná governess and protector

Neflatraceous		the capital of the Lìsztbrùnést Empire
Christine		Call girl on Azorloma working with the Trilateral Spies
Lìsztbrùnést Royal Space Yacht		

AUTHOR'S NOTE

This Novel is a work of fiction, none of the characters in the book exists except possibly one of the birds named Rascal. The purpose behind writing this Novel was to convey to the reader a sense of birds and their behaviors and traits.

A lot of people have pet birds and develop a relationship with those wonderful bird pets. After observing birds for quite a few years, I think I've discovered a few things.

Here's some examples. When I'm walking 10 miles in the morning which I used to do quite often in the past and accomplished again just a few days ago, I encounter a lot of birds.

There have been times (as I explained in the drama in the Novel) where at the eight-mile mark I was exhausted and seriously thinking of walking to my car and leaving the park and go home. Suddenly a couple Mallard Ducks who know me descended upon me wanting some treats, which they probably received. After dealing with those Mallard Ducks, I suddenly felt invigorated. Did mother nature do something, perhaps give me special energy so I could continue my 10 miles and complete it?

I do in fact have a pet bird who lives in the wild I named Rascal. This blackbird, a crow comes right up to me. Has no fear whatsoever. When I'm near the Mallard, Rascal moves in between us and tries to force the Mallards away. But I know if I give Rascal a treat, he'll go to nearby water in a gutter on the road to dunk it and eat it. But he always comes back to hassle the Mallards some more.

Just like in the Novel, the coots come up to me. They are lovely birds and normally will not get near a human. The pigeons know me well and sometimes follow me around the park. Pigeons are very nice birds, and they adopt humans who treat them right.

You might think it gets boring walking 10 miles every day, but I never allow it to get boring because I'm dreaming up new Novels as I go. Sometimes I receive golden nuggets from the ether and plug them into my Novels. If you take the time to read my Novel Endless Travels, Reincarnation and Remembrance, you will see some of those golden nuggets that authors rarely use in their Novels because they don't normally appear in regular conversations and rarely used in unusual circumstances. It's a good thing I always have my cell phone with me to take notes when one of those golden nuggets drops out of the ether and into my brain.

There are some heavy doses of telepathic communication in this book. A lot of people who were abducted by Aliens claim they communicated via telepathic means. I just talked to a woman yesterday who claims she's alien and her alien connections didn't need cell phones because they used telepathic communication. I'm fascinated with the subject of telepathic communications and have put telepathic activity in several my Novels.

There are numerous sources that discuss deep brain photoreceptor cells. [Enlightening the brain: Linking deep brain photoreception with behavior and physiology - PMC (nih.gov)]

In my travels and literature, I've explored there are some theories those deep brain photoreceptors in the center of our brains has two purposes, one if a high-speed conduit between the brain hemispheres. That makes sense. Another is it's for telepathic communications that humans have seemingly lost the ability to perform.

I suggest that if Aliens do communicate telepathically, it makes sense we have the ability to hear them because of we are very distant descendants of higher beings.

The Monroe Institute developed "Hemi-Sync" a means to

meditate to the point of the brain traveling to the universe. Some suggest that interface to the universe is through those deep brain photo receptors when we reach Hemi-Sync.

Did the CIA use Hemi-Sync while training spies? Hemi-Sync is sometimes referred to as the Gateway experiment [In 1983, The CIA Wrote A Bizarre Report About Transcending Spacetime With Your Mind | IFLScience].

The Monroe Institute has definitely advanced the Hemi-Sync process and I'm surprised the public is not more aware of Hemi-Sync. [DECLASSIFIED: CIA Explains Consciousness, The Matrix, Meditation, Holograms, Telepathy - In5D : In5D] This document gives some rather interesting information on the Hemi-Sync process.

I wonder if that's the source of the Movie named "Matrix?"

I'm mentioned in Wikipedia for my application of Hemi-Sync in a Novel "Pluto II":

Literature

Wolf's piano concerto was mentioned in Paul D. Escudero's Pluto II: Voyage to the end of the Universe when Greg listened to it to achieve a "Hemi-Sync Reality" during meditation. [33]

Pluto II - Google Books.

Now you know the genesis of telepathic communications used in this novel, *"Man of Birds."*

If you read this novel, then you know, how intricate scenarios were manifested by telepathic intrusion into the character's minds. It also gives way to how humans were able to interact with birds through telepathic ability.

In this novel the Aliens who meet Stanley at Ski Beach, have wings. Stanley's involvement and transformance with the Aliens was based on the love the birds felt for Stanley after many years of his walks on Ski Beach and interacting and observing all the types of birds mentioned in the story. It was through telepathic study of the birds' thoughts as well as Stanley that struck the Aliens that ultimately manifested that first meeting that resulted in Stanley soon experiencing travel through the galaxy and all the unique situations that followed.

There is romance and heart break in this Novel. The story explains how during the conduct of normal affairs, partners tear the hearts out of their loved ones that results in the possibility of the loss of that partner.

Some of us have gone through that process and the results were a permanent split. In this book when one of the partner's pushes the other over the brink, a permanent separation was likely. This was to convey to the audience the emotions associated with such a destruction of a partnership, when one of the parties unilaterally takes actions and doesn't quite comprehend the results that would soon be bestowed on them.

It's not until the stark reality of the potential loss, that a behavior is modified to save the relationship. But as some of you know in real life, people sometimes do not realize until the partner is walking out the door forever that its too late. The damage is done, and that person will be out of their life forever.

I'm sure that in such circumstances the partner that was left behind wishes they could unwind the time and fix the hemorrhage in the relationship. But unfortunately, they sometimes get bad advice from others that ultimately makes it permanent. Had they not taken the advice of their friends and relatives, the divorce might not have happened. *I want to congratulate all those people that helped out that destroyed marriages.*

In this book there is implied travel between star systems at incredible speeds to cover a great distance in a short period of time. Humans on Earth really do not know anything about the Universe unless the government is concealing information. Ben Rich a former head of Lockheed Martin's Skunk Works in his death bed confession, which is available on the internet, claims we already can travel to the stars, but it will never see the light of day in society because it's all locked up in black projects.

Let's drill down into Ben Rich's comment and see what the implications are.

Traveling to great distances between star systems implies speeds that exceed the speed of light. By the way what is the speed of light in a vacuum? If a spaceship was traveling at the speed of light in a vacuum and had a headlight shining light ahead. Would the photons that are leaving the headlight of a spacecraft travel faster than the speed of light? Or would those photons travel at the speed of light from a relative speed of the spacecraft in a vacuum. In a vacuum if nothing can slow down those photons, that means they would be traveling twice the speed of light since the spaceship is traveling at the speed of light and from a relative position in a vacuum from the spaceship would appear to travel at the speed of light. But an observer from a perpendicular position in space from the travel of the spaceship would probably see two different velocities, the speed of light relative to the space craft and the speed of light from the headlight relative to the observer offset to the side.

Has there been objects traveling faster than the speed of light? One German scientist claims stars traveling around the black hole at the center of our galaxy travels ten times the speed off light.

Another scientist has this to say: Faster than light travel is possible, scientist claims (nypost.com)   [https://nypost. com/2021/03/12/faster-than-light-travel-is-possible-scientist- claims/]

I have another explanation. God created the Universe in seven (7) days. In doing so none of the theories of scientists on this planet would really matter then because we know there are galaxies recently photographed by the Webb Space Telescope that are astonishingly far distances away. God's creation is proof enough things can go faster than the speed of light. Even people who believe in the big bang theory say it went faster than the speed of light. They must make that judgement, otherwise the Big Bang Theory loses all its credibility very quickly.

Suppose there are alien races one billion years more advanced than we are. Would they have figured out travel faster than the speed of light? Better yet did they figure out time travel. At the time this Novel is published another novel I wrote is now available: "A time for Memories and the Unthinkable, The Life of a Time Travel Spy." In that Novel I imply an enemy developing a time machine is worse than nuclear weapons because they could alter time.

As I said at the beginning of this author's note, this is a work of fiction, but as you read it, you get the sense of what situations would be like if there were plausible activities such as telepathic communication and travel faster than the speed of light to go long distances in a short period of time.

<div align="center">~~~~~~</div>

Near the completion of this book my mother passed away. She was 89 years old. She died from medical complications and COVID. I was lucky to see her the month before she passed.

I do the artwork for my books because if you leave it up to the publisher who will hire a great artist, you might get a book cover that is not in your frame of mind for what you want to project to the audience. I sent a copy of the book cover for this Novel to my wonderful sister Marilyn who was able to show my mother four days before she passed.

That makes this book special to me because it is in honor of my mother.

Just back from Ski Beach where I meet Rascal
daily.

Paul D. Escudero

保罗·道格拉斯·埃斯库德罗

Bǎoluó ·Dàogélāsī ·Āisīkùdéluó

San Diego, California

August 2022